QUEEN'S QUEST

*To Ann McEntire my Alaskan friend,
Beta Reader for the VarTerels' Universe,
and favorite walking partner.*

*Thank you for your support of my writing,
for fun and laughter,
and for great conversations.*

*Each book you've worked on,
contains a shining moment of you!*

THANK YOU

Thank you for picking up my book.

Join my readers group and
I will update you about my writing.

https://www.skrandolph.com/readers-group

Learn more about my books at my website.

www.SKRandolph.com

S.K. Randolph

Let the adventure begin!

ALSO BY S.K. RANDOLPH
VARTERELS' UNIVERSE

~Novels~

Part I - UnFolding

1. *DiMensioner's Revenge*
2. *ConDra's Fire*
3. *MasTer's Reach*
4. *Jaradee's Legacy*

Part II - CoaleScence

5. *Incirrata Secret*
6. *Corps Stones*
7. *Mocendi's Gambit*
8. *Queen's Quest*

~Companion Shorts~

Gifts, Discovery, Rescue, Encounters, Metamorphosis, Fishing, Lessons, Wanted, Duplicity, Tomorrow, SnowScape, Destiny

This is a work of fiction, and the views expressed herein are the sole responsibility of the author. Likewise, certain characters, places, and incidents are the product of the author's imagination, and any resemblance to actual persons, living or dead, or actual events or locals, is entirely coincidental.

Queen's Quest: Illustrated by the Author (VarTerels' Universe Book 8), First Edition

Copyright © 2024 by S.K. Randolph
Cover design and art copyright © 2024 by S.K. Randolph
Edited by L.S. Lane
Illustrated by S.K. Randolph
Book design by T. Krantz

ISBN
978-1-962777-11-7 (Paperback)
978-1-962777-12-4 (Hardback)

Self Published by S.K. Randolph
CheeTrann Creations LLC
Suite 316-160
1410 Valley View Drive
Delta, CO 81416

Email: sk@skrandolph.com
Web Site: www.skrandolph.com
Substack: skrandolph.substack.com
Facebook: http://facebook.com/S.K.Randolph11

All rights reserved. No part of this book may be scanned, uploaded, reproduced, distributed, or transmitted in any form or by any means whatsoever without written permission from the author except in the case of brief quotations embodied in critical articles and reviews. Thank you for supporting the author's rights.

No generative Artificial Intelligence (AI) was used in the creation of this book - the words and images were created by the author, a certifiable human being.

Publlished 2024 | 24-034 VU08-E1

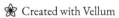

QUEEN'S QUEST

ILLUSTRATED BY THE AUTHOR

VARTERELS' UNIVERSE
BOOK EIGHT

S.K. RANDOLPH

Cover and Illustrations by
S.K. RANDOLPH

Soputto

Dia Bandia

Nira

Laich Gea

STRAIT OF NÂGRI

Reachti

Igran

Canniple Mt

Astong Wood

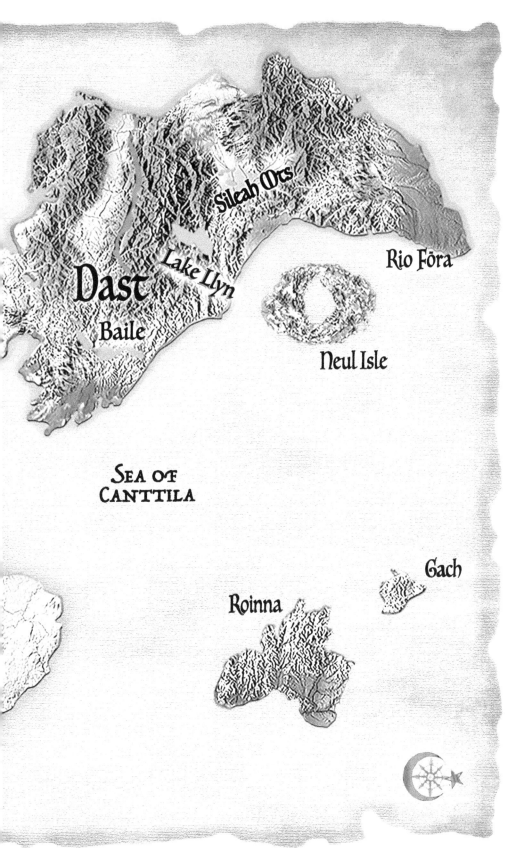

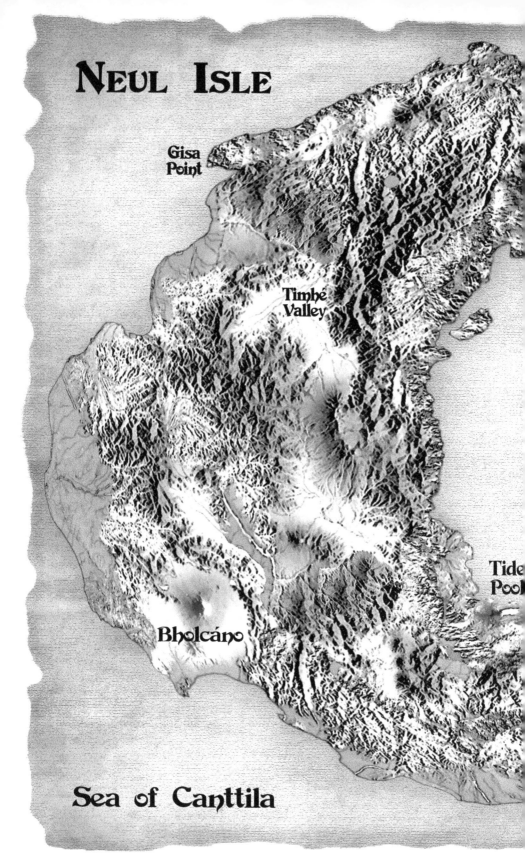

Prologue
Shiór Ridu

*The CoaleScence Spins
A web of intrigue thread by thread,
A circle that begins its ending
Opening portals that are pending...*

An increasing sense of unease ushered the Sun Queen Abellona into her private, palatial rooms. Her fire-opal eyes narrowed. *Somewhere in the Spéire Solar System, a change has occurred.* Sinking into a red velvet chair, she fixed her gaze on an exquisite portrait of her, a recent gift from SparrowLyn AsTar. As she watched, delicate brush strokes appeared, blurred, and reformed to show Neul Isle, the most sacred place on the planet of Soputto, hidden beneath an opaque dome.

Rising, she stepped closer. The island wavered. Once more, her portrait emerged, filling the room with regal beauty. She ran a finger along the edge of the frame. *Thank you, SparrowLyn, for sharing your prophetic gift.* A slight smile curved. *And thank you, Relevart, for delivering it to me.*

Seriousness enveloped her as she walked into a long, elegant corridor. *Now, I require more information.*

After contacting the Galactic Council, she returned to the quiet of her personal rooms to contemplate what she had learned. *Raiherr Yencara and his band of Vasro warriors have invaded Neul Isle.* Creases lined her brow. The Council had shared that these wanna-be DiMensioners awaited the return of Inōni, the granddaughter of Dri Adoh, the K'iin shaman, and her three companions. Abellona's fire-opal eyes narrowed. *Inōni and her escorts are each important to the successful progression from the CoaleScence into the next phase of Universal growth.*

Gripping the velvet arms of her chair, she expressed her growing concern aloud. "If even one falls into the hands of those who prioritize personal power and wealth over universal growth, disastrous consequences will follow." Her spine lengthened; her chin lifted. "I have sworn to remove the dome and banish the Vasro invaders once and for all."

Abellona gazed at her portrait, pursed her lips, and nodded. "Since the Council has asked me not to leave Shiór Ridu, I know exactly who must join me in my quest to save Neul Isle. Their last visit to the island brought the Unfolding to a close and the CoaleScence into being. Their intertwining destinies will not only rid this solar system of our enemies, but will usher in the Quickening."

A slight smile tugged at her full lips as she walked to the center of the room and announced, "My quest begins."

Closing her eyes, she raised her arms.

"I call forth those who must help me to win
Freedom for Neul Isle and that of the K'iin.
Each warrior will hear my call, my behest,
To join me now in achieving my quest."

1
El Aperdisa

Garon Anaru sat on the edge of the couch in the quarters he shared with his cousin. On his palm, black-rimmed spectacles glowed, vanished, and reappeared glowing brighter. He blew out a frustrated breath and looked down at the small rat terrier curled beside him. "I don't know what's going on, Spyglass."

The dog's eye, surrounded by the patch of black fur which had inspired his name, gleamed; and his pointed ears twitched.

Gar frowned. "This is the third time my spectacles have appeared without me calling 'em." Confusion pursed his lips. He stared unseeing at the terrier. "Do ya think the Sun Queen knows we already rescued Brie from Karlsut Sorda's ship?" Spyglass lifted his head and perked up his ears. Gar puffed. "Of course, she does, Spy. So..." He nibbled his bottom lip. "I wonder if—"

The entry hatch buzzed. Gar sent his spectacles into hiding and came to his feet. Spyglass yipped, jumped to the floor, and, tail wagging, trotted to the open entry hatch.

Esán stepped into the space, patted the frisky terrier on the head as the hatch closed, and straightened. "Gar, I'm so glad you're here. Do you know where Torgin is?"

"Nope. I was hoping you'd know, 'cause something weird is going on."

Esán squeezed his shoulder and guided him to the sitting area. "I understand. That's why I'm here." Once they were both seated and Spyglass had curled up beside him, Esán withdrew a small gold key from its pocket. "Tumu Noci keeps growing, even when it's in my pocket."

Gar peered closer as the key grew to span Esán's palm. He squinted and whispered, Repapa, the word to call his specs into being. They materialized on his palm, the frames already blazing like embers in a fire. "Hey! Your key grew to size and my glasses are glowing. What's up?"

The entry hatch opened and Torgin ducked through, his gaze darting from one face to the other.

"Sure glad to see you." Gar tilted his head. "You look kinda worried."

Pressing his lips into a thin line, Torgin withdrew the Sun Queen's book on the space-time continuum from behind his back. "This has appeared on my desk three times in the last chron-circle." His intense gaze darted from Gar's glowing spectacles to Esán's full-sized key. "*What* is going on?"

Esán moved over. "Sit down, and let's solve the puzzle."

Torgin placed the book on the side table. Settling beside the terrier, he scratched the dog's ears. His brows bridged in thought, then arched. "Den, Penee, and Brie left three turnings ago to escort Inóni to her village on Neul Isle, so she could birth her baby at home. They should be back by now."

Realization lit Esán's stormy blue eyes. "Something must have happened to keep them from delivering Inōni safely to the K'iin."

An agitated squirm brought all eyes to Gar's face. "I'm betting you're right." He held up his spectacles. "My specs, the key, and the book are acting real strange. We oughta tell—"

The buzzer buzzed, the entry hatch vanished, and Relevart ducked through. Shrewd amber eyes held a warning. As the hatch closed, he motioned them into a circle. Silence enshrouding them, the trio joined him. A shield shimmered up around them. The living area blurred and refocused into a round, stark white space, where Henrietta and Thorlu waited.

Spyglass scampered over, licked Henri's hand, and sniffed Thorlu's shoes.

Gar called the excited terrier to heel and tipped his head to peer up at Relevart."

Relevart moved to his life-mate's side. "We can talk here. Henri, please share what you know."

Amethyst-rimmed spectacles magnifying her violet eyes, Henrietta Avetlire studied each face. "I keep hearing partial telepathic messages from Abellona. Each of you has been alerted with the appearance of the key, the book, and Gar's spectacles. Something is wrong on Neul Isle. The Sun Queen has sounded the alarm. We need to develop a plan our enemies will not expect."

Relevart turned to Thorlu. "Who do you believe is on the island?"

Thorlu, whose recent initiation to the rank of High DiMensioner in the Order of Esprow had amplified his talents, stared into the distance. With a slight nod, his steady gaze moved to the VarTerel. "This is the work of Karlsut Sorda, which means Raiherr Yencara and his sidekick, Zori Sedrin, are on the island."

"What has convinced you they are the invaders?"

Thorlu answered without hesitation. "Before I left the *Surgentin*, I discovered Raiherr has recruited a group of wannabe DiMensioners. I also learned his SorTech, Callum, has invented several new innovations for the SorTechory Box. Regrettably, I didn't find out what they were before I left."

Henri peered at him through her lenses. "You trained Raiherr, correct?"

"I did." Thorlu nodded. "And, yes, I can predict his next move. My association with Karlsut also gives us an advantage."

Relevart scanned the group. "Thorlu, please stay. The rest of you teleport to a place you rarely frequent and then assemble in the mess hall for mid-turning meal. Meet back here in two chron-circles."

Gar scrubbed his dark curls with a hand. "Wait. What about Ari, Elf, and Rethson? Why aren't they here?

Relevart's amber eyes hardened. "Like you, they have an important job to do. We will be filling them in after mid-turning meal. Briefly, we have spies onboard, and they will help us to find them."

Henrietta gave a soft whistle. Spyglass ran to sit at her feet. She smiled down at the terrier. "You stay with me, Spy, until things calm down."

Gar looked from Henri to his canine companion. "Ahh...thanks." He put his hands on his hips and squinted up at Relevart. "Don't you want us to help make plans?"

A crooked smile flashed. "I do, young Garon. However, let's do the work of fooling our enemies first." Relevart snapped his fingers.

Gar found himself, alone with Torgin, gazing out the oval view-portal of one of the three observation decks on *El Aperdisa.*" With a shrug of acceptance, he tipped his head and grinned. "Nice to see ya, Torg!"

His cousin grinned back. "Good to see you, too." He chuckled. "I love it when you get excited and slip into your New York speech patterns. It reminds me of our time together in 1969." Bending down, Torgin studied the logo on his shirt. "Isn't that the t-shirt you were wearing when we left the city?"

Gar ran a hand over the 'I love New York' logo. "Yep. This is the only new shirt I ever owned until you found me. Gin got it for me special. Sure glad it was too big then 'cause it fits great now." He let out a breath heavy with emotion.

Torgin put a hand on his shoulder. "I wish I had met Gin."

"Me, too. You woulda liked each other." Gar glanced at the door. "I think it's time to eat."

A flash of light in the middle of the ship's Holographic Center faded, leaving Ari, Elf, and Rethson staring at the Universal VarTerels. Ari frowned and fixed her attention on Relevart. "How did we get here?"

Henrietta held up her spectacles. "I brought you, Arienh. Relevart has something important to share.

The Universal VarTerel studied the trio in silence, then spoke with utmost seriousness. "We have spies on *El Aperdis*a."

Ari slipped a hand into Elf's. "How many?"

"We aren't sure. What we know is—" Relevart's gaze traveled the group. "—someone is eavesdropping on our discussions and passing the information to our enemies."

Rethson spoke up. "How did you discover there are spies?"

Henrietta replaced her spectacles on her nose. "Only those of us gathered here plus Esán, Torgin, and Gar knew Brie was taking Den, Penee, and Inōni to Neul Isle. Since they left, all attempts to contact them have failed."

Impatience made Ari cleared her throat. "Why aren't the others here? Have you told them what's up?"

Henrietta's magnified violet eyes glinted. "The Sun Queen has summoned them. There is once again trouble on Neul Isle. You three have an important task to accomplish on *El Aperdisa*. Karlsut has his spies on this ship. Since you have each encountered Karlsut and his methods, you are the best prepared to find them."

Ari's chin jerked up. Her hands curled into white-knuckled fists. Stubbornness firmed her jaw. Her aunt's raised brows made her take a breath and relax her hands. "You understand I want to go to Neul Isle after Brie, Aunt Henri, but I will listen to your plan and then decide."

"Thank you, Arienh." Henrietta removed her spectacles and slipped them into their hidden pocket. "So far, Karlsut's men don't realize we know they've invaded the ship. You have already helped us leak the word that Skylyn has returned to her regiment to receive an award. They've learned via ship's gossip about your training missions to prepare for the trip to El Stroma." She paused and turned to Relevart.

He continued. "Commander Odnamo sent word that one of his men overheard two crewmen talking about Brie's departure with Penee and Den to return Inōni to Neul Isle. We cannot allow them to continue putting all of us in danger. Ari, you and Elf and Rethson will appear to leave for DerTah to work with Wolloh. Instead, you will remain on board in shifted form, infiltrate the crew, and uncover Karlsut's spies."

Ari felt a strong urge to defy the VarTerels. Instead, she switched her attention from her aunt to her friends. "What do you think? Can we pull this off?"

Elf grinned and shifted to a uniformed crew member with a dirty-blond crewcut and features so neutral others might not notice him. "Name's Tezeeni Zakeron. My friends call me Zak. I'm from DerTah, and for sure we can work undercover. All we need is a good plan." He spoke in a gravelly voice with a slight accent and then returned to his own form.

Rethson frowned. "Karlsut's men know me. How can I fool them?"

Ari faced him, her eyes unblinking and her voice calm. "You're as talented as Elf and me, and you know the enemy! I bet you'll spot them before we do. So, show us your new persona."

Head bowed, Rethson stood in silence. A long inhale later, he squared his shoulders and morphed into a sturdy, freckle-faced, blue-eyed man with military-short reddish hair. A faded scar ran from below his elbow, down his arm, and over his hand. He licked his thin lips. "Will this do?"

Ari's grin of approval brought Rethson back to himself. She chuckled. "You're amazing. What are you called?"

A twinkle sparked. "I'm from the planet of Persow. Name's Rily Bailith."

Ari glanced up at Relevart. "I can't shift to Ira because Karlsut knows me in that form. So, how about this?"

Light flashed. In her place stood a youthful version of Paisley James Tobinette. Smooth, black skin aglow and brown eyes gleaming, he grinned down from his tall, muscular height. "I'm called Jem, and I grew up in the Central Mountains on Thera." Returning to her natural form, she looked at the Universal VarTerels. "What's the plan?"

Relevart addressed each of his assets. "Ari, you will take the lead and report to your aunt, but only in your Jem form. Let's make some decisions."

A short time later, Jem paused in the hatchway to the bridge. Commander Odnamo waved him forward.

"This is AeroTech Jem Taisley. He will assist our communications officer. Please, introduce yourselves."

Esán, fear for Brie demanding his full attention, gulped his mid-turning meal without tasting a bite. After leaving the mess hall, he searched for Torgin. Frustrated that his friend was nowhere to be found, Esán did a mental scan of the surrounding area, teleported to the Holographic Center, and paced the stark white emptiness. *Where are you, Torgin Whalend?*

All senses tingling, he stopped. The white walls vanished, leaving him standing at the top of an unfamiliar mountain. Every nerve on fire, he made a slow rotation. Torgin, Gar, and Thorlu Tangorra materializing beside him brought him to a standstill. "What the..." He pinched Torgin.

"Ouch!" His friend jumped back. "What did you do that for?"

Esán shot him a lopsided grin. "I didn't know if you were real."

Torgin rubbed his arm. "All you had to do was ask."

Thorlu cleared his throat. "This is all real. Relevart and Henri created a fold in space-time from TreBlaya to its neighboring solar system. Then with Torgin's help, they transported us through it to the planet of Soputto. We are at the top of Dia Bandia Mountain, where we can access the portal to the Sun Queen's realm in Shiór Ridu." He rested a hand on Gar's shoulder. "Get out your specs, Garon, and tell us what you see."

Gar whispered, and the spectacles appeared. Resting the temple arms on his ears, he made a slow pivot. "I see tall cliffs covered with trees. Below us is a canyon with a river." He lifted his chin and gazed upward.

Torgin exclaimed softly. "Look! The frames are glowing like embers and his eyes are the color of fire opals."

Esán pointed. "Over there."

As one, the group turned. High above the forested mountainside, an oval of shimmering amber light glowed brighter and brighter. An obsidian staircase descended from its center. Followed by two attendants, Abellona, the Sun Queen of the Spéire Solar System, stepped free of the portal and smiled at Thorlu.

"It is good that we meet again as allies, Thorlu Tangorra. Congratulations on your decision to leave the Mocendi behind. Achieving the level of High DiMensioner in the Order of Esprow is a sign of your integrity and your power."

Thorlu bowed his head and touched his heart. "I am honored to fight at your side, Your Majesty."

Abellona inclined her head and addressed the group. "Welcome, Garon Anaru, Esán Efre, and Torgin Whalend." She scanned the mountain and the canyon. "We are not safe here. You must come with me to Chadēta Apól, my realm in Shiór Ridu." Opal eyes regarded each of them in turn. "I must blind you for the journey. Do not fear. When it is safe, your sight will return. Please move closer together." She raised a hand.

> *"Protect the eyes of those who travel*
> *To my domain to help unravel*
> *Why dreaded danger stalks the land,*
> *And how to thwart its evil plan."*

Torgin's hand flew to his eyes. Esán gasped, and Thorlu swore softly.

Gar touched the ebony rims of his spectacles. "I can see. Is that okay?"

The Sun Queen smiled and offered her hand. "As long as your rims glow, your eyes are safe, but, young Garon, you must not share what you observe unless I give you permission. Do you understand?"

"I do. I promise not to breathe a word." Gar crossed his heart the way Gin had taught him as a kid in New York.

"Good. Stand with your friends, so you can guide them onto the staircase."

Abellona mounted the stairs. Her attendants waited for Gar and his friends to follow the Queen and then closed in behind them.

Gar gasped. The steps, moving like an escalator in New York City, carried them upward and stopped at the top, where an elegant, open carriage with a brilliant, fire-opal sheen waited.

Four long-legged ebony creatures, their horse-like manes and tails ablaze, turned regal feline heads and purred a welcome as the Sun Queen approached. A uniformed man with glowing black skin and fiery orange eyes helped the Sun Queen to mount the steps.

Before she took her seat, she addressed her guests. "Gentlemen, my footman will assist you up the four stairs into my carriage, and Gar will guide you to your seat. Once we are beyond the palace gates, your sight will return. Thank you for your patience." The queen's four attendants waited for them to settle in their seats before climbing into a second carriage.

At a sign from Abellona, the cavalcade set forth along an obsidian-black road. Gar stared with awe-filled attentiveness at a world unlike any place he had ever been. Surrounding the carriage on all sides, a firestorm of orange, red, and gold flickered around obsidian statuaries, creating fiery. sculpted pictures of life in the Sun Queen's domain in Shiór Ridu. Overhead, a cupola of sunset-colored clouds defined and protected the Sun Queen's realm.

Gar shook his head in wonder. "Thank you for letting me see your land."

Abellona smiled. "Your spectacles allow you to see what few Humans have seen. Without them to protect your eyes, the sun's fire would have left you sightless."

She gazed ahead as they approached a shimmering, garnet gateway, bearing the gold and fire-opal seal of the Realm of the Sun Deities. Silence in the carriage and beyond escorted the cavalcade through the open gates and along a boulevard lined with exotic, flame-colored flora.

Torgin gasped and rubbed his eyes. "My sight has returned!"

Esán heaved a sigh of relief.

Thorlu bowed his head. "Thank you, Sun Queen, for the return of our sight."

Abellona smiled a gracious smile. "I apologize for your temporary blindness, but it is the law of the land. Humans are rarely welcome in Shiór Ridu, and those who are must accept our rules." She turned to Gar. "You, Garon Anaru, are an exception because you wear spectacles gifted to you by Henrietta Avetlire, the Universal VarTerel, and blessed by me."

The carriage rolled to a stop outside an exquisite palace with sculpted turrets rising into the clouds. Gar felt a flood of emotions. He touched his t-shirt and remembered Gin reading to him about castles and queens and knights. He sighed. *I miss you, Gin.*

A footman lowered the carriage steps; a man with skin as dark as Abellona's and deep brown eyes with flashes of opal assisted the Queen to alight. When her companions had joined them, she introduced him. "This is my oldest son, Nimah." Her brilliant smile encompassed them all. "We welcome you to Chadēta Apól. Nimah will escort you to a meeting room. Please make yourselves comfortable, and I will join you shortly."

Nimah's curious gaze moved over the group before he preceded them up the stairs and into an elegant reception area. He led them down a long corridor, where the striated stone walls turned from black to silver and back as they passed. Partway down, Nimah stopped, faced the wall, and spoke a soft word. A black garnet door materialized and opened. The companions filed into a large, high-ceilinged room with the windows lining one wall, providing a view of a fiery-red mountain range.

Nimah led them to a sitting area. "Please make yourselves comfortable. My esteemed mamai will join us soon."

Gar sank into a soft seat. *I can't believe I am in the Sun Queen's palace. Wonder what will happen next?*

2
Neul Isle

Rina, the Guardian Incirrata of Neul Isle, had discovered an impenetrable dome arching over the island. Neither sun nor rain could penetrate to the land beneath, a deafening silence smothered all sound. No birds called, no animals cried, no sea life made itself known above the still, pale, pewter-colored water of the lagoon. For the second time, enemies had invaded the sacred Isle of Neul.

Her responsibility to protect the island prompted her to deliver her Phantom Stannag partners, the Astican, Abarax, and La, the Luna Moth, to the shore opposite Rina Island, where she first sensed the presence of danger. Now, she must wait.

Abarax and La floated through the night-dark silence of the forest and hovered at the clearing's edge. Their attention fixed on four men sitting around a campfire, they listened with growing dismay as they plotted their next move.

La fluttered up to the Astican's shoulder. *"I check K'iin Village."* A wing brushed its cheek. Lifting into flight, its true love made her way over the clearing. With faint flickers of firelight patterning her translucent wings, she faded from sight.

Abarax experienced a moment of dread. *Her goal will take her to their village high in the San Crúil Mountains.* The gray scales on its body quivered. *Be careful, my beautiful Luna Moth.*

The Astican's attention switched back to the men around the fire. What it learned sent a shiver through its huge translucent wings. The invaders were on Neul Isle to intercept four people who were important to their leader. Frustration filled the discussion. Thus far, their prey had eluded them.

One man stood, looming over the others. Steely eyes glinted in the firelight. "Karlsut will not tolerate failure."

His companions squirmed and muttered under their breath. A growl from their leader ended the dissatisfied grumbling. He pointed. "Callum, check on the SorTechory Box. We can't afford a mistake."

With keen interest, Abarax observed the short-stocky man called Callum rise, walk away from the fire, and stop in front of a plain brown, cabinet-like box on the far side of the clearing. A raised hand produced a low humming. The box glowed, illuminating the area with mid-turning light.

Easing further into the trees, Abarax pressed the full lips of its rosebud mouth into a tense line. Realization made its ghostly wings tremble. *Callum is a SorTech. His SorTechory Box created the darkness and the dome over the island.*

The Astican frowned, its thoughts racing. Brie rested in the basement room in Penee's proxy parents' lakeside cottage. Located in a sparsely populated area on Soputto's continent of Dast, it provide the perfect environment for her active mind to retrace the choices of the past two turnings.

At Relevart's direction, Brie gathered Penee, Inōni, and Den together and entered Mittkeer's timeless night. When they regained their equilibrium, a successful search for the Incirrata Constellation guided them to their destination.

Brie contemplated the star-studded endlessness. The Star of Truth's faint tingle made her hesitate.

Den peered down at her. "What's worrying you, VarTerel?"

Brie clenched and unclenched her fist. "Something is not right at Neul Isle." She gazed up at Musette, the tourmaline crystal topping her staff. A rush of confidence steadied her. "I'm going to create a time window. With luck, we'll discover what's going on." She lifted her staff and drew a large oval in the night sky.

Below them, only part of the island's shoreline came into focus. Inōni pressed closer. "Brielle, what is hiding my home?" Tears slipped from the corner of her eyes. "It reminds me of your first visit to Neul when clouds covered the island."

Brie heard and understood her dismay. "We'll figure out what's happening, Inōni." She tapped the time window. The image zoomed out, highlighting an opaque dome of vibrating energy covering most of the isle. Brie glanced at her companions. "We can't exit Mittkeer onto Neul Isle until we know what's going on."

Den peered at the dome, then at Brie. "I'm certain this is SorTechory at work, which suggests that Karlsut Sorda and his Vasro are involved." He put his arms around Penee and Inōni. "We are all too important to our enemies to walk into a trap. Where do you suggest we go to regroup?"

Brie snapped her fingers. The imaged changed. A cottage sitting at the edge of a lake took shape.

Penee nodded. "My proxy parents' summer home. Let's depart Mittkeer into the hidden basement room, so we won't broadcast our presence." She peered around Den. "Don't worry Inōni. We'll solve the mystery."

Moments later, they huddled in the light of a single lantern in the basement hide-away. No one moved.

Penee touched Brie's arm. *"Are we safe to talk?"*

The tension in Brie's body eased. "We are. I don't sense anyone else in the cottage." A frown creased her brow. "Whatever is shielding Neul Isle clearly denotes trouble." She looked at Den. "Any ideas?"

The amethyst flecks in Den's blue eyes glistened in the dim light. "I'm guessing Karlsut has a spy on *El Aperdisa*. That's the only way he would know we were bringing Inōni home." He pressed his lips together and studied the girls. "All of us are important to the successful completion of the CoaleScence." His focus switched to Brie. "You have the MasTer's gene, something Sorda and his followers covet. It is vital that we avoid playing into their hands. You're a VarTerel, Brielle AsTar. What do your instincts tell you?"

Brie touched the Star of Truth, savored the faint warmth spreading over her skin, and returned her attention to her companions. "If you were Karlsut, Den, where would you direct your men to set up camp on Neul Isle?"

Den's serious expression brightened. "I'd send them to a place I was familiar with...either the clearing near the tide pool on the southern end of the central lagoon, or some place on the eastern shore near Rina Island."

Inōni pressed a hand to her rounded belly.

Brie felt her tense. "Are you alright?"

She sighed. "Just tired. I need to rest."

Plans formed in Brie's mind with the speed of inspiration. "Penee, you will stay at the cottage with Inōni. Den and I will do some reconnaissance. We must determine the origin of the dome and who constructed it. But before we leave, please take Den and make sure the cottage is safe, so you and Inōni can relax while we're gone. Inōni and I will wait here until you call us."

A glance at Inōni made her smile. The mother-to-be slept peacefully on a cot. Stifling a yawn, Brie stiffened her spine and prepared to watch over the mother and her unborn baby.

Penee led the way up the stairs to the hidden entrance into her proxy father's Trophy Room. When a mental probe produced nothing to alarm her, she pulled the lever and stepped through the open door.

Motioning for quiet, Den moved ahead and slipped into the hall. Moments later, he returned. "Everything's good." He studied her face. "Are you alright staying here with Inōni?"

"I wasn't, but then I realized my knowledge of the cottage and the area makes me the most suitable person to protect her. Take care of Brie, Den. She's important to the CoaleScence's successful transition."

Den's muscular arms wrapped around her in a gentle embrace. "We all are, Penee, especially you. Without the Girl with the Matriarch's Eyes, El Stroma might never achieve its true glory." His expression grew even more serious. "Brie and I are going to make plans, but we won't share them with you and Inōni. Knowing them would put you at risk." He released her, his gaze fixed on her face. "Do you have an escape plan if you need it?"

She raised a brow and smiled. "I do."

The twinkle in his eyes suggested he understood. "I'm not sure how long Brie and I will be gone, but I know we need to eat and rest before we go."

"I'll check the pantry; you fetch the girls." She watched him go, then hurried to the kitchen. Humming to herself, she prepared a healthy meal.

Penee gazed out the windows at the sun-created diamond sparkles on the surface of the lake. Her thoughts registered the contrast between the beauty of morning here at Llyn Lake and the sense of doom encapsulated within the dome over Neul Isle. She shivered.

Den and Brie had chosen to stay overnight and had left right after breakfast. When she last saw them, they were headed to the boathouse by the lake to make plans. She felt instinctively they were still there.

A faint but familiar sound yanked her full attention to the lake. A shiver of fear raced up her spine. *I knew Karlsut would send someone to check the cottage.* Her fearful reflection in the window brought her up short. *My job is to protect Inōni. I'd better get her and warn the others.*

In the boathouse, Brie and Den discussed and discarded one plan after the other. Their primary concern was how to enter the dome over Neul Isle without alerting their enemies. Brie twisted a curl around her finger. "I'm certain they'll expect us to arrive via the Land of Time."

Den scanned the lake to the mountains on the opposite side. "What about teleporting to somewhere on the island that we both know?"

Brie frowned and shook her head. "I think that's as dangerous as using

Mittkeer." The rowboat tied to the wooden dock sparked an idea. "They know we're coming. Let's do what they'll least expect." She grinned. "Like arrive in a boat!"

Den laughed. "Great solution." Seriousness stripped his smile of humor. "Then what?"

"When we discovered the dome from Mittkeer, I looked for whether it rested on the land, in the water, or both." Her nostrils flared. "It appears to rest on the shore. What did you notice?"

"Like you, I checked both. The dome enters the water near Rina Island. On the opposite side, it rests on the ground inland, a walkable distance from the Forest of Deora. To truly understand what it is, we need to see it. Let's get in the rowboat, go into Mittkeer, and exit a safe distance from the shore. Worst-case scenario—we find no way in and have to return to Dast to determine our next move."

Brie pursed her lips. "I have a better idea. Let's—"

Penee and Inōni materialized, panic encircling them like hornets in a frenzy. Pointing upward, Penee touched her ear. A familiar whooshing sound over the lake shouted a warning. She put a protective arm around Inōni and hissed, "A hot-air balloon! We can't stay here."

Brie jumped into action. "Den, help the girls into the boat. I'll untie the lines."

After they settled, she climbed in, tossed the forward line in the bow, and sat down. Her staff materialized in her hand. "How far away is the balloon?"

Den grew still. His eyes glazed over, then refocused on her. "It's almost reached the center of the lake. What are you thinking?"

"You and Penee will help me teleport us to the other side of the Sileah Mountains." She tensed. "Penee, put an image of the dunes beach in Den's mind." Another whoosh added urgency to her next statement. "Everyone hold on. Penee, now!"

The boat landed with a thud in a trough between sand dunes and tipped to one side. Brie gripped the gunwale and gulped a breath. Penee grinned and squeezed Inōni's hand. Taking a moment to ensure no one had followed, Brie raised her staff. Mittkeer's night sky, studded with stars, constellations, and distant galaxies, enclosed them in endless time.

Zak lay on his bunk in the crew's sleeping quarters on *El Aperdisa*. His first turning as a Trainee on the engineering team had been interesting. One of his fellow crew members, a guy named Reedan, had grilled him on why he had joined the crew so late in the game. Later, the man volunteered to take him on a tour and to show him the ropes.

Zak glanced at an empty bunk across the way. Earlier, Reedan had slipped from his bunk and had not returned. Zak's brow wrinkled in thought. *The curiosity and constant questions make me wonder if he might be one of our spies.*

Eyes mere slits, he scanned the space. Careful not to disturb his neighbors, he pushed his blanket aside, slipped from his bunk, and, accompanied by a chorus of snores, made his way to the access hatch and into the passageway.

He looked one way and then the other. *If I were Reedan, where would I look first? The crew's head is inside their sleeping quarters, so not—*

The murmur of approaching voices sent him scurrying into a utility compartment across the way. Hidden in the darkness next to the open hatch, he waited. Two men came into view. One of them was Reedan. Pressing further into the darkness, Zak strained to hear their conversation.

In Shiór Ridu, Torgin stared out a palace window, his anxiety mounting. Behind him, his friends sat talking in subdued voices. A chill of anticipation traveled from his sacrum to the top of his head. *Karlsut Sorda lacks any form of integrity. He wants Brie and Penee to use for personal gain. I'm certain he planted the traitors on El Aperdisa. We have to find Den and the girls first.*

Before he could share his concerns, Aahana, the Sun Queen's daughter, entered the palace room where they waited. Her beautiful smile warmed them. "My mamai has asked me to bring you to her. Please come with me."

They filed from the room, crossed an open courtyard, and entered another wing of the palace through a plain, burnt-umber door. Aahana led them partway along a corridor and paused. "I will leave you here. You are about to enter a room only one Human has ever seen."

The door swung inward. Thorlu took the lead, followed by Esán. Gar hurried after him and wiggled between them. Torgin's attention fixed on a three-dimensional depiction of the planet of Soputto carried him ahead of his companions.

The Sun Queen met him with a smile. "I knew, Torgin Whalend, you would find this laboratory fascinating. Gar, Esán, and Thorlu, please join us. We have much to discover."

Seriousness cloaked her. "The Council of Deities received a threat stating if they interfere and remove the dome over Neul Isle, the planet of Soputto will cease to exist. Until the Council knows who sent the message and how they created the dome, they are remaining aloof from the situation and directed me to contact The Universal VarTerels. For several reasons, Relevart, Henrietta, and I decided that I must bring you here. I will help you find out who our enemies are and do what I can from a distance."

While he listened, Torgin split his attention between the Sun Queen and the laboratory. His scientific knowledge clambered to catch up with the technology surrounding him. Fascinated, he noted the detail on the Soputton globe. A glint of light drew him a step closer. A sudden silence caught him like a salmon on a hook. He switched his focus to the queen.

Abellona's regal features registered interest. "What, Torgin Whalend, have you discovered?"

His cheeks warmed. "I apologize for being so rude."

"I felt you listening, but the technology fascinates you. So, what did you learn?"

Eagerness and excitement replaced his embarrassment. "The globe is a hologram. My instincts suggests that it can change its position, but I'm not sure how."

The Queen moved to his side. "We must know who our enemies are without alerting them, so I asked Shācor, my Holographic Specialist, to prepare this platform for our visit." She whispered a soft command in her own language.

The spherical object shimmered and reformed. A three-dimensional holographic image of Neul Isle covered by the opaque dome hovered knee high above the floor. Torgin examined it, gazed at his friends, and then at the queen. "That's a real-time depiction of the island, correct?"

She smiled. "It is. Shācor informed me we can see through the dome, at least for now. Let's see if we can pinpoint where our enemies are."

Above the image, a large, round window framed in black obsidian took shape. Like a zoom lens, it zeroed in on the island. As the group watched, it displayed the shoreline around the lagoon, then zoomed in tighter. A tree-surrounded clearing, where four men gathered around a campfire, came into focus on the shore nearest Rina Island. To one side, a brown box sat hidden in shadow.

Thorlu moved closer and stared into the lens-like window. "One man is a SorTech. That is a SorTechory Box. Can the lens show us the men's faces?"

Gar inched closer to Torgin and adjusted his spectacles. "I see four men gathered around a fire. Another one is hiding in the trees."

The Sun Queen whispered, "Dûnoon!"

The huge lens changed angles and zoomed in on the four men.

Thorlu and Esán exchanged glances. The High DiMensioner pointed to each. "Raiherr, Zorin, and the SorTech Callum. I don't know the fourth man, but he is most likely one of Raiherr's recruits."

The lens changed its angle to show the hidden observer.

Thorlu's brows arched. "The man in the trees is Hossela, a Pheet Adolan Klutarse employed by Skultar Rados. My guess—he's spying for his boss." Thorlu faced the queen. "I have heard that Callum upgraded The Box and added new technology. It wouldn't surprise me if he used it to create the dome."

Torgin cleared his throat. "Can the hologram's remote feed provide a closer look at the shoreline outside the dome?"

Again, Abellona whispered. The map shifted.

Torgin moved closer. Neul Isle grew smaller; the continent of Dast formed, its southeastern coast curving around the island's northern and eastern shorelines. As they watched, a rowboat materialized midway between the shore and the island off what Torgin knew was Rio Fōra Point. Four people huddled in the boat.

Esán choked. "Brielle!"

Torgin turned to the queen. "Those are our friends, the ones Raiherr is after."

3
Neul Isle

Mittkeer released the boat into the Sea of Canttila near the point of Rio Fōra. Settling with a splash, it rocked gently. Brie savored the feel of her VarTerel's staff in her hand and exhaled a relieved breath. *I'm certain we didn't leave a trail for Karlsut's men to follow.* A whispered word dimmed the rainbow crystal. The staff vanished.

Den flexed his fingers, rubbed his palms together, and grabbed the oars. Schooling himself to do what must be done, he waited for her signal.

Brie opened to her love of the sea and her learned knowledge. As long as the slight chop remained steady, the light, easterly wind would help them. She nodded.

Den dipped the oars and, focused on his goal, rowed toward the island. In the stern, Inōni hugged herself and gazed with rapt attention at the approaching shore. Penee tipped her head back, inhaled the sea air, shivered in delight, and grinned.

Brie scanned the water ahead, searching for floating debris or changes in the surface that might indicate rocks hidden beneath. They had almost reached the halfway point when an exclamation of pain and the boat swinging in the current brought her around to find Den doubled over in agony. Penee's tormented groan added to the chaos.

Inōni stared at the girl next to her. "Penee are you—"

A sudden gust angled the boat's starboard side into the wind. The ocean's choppy waves set the boat rocking.

Penee's mismatched eyes, glistening with tears, beseeched Brie to help.

With focused concentration, Brie steadied the boat and returned it to its original course. "I've got the boat. What just happened?"

Penee and Den peeled back their sleeves to reveal their octopus tattoos glowing scarlet. "The Incirrata knows we are here." Penee wiped cascading tears from her cheeks. "She sent us a warning. What do we do?"

Den gripped the oar handles. "Do we go back, Brie, or keep going?"

Brie frowned. A rush of confidence directed her response. "We get to shore and find shelter for the night."

He inhaled a steadying breath, dipped the blades, and began to row.

Brie switched her attention to the stern. The octopus tattoo on Penee's arm now glowed blue. Relief infused her friend's expression as she showed Inōni the Incirrata's gift.

Resuming her position as outlook, Brie turned and again scanned the water for any hidden danger. Her mind filled with images of the Incirrata. *We will get to shore, Rina. I promise.*

Esán pulled his gaze from the hologram of Brie in the rowboat and forced calm control into his voice. "Your Majesty, we need to reach our friends. Can you help us?"

"I cannot." Abellona's fire-opal eyes hardened. "The Council asked me to stay here and visible in the event the SorTech's Box can penetrate Shiór Ridu's shields." Her gaze darted to the entryway. A smile brightened her features.

Aahana entered. "You are ready for me, Mamai?"

The Queen beckoned her daughter to her side. "I cannot act, but Aahana has reached out to Kat, the Goddess of Small Creatures. With her help, Aahana will take you to join your friends unnoticed by Raiherr and his men."

Torgin acknowledged Aahana and then spoke to her mother. "Can we see if the K'iin are safe so we can return Inōni to her family before we tackle our enemies?"

Abellona studied him with renewed interest. "You are always one step ahead. I like your mind, Torgin Whalend. Let us see what we can discover."

A whispered word and the lens rotated and focused on the San Crúil Mountains and the Valley of Tá Súil, where the K'iin had lived for the past centura. A slow zoom showed Dri Adoh and Artānga imprisoned in individual huts, each guarded by two men. Four others were stationed around the village. No tribal members were visible.

Thorlu frowned. "Raiherr brought a small army with him. Is it possible to bring Inōni to Shiór Ridu without putting you at risk?"

Abellona seemed to grow taller. Her voice rang out. The authority of her royal position filled the lab. "I am not at risk from the likes of Raiherr Yencara and his SorTech. They do not know with whom they are toying. When the council is ready, he and his men will regret joining forces with Karlsut Sorda."

Her gaze encompassed the group. "Before we make our plans, I wish to share something with each of you." She regarded Thorlu with respect. "You are here, Thorlu Tangorra, to exercise the new power you carry. Use it with integrity, and it will increase in ways that will surprise you."

Thorlu touched his heart. "I will strive to make those who trust me proud."

The Sun Queen's attention moved to Esán. "The Seeds of Carsilem continue their journey to full power. Do not become complacent, Esán Efre. Keep Tumu Noci, the Key to the Space-Time Continuum, until you have safely returned Inōni to her tribe."

She gazed at Gar. "You, like Abarax and La, belong to my family. Use your spectacles with care. The power they contain will grow as your talents mature." Her radiant smile washed over him. "Garon Anaru, I will always come to your aid when I deem it appropriate to do so."

A slight rotation brought her around to face Torgin. "Torgin Wilith Whalend, I admire your intelligence, your curiosity, and your musical talent." The Sun Queen raised her hands. The book, *The Secrets of the Space-Time*

Continuum, appeared on her upraised palms. "Please, place your palms on the book and close your eyes."

Torgin rested his hands on the book's ancient cover.

"Clear your mind and prepare to receive my gift. A reddish aura formed around Torgin as the Sun Queen whispered,

*"Book of Space Time intertwine
All your secrets within this mind.
Weave them through with sacred fire,
And this intellect inspire."*

With the last line of the verse fading into silence, the book vanished and Abellona's scepter appear in its place. Touching it to Torgin's chest, she spoke once more.

*"Sacred Scepter, leave your mark
Over Torgin Whalend's heart,
As a sign that he is blessed
With this power at my behest."*

"Open your eyes."

Esán suppressed a grin when Torgin's spine lengthened and his chest broadened. The boy he had first met on Myrrh over four sun cycles ago provided a stark contrast to the young man who faced the Sun Queen. *I remember when you were terrified of anything new or different, Torgin Whalend. Now, look at you!*

Torgin smiled. "Thank you, Your Majesty."

The queen studied him with an intense and questioning expression. "How do you feel?"

"As though you released me from a prison of my own making. Freedom of thought, eagerness to learn more, to compose new musical works, to live like I have never lived." An exhaled breath ended in a bemused smile. "The blood in my veins is throbbing in response." He scanned the group with heightened senses. "Awareness of my surroundings has magnified tenfold. Confidence fills me in ways I have not previously experienced. Thank you, Sun Queen, for the gifts you have given. I vow to use them for the benefit of all."

Abellona nodded her approval. Her gaze encompassed the group. "It is now time to act. To conquer our enemies, we must work together. Torgin, you will remain here to help develop a plan to remove the dome from Neul Isle. You will also be my line of communication to your companions."

"Aahana, you and Kat will take Gar and Esán to intercept Brie and her charges. Esán, please be prepared to act as my point person on the island. Explain to your friends what has occurred."

"Thorlu, you will accompany them and return here with Inōni. I have an important role for you to play."

An attendant entered and presented supply-packs to Gar and Esán and handed Thorlu a knapsack with packs for Den, Penee, and Brie.

The Sun Queen's gaze once again encompassed the group. "It is time. Remember, our enemies must not know you've visited the Realm of the Deities."

Gar gave a surprised squeak. "Holy Cow, where are we now?"

Esán grinned at the Old Earth expression and smiled at the beautiful woman standing next to Aahana.

Rethson, in the persona of Rily, stood unnoticed in the galley of the living ship, *El Aperdisa*. In his dual roles of server and assistant to the dessert chef, he could pick up bits of conversation throughout the mess hall. Nothing raised his suspicions until two men entered, filled their plates from the food bar, and sat down. Recognition hit him like a bolt of lightning. A shiver of dread chased up his spine. He was far too familiar with one of them.

Breathe. Don't give yourself away, Rily. With hard-edged control, he calmly replenished the dessert case. Empty tray under his arm, he walked to the galley, placed the tray on a countertop, and gripped the side of the sink.

The dessert chef looked up from preparing a plate of pastries. "Rily, you alright?"

With a tired smile, Riley nodded. "It's been a long turning, sir. Is there anything you need before I log out?"

"Go. Get some sleep. I'll see you tomorrow." The chef returned his attention to his work in progress.

Rily strolled from the galley, his mind buzzing. *Later, after lights out, I'll slip away to meet with Zak and Jem. They must know the identity of the person we're dealing with.*

⸻

Den Zironho put all his formidable strength into rowing the boat and its passengers toward Neul Isle. Knowledge gleaned from his previous visit to the island enabled him to plot a course to ÁFini Sacu, the first sheltered cove on the southeastern shore, where an inlet east of the cove's entrance would provide the perfect shelter for the night. Grateful to the youngest VarTerel for easing the pain in his arm, he focused on rowing.

Silence but for the occasional call of a bird and the dip and lift of the oar blades filled the boat. The island drew closer and closer. At the bow, Brie pointed to starboard and called over her shoulder. "Den, something beneath the surface!"

Making a course adjustment, Den projected his deep voice forward. "We're closing in on the mouth of the cove, Brie. Let me know when you see it."

Brie nodded, smoothed several unruly, copper-red curls back into her low ponytail, and concentrated on watching the water and the shoreline.

Den squinted up at the sky. The sun had reached its zenith and begun its slow glide toward the horizon. Fueled by determination and the need to arrive at their destination long before the sun set, he concentrated all his energy on reaching ÁFini Sacu.

Brie pointed, then announced over her shoulder. "Cove ahead. Stay your course."

Den smiled at her use of nautical terms and remembered she had spent time on a sailboat. A frown took the place of his smile when he glanced back at Penee and Inōni. The K'iin shaman's granddaughter carried a baby placed in her womb by the Protariflee experts on *El Aperdisa*...Penee's egg fertilized by his sperm. The child was a thank you gift to the K'iin for saving and protecting the VarTerels Henrietta and Irstant. A chill skittered over his skin. *Inōni is not safe as long as our enemies roam the island.*

"Den, steer to starboard! We are at the cove." Brie's voice jerked him back to the job at hand.

He shoved all concerns to the back of his mind and gave his full attention to rowing. Once inside the cove, he made good time in the calm water. Soon, the girls were helping him beach the rowboat at the head of the inlet. When they finished, Inōni and Penee began to gather edible plants, while he and Brie gathered dried wood to build a shelter.

"Look!" Penee's startled cry brought everyone's attention to two figures walking from the trees.

Brie dropped the piece of wood she held, ran, and threw her arms around Esán. Den strode to Inōni's side and smiled as Gar hugged Penee and grinned up at him.

"The Sun Queen sent us, Pen." Gar bit his lip. "Don't tell anyone."

Esán kissed Brie, brushed a curl off her forehead, and, gripping her hand, escorted her to join them. "Gar and I have a lot to share, but first..." He gave a soft whistle.

Thorlu stepped from the trees with two exotic beings flanking him on either side. After a brief conversation, the High DiMensioner walked over to join Den, Esán, and Gar.

Penee, Brie, and Inōni hurried over to Aahana and Kat, smiles of delight lighting their faces.

Den enjoyed their obvious pleasure at being reunited for even a short time before focusing his attention on Thorlu. "I know why Esán and Gar are here. What brings you to Neul Isle?"

Thorlu glanced at the women. "I am here to take Inōni back to Shiór Ridu." He explained the queen's request.

When the girls joined them, Thorlu took the lead. "Aahana, Kat, and I are here, Inōni, because you are not safe on Neul Isle. The Sun Queen has asked us to escort you to the safety of her palace until our enemies are dealt with. The sooner we leave, the better."

Den looked from the two young deities to the High DiMensioner. "How did you get here. Do you think you were noticed?"

Aahana smiled. "Kat and I combined our knowledge to create a shield. It erased our energy signatures and kept us invisible to the human eye." Her gaze darted over the cove. "We need to leave. Our power is a beacon for Raiherr and Callum. The longer we are together, the stronger our vibratory presence will be." She turned to Inōni. "Are you willing to come with us to Shiór Ridu?"

Inōni, her expression filled with awe, pressed her hands to her belly. "I am." She hugged Penee, Den, and Brie, bid Esán and Gar goodbye, and followed the Goddesses and Thorlu into the trees.

Moments later, a soft glow shimmered. Four figures floated from the treetops and faded into the colors of the summer sun.

With a sigh of relief, Den turned to his companions. "Are we safe here for the night?"

Esán surveyed the cove and surrounding shoreline. "The Seeds are quiet. I sense nothing moving our direction. Brielle?"

Brie walked to the boat, scanned the cove and the forest, and closed her eyes. When she opened them, she smiled and rejoined her friends. "Although I perceive nothing alarming, we still need to shield our energy. As Aahana noted, we are all powerful. Let's try not to attract our enemies to us by accident."

Gar's gaze darted one way and then the other. "How do we do that? If we all put up shields, won't that be like shouting that we're over here?"

Brie nodded. "You're right, Garon, and I believe I might have a solution." She turned to stare at the forest bordering the beach. "A hemlock tree called to me from deeper in the woods. I'm betting, since it communicated, it is like the hemlocks in the Terces Wood."

Gar stepped to her side. "So, how can a hemlock help us?"

She smiled. "If we each carry a sprig from a hemlock tree, it will shield our powerful presence, without giving us away. Now, you help Den and Esán find the best place to camp, while Penee and I look for it." She kissed Esán on the cheek and led Penee into the woods.

The urge to follow them made Den gulp a breath.

Gar stared up at him. "It's okay, Den. Brie will take care of Penee. They'll be back before you know it."

Smiling at the boy from Old Earth, Den joined him and Esán in a search for just the right campsite.

Brie and Penee hiked along the shoreline of the creek to a small mountain lake. Following the curve of the lakeshore, they ducked beneath low branches, climbed over big surface roots, and skirted large rocks. As they rounded the trunk of a massive deciduous tree, they came to a halt.

Brie laughed softly. "I knew we'd find a grove of hemlocks. Let's take a closer look."

Penee followed Brie between two trees and stopped beside her. "The clearing is big enough for us to camp here tonight. What do you think?"

Brie gazed up at the canopy of hemlock branches overhead. An ancient tree on the opposite side of the clearing lured her closer. Scattered at the base of the tree were five sprigs of hemlock. Brie picked them up, placed a palm against the trunk, and whispered,

> *"Hemlock, thank you for this gift.*
> *It will help us each to shift.*
> *Our power and essence will be hidden*
> *From those who come for us unbidden."*

She handed Penee a sprig. "We need to return to the boys before their presence is discovered."

Penee hurried after her. "Aren't we going to camp in the grove?"

Brie stopped. "Cast your thoughts back to the grove and see if it feels right to return."

With her hemlock sprig next to her heart, Penee closed her eyes. When they blinked open, surprise registered in their blue and green depths. Her voice vibrated with awe. "The old tree told me we will be safer closer to the beach. How does it know that?"

"Hemlocks hold an ancient magic that we must respect. Do I understand it?" Brie shook her head. "No, but I realize the truth and power of it. That it spoke in your mind says it honors you as its equal. Heeding its advice is vital to our safety. Come on. Let's get back to the beach."

4
El Aperdisa

Zak pressed further into the darkness in the engineering compartment on *El Aperdisa*, his heart pounding. A lanky crewman he did not recognize stopped under the passageway light near the hatch to the crews' quarters. Reedan joined him, his expression frosty and his eyes as hard as steel. Tension flashed between them.

The first man scowled. "This had better be good, Reed. I need my sleep. So, what's up?"

Reedan's return scowl accented the toothless gap in his front teeth. "You think I'd wake you if it weren't important?" His harsh expression skidded into a glare. "There's a new guy in engineering. He don't know much, so why'd they hire him, Nesen?"

"What did the Chief say?"

Nesen's hard-edged question made Zak strain to hear more and produced an odd expression on Reedan's face. Pinched lips and narrowed eyes scrunched his features together. His nostrils flared. "He introduced him as a Private but shared that he is a trainee in engineering. Who hires an untrained man to apprentice on a ship that's about to leave orbit?"

"Guess the Chief thinks he's got potential or—" Nesen chewed his bottom lip. "Keep your eye on him, Reed. See what you can learn about him. I doubt anyone realizes there are Vasro spies onboard, but you never know. Keep me posted." He yawned and walked back toward the T-lift.

Reedan's jaw tensed. Shaking his head, he hit the touch pad to the crew's quarters. Shoulders hunched, he stepped through the open hatch and into the shadows as it closed behind him.

Caution held Zak quiet, his attention fixed on the hatch across the way. *If he is truly one of our spies, he'll notice I'm missing and come looking for me.*

Seconds later, Reedan returned, his face a picture of frustrated annoyance. An angry scan of the passageway stopped at the utility compartment's open hatch.

Zak pushed further into the dark corner and melded into his surroundings.

Reedan stuck his head in the entrance, stepped in, and turned slowly. With a profane utterance, he marched across the passageway to the entry hatch and disappeared into the crewmen's quarters.

Zak remained hidden, waiting until Reedan's energy changed from anger to sleep.

Thorlu Tangorra returned to the Sun Queen's palace in Shiór Ridu with Aahana and Inōni. Kat, the Goddess of Small Creatures, deposited them near the portal at the top of Dia Bandia Mountain, bid them farewell and good fortune, and returned to her homeland. Aahana teleported them to the palace and escorted him to the Queen's reception area.

Impatient to learn what role Abellona wished him to play in the removal of Karlsut Sorda's men from Neul Isle, he forced himself to stand still and gaze out the window at the queen's domain in Shiór Ridu. Fascinated by the exotic, alien landscape of Chadēta Apól, he observed the fiery red of the sun painting highlights and shadows over mountains and plains. *It is as beautiful as it is alien.*

A noise behind him made him turn and smile. "You look excited, Torgin Whalend. What have you discovered?"

Before Torgin could reply, the door to the inner sanctum opened, and a female attendant entered. "I am Queen Abellona's receptionist. She will see you both now. Please follow me."

The receptionist led them across a large open area to a double door engraved with the Sun Queen's ancestral symbol. After knocking softly, she entered. "Your guests are here, My Lady. May I show them in?"

"You may, Miâseena."

The young woman moved aside. Thorlu and Torgin walked into a room glowing with the light of the immense Soputton sun. Abellona sat on a throne, her regal presence washing over them. With reverence and respect, they bowed their heads and waited.

"Welcome, honored guests." The Queen rose, descended the two steps, and scrutinized Thorlu and then Torgin. "Miâseena, you may go. Gentlemen, please come with me." Her coal-black braids afire from the sun's radiance, she led them to a sitting area and lowered elegantly into a ruby-red velvet chair. Indicating two chairs opposite her, she smiled. "Please be seated."

Her fire-opal gaze examined first Torgin and then the High DiMensioner. "Thorlu, thank you for escorting Inōni to the safety of Shiór Ridu. I know you are eager to learn more about my plans for you. Please be patient while Torgin shares what he has learned. You will, I assure you, find it interesting. Torgin..."

Excitement glinting in Torgin's eyes, he met Thorlu's intense gaze. "I replicated Callum's SorTechory Box and traveled back in time to before he made the changes. Indeed, The Box is the means by which he created the dome over Neul Isle." Torgin withdrew the time whistle from beneath his tunic. "He does not realize there is a flaw in his new design. Using this..." He held up the fire-painted whistle. "...and Tumu Noci, I can create a doorway through the side of the dome. When we are ready, I can remove the dome altogether."

Thorlu's brows bridged. "Why didn't you just destroy The Box before he changed it?"

Abellona interjected. "Altering the workings of what occurred in the past only creates bigger problems. Making changes is much safer in the present." She smiled. "You have done well, Torgin. What else did you discover?"

"Raiherr and his men arrived on Neul Isle in a jumper craft, which is hidden on the Plains of Cârthea."

Thorlu turned narrowed eyes to scrutinize the Sun Queen. "What now?"

"You and Torgin will return to Neul Isle and work together to neutralize Raiherr and his men. The Council of Deities is certain Karlsut Sorda sent the message threatening Soputto. Although, like the Inner Universe's Galactic Council, they will not interfere, they would like this confirmed. Which does not mean they will allow a devious, self-serving Human to threaten to destroy a planet. Thorlu and Torgin, with the help of your friends, you will do this work. When it is safe to do so, you will return Inōni to her people."

Torgin pursed his lips in thought. His gaze moved from the Sun Queen to Thorlu. "You can shape shift, correct?"

"I can. Why?" Thorlu waited, his curiosity peaked by the young man opposite him.

"Unless you have a better idea, I believe we should not enter the dome in our human shapes. My preferred shifted form is the bald eagle. What's yours?"

Abellona smiled, raised a hand, and shifted. A fire eagle soared through the room, landed on the throne, and returned to humanesque form. The queen's fire-opal eyes gleamed. "The Soputton fire eagle is known for its beauty and its powerful presence. It is also endemic to this planet. I suggest you use its shape. It will hide your human essence and allow you to enter the dome undetected. If you agree, I will alert Abarax and La to watch for you in fire eagle form. They will provide for your needs once you arrive."

Thorlu rose from his chair. "May I attempt a shift to it here, Your Majesty?"

She smiled her gracious smile. "Please, make the shift."

He looked from Torgin to the Queen. "What is the most important thing to know about this bird of prey?"

Abellona smiled and again lifted her hand.

Thorlu's hand flew to his heart. The power of eagle coursed through his brain. Mental clarity and extraordinary vision helped him to shift and take flight. A laugh of pure delight accompanied his return to Human. He smiled at the Queen. "What an incredible bird! I see why you chose the eagle."

The Sun Queen rose. "Aahana will take you to Lake Llyn on the continent of Dast and leave you at the cottage of Penee's proxy parents. From there, you can fly to Neul Isle. Torgin's compass will guide you. Since the dome appears to obscure anything or anyone outside its walls, you can explore the exposed shore for the best place to enter the dome. I suggest you find and deal with The Box before you do anything else. Trust your instincts. Your friends have their goal—to free the K'iin. When that is done and you have Raiherr and his SorTech under your control, I will have Inōni brought to you."

A tall, dark-skinned male attendant entered the room and bowed. "You called, My Sovereign Queen?"

"Please take my guests to their suite. Make certain they are well-fed and have everything they require for their upcoming adventure."

With a gracious bow, the Sun Queen of Soputto vanished.

On Neul Isle, Rina, the Incirrata, met with her Stannags deep beneath Rina Island. Telepathic messages flew among them. Abarax reported that a Human it recognized as a low level Mocendi and his SorTech had created the dome. La informed them she had discovered the Mocendi's men had taken over the K'iin's village and imprisoned the Shaman, Dri Adoh and the K'iin chief, Artānga. When they finished, Rina shared that Brie and her friends rowed toward the far side of the island.

As they conversed, Abarax's chest glowed red. Its phantom essence quivered; pale blue eyes changed to fire-opal greens and reds. When the glow faded, the Astican's blue eyes blinked open and focused on the Incirrata. *"The Sun Queen is sending the Humans, Thorlu Tangorra and Torgin Whalend to assist us in our fight. We are to provide them with whatever they require."* Its huge wings spread in response as it expressed its delight and then folded into place. *"Even as Stannag, I am too big to exit through the dome to meet them. If I tried, it would change the dome's frequency and alert our enemies."*

La landed on a piece of coral. *"I make me smaller. Go through dome. No change.* Silence held her momentarily still. *"What message me share?"*

Rina's Incirrata brains sought the best response. *Tell Torgin and Thorlu what we know. Advice them to enter the dome near the Forest of Deora. Then you will both join them in the fight to free the K'iin and rid Neul Isle of the enemy."*

When they had defined their basic plans, Rina sent Abarax and La to intercept the two incoming Humans. Putting her nine brains to work, she focused on her first priority—the defense of the sacred isle. After alerting Penee and Den by igniting their tattoos, she established a mental screen around the camp near Rina Island. *Knowing one's enemies is paramount to the success of any attempt to bring them to their knees.* With all brains alert, she began to listen.

On the beach bordering the inlet in ÁFini Sacu, Brie placed an invisibility charm on the rowboat and helped her friends to build a makeshift shelter for the night within the trees nearby. In the supply-packs provided by the queen, the companions discovered sleeping pads, weather blankets, energy snacks, and canteens of water. They arranged everything for the night, then gathered on the beach in the late afternoon light.

Brie slipped a hand into Esán's. "Thank goodness for the supplies Thorlu brought from Abellona."

Gar rubbed his rumbling stomach. "The Sun Queen thought of almost everything. What're we gonna eat?" He held up an energy packet. "This won't fill me up."

Den chuckled. "How about we go fishing?"

"Nice thought, but we can't build a fire, right?" Gar puckered his mouth in a pout.

Penee bent down to look him in the eye. "When I was a girl, my cousin, Skultar, locked me in a stall in the barn. He said it was to keep me safe." She scrunched up her nose and glanced up at Den. "A boy helped me a couple times. One night after everyone was asleep, he snuck into the barn, taught me how to build a fire in a pit, and then showed me how to cook vegetables on a pointed stick over the coals." She straightened and flashed a smile at Den.

Gar grinned. "I bet it was you, Den. You gonna show us how to cook fish over a fire pit?"

Den's blue eyes flecked with amethyst sparked with laughter. He tapped his chin and gazed at the group. "Our problem..." His tapping ceased. "There will be some smoke, and it might give our position away."

"I know!" Gar clapped his hands. "Our VarTerel can make the smoke go away. Right, Brie?"

Brie stared out at the cove. Her eyes narrowed; her lips pursed. A soft laugh released the facial tension and left her smiling. "WoNa taught me a charm to fool anyone pursuing me in the desert. I'm certain I can make it work with a fire, so let me know when the pit's ready."

Gar gave her a quick hug. "Thanks, VarTerel!"

Den grinned and took charge. "I'll prepare the pit. Gar and Esán, see if you can catch some fish. I thought I saw some brook charrs in the spot where the stream widens. Check your pack for some fishing line. Brie, you can help Penee with the edible plants she and Inōni gathered and look for some clams. I'll let you know when I'm ready for the charm."

He pulled a foldable shovel from his pack, and, humming to himself, began to dig. When he was satisfied with the size of the pit, he lined the bottom with rocks, then built a teepee of driftwood over a pile of dry grass, moss, and twigs. Next, he searched for forked branches, which he cut to size with the hunting knife from his pack and positioned one in each corner of the pit. Laying two more straight sticks aside, he stood up, surveyed the beach, spotted Penee and Brie, and gave a low whistle.

The girls arrived beside him, looking more relaxed than he'd seen them in several turnings, their hands filled with clams. Gar and Esán strode from the trees at the mouth of the stream, carrying five silvery charrs and sporting happy smiles.

Den waved. "Fire's laid and ready to start." He plucked several large leaves from a nearby bush and laid them on the ground near the pit as his companions joined him. "Put your bounty on the leaves. We're about to have a feast. What do we need to do, Brielle?"

After depositing her treasures on the leaves, Brie gazed at the laid fire. "I'll say the charm. As soon as I'm finished, I'll signal you to light the fire. Position yourself where you need to be, Den. Esán and Gar, please stand behind me and give me your support. Penee, please join Den."

Penee nodded and went down on her knees next to him.

Den rubbed his hands together. "I'm ready when you are, Varterel."

Brie knelt and held her hands, palm down, over the pit. Taking a breath, she recited WoNa's charm.

> *"Smoke that rises from this fire*
> *Catch the wind, let it inspire;*
> *Waft and float into the sky,*
> *And shift into a dragonfly.*
>
> *On wings of light, fly through the dome.*
> *Discover where our enemies roam;*
> *Fill their minds with secret fear*
> *That magnifies as we draw near."*

At her signal, Den again rubbed his palms together three times, ending with his right index finger pointed at the teepee of wood. "Dencinio!" A mini zigzag of blue lightning shot from his fingertip, sending a shower of sparks between two sticks in the driftwood teepee. Dried moss burst into flames which curled the dry grass and licked along each twig until the driftwood caught. Beside him, Penee gasped. He looked up in time to see smoke wafting upward. One-by-one, five azure-blue dragonflies materialized. Silvery wings shimmering, they hovered above the flames, dispersing the smoke.

Once the fire burned down and smoke thinned to occasional wisps, the dragonflies flew toward the dome and disappeared.

Gar's smile filled his face. He hugged Brie. "Knew you could do it! Now, tell us what to do, Den. My stomach can hardly wait!"

Pulling out his knife, Den showed his friends how to slit the fish's belly open and remove the internal organs and then the gills. Once the fish were ready to cook, he demonstrated how to sharpen the end of a straight stick. By the time they had accomplished these tasks, coals glowed red-hot in the pit. He placed the two straight sticks in the forked Vs on the two longest sides of the pit, and picked up a charr brook. "Take a fish and slide the stick into its tail and out its mouth." When his demonstration was complete, he rested the ends of the stick on the makeshift rack with the fish over the coals.

Esán finished, balanced his on the rack, and helped Gar. Brie set her fish next to theirs, and Penee positioned hers at the end. Den then placed the clams around the edge of the coals while Brie helped Penee arrange their collected greens on two large round leaves.

Dusk's light crept in while they feasted. Ever-vigilant, Den sent a mental probe throughout the cove. When nothing suggested trouble, he chewed another bite of fish, savored a clam, and allowed himself to enjoy the moment.

5
El Aperdisa

Observation Deck 3 on *El Aperdisa* was one of Ari's favorite places. When her watch on the control bridge ended, she had slipped away. Still in Jem's form, she now stared out an oval view-portal into the vast darkness of space. *Where are you, Brielle? Are you safe?*

Forcing herself to focus on her Jem persona, she took a moment to embrace it fully before leaving.

Jem shook off a growing sense of malaise, strode from the observation deck, and headed for the one of the newly engineered T-lifts. As the doors slid open, an officer greeted him with a nod. Jem returned it and stepped into the car. A quiet whoosh later, the lift stopped. The officer smiled. "Sure like our new transport system. It's about time they replaced the old Drops." He exited—the doors closed. Jem gritted his teeth, massaged his painful thumb, and frowned. At the level of the passenger quarters, he stepped from the T-lift and hurried along the corridor. He had almost reached Penee's entry hatch when he gasped.

A ri flashed into being. Mortified by her lack of control, she hurried the last stretch to the touchpad, put in the code, and dodged inside.

A shaky breath later, she sank into a chair and buried her face in her hands. *What made me shift like that?* Her thumb tingled. She blinked, and smoothed her hair back from her face. *Of course! Mira had Ira's thumb sting when he needed to shift to me. The trigger is still working.* She frowned. *Wish I'd thought of it before. I hope no one saw me.* Lowering her hands, she stared at her thumb. *I won't ignore your warning again.*

The hatch light flashing brought her to her feet and into Jem form. On the viewer screen, two crew members stood, backs to the screen, arguing. Tuning her hearing to the passageway, she listened.

"I'm telling you, I saw Arienh AsTar enter these quarters."

"Ya, right. She's not even on board the ship. You seein' ghosts or something?"

His features in shadow, the first man turned to stare at the hatch. "What if she is in there? She can tell us where her friends are. I'm going in."

"Sure you want to end up in the brig for a 'what if?'" The second man shoved his hands in his pockets and strode from sight.

Still in Jem form, Ari held her breath as the first man moved from shadow into light. His unfamiliar features—hooded, dark eyes rimmed with gray; a thin, crooked nose; and cruel mouth—etched itself into memory.

"I'm gonna find out if you're on board, Arienh AsTar. And if you are—" He shook his fist at the viewer and, muttering to himself, walked down the passageway.

Dizzy with relief, Ari shifted and slumped onto the edge of the chair. The accidental return to her true form had almost gotten her caught. "Ari, you are an idiot." She sat up straighter. *On the positive side—I got a peek at a potential spy. Now, all I have to do is pick his face out of the crowd.*

Inōni sat in an elegant sitting room, gazing over the ember-bright landscape of the Sun Queen's domain. *My life has changed so much since the VarTerels arrived in our village several sun cycles ago.* She gazed down at her belly. *Who would have imagined, little one, we would be guests in Shiór Ridu?*

Pressing her hands to the roundness, she whispered, "I can't wait to hold you in my arms." A kick made her smile. Humility moved her to tears. "You carry powerful genes and will grow to be a wise woman, a spiritual leader of the K'iin. Protecting you is my sole purpose in this life."

She closed her eyes and sang a sacred song.

> "Baby nestled deep inside,
> You are my love; you are my pride.
> You share my blood, my heart, my soul;
> Each will help you become whole.
>
> Ancients bless this sacred being.
> Give her the gift of future seeing.
> Grant her wisdom and the talents
> To maintain Neul Isles' balance."

As she finished, she blinked and looked up. Her eyes rounded. A gentle hand touched her shoulder as she prepared to rise.

The Sun Queen smiled at her. "You have a beautiful voice, Daughter of the K'iin." She sat down. "I realize the wee one you carry is from the seed of Penesert el Stroma and the sperm of Den Zironho. They granted you this gift as a thank you to your tribe for saving the VarTerels, Henrietta Avetlire and Irstant. How were you chosen to be the host mother?"

Inōni smiled. "My grandfather asked for a tribal woman to travel with Den and Penee to the ship *El Aperdisa* to undergo Protariflee. I volunteered. It has been several moon cycles since I left the village."

The queen turned toward her, a thoughtful expression on her regal face. "May I place my hands on your abdomen?"

Inōni smiled. "Of course, you may."

Gentle hands rested on her baby-rounded belly. The Queen closed her eyes and quieted her breathing. The baby kicked. A soft laugh, cut short by a startled inhale, brought the queen's head up and her hands to her heart. She examined Inōni with glowing opal eyes. "You know the gender of the child?"

"I do." Inōni lowered her gaze to her belly. "I carry a girl."

The queen smiled. "I would like to bless your child, Inōni, but I must first gain the permission of Dri Adoh. When our enemies are gone and Neul Isle is once again safe, I will return with you to your village. Until then, you must remain here."

Queen Abellona's eyes flashed green, then scarlet. "Come in, Xairā."

Inōni turned as a young woman about her age entered. With one hand on her heart and the other resting on the hilt of her sword, she bowed before her monarch. When she straightened, she snapped to attention and waited.

"You may relax, Xairā. I have an assignment for you. Please listen with care."

While the queen explained Inōni's presence and the importance of the child she carried, Inōni studied the young woman. Her deep red and gold uniform marked her as part of the Queen's Personal Guard. Black hair streaked with red and slicked back into a bun framed a warm brown face that reminded Inōni of her tribal members. Respectful adoration for the queen gleamed in dark chestnut eyes flecked with indigo and amber. She listened with total attention.

The Sun Queen paused, then nodded at her guard and spoke to Inōni. "This young woman is one of my personal guards. Her name is Xairā. I have asked her to remain at your side until we take you back to the Valley of Tá Súil and your tribal clan. Since it is vital she not call attention to her position, she will dress as you dress and learn from you the ways of your people." With that, she rose from her seat and faded, first to a figure of fire, and then to a swirl of light that grew smaller and smaller until it vanished.

Xairā offered Inōni a hand. "Why don't we go to your quarters and get to know each other? My queen shared that her dresser left new clothing there for both of us." She stroked the tailored fit of her jacket. "It will be interesting to dress as a woman instead of one of My Lady's guards."

A comfortable silence engulfed them as they left the sitting room.

Abellona materialized in her private study, seriousness engulfing her like a cloak. She crossed the room to stand in front of her portrait. Her visit to Inōni had magnified her desire to be rid of the interlopers on Neul Isle. *The stakes are much higher than anyone realized.*

SparrowLyn's painting did not provide an answer to her primary question... how to remove the dome.

She touched the frame and whispered, "I have much to contemplate. Time is the key. I must watch and wait and not allow the situation to escalate."

After a long nap and a hardy meal, Torgin and Thorlu changed to camouflage-patterned clothing provided by order of the queen and prepared to depart Shiór Ridu.

Torgin tucked his compass and the time whistle beneath his shirt. "I'm ready to go whenever you are, Thorlu."

The former Mocendi stared out the window for several chron-clicks before he turned, his expression thoughtful. "Let's make a plan that's flexible enough to get us started on the queen's quest but can change as needed. Do you know the cottage where we are going?"

"No. I was doing research in the Galactic Library on Myrrh when Brie first took Penee there." He held up a key. "Pen gave me this in case. It will open the side door. Do you think we'll spend time there?"

Thorlu shook his head. "Karlsut knows the cottage, so we only want to stay there if necessary. I suggest we fly directly to Neul Isle and meet up with Abarax and La first."

Torgin nodded. "Hope they have information to share." He ran a hand through his hair. "My instincts are nudging. We need to go."

"I believe I am to be your guide." Aahana's pleasant voice brought a welcoming smile from the men.

Thorlu took the lead. "We're very glad to see you, Aahana."

"Mamai ask me to inform you the cottage is being watched. I am to take you to a beach on the eastern side of the Sileah Mountains. From there, Ostradio will guide you. Please follow me." She led the way to the balcony and stepped outside.

Torgin gasped as heat penetrated his clothing and sent sweat rolling down his neck. Beside him, Thorlu swore.

A blue aura formed around Aahana. "Stand close to me."

Striding forward, Torgin took his place on one side and Thorlu on the other. The moment the expanding circle of blue light touched him, Torgin felt coolness wash over his body.

Weightlessness carried the trio upward. Aahana whispered a command. A portal opened in the red sky, and the blue light carried them through it. Far below, the continent of Dast appeared and rose to meet them.

On the beach in Áfini Sacu, Brie and her companions awoke to the coolness of morning. The rising sun washed the sky in golden light streaked with pastel hues of pink and lavender. Breakfast, freshly picked berries and protein biscuits from the Sun Queen's supply-packs, provided a quick meal and gave them time to awaken fully before they prepared to row further along the coast.

When they were ready, Brie banished the spell of invisibility. While Den and Esán uncovered the boat and pushed it to the water's edge, she scanned the beach and the bay with squinted eyes.

Penee walked along the narrow beach to stand next to her. "What are you sensing?"

"Something's changed, but I'm not sure what." Brie frowned. "Right now, it's pretty far away." She linked her arm through Penee's. "Let's confer with Den and Esán. Perhaps one of them senses something."

As they hiked up the beach, Gar sprinted from the trees. "Hey! My spectacles just appeared, and they're glowing. What do ya suppose is up?"

The companions gathered next to the wooden boat. Esán's eyes narrowed as he studied Gar's face. "Did you just say your specs appeared on their own?"

"Yep. Just like before."

Esán frowned. "Brie, you sensed something, too?"

She explained her flash of insight and continued. "I don't believe we are in danger yet, but I think Abellona is letting us know via Gar's spectacles that we need to get moving."

Penee spoke up. "Den, you said there's a cove close to the Forest of Deora, right?"

Rubbing his tattooed arm, he nodded. "Créada Sacu is the closest access to the forest and to Lake Chittârine, where we can determine if swimming beneath the dome is possible. If we can't, we need to find another way inside that won't alert our enemies. He grimaced. "Pen, is your tattoo burning?"

Penee answered with a nod and showed the glowing incirrata tentacle spanning the length of her arm. "It is, though, not like yesterday."

Esán edged toward the boat. "We need to go. Grab your packs. Den, I'll help row, so prepare both sets of oars. You take the aft and I'll take the forward bench."

While Brie, Penee, and Gar climbed in and took their seats, Esán and Den rolled up their pant legs and positioned themselves on either side of the bow. Thankful for the slack tide, Esán scanned the calm bay and nodded at Den. Together they inched the boat over the gravel and sand until it was on the verge of floating free. Den swung a leg over the gunnel and climbed aboard. After setting both sets of oars in their oarlocks, he took his seat.

Esán pushed the boat out through the cool water until it was free of the bottom, then scrambled in. A couple of gulped breaths later, he gripped his oars, and signaled Den. Together, they maneuvered the bow toward the cove's mouth. Their synchronized dip, pull, and lift of the oars propelled the boat forward.

In the stern, Penee and Gar stared ahead as the mouth of the bay drew closer. From her seat in the bow, Brie prepared to warn Esán and Den of any hazards that might appear.

Within a grove of trees at the northeastern end of Dunes Beach on Dast, Torgin and Thorlu watched Aahana fade into the morning light. Moving to a better vantage point, they took stock of their location.

Torgin withdrew the Compass of Ostradio from beneath his shirt, and held it out toward Thorlu. "Let's see what we can discover."

The High DiMensioner stepped closer. "I've always wanted to observe Ostradio at work. What do we need to do?"

With his gaze fixed on the compass face, Torgin envisioned the map of the holographic island the Sun Queen had shared. "Show us Neul Isle."

The golden compass needle blurred into a spin and stopped, pointing south. A map formed above the compass face. Thorlu bent closer, then straightened. "If I were your friends, I'd be heading for the Forest of Deora." He frowned. "Even if they reach it, how will they get through the dome?"

Torgin pointed. "I expect they'll hike to Lake Chittârine to see if they can swim under it."

Again, Thorlu bent over the compass map. The sooner we locate and eliminate The Box, the better. What if we head for Gisa Point? It's close enough to Rina Island, but far enough from Raiherr and his gang's camp that they won't sense our presence."

"Agreed." Torgin took a last look. The map faded, and the compass went quiet in his hand. He had just tucked it beneath his shirt when Thorlu gripped his arm and pulled him deeper into the trees.

Swooping low over the beach was a Q-Seeker. It made several passes from the high cliffs to the towering rocks and back to the high cliffs. A final flight along the beach propelled it up and over the dunes between the beach and the mountains.

Torgin let out a breath. "Good catch, Thorlu. We'd better go before it comes back." Shifting to a fire eagle, he flew from the trees over the sparkling sea, landed on the furthest towering rock, and waited for Thorlu to catch up. After a short breather, they launched into the air and soared over the open ocean.

6
Neul Isle

Klutarse Hossela, Skultar Rados' personal assassin and spy, had arrived on Neul Isle in his own jumper craft shortly after Raiherr's craft had landed. Secluded in the thicket of long-needled pines covering the ridge above the Vasro's camp, he lowered a tree branch and peered at the men below. *Hope Skultar doesn't discover I'm working with his brother.* He shrugged. *Karlsut pays good.*

An argument below refocused his attention on the clearing. *Sorda doesn't trust Zorin and Raiherr or their low level Vasro comrade, Dulno.* He scrunched his brows in concentration. *Too bad he wants the Mocendi wannabe and his Vasro alive. I know just the way to make them wish they'd never been born.*

He gazed up through the dome-generated dimness and scowled. *What are you up to, Raiherr? Why the dome?* A movement near the SorTech's Box made him look closer.

Callum rubbed a flabby cheek, opened the front panel of the reddish-brown box, and stood fiddling with the controls. Light to the side of it wavered, faded, and refocused into a steady shaft. More fiddling produced a hologram of their jumper craft hidden close by.

Raiherr joined his SorTech. "So, you've got it working. Show us something we don't know."

The tide pool at the end of the lagoon replaced the craft. Callum touched a pale blue light pad with a stubby index finger. The Box hummed. The image zoomed-out, showing the empty clearing around the pool. "Brie and her friends are not hiding there."

The Vasro leader scowled. "I got a report they aren't at the Lyn Lake cottage either. So...where are they?"

Callum adjusted The Box's controls. "I'm still working on some changes. Right now, we can't see out and no one can see in. I need more time."

Raiherr's frustrated scowl grew threatening. "Our time is finite, Callum. My last update on *El Aperdisa* stated the commander sent the young people to different places to prepare for the trip to El Stroma. I don't believe it for a chron-click. Do you honestly think Ari and Esán don't realize Brie's heading for trouble? I need to know right now whether anyone is on or near Neul Isle."

The SorTech turned his back, his exasperation vibrating around him. Bending over The Box, he began to work the new controls.

In the trees, what Hossela had learned triggered an alarm. *What if they search under the dome?* He scowled. *My craft and my presence are at risk.* Lips pressed together, he glared at the men in the clearing. *What's more important...spying on these idiots doing nothing or making sure they don't discover they have unwanted company?* Muttering under his breath, he slipped away.

On the opposite side of the island, Brie and her friends had reached their goal and now stood on the beach at the west end of Créada Sacu. The rowboat was well-hidden in the trees near a narrow gully between two moss-covered hills. Brie shrugged her supply-pack into place, tightened a strap, and reached for Esán's hand. "Let's find out if it's possible to enter Lake Chittârine and swim under the dome."

Gar held up his spectacles. "I can lead us." He hooked the temples over his ears. "I'll tell you if there's any weird stuff in our way."

Den chuckled. "Lead on, young Gar." He followed.

Penee fell in line behind him.

Brie squeezed Esán's hand. "I'm so glad you're here."

Esán returned the squeeze. "So am I." He pointed up the gully where Gar skirted a large stone, then climbed onto a curved tree root. "Garon never ceases to amaze me. What an adventurous spirit he has."

The boy waved them forward, jumped to the ground, and continued along the gully.

Brie glanced over her shoulder. *Something's about to change. Hope it's—* She shivered and moved closer to Esán.

Torgin's eagle talons touched down at the water's edge west of Gisa Point. An eagle's screech close by heralded Thorlu's arrival. Both fire eagles surveyed the coastline and mountains rising above the trees behind them. Torgin laughed when he and the High DiMensioner materialized in the same instant. "How are you liking your fire eagle form, Thorlu?"

The High DiMensioner grinned. "I love it!" He sobered. "Let's have a look at Ostradio."

Torgin scanned the area once more with human eyes and withdrew the compass. "Show us the closest place to examine the dome."

The gold needle spun and stopped. A map rising above it highlighted Timhé Valley.

Thorlu studied the map, then glanced up at the sky. "At least it's still early. Let's go." He shifted and shot toward the mountains.

Memorizing the map's details, Torgin watched it fade, tucked the compass beneath his shirt, and changed to a fire eagle. Reveling in the delight of flight, he followed. At the top of a high plateau, he found Thorlu standing with his hand shading his eyes, staring at the dome blocking the way not far ahead.

After a long glide to a landing, Torgin shifted and gazed with a scholar's interest at the sun washing the dome and the opaque dimness, obscuring everything captured within it. A spark of crystal light caught his eye. "Thorlu —" He gripped the High DiMensioner's arm.

Both men held their breath as a tiny moth shimmered free of the dome and grew into a full-sized luna moth. Torgin held out a hand.

The moth landed. Her telepathic message filled his mind. *"I La. Abarax inside dome. Sun Queen say to help you. Rina say tell you Brie on other side of island. Abarax and I meet you in Forest of Deora."* She lifted into the air, brushed Torgin's cheek, then Thorlu's with the soft tip of her wing, shrunk to a pinprick of light, and disappeared through the dome.

Torgin repeated her telepathic message for Thorlu, who nodded and reached toward the spot where she disappeared.

Catching his arm, Torgin explained, "If you touch it, the dome frequency in that spot will change and alert Callum."

The High DiMensioner sighed. "I didn't realize how beautiful La was when I was here before. All I wanted was to catch her and—"

Torgin shook his head. "You are a different man now. Treasure that." He touched his cheek. "And treasure the kiss of the luna moth's wing."

"Thank you for the vote of confidence, Torgin." Thorlu stroked his beard. "If we get distracted and fly off course, do you know the way?"

Torgin tapped his temple. "Map's in here, so I'll lead." He shifted.

With strong eagle wings pressing the air and the eagle's keen sight picking out landmarks below, Torgin led Thorlu along the mountainous western coast of Neul Isle. They skirted the dome and swooped low over a river east of Bholcàno, the island's dormant volcano, and stopped for a quick break.

When they were ready to continue, Torgin's eagle soared upward, leading the way. With the freedom of flight engendering a wave of delight, he caught an air current and leveled off. A faint warning tingled through his feathers. Eagle-acute hearing picked up a low hum. Swooping past Thorlu, who had taken the lead, he landed in a crevice between two high mountain slopes and shifted. As soon as the High DiMensioner stood beside him, Torgin pressed a finger to his lip.

Thorlu listened intently, then whispered. "A Quest-Seeker, more commonly know as a Q-Seeker, Raiherr's favorite toy." He pulled Torgin beneath an overhang. "Which means he has someone working outside the dome."

Torgin clenched his teeth and exhaled a shuddering breath. "We have to warn the others." His brows bridged. "Because eagles mate for life, two flying close shouldn't alert the enemy. I know where Brie and the gang are heading. If we can intercept them, we might all be able to hide before we're seen."

"If we destroy the Q-Seeker..." Thorlu pressed his lips together. His negative expression brightened. Certainty filled his voice. "...Raiherr will know there's someone on this side of the island and focus on finding out who."

"That would give Brie and the others time to reach the lake without being discovered." Torgin squinted into the distance. An idea took shape. "What if one of us leads the Seeker out over the ocean and forces it into the water?"

"Good idea, but..." Thorlu inhaled. "...I don't think we should separate. I'm betting the controller has several types of Q-Seekers."

Torgin frowned. "Hope he doesn't have any Stalker-Rangers."

"Agreed. Especially the S-Ranger know as a Howler—an even better reason to stay together."

"Alright, let's do this before it gets any later." Torgin ducked into the ravine.

Thorlu followed, shifted, and flew upwards.

Torgin embraced his fire eagle and soared from the ravine.

Outside the dome near the tide pool at the south end of the lagoon, Pakdon, one of Raiherr's recruits, brought the Quest-Seeker in for a landing. *I've found nothing, and I've been at this for chron-circles. Maybe it's time to quit.* He tapped the control sensor implanted in his palm to power off the haptic holo's remote feed and gave the silver holo lenses covering his eyes a moment to withdraw. *Better not make the boss angry. He can be pretty nasty.*

Pakdon chewed his bottom lip. *Raiherr hired me because I'm an expert Haptic Holo Controller and helped to develop this latest Quest-Seeker. Not just any HHC could accomplish what I have.* He pinched the bridge of his nose. *If only I'd known more about the Vasro movement before—* A yawn left him watery-eyed. "Resting will have to wait." With a quick series of taps, he powered up the haptic sensor array, touched his fingertips to his thumbs, and waited for the silvery holo lenses to cover his eyes. He adjusted the Q-Seeker's settings to autonomous, set the launch course, and activated it. A bird's screeching brought his head up and his gaze darting skyward.

"What the—" He ducked, barely missing the wingtip of an enormous fire eagle swooping over the clearing. Swearing, Pakdon scrambled to regain his footing and prepared to launch the Q-Seeker. Wing-wind whipped around him. A second eagle's black talons filled Pakdon's vision, then snatched up the Quest-Seeker and soared upward. "Hey! Stop! Bring that back—"

His shout followed the disappearing eagle over the mountains toward the sea.

Aghast and vexed at his failure to out-maneuver the two birds of prey, Pakdon moaned. *Raiherr is going to kill me.* His holo lenses showing him the Q-Seeker plummeting downward into the water triggered a full-body shudder.

He put the remote power feed on pause and waited for his lenses to clear. When he could see the world around him, he grabbed his pack and pulled out the Stalker-Ranger known as a Howler. A quick check later, he put it on the ground, tapped his fingers to his thumbs, and waited for the holo lenses to cover his eyes. When they were in place, he touched his palm controller to set the Howler's weapons on locate and stun, pressed his index fingers to his thumbs, and through his holo lenses watched it rocket skyward.

Torgin's eagle form released the Q-Seeker into the sea and banked back to the shore. Halfway there a stalker-ranger he recognized as a powerful Howler shot over his swooping body and angled upward.

High above, Thorlu's eagle led the S-Ranger one way and then the other. No matter how unexpectedly the High DiMensioner's eagle form changed direction, the Howler steadily closed the gap between them. Taking emergency evasive action, Thorlu pressed eagle wings close to his side, pointed his beak downward, and made and abrupt arrow-like swoop.

A streaking ray of red light narrowly missed the eagle's tail feathers. The Howler dropped lower. A predatory wail accompanied its change of trajectory, all sensors focused on the underbelly of Thorlu's eagle.

Torgin hovered on outstretched wings outside the bounds of the Howler's far-seeking telegenic eye. A soft tingling sensation beneath his back feathers alerted him to his fellow eagle's call for help. Soaring higher, Torgin streaked toward the Howler and his good friend.

Thorlu's wings pressed harder, sending him in an upward curve leading back toward Bholcàno. The Howler sped up, its aggressive roar echoing off the fast approaching mountains.

Banking to the east in a widening circle, Thorlu swooped beneath it, leading it ever closer to the volcano's craterous mouth.

High above, Torgin, his wings flattened against his muscled eagle body, shot straight for the Howler. Once in range, he unfurled his massive pinions to decrease his speed. Feathered legs outstretched, he primed his talons and gripped the streamlined Howler. A long, low glide positioned him to release it against the jagged, lava-blackened side of the volcano. After several attempts to right itself, it lay still, a gaping crack in its rounded, metallic silver canopy.

Torgin's eagle swooped into positioned over it. Executing a series of smooth, connected movements, he wrapped strong talons around the unresponsive stalker-ranger, flew up and over the volcano's cavernous mouth, and released it. Perched on the crater's edge, his acute eagle sight picked out the once powerful Howler tumbling into darkness and shattering on the scabrous blackened stones below.

Pakdon watched his stalker-ranger, clasped in eagle talons, disappear toward Bholcàno and groaned. He turned to stare at the dome only a short distance away. "Callum will realize something happened when he loses the Howler's signal." Again, he studied the dome. "Good thing I brought several more."

He scrambled to his feet. "Raiherr's short on patience. Shoulda brought another backup with me for this run." A muttered string of profanities escorted him into a narrow ravine which zigzagged toward the ocean. In a valley flanked by steep cliffs on one side and a gentle slope leading to the sea on the other, a small jumper craft rested midway to the shore.

Flipping up the cover to the ship's entry pad, Pakdon entered a frequency code. A hatch slid open and closed automatically behind him. He stood in the dim coolness of the ship, absorbed the quiet calm, and sighed. The pilot's seat beckoned. Hands resting on its back, he gazed into the distance.

"Why did I sign on with Raiherr Yencara? He is as deceitful as his boss and more power-hungry."

Again, the seat called to him. He sat down and examined the ship's control panel with squinted eyes. Leave or stay and become more entangled in Yencara's web. Leave and find a new life—

The ship's radio flashed. Raiherr Yencara's demanding voice filled the cabin. "Pakdon, where in Hades are you?"

Pakdon glared at the controls. *If I run, I'll be running for the rest of my life.*

Thorlu materialized at the foot of the volcano and stood watching small wavelets dance up the beach and vanish, sucked down into the sand. An eagle's cackled screech alerted him to Torgin's arrival and shift to Human. Thorlu's mouth curved into an appreciative smile. The tall, young man intrigued him. His intelligence, his talents, and his growing confidence made him a powerful ally.

"Good work, Torgin. What's our friends' location relative to ours?"

Torgin withdrew the compass and cupped it in his hand. "Ostradio, show us the way to Lake Chittârine."

The needle spun and stopped, pointing east. A map of the island took shape.

Torgin angled it for Thorlu to see and pointed. "We are here." He pointed at a large lake. "Brie and the others are heading for this lake, almost due east of here." His index finger traced the way from the volcano. "I suggest we follow this route." The map faded; the compass disappeared beneath his shirt.

Thorlu tilted his head. "Torgin Whalend, I am so glad we are on the same side."

White teeth flashed in a beaming smile. "So am I, Thorlu Tangorra. Shall we find our friends?"

"Lead on." Flashing into eagle form, Thorlu stretched his wings and waited until Torgin had shifted.

Together, they soared skyward. Below, an intermittent crevasse provided a visual guide through the rough mountain terrain. Wing stroke by wing stroke, they closed the gap between Bholcàno Volcano and Lake Chittârine.

7
El Aperdisa

Ari sat on the grassy floor in Elf's secret room off the Plantitarium. Plucking a blade of green, she twirled it between her fingers. *Sure hope the past two turnings of playing spy have produced some interesting results.* She flicked the blade of grass into the air. *I'll learn more when Elf and Rethson get here.*

A flicker of light and a kiss on the cheek sent happiness racing through her. She faced Elf and returned his kiss. "Nice to see you in your true form, although..." Her sense of humor ignited. "...Zak is sure good-looking."

Elf's shoulders shook with a silent laugh. "I do love you, Arienh."

Rethson materialized. "Enough of the mushy stuff, you two. We have work to do." He sat cross-legged on the ground in front of them. "Who wants to start?"

Ari studied his serious face, recognized the fear at the back of his eyes, and resisted the urge to touch his knee. "Tell us what has scared you, Rethson. What have you discovered?"

He clasped trembling hands in his lap and licked his lips. "I recognized one of our spies, and he knows me." His head tipped back as he blew out a shaky breath. With a gulped inhale, he straightened and met her gaze. "Vygel Vintrusie and Roween Rattori employed the crewman known as Reedan. His job with them was to ensure my strict compliance to their orders. He was on the boat pursuing you in TheDa Fiorde on DerTah when Elf's sea creature brought me to you."

Ari leaned forward. "Breathe. We're right here, and we won't let him near you."

Elf wiggled closer and looked him in the eye. "Rethson, tell us why he scares you so badly."

"He is conniving, merciless, and meaner than anyone I have ever met. If I displeased him, he beat me with a whip until I could hardly stand. How in the Universe did he end up on *El Aperdisa*? Never mind. I bet Karlsut recruited him and maneuvered him on board with his other spies."

Elf frowned and rubbed his hands on his thighs. "Reedan works with me in engineering. The chief engineer asked him to show me the ropes. As soon as we were alone, he grilled me on why I joined the crew so late. He asked me since I was a Private what my true area of expertise was, and why I was apprenticing in engineering. Also, he asked who recommended me to Commander Odnamo.

"I explained my training's in weapons operation, but I volunteered to learn engineering because it has always intrigued me. By doing so, I cemented my place on the crew. As to who recommended me to the Commander, I told him my previous unit leader informed me, I'd been offered a transfer to *El Aperdisa*. I accepted.

"Last night after lights out, he slipped away. I followed him and almost got caught when he and Nesen returned to the crew's quarters together. I hid and played spy. Nesen's definitely Reedan's boss. Do either of you know anything about him?"

Rethson frowned. "Nothing." He looked at Ari. "You're awful quiet, Arienh. What's up?"

Ari bit her lip. "I almost gave us away." She shared her experience in Penee's quarters. "I bet the crewman who almost caught me was one of your two men. Can you put their images in my mind?"

Rethson hunched his shoulders. "Elf, you do it."

Facing her squarely, Elf took her hands in his. "Tell me when you're ready."

Ari exhaled and looked him in the eye. "Ready when you are."

"First, I'll show you Nesen."

A man's angular face and dull, almond-shaped, gray eyes focused. Nothing about him was familiar. She shook her head. "He wasn't there."

Elf squeezed her hands. "Ready for Reedan?"

She nodded. His image produced a gasp of recognition. "That's the man who saw me." She shuddered. "I don't believe the other man was involved. He seemed totally uninterested and left before Reedan threatened to make me sorry."

Elf exchanged glances with Rethson. "Ari, you'd better inform Henrietta as soon as you can."

Rethson climbed to his feet and gazed at Ari with fear pulsating in waves. "Ari, be careful. You don't want to meet up with him on your own. I better get back to the galley before I'm missed." He flashed from view.

Elf stood and helped her to her feet. "Duty calls, so I'll tell Commander Odnamo what we've learned." He kissed her. "Like Rethson said, be careful. I'll meet you in Brie's quarters later." He faced the wall, listened intently, and then stepped through it into the Plantitarium.

Ari calmed her exploding anxiety. Brie always tells me I'm as talented as she is. Now's the time to prove it. First step...inform Aunt Henri and ask her advice." Determination lifted her chin.

A short time later, AeroTech Jem Taisley stood on the bridge, accepting a message tab from Commander Odnamo. "When you have delivered this, please return to your station."

Jem saluted and turned to leave as the hatch opened and Nesen, a low-ranking officer, blocked his way, glanced at the Commander, and stepped aside. Jem left without a backward glance.

Making certain no one followed, Jem arrived outside the VarTerels' quarters, his uniform hat under his arm and the message tab in his hand. Henrietta answered his buzz and motioned him inside.

In the gully leading from Créada Sacu, Brie accepted Esán's help to climb over a hip-high rock, straddled it, and peered at the misty haze floating over the terrain up ahead. Swinging her leg over the stone, she reached for Esán's shoulders. His strong hands gripped her waist. A grin flashed as he lifted her down and hugged her close. She chuckled and slipped her hand into his. "Lead on."

Gar, who had led the way from Créada Sacu, stepped free of the gully's protection and stopped. Den and Penee halted to one side. Brie caught her breath as she and Esán joined them in the soft grayness floating over the wide-open space. Not far ahead, bubbling water flowed through a rocky stream bed, its gurgling song carried away on a cool breeze. Beyond it, knee-high grass and wildflowers carpeted rich wetlands. On one side, rolling, tree-covered hills continued to the seashore, and, on the other, steep mountains towered high overhead. The entire view created a breathtaking panorama.

Brie breathed in the damp air. "I'm never bored by the extraordinary diversity of Neul Isle." She faced her friends. "Our destination is on the far side of the wetlands. If we cross on foot, we are visible to anyone hunting for us."

Penee frowned. "So, what do you suggest?"

Esán answered, "Let's fly across. We can all shape shift. If we change to birds that flock and fly together, we might arrive at the lake unnoticed."

Gar, his glasses gleaming, scanned the cloud-covered sky. "Are there sea gulls on Neul Isle? On Earth, I used to watch them gather in huge groups and fly together one direction and then the other, squawking the whole time."

Den chuckled softly. "You never fail to amaze me, Gar. There are plenty of gulls here." He smiled. "Did you know their erratic flight pattern is called jinking, and they use it to confuse their enemies?"

"Nope. I didn't." Gar grinned. "Sounds like the right bird for us!"

Den sobered, turned, and gazed ahead. "I suggest we all change and remain still until I give the signal. Then we fly over the wetlands…" He grinned at Gar. "…squawking our "delight" and jinking. When we reach the other side, all of you land and stay hidden while I scout ahead." He faced them. "Sound good?"

Soft affirmatives floated around them. Brie smiled and shifted. With a flutter of wings, her friends changed. Den in the lead, the colony of gulls launched over the wetlands, a chorus of squawks echoing through the mist.

Pakdon landed his small jumper craft in a clearing north of Áfini Sacu. Still angry at himself for getting involved in Raiherr's villainy, he switched off the controls and sat torn between escape and compliance. *I'm stupid if I stay and even stupider if I leave.*

Squinting his eyes, he searched the terrain in front of him. *I'm certain the two eagles are shape-shifters.* He shuddered. The Vasro leader had tried to persuade him to study the Arts of DiMensionery. Teeth clenched and nostrils flaring, Pakdon sneered his distaste. *Nothing about the Arts intrigues me. I'd rather fly Quest-Seekers and explore unknown places and be free to be me.*

With a huff, he rose, crossed to the Seeker Center, and selected the one he preferred for this next mission. Murmuring to himself, he studied the map of the island on his v-screen and reviewed the areas he had explored so far. "On the continent of Dast, I searched Lyn Lake and the beach beyond the Sileah Mountains. Since arriving on Neul Isle, I've explored every crack and crevice between Gisa Point and the volcano. A change in the wind prompted me to move my ship further southeast along the coast. I landed here and continued my search from this point..." He touched the screen. "...back toward the volcano. So, what now?"

Plans solidifying, he accessed the Haptic Holo Con and went to work, plotting a course from his current position west along the coast over Lake Chittârine to his previous landing site and back.

He exited the ship and stood in sunlight burning through a thin mist. A scan of the sky assured him the fire eagles were elsewhere. He shivered. *Wonder what it's like to fly like that?*

With a quick shake of his head, he focused on the job ahead.

Memories of colonies of gulls soaring over the seaside capital of Reachti when he was a boy guided Den over the grassy expanse below. With a constant speed and somewhat erratic flight pattern, he led his small colony over the wetlands and across Lake Chittârine. Near the shoreline, where the side of the dome entered the water, a copse of deciduous trees provided the perfect, sheltered hiding place.

After assuring himself his fellow gulls blended into the leaf-covered ground, he flew over the pale blue lake, where thinning mist allowed the late afternoon sun to form patches of sparkling light on the calm surface. A low swoop carried him closer to the spot where the grim dimness of the dome's side disappeared. He landed on the water, shifted to a fish, and dove deep, hoping to discover how far the dome descended.

Frustration sent him swimming to the surface and back into gull form. Wings flapping hard lifted him free of the water. He shot skyward. A circuitous flight over the lake and surrounding shore satisfied him the enemy had not found them. A long glide ended beyond the edge of the copse with his shift to Human. Quiet voices drew him deeper into the trees.

His friends, who gathered in a group listening intently, parted as he walked up. Relief triggered a welcoming smile. "Am I glad to see you, Torgin Whalend!" He glanced around. "Is Thorlu with you?"

Gar edged closer to his cousin. "Thorlu's keeping watch, so Torgin can fill us in. He's got news to share."

Torgin smiled at his young cousin and returned his gaze to Den. "Esán shared your plan and said you were doing a reconnaissance flight. What did you discover?"

Den frowned. "I landed at the point where the dome enters the water, shifted to a fish, and followed the side down to the lakebed. I found only a slight gap between the edge and the sandy bottom, so there's no way to swim under it. We came all this way for nothing." He shook his head. "Let's hope Ostradio will guide us to a better place. Please, Torgin, share your news. Then we need a new plan."

He listened to Torgin's summary of what had happened since they had last been together. When Torgin described the Q-Seeker on the continent of Dast and shot a quick glance at the sky, Den froze. Swallowing the lump of dread edging up his throat, he spoke up.

"Are there Quest-Seekers on Neul Isle?"

"There are." Torgin's summer green eyes hardened. "Thorlu and I destroyed not only a Q-Seeker but also the Stalker-Seeker called Howler. We don't know how many more there might be." His gaze encompassed the group. "What's important is that we are well prepared to destroy another one if necessary."

He withdrew the time whistle and held it up. "Let me share my most important discovery. Because of the Sun Queen's advance technology and my ability to make use of the space-time continuum, I discovered a way to get us inside the dome and to destroy it when the time is right." A quick explanation later, he tucked the whistle away and scanned the sky.

When the murmurs of amazed interest died down, Den spoke up. "How do we proceed?"

Torgin smiled. "I have one more thing to share. La and Abarax are meeting us in the Forest of Deora. Thorlu and I checked the area on this side of the dome on the way here. That's our next destination."

Gar raised a hand holding his glowing spectacles. He perched them on his nose and gasped. His fire-opal eyes widened. Abellona's voice filled the copse. "A Quest-Seeker approaches the lake." Gar removed his specs and sent them into hiding. "The Sun Queen just spoke through me." He touched his throat in amazement. "What now?"

Den looked at Brie. "VarTerel?"

Her attention shifted from the sky to Torgin. "You've just dealt with two. What did you learn?"

"Destroying a third Quest-Seeker will let Raiherr and Callum know for certain someone is here, and an intensified search will begin." He fingered the compass under his shirt. "With luck, if we can enter the dome while the Q-Seeker continues its search. When it discovers nothing, Raiherr might assume the other losses were accidental."

Penee's urgent voice interrupted. "The Q-Seeker's closing in. We can make plans once it passes us by."

A small, Neul hawk dropped into their midst, and Thorlu appeared. "You need to hide now."

Esán drew Brie closer. "Torgin, tell us what to do."

"Den and Thorlu, shift to hawks so you can perch on a high branch and keep watch. When we are out of danger, one of you let us know."

Den hugged Penee and stepped away. "You'd best go deeper into the trees to hide."

To the soft whisper of gull wings, Den and Thorlu flew to separate branches under the canopy of leaves. Beneath them, as stealthful as a prowling ludoc cat, their friends skulked through the copse of trees.

8
Neul Isle

Esán forced his racing thoughts to a slow trot. Up ahead, his friends crept forward. In the distance, a faint hum snapped his senses to high alert. *"Close!"* The one word telepathic warning sent the companions to the ground to blend into the forest's leaf-carpeted floor.

The Q-Seeker's high-pitched hum peaked and then grew more distant. Wildlife hushed into silence. His friends held their breath. Tension in the copse eased. Esán tightened the mental reins on his friends. No one moved.

Birds twittered a chorus in the treetops. A tinimunk skittered through the dried leaves and up the trunk of a rough-barked tree. Soputto's sun slipping toward the horizon turned approaching dusk to a soft, tenebrous blue. The silent arrival of a hawk and Den's somber-faced appearance in human form prompted a relieved sigh from the group. Everyone stood up, brushing leaves and twigs from their hair and clothing, and gathered around their friend.

Den spoke in a low-pitched voice. "When Thorlu and I saw the Q-Seeker pass overhead, I flew in the direction it came from. North of the cove where we spent the night, a small, silver-gray spacecraft sat half-hidden in the shadows."

Esán edged closer. "Did you see the pilot or a Haptic Holo Controller or..." He shrugged.

"A man with silver eyes sat on the exit steps, working with the sensor in his palm. He seemed to be testing the remote controls in his fingers. I did a brief mental probe. He's not a Mocendi or a Vasro." Den released a soft breath. "The Q-Seeker is doing recon between the ship and the volcano and back to the ship. Thorlu will warn us when it's headed our way."

"Torgin, is the Forest of Deora still the best place to enter the dome." Urgency infused Esán's statement.

Gar frowned. "Why can't we enter right here?"

Torgin pointed at the tree branches bushing the dome. "Because we would find ourselves on the steep side of a mountain with no way to go but up. Besides, Abarax and La are expecting to meet us in the Forest of Deora with the latest information on our enemies. Let me show you the best route." He pulled out the compass and gave it instructions.

Everyone moved closer. The compass needle pointed west. A map appeared. Torgin traced the route with the tip of an index finger. At his command, the map vanished. Still clutching Ostradio, he said, "We know the Quest-Seeker is now heading for Bholcàno. The dome near Deora divides the forest...the majority inside and a cluster of trees outside. Once the Q-Seeker passes us on its return journey, we head straight for that group of trees."

Thorlu flashed into being. "Time to hide. It's almost here." A hawk took his place and flew skyward.

Esán pulled Brie down beside him as their companions melted into leaves and moss.

The Q-Seeker's piercing hum once again cast a spell of silence over the copse. Like her friends, Brie strained to hear. When it passed overhead without a pause, everyone exhaled in relief and scrambled to their feet.

Penee's unique eyes scanned the sky and then sought her companions. "What is the quickest way to the forest? Do we teleport?"

Brie shook her head. "Teleporting this large a group might alert our enemies."

Den brushed a stray leaf from his hair. "We've already established our colony of gulls, so I believe it's our best bet. Torgin, please take the lead—"

"I'd rather fly ahead and be ready to create the opening as soon as you arrive. Esán, you still have Tumu Noci, correct?"

"I do."

"Good, you come with me. Gar, you stay and keep our colony alerted to any trouble. Den, follow the dome until you reach a valley with rugged hills on two sides. Esán and I will meet you there. If you fly over a small lake, you've gone too far."

Den turned. "Thorlu, do you have anything to add?"

The High DiMensioner smiled. "I'll help our VarTerel track you."

Returning the smile, Brie glanced up through the leaf-filtered sunlight. "I'm glad we're on this side of the island so we won't be in total darkness until after we reach our goal. Go. We'll follow."

A quick shift, and Torgin and Esán disappeared through the loosely woven branches overhead to soar high above the trees.

Shoving her growing edginess to the back of her mind, Brie assessed her options and made a decision. "Den, you're on."

He took command. "Assemble in a loose colony behind me and stay alert. If anything feels wrong, let me know. When I give the word, shift." He surveyed the remaining companions. "Now!"

The colony of Neul Gulls lifted into flight as Soputto's sun edged lower. Aware of everything around her, Brie flew toward the turning's end and what she knew would be a new adventure.

Their focus on arriving safely in the section of the Forest of Deora outside the dome, Torgin and Esán soared high above the Isle of Neul, their senses alert. Golden light turning to deep bronze tinted Lake Chittârine as the sun crept closer to the horizon. Long shadows stretching over the land from the west nudged Torgin to pick up speed. The opening in the dome would be more challenging to create in the dark.

A telepathic message from Brie flashed through his mind. "The colony is in the air."

He squawked. Esán responded in kind. Together they dropped lower, swooped over the last of the wetlands, and landed in the valley a short distance from their goal.

As dusk's glow softened, Torgin signaled his friend closer and pointed at a ravine wide enough for them to walk side-by-side. Relieved that Esán needed less explanation than most, he started forward.

Their brief hike ended at the dome hidden behind tall evergreens. Moving a low tree branch aside, Torgin whispered the charm, "Dreelish" and pressed his splayed fingers against the dim side. A slight tingling sensation raised the hair on the back of his neck. He stepped to one side. "Say the word Dreelish to shield your energy essence, and touch the dome, Esán. Memorize its vibrational pattern, then get out Tumu Noci."

Esán, eyes narrowed in concentration, did as instructed. After whispering the charm, he rested a hand on the dome's shimmering surface, experienced the tingling effect, and then removed it. "Interesting. I wonder what technique The Box used to create it?" Not waiting for a reply, he held up the Key. "Tell me what to do."

With the compass and the time whistle in hand, Torgin experienced a flicker of his old self-doubt. "How did I arrive here, Esán? You listen; the others listen to me; the Sun Queen placed the information from the book on the space-time continuum in my memory." He blew a soft note on the time whistle. "And I have this."

Esán grinned. "Don't question. Just accept your amazing gifts and tell me how we create the opening in the dome."

Torgin's thoughts organized themselves into a concrete plan. After a quick explanation and rehearsal, he and Esán arrived in the clearing as the colony of gulls landed and shifted to Human. Together, they guided their friends through the ravine to the forest patch on their side of the dome.

"Den and Thorlu, please do a mental sweep of the area so the enemy doesn't take us by surprise. When they've finished, Brie and Penee, you can create a subtle ward around this small grove."

The group grew silent while Den and Thorlu conferred and then, facing opposite directions, scanned the coastline of Neul Isle. Den, whose mental probe encompassed the Southeastern shore, finished first.

When Thorlu had completed his probe from their position to the volcano and back, he nodded at Torgin. "All clear and calm."

Torgin blew out a quiet breath. "Looks like we're ready to go." He turned to his cousin. "Gar, put on your specs and make certain the area next to the dome is safe. Esán, when I give you the sign, focus on the dome's vibrational pattern and draw the opening with Tumu Noci." As he spoke, he withdrew the compass and whistle.

Gar, his spectacles in place, faced the dome. A gasp of surprise froze the companions mid-motion. He turned slowly. On his hand perched a little luna moth, the soft blue-green of her wings glowing in the last light of the sun.

La grew to full size and landed on Torgin's shoulder. *"Abarax say wait. Strange movement in forest. I return when safe."* She shrunk to a miniature of her normal size and vanished through the dome.

Torgin shared her telepathic message with the group before addressing Den and Thorlu. "You're sure neither of you sensed anything out of the ordinary?"

Thorlu shook his head. "No, nothing. What now?"

"We wait for La to return and tell us it's safe to enter."

Silence settled over the stand of trees. Night shadows crept nearer, magnifying the growing tension in the group. Brie moved closer to Esán. Penee slipped a hand into Den's.

Gar's specs materialized on the bridge of his nose. Flecks of fire-opal red and green gleamed in his dark eyes. He stared at the dome, tipped his head, let out a quiet breath, and pointed.

A glint of crystal light penetrated the dome's dimming side. La shimmered into being, grew to full size, and once again landed on Torgin's shoulder. *"New friend awaits. Come now."* With a flutter of her wings, she diminished to a sparkle of light and vanished into the world beneath the dome.

After sharing La's message, Torgin withdrew the compass and the time whistle and motioned Esán forward.

Doubt etched a frown on Thorlu's face. "What if this is a trap?"

Brie's trust-filled gaze met the High DiMensioner's. "Abarax and La are our friends. They work with Rina, the Incirrata protector of Neul Isle. Rina sent them to help us. If we were in danger, La would have given us a warning. I sensed nothing suggesting trouble, simply surprise and relief."

He stroked his beard and studied her for a long moment. "I trust your knowledge of the situation, VarTerel. Thank you for humoring me."

Torgin took charge. With the compass on his palm, he whispered instructions. The needle gleamed, spun in a blur of gold, and stopped, pointing directly at the dome. A soft note on the whistle and Tumu Noci grew to size and glowed golden. With its tip, Esán drew an arch on the side of the dome.

Penee's subdued gasp highlighted the scintillating change as the surface melted away, forming an entrance into the murkiness beyond.

Torgin motioned Den through first. "Make sure it's safe."

Den stepped into the dimness, vanished, then reappeared. "Let's go."

Gar darted through. Brie and Penee filed in after him. Thorlu cast a last glance at the sky and stepped through the opening, followed by Torgin and then Esán, who reversed the process. Everyone watched as the entrance arch vanished and the dome's side reformed.

At a nod from Torgin, Esán whispered "Dreelish" and pressed his palm to the reestablished section to affirm it vibrated at the correct frequency. Removing his hand, he wiped the palm on his pant leg and smiled at the group. "It's solid."

Gar gasped and stared into the dimness, his opal eyes magnified within the ember rims of his specs, and pointed. "Look!"

Torgin clutched his cousin's shoulder and swallowed. In the dim light of the inner dome, an extraordinary creature sat on its haunches observing the group.

"All is safe, young Gar." The Sun Queen speaking in his mind made Gar shrug off Torgin's hand and adjust his specs. Her presence calmed his fear. The curiosity swirling in the group gathered behind him, urged him a step closer to the creature. Through his spectacles, he examined the three distinct faces staring back at him from a body covered in what resembled the seaweed lining the shore at low tide. He tipped his head to one side, then walked forward to gaze into the sea-blue eyes of the bear-like head topping the body. A squat brought him in line with the blue eyes of a smaller face perched above a third lava-dark face with golden eyes.

He stood and addressed the top head. "Are you three creatures or one?"

The creature lifted its snout. Its deep voice rumbled. "I am Sea Wee Vala, the Totem Spirit Guardian of the K'iin."

Abarax, the Stannag Astican, shimmered into existence. "Dri Adoh sent Sea Wee Vala to help you retake the village. La and I must rejoin Rina to collect the information you require to succeed." The beautiful luna moth landed on its shoulder. "La will be our go between." Abarax bowed its head. "May the power of the Sun Queen flow through you." The Phantom Stannags faded from view.

Gar refocused on Sea Wee Vala. "How can you help us?"

The Totem Spirit straightened to his full, magnificent height and gazed down at the group. "You must first rest. Please gather close. I will transport you to a well-hidden place."

Thorlu glanced at Gar. "Does the Sun Queen say we are safe with this creature?"

Gar's throat tightened, then relaxed. Abellona's voice whispered through the forest. "Sea Wee Vala is my kin. Trust him. Rest. Then rid Neul Isle of our enemies."

Her voice faded. Gar grinned and held out his hand to the Totem Spirit. His friends gathered around them. The Forest of Deora vanished, replaced by tall, ancient trees at the base of a mountain.

The Spirit Guardian gazed down at him from blue eyes. "Use your spectacles, young Gar. Lead us to our goal." It pointed through the stand of trees.

Gar turned and stared. A rough path came into focus. Curiosity nudging him forward, he led his friends between the age-old trunks. The motion of a tinimunk scurrying ahead of him drew his attention. Not wanting to lose sight of it, he hurried around a tree and stopped, his eyes rounded with astonishment. Behind him, Den gave a surprised whistle as the companions halted.

In front of a dark wooden door framed by large stones set into an ivy-covered wall sat the tinimunk. Tiny nectar-seekers fluttered around a carving of the Totem Spirit Guardian's bear-like head, staring down at the group from above the door. A green lizard climbed a mossy trunk to one side; the hiss of a snake sent Gar back a step. "Where are we, Sea Wee Vala?"

"We're at Orāk Cavern, a secret hide-away known only to the K'iin. Focus to the right of the door and describe what you see."

Gar peered through his lenses and pointed. "There's a reddish glow in that crevice."

"Between those stones, you will find a small, smooth rock. Turn it toward the sunrise."

A tingle of doubt made Gar glance back at Torgin. His cousin's affirming nod and his gesture to the east gave him the courage to move close to the wall. He reached into the crevice. Searching fingers found the round rock. A quick turn toward sunrise and the door swung inwards. Gar exhaled a shaky breath.

The K'iin's totem spirit spoke to the group. "Please enter, my friends. Follow the path to the dead end. Gar, with his spectacles, will find another crevice and move the round stone straight up. A new way will reveal itself. Once you are through, close the opening." He studied each individual face and stepped to one side. "Allow your instincts to be your guide. Please enter."

Gar smiled at Torgin, who ushered him through the doorway. They walked a short distance along the smooth path between crystal-flecked stone walls and waited for their friends. Esán and Brie came next, followed by Penee and Den. Thorlu hesitated, caught Torgin's eye, and, at his nod, entered. As the door closed, the walls surrounding them glistened brighter.

Penee stepped up behind Esán and Brie. "How do we navigate in a dark tunnel? Oh! Look at Gar."

Torgin squeezed his cousin's shoulder. "The rims of your spectacles are glowing like embers—a sign you should take the lead. I'll be right behind you."

Gar started down the tunnel. With each step he took, the glistening crystal specks in the walls gleamed brighter, emphasizing the path. He looked back and grinned. "We've got all the light we need, Pen. Come on!" Cloaked in confidence, he strode along between the walls.

The only sounds in the tunnel were his companions' quiet footsteps. When they reached the dead end, they stopped a short distance behind him and waited.

Brie moved to his side. "Do you see the crevice Sea Wee Vala told us about?"

Gar peered at the dark stone and shook his head. He glanced toward Brie.

"I don't see—" He gulped a breath, stepped past her, and examined the wall. A soft laugh escaped. A crevice, just big enough for his hand, glowed silver. "Got it!"

He reached in, found the smooth, round rock, and leveraged it upward. A door-sized rectangular section of stone opened inward, exposing a dark tunnel.

Torgin move past him. "I'll scout up ahead." He had taken only a few steps when he stopped and stared up a steep stairway. Gar, his curiosity brimming over, hurried to stand at the foot of the stairs, his bespectacled-eyes exploring. "They go up and up, Torg. Does it feel safe to you? It does to me."

Torgin smiled. "It does to me, as well." He turned and waved the group forward. "We have some climbing ahead of us."

Thorlu moved to the front of the group. "Let's have our VarTerel confirm our safety."

Brie climbed the first two steps, closed her eyes, and breathed. "Nothing suggests a threat. Does anyone else have doubts?"

Penee shook her head. "I only sense anticipation."

Den nodded. "I agree with Pen. Esán?"

"I'm ready to find out where the steps lead. If you're satisfied, Thorlu, I suggest we begin the climb."

The High DiMensioner's gaze embraced the group. "I don't doubt you. Our safety is my primary concern."

Gar raised a hand and listened intently. "The Sun Queen says you keep us in balance, Thorlu." He removed his specs and held them out. "She suggests you try on my spectacles and look up the stairs. She says you will discover more than the rightness we are feeling."

Thorlu took the spectacles, settled them on his nose, and stared up the staircase.

When he remained unmoving, Gar climbed the steps, turned, and looked back at him. The High DiMensioner's magnified eyes widened. A slight smile curved into a surprised grin. He removed the spectacles and studied them with awed delight before handing them back.

His gaze moved from one companion to the next. "I knew I was in talented company, but I did not know how talented. Now, I have discovered I am every bit as gifted." His delight morphed into seriousness. "We are safe to climb the stairs. At the top, we will discover another door, which Gar must open. What lies beyond..." He looked over the group. "We will discover together."

Gar, glad to have his spectacles back in place, took the lead. One stone step after the other, he climbed higher and higher, with the silvery glow of the walls lighting the way and his friends in single file behind him. *I wonder what you saw, Thorlu Tangorra?*

9
El Aperdisa

In the clearing near Rina Island, Raiherr Yencara stood beside The Box, glaring down at Callum. "How soon will you be ready to test it? What's taking so long, anyway?"

Callum set down his small tool, took a deep breath, exhaled, and turned. His blank expression and the tension in his neck and shoulders broadcast his frustration at the intrusion. "If you want to see beyond the dome, let me complete the upgrade. I'll let you know when I'm ready."

Raiherr's nostrils flared. Suppressing the urge to confront his SorTech, he strode from the clearing, muttering his annoyance between clenched teeth. Emerging from the shadowy trees into the dimness cast by the dome, he followed a rough trail to the shoreline of Bolcán Murloch and paused across from Rina Island.

Gray plains...gray water...a SorTech who is wasting my time... A scowl distorted his uneven features. *Nothing is going my way. Karlsut's breathing down my neck. Callum is too slow.* He glanced up at the gray sheen of the dome high overhead. *I'm sick of gray. A little sunshine, a cool breeze...* He muttered, "I thought Callum had everything under control. I shouldn't have believed his claims about making all the changes in The Box."

A movement on the pewter-gray water snatched his attention. A large fish surfaced, then dove deep, leaving a circle of bubbling ripples roiling in its wake. He fixed his squinted gaze on Rina Island. "I'm going to find a way to catch you, Incirrata. Just you wait."

A slow scan of the lagoon ended at the hidden trail leading to the K'iin's village. *Where are Brie and her friends? They should be on the island by now.* Again, disgust twisted his mouth. Sputtered profanities carried him through the dim grayness to camp. He shouted across the clearing, "Callum, I want to see beyond the dome, now!"

Paying no attention, the SorTech kept on working.

Raiherr strode across the clearing, grabbed his shoulder, and yanked him around.

Callum's angry glare devoured Raiherr's face. "Don't touch me when I am working on The Box. You could have killed us both. Now, leave me alone and let me try to undo the damage you've done.

The Box flashed. The dome overhead shimmered and dissolved. Dim dusk light and fresh air flooded the camp. Callum gave an angry shout and turned back to The Box. Working frantically, he tapped buttons, toggled switches, and twisted knobs.

Raiherr stared up at the sudden appearance of the night sky. "Can you fix it, Cal?"

The SorTech mumbled, groaned, and shook his head. "Go away. I can't concentrate with you breathing down my neck."

Raiherr turned to find Zorin smirking and his sidekick, Dulno, staring up at the sky. Anger flashed, flooding his expression, his body language, and the clenching and unclenching of his fists. Zorin's snide expression vanished. He elbowed Dulno, who took a step back and shoved his hands into his pockets.

"Make yourselves useful." Raiherr pointed at the food packs. "Prepare a meal and be quick." While the two men hurried to do his bidding, Raiherr returned his attention to Callum.

The SorTech pulled out a hand cloth and wiped away the sweat beading on his forehead. After tucking it into his belt, he gulped a breath, tapped a button. Above them, the dome shimmered back into place.

Callum faced his boss. "You understand your interference caused everything I've accomplished in the last three turnings to be erased. I have to begin again. And, Raiherr, I was ready to run a test." Shaking his head, he walked over and joined Zorin and Dulno.

Disgust and frustration dancing a tango in his mind, Raiherr stared at The Box.

On the far side of Neul Isle, Brie rubbed her aching back and wondered how long she'd been climbing the stone steps. Memories of descending the steep stairway of Retu Erath in the Cavern of Tennisca on Myrrh made a momentary appearance. She gulped a breath. *Sure is easier to go down than to climb almost straight up.*

Pen's labored breathing pulled her back to the present. She paused and called out, "Gar, we need a break."

A chorus of relieved sighs floated upward. Penee sank onto a step and covered her face with her hands. Torgin pulled out a hand cloth and wiped his face and neck. Den unhooked his water flask and offered it to Penee, who drank deeply and managed a smile as he helped her to her feet. Several steps below, Esán and Thorlu conversed in subdued voices.

Gar looked at the adults and shook his head. "I'm not tired."

Brie smiled. "Give us a bit longer, Gar, and then we can go."

He nodded, leaned against the wall, and resettled his specs on the bridge of his nose. "I just wanna—"

Den chuckled and gave him a clipped salute. "We're ready when you are, Gar."

With a grin and a return salute, Gar started climbing.

Step up, step up, step up… Brie's attention wandered, then snapped back to the moment. A change made her pay closer attention. The tunnel making a gentle curve to the left registered first. She placed her foot on the next step and frowned. *What is happening to the stairs?* Her hand brushed a wall no longer composed of cool stone, but rather of something rough.

Ahead of her, Gar stopped, adjusted his spectacles, and turned. "Hey! The steps aren't stone anymore." He stamped his foot. "They're made of wood!"

Thorlu called from back of the line. "Keep going. We're good."

Brie grinned. "Gar, we are almost at our destination. Lead on!"

From that point, wooden steps carried them upward. The rough bark, which glowed like the stone wall, gradually shifted. Brie squinted at the rounded sides of tree trunks replacing the stone walls. As the tunnel curved, the trunks grew larger, and the ground leveled out.

Brie joined Gar. Together, they walked up to a wall of low-hanging, leafy branches, obscuring what lay beyond.

Gar pursed his lips, tipped his head to look up at her, and shrugged. "Now what?"

Their companions' edgy impatience felt like a hot breeze on the back of Brie's neck. The Star of Truth responded with a warm tingle. She clasped a branch and pushed it aside. A faint rustling started softly and grew louder. The branches lifted, creating an arched canopy above a suspended foot bridge wide enough for two people to cross side-by-side.

Gar peered around her. "Shall I go?"

"Let me explore first." Brie took several tentative steps. Surprised by sturdiness of the bridge, she gripped the rounded railing and looked down. Peering through the branches of a red Bāoba tree, she spotted the dimly lit ground far below. Straightening, she discovered Esán standing beside her.

He smiled and took her hand. "Thought you could use some backup."

Hand-in-hand, they walked along the bridge until a door similar to the Orāk Cavern entrance took shape between leafy branches.

Amazed once again by the magic of Neul Isle, Brie gazed into Esán's stormy blue eyes. "Shall we get the others?

Thorlu stood apart from the group. Gar's spectacles had let him see this far. Now, like everyone else, he waited, anticipation and fatigue vying for first place. *I hope we didn't climb all those steps for nothing.*

Torgin joined him. "Any idea what's behind the door?"

"No. I saw up to the trees covering the bridge. I'm not really worried...just ready to rest and make some decisions."

Torgin glanced at the others and back at Thorlu. "We all need a rest. What a strange turning. It feels like it will never end."

Thorlu glanced at the trio by the bridge. "It's time to discover what's beyond the door. You get Den and Penee." He walked up to Gar and rested a hand on his shoulder.

Torgin, Den, and Penee joined them, their curiosity igniting as Brie and Esán reached the path.

Thorlu took the lead. "Are you satisfied it is safe to cross?"

Esán put an arm around Brie. "The bridge is solid. Since the Queen trusted you to see ahead, you and Gar should cross first. I expect the door will open like the others, so Gar is our "key". He smiled at the boy peering up at him.

Thorlu squeezed Gar's shoulder. "Are you ready, Garon?"

Bespectacled eyes gleamed. "This is the best mystery yet." He strode forward. "Come on, Thorlu. Let's solve it."

Amused by the boy's enthusiasm, Thorlu smiled to himself and hurried onto the bridge.

When he caught up with him, Gar stood motionless, his magnified gaze scanning the door's wooden surface. "I examined both sides." He shook his head. "No crevice, Thorlu. What do we do?"

The High DiMensioner's memory of what he had seen through Gar's spectacles came into focus. "Gar, touch the door."

Gar stepped closer and pressed splayed fingers against the rough wood. A blue light began to glow, outlining each finger, the edges of his palm, and finally turning his hand and wrist blue.

Thorlu edged closer. "Garon, remove your hand."

Biting his lip, Gar lifted his hand, curled the fingers into a fist, and pressed it against his heart.

Thorlu tensed. The door opened inward. A lantern's warm glow accented the features of an older woman with warm, brown skin. Dark eyes with pupils encircled in orange-gold gazed into his, then made a slow, steady inventory of those gathered on the bridge, ending with Gar.

"I am Cadhōla, wise woman of the K'iin. Sea Wee Vala told me of your coming." She smiled at Gar. "The Totem Spirit said I would know you by the Sun Queen's eyes."

Gar squinted through his specs. "How come you speak like us?"

Her smile widened. "The Universal VarTerel who gave you the spectacles taught me your words."

"You mean Henrietta, right?"

Her white teeth gleamed. "I do. Please show your friends your eyes."

Gar turned.

Thorlu marveled at the glowing ember frames of the spectacles and the boy's magnified, opalescent eyes. The wise woman's mention of Henrietta erased his remaining doubt. He placed a hand on his heart and introduced himself. "I am High DiMensioner Thorlu Tangorra. Sea Wee Vala sent us to you, so we might rest and refresh ourselves in safety. May we enter?"

Cadhōla smiled. "You may once I have confirmed the authenticity of all." Holding the lantern high, she moved onto the bridge and stopped, her gaze fixed on Brie. "Welcome back to Neul Isle, Brielle AsTar, youngest VarTerel in the Inner Universe. We are grateful to have you with us again." She moved to Esán. Seriousness clothed her. "Esán Efre, Bearer of Dual Seeds of Carsilem, I welcome you to Nûsini, the sacred sanctuary of the K'iin." Hand to heart, she faced Den and Penee and drew an infinity symbol in the air. "Givers of the gift of life, we embrace you as honorary members of the K'iin. Thank you for all you have given." After offering her hand to each, she fixed her attention on Torgin. "Sea Wee Vala told us of your musical soul and the many gifts you carry. We welcome you and your companions to Nûsini." She returned to the door. "Please follow me into the heart of the Bāoba tree, the entrance to the sanctuary."

Thorlu stepped to one side to let his companions enter first. *I wonder if the K'iin realize I was once their enemy?*

At the center of the Holographic Laboratory, Abellona peered at a hologram of Neul Isle. The whispered command "Dûnoon!" prompted the huge lens above the platform to change its focal range and zoomed in on the Bāoba trees containing the K'iin's Sanctuary Pods. As Brie and her friends disappeared into the hollow trunk with Cadhōla, the queen breathed a sigh of relief, thanked the specialist for his help, and glided into the corridor.

Ferêlith, her personal attendant, hurried to meet her. "The Universal VarTerel awaits you in your private study. Shall I prepare his favorite tea?"

Abellona smiled. "Please do." She flashed from view and reappeared outside the study door. Curiosity brimming, she walked into the most secure place in her land.

Relevart stood and bowed over her offered hand. Releasing it, he smiled down at her. "Thank you for seeing me, Queen Abellona. I believe we have much information to share."

She motioned toward two comfortable chairs and took a seat. When he had settled across from her, she created a shield around them. "Shall we begin?"

10
Neul Isle

Brie smiled at Gar's eager curiosity. Without hesitating, he strode into the hollowed trunk and rotated slowly, his spectacles glinting with ember-light.

Den and Penee followed.

Esán clasped Brie's hand and escorted her inside, where Cadhōla's lantern illuminated the trunk's red wood interior.

Torgin ducked through the doorway and stepped aside to make room for Thorlu.

After closing the door, the wise women guided them to a staircase built into the curve of the trunk. "At the top of the stairs, you will enter the sanctuary pod. Several of my tribal members await your arrival. Only two of them know your words. They will translate if needed. VarTerel, please lead the way."

Brie mounted the steps. When she reached the top, warmth and gentle light greeted her. Esán stepped to her side. Gar and Torgin followed, with Thorlu close behind.

Eight tribal members, waiting to receive them, studied them with restrained curiosity until Den and Penee appeared at the top of the stairs and entered the sanctuary pod. As one, the tribal members drew an infinity symbol in the air, knelt, and bowed their heads.

Cadhōla walked to stand with her tribesmen and chanted a song in the tribal language. To her rhythmic cadence, they rose, linked arms and swayed.

"We honor the givers of life to the K'iin.
They foster your child that all life may win.
Her focus will be on our sacred laws.
Beauty and Light are her hallowed cause.

The K'iin are the children of K'inichi, the Sun.
We shine with the brilliance of this blessed one.
Neul Isle, our home, is our gift of life's seeing
And opens our hearts to the beauty of being."

Brie inhaled in surprise at her understanding of the words flowing through her mind in the language of the K'iin. Beside her, Esán nodded and touched his temple.

When the last line had merged into silence, the K'iin moved into single file. At a sign from their wise woman, they approached Penee and Den and, one-by-one, looked them each in the eye; touched their heart; and move to the side.

Cadhōla faced the tribal members. "We have greeted our guests. Let us share our bounty with them." As they dispersed, she turned. "My people have prepared food. After we eat, we will show you where you may rest. With the rise of K'inichi, our glorious sun, we will make plans to rid Neul Isle of our enemies and return Inōni and the child she carries to her tribal family." She smiled at Thorlu. "You have many questions, High DiMensioner. We will talk after we eat. Please, everyone, come with me."

As they moved further into the Sanctuary of Nûsini, Brie's wonder-filled gaze absorbed its exotic beauty and harmony. Symbolic etchings circling the spherical structure outlined blank ovals of soft light on the warm creamy-beige walls. Midway to the rounded ceiling, a balcony-like structure divided into cubicle spaces encircled the interior. A raised stone fire pit at the pod's center cast shadows like hovering sentinels over two semi-circles of low seats. To one side, a long table heaped with food drew the group forward. Brie inhaled and slid onto the seat indicated by Cadhōla.

When all were seated, the wise woman turned to Brie. "Please, VarTerel, honor us with a blessing over this meal."

Brie hid her surprise and bowed her head. The blessing the Wood Tiffs of the Terces Wood always said came quickly to mind.

> *"To the Plants, to the Tree, to the Flowers and Vine,*
> *For the food on our table, these presents divine,*
> *We thank all who've given of body and soul*
> *To keep our lives healthy, abundant, and whole."*

Cadhōla smiled. "Thank you, Brielle." She gazed around the table. "Help yourselves and enjoy."

While Brie savored her fresh vegetables, just-baked bread, and wedges of smoked fish, she studied the tribal members across from her. Each bore two tattoos on their forehead, denoting their clan and their family. The females' short hair curled softly around their oval faces. All the men wore their long hair braided and coiled at the back of their necks. Like their wise woman, a ring of golden orange circled the pupils of all the tribal members. One thing struck her above all else—the fear and sadness cloaking them all.

A shiver chased up her spine. *We have to help them save their village and their island.*

After the meal, Esán helped a younger tribesman rearrange the seats around the fire pit and then took a seat across from Cadhōla and two female K'iin. Brie and Penee sat beside him. Den, Torgin, and Thorlu, the tallest members of the group, sat behind them. Gar, his spectacles in place, sat cross-legged on the floor at his feet.

While they settled, a tribesman tapped the center of a glowing oval on the wall. The light in the inner walls dimmed, and the oval became as clear as glass. Dim gray light pooled on the floor and then vanished when a second touch returned the oval to a warm, impenetrable beige. When interior light returned, he moved to the wise woman's side and spoke to her in Inik, the tribal language.

She responded in kind. "Achōsi Tu, Pedar."

The tribesman then crossed to narrow steps and climbed to the second level.

Cadhōla addressed the group. "Pedar shared that we are safe for the night. Only thick branches covered with leaves are visible to our enemies. What are your questions before we show you to your sleeping pods?"

Gar raised his hand. "I have two questions. What is this place made of and why are there no windows?"

A twinkle lit Cadhōla's dark eyes. "We are sitting inside a special seed pod from a plant found only on Neul Isle. I need you to be patient, young Gar. When we have banished our enemies, I will share how we grow them in the Bāoba tree and why we don't need windows. Your second question?"

"You said thank you to Pedar, right?"

"I did."

"Will you teach us how to say it, so we can thank you and those who help us?"

Cadhōla gazed at him with solemn eyes. "Thank you in Inik is A-chō-si Tu." She pronounced it with distinct accents. "I will say it; you repeat it after me. A-chō-si Tu."

Gar sat up straighter. "A-chō-si Tu. Achōsi Tu." He grinned. "Achōsi Tu, Cadhōla."

The wise woman returned his grin. "Achōsi Tu, Garon, for your eagerness to learn Inik." Her attention fastened on the adults. "It is late. What is your most important question?"

Esán leaned forward. "The Sun Queen showed us your village. We saw that Raiherr's men had captured Dri Adoh and Artānga, but there were no other tribal members visible anywhere."

Cadhōla sighed. "When the enemy captured Dri Adoh and Artānga, our chief, our women and children fled to a secret hide-a-way in the catacombs beneath the mountains. The Sun Queen ordered my tribesmen to wait for your help to plan the rescue. They are hiding near the entrance to the catacombs."

Penee yawned. "Don't you think sleep would help us think more clearly?"

A murmur of assent brought Esán to his feet. "Achōsi Tu, Cadhōla. Your sharing will help our minds to make plans as we sleep. Unless anyone else has a pressing question—" When no one responded, he let out a sigh. "Please show us where we may rest."

The wise woman and the women with her stood. "We have three sleep pods ready." She paused while her guests reordered into three groups. "I will show Penee and our VarTerel to their pod. Yina will guide Torgin and Gar. Seméa will take Den, Esán, and Thorlu."

Esán hugged Brie. "Sleep well. I'll see you in the morning."

She kissed his cheek. "You, too."

Smothering a yawn, she followed Cadhōla and Penee to a rectangle outlined with symbols. The wise woman touched the center, and an opening appeared. Once they passed through, the pod wall reformed.

Seméa led Torgin and Gar to a rectangle on the eastern side of the pod and tapped the symbol-accented rectangle. They followed her through the opening.

Yina waited, her gaze on Esán. She licked her lips. "Sleep now?"

He smiled. "Yes."

She led them to their rectangular exit and onto the wooden platform. While they gathered behind her, she raised a hand. Leaves rustled as branches lowered into place to form a bridge between the main pod and a smaller one attached to a higher branch. Yina stepped onto the bark covered bridge, crossed with confidence, and touched an area defined by symbols of the night sky. The smaller pod's opaque side shimmered into an arched opening. She turned and waved them forward.

Esán scanned the bridge and took a tentative step. He smiled over his shoulder. "It's solid. Come on."

The trio filed across and into the pod. Yina spoke to Thorlu, who was closest to her, wished them all a pleasant night's sleep in a halting rendition of their language, and exited. As she waved from the other side of the bridge, the branches shivered and lifted elegantly back into place in the Bāoba tree. Esán reached toward the arched opening. It shimmered into opacity, leaving them alone in the pod.

Den took a step forward and grinned as warm light glowing from overhead illuminated four sleeping cots spaced around the interior walls. "I am so tired. Hope there's a personal space in here.

Thorlu searched the rounded walls. "Yina told me there's one on the opposite wall." He crossed to a curtained doorway and peeked inside.

Esán yawned. "You go first, Thorlu." He yawned again. Selecting a cot, he pulled off his pack. "You're next, Den."

The light dimmed when everything was quiet and the trio had settled on their cots.

Esán lay staring up at the faint glow overhead. *Wonder what Brie is thinking?*

"I love you, Esán Efre. Go to sleep."

"I love you, too, Brielle AsTar." He smiled and rolled onto his side. *And I love telepathy.*

To the soft snores of his pod-mates, he slipped into a deep and dreamless sleep.

In the solar system closest to the Décussate, *El Aperdisa's* orbit around the planet of TreBlaya carried the ship into the glow of the rising sun. Ari, as Jem, gazed out the view-portal on the observation deck and sighed. *I wish I were with you, Brielle. Since I'm not..."* Jem's fists clenched. *I will do—*

Reedan sauntered across the deck and leaned casually against the wall. "Hi. Names Reedan. How's the view?"

Jem shrugged. "I enjoy seeing the changes as the ship orbits the planet."

"You're new, right?"

Jem modulated his tone to bland. "New to *El Aperdisa* but not to ship's communications. Why do you ask?"

Reedan scooched closer. "No reason. I just heard that three new guys joined the ship's crew. I met Zak. Do you know him?"

A wrinkled brow and a shake of the head preceded Jem's response. "Nope. Don't think so. What does he do?"

"He works in engineering with me. I thought you might have met since you arrived at the same time." Reedan fixed his cold gaze on Jem.

Jem cast a casual look at the chronometer on the wall behind him. "Gotta go. My watch begins in a few. Nice meeting you, Reedan. See you around." Without a backward glance, he walked to the hatch and stepped through.

Behind him, he sensed Reedan's frustration and almost smiled—almost.

The memory of Rethson's fear of him kept Jem from feeling smug. He knew Reedan would try to trip him up again.

Grateful to have gotten away from him, he waited at the T-lift. When the door opened, Nesen, Reedan's boss, greeted him with an absent smile. Jem ignored his desire to walk away and stepped inside. Footsteps hurrying down the passageway sent a chill up his spine.

Reedan strode on board. "Thanks for holding the lift for me, Jem. My shift's about to start. Don't wanna be late." He nodded at Nesen and pressed the down tab."

The T-lift shot downwards. Jem held his tongue and hoped both men would leave the car on the engineering level.

A silence fraught with tension tightened as the T-lift slowed to a stop. Reedan touched the close tab and faced Jem. Nesen took a step nearer. Neither man said a word.

Jem looked from one to the other. "Can I help you with something?"

Reedan lifted a clenched fist. Nesen frowned. The fist lowered. "I'm Nesen. We've been tasked with locating a crewman who sneaked on board around the time you arrived. We thought you might have run across him. His name's Dufar. We don't know his last name or the rank he has adopted."

Letting curiosity creep into his expression, Jem shook his head. "I don't remember meeting anyone of that name. If I do, I'll let Reedan know."

Voices outside the T-lift changed the atmosphere in the car to easy. Reedan pushed the open tab.

Nesen said, "Thanks, Jem. Nice to meet you." With a nod, he led the way into the passage.

Two crewmen entered, the hatch closed, and the lift shot upward. "You're Jem Taisley, correct? The taller crewman studied him with a questioning gaze.

"I am. And you are...?"

"Henrietta Avetlire sent us to find you. Name's Torlad. My buddy is Equis. We are members of the task force helping to find unwanted visitors on *El Aperdisa*."

The T-lift whooshed to a stop at the bridge. Torlad stopped the door from opening. "I am telepathic. Commander Odnamo will give you my code name. Share it with your friends. If you need help, alert me via telepathy."

The hatch opened. Equis said, "After you..."

Jem exited.

Equis followed. "I'm in navigation, so I'll see you on the bridge." He hurried away.

Jem walked to the men's head, entered a stall and closed the door behind him. Pressing his hands against the wall, he shifted. Ari gulped one breath and another, then returned to her male form.

A flush later, Jem walked over to the hand cleanser. Hat in hand, he studied his features in the mirror. Dark skin and eyes, a smile that revealed straight white teeth, and hair shaved short made him stand straighter. *I intend to be every bit as brave as you, Paisley James Tobinette.*

11
Neul Isle

Raiherr Yencara scowled at the Quest-Seeker sensor screen in his small spacecraft. Footage from his personal Q-Seeker of his Vasro fighters partying around a campfire in the K'iin village stirred the smoking coals of his ever-present anger. *I sent you an order via the Q-Seeker to find the villagers and herd them back to their homes.* Though clenched teeth, he growled, "The footage shows no activity, so what in Sedah are you doing, Relno?"

Raiherr let out a hissed exhale, examined his Q-Seeker, and placed it back in its holder. *Pakdon showed me how to program the darn thing, but I'm beat. Better send it off in the morning.*

Consternation wrinkled his forehead. Although Pakdon, his hired HHC, was the best on this side of the galaxy, he was not a Vasro. Chewing his bottom lip, Raiherr considered Pakdon's recent messages, which were sketchy. *Wish I could check in with you in person.* The thought deepened his current frustration. *Callum says he's close to completing the changes to The Box. They'd better be done.*

Raiherr exited the jumper craft into the gray dimness and shot an impatient glare at the opaque dome, obscuring his ability to see beyond it. *I want to know what's happening outside the dome, and I want to know now.* He ground his teeth. *Callum's changes are taking far too long.*

A tactile frequency code secured the spacecraft. With a final embittered glance at the dome, he marched toward the clearing. When he arrived at camp, his men slept soundly on their mats. Callum's intermittent snores stoked Raiherr's dissatisfaction.

Two long strides carried him to the SorTech's side. A sharp nudge with the toe of his boot brought the man upright.

Callum gawked up at him. "What the—"

Raiherr growled low in his throat. "I presume the changes to The Box are complete."

The SorTech pushed up to sitting and squinted through sleep-heavy eyes. "I'll finish in the morning. Right now, I need my rest."

"I want it done now." Raiherr gripped Callum's arm and yanked him to standing. "You will complete the changes within the chron-circle." He bent low and put his nose so close to the SorTech's he could feel the other man's breathing. "Do I make myself clear?"

Callum brushed Raiherr's hand off his arm and returned the glare. "If I try to finish now, I cannot guarantee I won't ruin what I've already done. Let me sleep, Raiherr, or you won't have me or The Box in working order tomorrow or any other turning." He sat down, grabbed his blanket, and, turning his back, lay down.

Anger roared through Raiherr's whole being. Stifling the urge to kick the SorTech senseless, he marched from the clearing. When he came to his senses, he stood on the shore of Tibêth Cove by Rina Island, staring across the lagoon. His gaze roamed the opposite shoreline, then lifted to the darkness beyond the dome. *Tomorrow you'd better get the job done, Callum, or...* He shook himself. *Or what... He knows you know he's all you've got.*

A filthy string of words garnered throughout the galaxy streamed from his mouth. He kicked a rock into the water, watched the ripples fade into nothing, sent a wad of spittle after it, and murmured, "I need a goal. Waiting around for Callum to finish is a waste of my time, so I will begin my search for Penesert El Stroma in the morning. She's on the island. I know it." He stroked his chin. "Sorda wants Brielle. He can have her. I want the Girl with the Matriarch's Eyes."

The memory of the final meeting he had with his boss before departing the spaceship *Surgentin* surfaced.

Raiherr sat in a private conference space on the spaceship *Surgentin*, with Karlsut Sorda glaring down at him. His boss' narrow face, accentuated by a long, pointed nose and squinted eyes, conveyed a message impossible to ignore... *Obey me or—*

Sorda put his hands on the chair arms and leaned closer. "Lest you forget, Yencara, I am your boss, and I pay you good money to do **my** bidding. If you want me to keep filling your pockets, do as I tell you, or I'll find someone who will. Am I clear?"

Raiherr ground his teeth, but kept his mouth shut, and nodded. The anger roiling inside him would explode in the man's face if he tried to speak.

Karlsut straightened and chortled. "Too angry to answer me? I admire your control." He held out a mini data-tab. "Read the contract. I want a verbal acceptance and a signature. Let me know when you are ready to continue our meeting."

Curbing his desire to get up and walk out, Raiherr focused on the detailed contractual agreement. The more he read, the less he wanted to sign it. Karlsut Sorda's document provided him with no wiggle room to interject his own needs into a situation.

Across from him, his boss' scrutinizing gaze dripped with disdain. "One more thing to consider before you sign, Yencara. If I discover you are scraping funds off the top behind my back, I doubt you will like what results."

Arrogance lifted Raiherr's chin. "I don't cheat the people who hire me, Karlsut."

A raised brow and a condescending sneer were Sorda's only response.

Rather than dig the hole deeper, Raiherr tapped record on the data-tab, and stated clearly, "I, Raiherr Yencara, accept the terms of this contract and swear to honor them in good faith." He then signed it and handed the data-tab to Karlsut.

Sorda glanced at the small screen and set the data-tab aside. "Let's get down to work. I have a job for you and your SorTech, Callum."

. . .

Raiherr chuckled to himself. "Just wait, Karlsut Sorda. You think you own me?" Penee's lovely eyes filled his memory. "Well, you don't."

His spirits on the rise, he hiked back to the clearing, where Zorin, Dulno, and Callum slept. Settling on his mat, he forced his eyes to close. Arrogant mind-chatter kept him awake until slumber stole through him. His body relaxed; his worries slipped away. *Tomorrow...* He slept.

La, the Luna Moth, fluttered into the air. Raiherr's murmurings, heard from a bush next to the water, sent her flying toward the Incirrata's island. Informing Rina and the Sun Queen of the Vasro's plan was her immediate goal.

She arrived at the shore above the Incirrata's lair to find the Astican materializing, its hand held out and its cherub blue eyes filled with questions. When she landed, it lifted her to eye level. "Rina sent me. We are to meet her on the far shore of North Tibêth Cove. She awaits your news."

Abarax spread its massive wings and flew beside her, their phantom luminescence a faint glow in the dimness.

The Incirrata, her eyes above the water's surface and one blue tentacle resting on a rock, waited in the shadow of the trees lining the shore. La fluttered down to land on the tentacle and, using telepathy, shared Raiherr's plans with both Rina and Abarax.

In the sleeping pod in the Bāoba tree, Penee sat on the edge of her cot, her beautiful eyes focused on the floor. Nothing in her world felt right. Her search for a concrete reason left her heartsick and weary.

A pair of feet appearing in her field of vision made her raise her eyes to meet Brielle's questioning gaze. "I-I-I..." A shaky hand scrubbed through her short hair.

Brie sat down beside her. "Since we arrived on Neul Isle, you have been more withdrawn and quiet than I have ever known you to be. Please share what's going on, so I can help."

Again, Penee ran her hand through her hair. "Ever since Healer De Dilliére told Relevart that Inōni was ready to return to Neul Isle, I've been miserable. I'm happier when we're together. When Thorlu took her to Shiór Ridu, something inside me shattered. Brie, she is carrying my child and Den's. I want to be with her when the baby is born. Skylyn is carrying your babies. Imagine never knowing them, and them never knowing you. How would you feel?"

Brie's chestnut eyes glistened with sympathy. She sighed and folded her hands in her lap. "Like you, Pen, it would devastate me. I hope that both Skylyn and I will be a part of my babies' lives. Our destinies and that of Thorlu, who is the father of my girl child, will define what happens to them." She pulled her long, coppery ponytail over her shoulder and ran her fingers through its length.

Penee watched her. "At least you understand." She shook her head. "I'm at a loss. What do I do, Brie? I can't seem to shake the lethargy and sadness drowning me. I wish I could go to Shiór Ridu and be with her while I can, but..." A tear slipped down her cheek.

Brie moved closer and put an arm around her. Brushing the tear away, Penee looked at her friend. "If you were in my position, what would you do?"

"I am not sure what I'd do, Pen. If I could move beyond the dome without Raiherr and his men knowing, I'd take you to the Sun Queen's palace. For now, we need to sleep, so we are ready for tomorrow. Do you think you can doze off?"

Penee sighed. "I'll try." She stretched out on her cot. "Don't worry about me, Brie. I'll see you in the morning.

Forcing herself to focus on the present moment, she listened to Brie prepare for bed and settle on her cot. Soon, a chorus of soft snores wafted through the sleeping pod.

Penee closed her eyes and concentrated on her breathing. Sleep crept closer and closer. Her body relaxed, tension melted away, and a dream tip-toed into being. Inoni's beautiful face smiled down at her, a harbinger of life-altering change.

Inōni lay on her bed, trying to make herself settle down for the night. As much as she appreciated the Sun Queen's hospitality, she missed Penee more and more with each turning.

An unexpected wave of guilt made her glance at Xairā's door. The Queen's personal guard watched over her day and night. It had taken Xairā time to relax and enjoy a job not predicated on protecting her queen. Inōni, smiled and pressed her palms to the roundness of her belly. "She becomes more fun each turning, doesn't she, wee one?"

A small kick made her laugh and think once again of Penee. *I wish you were here, Pen. Sharing my joy with you makes this pregnancy even more meaningful.*

She kissed the tip of a finger, then touched the spot where the small kick had left her skin tingling. *Good night, wee one. Tomorrow will be another turning.*

Sun streaming in the windows of her room woke her to Xairā smiling down at her. "After morning repast, I suggest we do something different from usual. What do you think?"

Inōni stretched and sat up. "Give me some time to wake up and get dressed, and I'll meet you on the terrace."

A quick cleanse later, Inōni donned the dress given to her by the queen and sat brushing her short curls. Her reflection in the mirror demanded her attention. It blurred and Penee's image took shape. Behind her friend, a dark shadow loomed. Inōni caught her breath. Her hands flew to her belly. *Penee is in danger. I must tell the Sun Queen.*

She stood and hurried to the terrace. As she stepped into the enclosed area, Xairā, who sat nibbling a piece of fruit, dropped it and came to her feet. "You appear frightened. What happened?"

Inōni fought to calm her rushing emotions. "I must speak with the Queen. I'll tell you on the way."

They arrived in the Queen's reception area to discover she was not available until later in the turning. Inōni cast a dismayed look at her companion. "What should I do?"

Xairā escorted her from the room. "It wouldn't surprise me if the Queen already knows something is amiss. Why don't we go for a walk in the

Memorial Garden? Our cooler weather will allow us to enjoy the beauty of the statuary and flora. I've already told the Queen's assistant where we will be."

Inōni sighed. "I could use a walk. I can tell you more about my friend, Penee, and her importance to the Universe.

Her companion guardian led her down a long hall and out a bronze door. A breeze rustled through her curls as the beauty of the garden drew her forward. Enchanted by the elegance of the statues and the vibrant colors of the flowers and trees, she allowed herself to relax. Penee, you are with Brie and Den. They will take excellent care of you.

12
Neul Isle

Penee gasped and stared up at the Totem Spirit Guardian of the K'iin, where it stood at the center of the sleeping pod. Gar, astonishment widening his dark eyes, stood in front of it. Sea Wee Vala touched the boy's shoulder.

Gar tiptoed to her side, looked at Brie sleeping across the pod and put a finger to his lips. He pointed at Penee's clothes on the end of the cot. "Get dressed."

"*What is going—*"

He shook his head. *"Important. Hurry."*

Penee gathered her clothes and hastened to the cleanse space. She tossed her sleep shirt in the corner, put on her sweater over the chain mail shirt the VarTerel Irstant had made for her, and pulled on her pants. Sitting down, she slipped stocking feet into her boots. All the while, her imagination chased its own tail, trying to second guess the situation.

The minute she stepped into the sleeping area, the world around her blurred. She groped for Gar's hand and held her breath. The world steadied.

Dark sapphire-blue stone enclosed them at the bottom of the steep stairway leading to the Bāoba tree.

Ahead of them, Sea Wee Vala opened a vast network of tunnels and selected one. Gar scurried after him. Penee followed them along a rough-hewn path that twisted its way down one tunnel after the other. She tried to suppress her rising fear. *If I get lost I'll wander forever in this unending labyrinth.*

Gar slowed to walk beside her, his spectacles perched on his nose. The dark rims glowing in the dim light cast by Sea Wee Vala's blue aura. No fear emanated from him, only intense curiosity.

Choosing to emulate his courage, Penee squared her shoulders and set her "what ifs" aside.

Startled into wakefulness, Brie bolted upright. Her chest heaved. Her heart raced. The Star of Truth sent faint tingles up her neck, but nothing more alarming. A confused glance around left her staring across the room at Penee's empty cot. She threw back her blanket and pressed her feet to the floor. Her frantic gaze searched the pod and stopped on the open curtain of the clean space. Brie's alarm intensified. *Where in the universe are you, Penesert El Stroma?*

For a long moment, she studied Penee's cot, then nodded to herself. *"Esán, I need you!"*

Arriving in the middle of the pod, sleep fading from stormy blue eyes, he hurried to her and rested his hands on her shoulders. "Brielle, what's wrong?"

She pointed at the empty cot. "Something woke me, and I found Penee gone. I don't understand why I didn't hear her leave. Did she visit you and Den?"

"No. Den was just stirring when I left to come here." He drew her down on the cot beside him. "I woke up because something important changed. Then I received your telepathic message. Have you done a mental scan?"

"Not yet." She clasped his hand and inhaled one relaxing breath, followed by another. Closing her eyes, she scanned each sleeping pod, then moved on to the main sanctuary pod. Her eyes flew open, and she turned to Esán. "Penee isn't the only person missing. Gar is gone, too. What do we do?"

He stood and pulled her to her feet. "We ask Cadhōla if she knows anything."

The entrance arch shimmered open. La flew through and landed on Brie's shoulder. Cadhōla entered, turned, drew a symbol in the air, and faced them. "La has a message from the Sun Queen. When she is done, please come to the Sanctuary Pod. We will nourish ourselves, and you can tell us what we need to know." She opened the arched entryway. "Since your companions are on the way here, I will leave Bāoba bridge in place."

Brie watched the wise woman cross to the Sanctuary Pod and grabbed her clothes. "I need to get dressed."

La fluttered to Esán's shoulder. *"I wait till all here."*

From behind the closed curtain, Brie sensed Torgin's arrival. He and Esán conferred in low voices, an occasional word, louder than their quiet murmur, drifting her way. Torgin's frustration-laced tone made her rush to finish dressing.

As she walked from the cleanse space, Thorlu and Den entered and joined them. Their worried expressions increased her growing concern.

She sank onto her cot. "I suggest you have a seat. The Sun Queen has sent La to help us understand what has transpired."

The men moved two cots closer and sat down, their gazes questioning and alert.

La landed on Brie's upturned palm and telepathically shared Raiherr's conversation by the lagoon. After Brie repeated the Vasro's goal to find and capture Penee and her companions, La provided additional information, fluttered from one person to the next, and exited the pod.

Torgin cleared his throat. "What else did La tell you?"

Brie brushed a hand across her eyes and looked at her friends. "La shared Raiherr's plans with Abarax and Rina, who contacted the Sun Queen. Abellona ordered the Stannags to spy on the Vasro leader and his men and to keep her informed. She then contacted Sea Wee Vala and asked him to remove Penee and her young guardian, Garon, to a safer hiding place." Brie rubbed the back of her neck. "I need a moment."

While her friends digested La's information, she focused on the Star of Truth. Its intense pulsing, stronger than she had experienced since her escape from *Surgentin*, unnerved her.

Esán caught her eye. *"Are you alright?"*

She lowered her hand. *"I am."* Her attention returned to the entire group. "Our job is to rid the island of our enemies and to destroy the dome. The K'iin will help. Abellona will do what she can." Brie shivered. "One more thing…Relevart visited Shiór Ridu to warn the queen the *Surgentin*, Karlsut's ship, travels this way."

A silence thick with meaning filled the pod. Thorlu broke it by rising. "We need food and to strategize with Cadhōla and her tribesmen. He looked at Den, whose fear for Penee flashed like a beacon. "Panic won't get us anywhere, my friend."

Den squeezed the bridge of his nose and stood. "You're right." He swallowed. "We will do what must be done. Let's join the K'iin."

Thorlu led the way across the Bāoba bridge with Den at his heels. Torgin pressed his lips into a thin line and followed. Brie took a moment to regain her composure before preceding Esán to the Sanctuary Pod.

From her favorite chair in the main room of her private wing, the Sun Queen regarded her portrait. "I have done what I can do, SparrowLyn AsTar. It is now up to your daughter and her friends"

Impatience brought her to her feet. The desire to act constricted by the Council of Deities' order not to draw attention to herself made her ill at ease. She paced to the window. *Others must execute any action I wish to take.* Her fire-opal eyes narrowed. *I am fortunate. Trustworthy players stand by, ready to act. Still, I wish—*

A soft knock made her inhale a calming breath and turn. Ferêlith and Inōni waited beyond the door. Another breath erased her agitation. "Come in."

Her attendant entered first. "The shaman's granddaughter and her personal guard are here. May I bring them to you?"

"Show them in, and, Ferêlith, please serve our morning meal in here."

Ferêlith curtsied and stepped aside. Inōni, followed by Xairā, entered.

Abellona motioned her guests forward. "Inōni, let us get comfortable. Xairā, please join us. I have received some troubling news I would like to share with you both."

Inōni pressed a protective hand to her distended belly. "Are my friends in trouble?"

Abellona led her to a sitting area by the sun-washed windows. "Please, Inōni, take a seat, and I will share what I know."

Xairā helped Inōni to lower her encumbered body onto a chair and sat next to her.

Inōni smoothed her long skirt and lifted eyes filled with apprehension. "I had a dream last night. Penee is in trouble, isn't she?"

The Sun Queen chose not to mince words and described the conversation La had overheard. "I have already taken action. La will warn the companions, while Rina and Abarax devise a plan to monitor Raiherr and his men. They will update us as things develop. It is crucial, Inōni, that you do not panic. Your friends are better prepared to deal with the situation on Neul Isle than almost anyone in the Inner Universe. Now, I suggest we eat, and we'll go from there."

Ferêlith entered and set out breakfast on an elegant wenge wood buffet. Xairā assisted Inōni to a chair at a matching table, and glanced at the queen.

Abellona took her seat at the head of the table and motioned Xairā to a seat opposite Inōni. Ferêlith served a delicious-looking meal and stood back, ready to help if needed.

For a time, no one spoke. The queen watched her young guest move the food on her plate from one spot to the next, never taking a bite. "Inōni, you must not let your fear for your friends keep you from nourishing yourself and your unborn child. She needs all the nutrients you can provide."

Inōni nibbled one small bite and then another. "The food is delicious. Thank you, Abellona."

The Sun Queen smiled. "When we've finished our meal, Xairā will take you for a walk. Then you must rest, Inōni. I promise to watch over your friends."

👁 👁

Penee's anxiety increased with each step as she and Gar followed the Totem Spirit of the K'iin down one tunnel after the other. She considered demanding to know more, but pressed her lips together and kept walking. *Sea Wee Vala will share when we're safe.*

A fork in the tunnel ended in a cavern where massive quartz crystals shot down from high overhead to line the walls. The Totem Guardian of the K'iin stopped and turned. Its three faces glowed, their eyes shining with an inner light. Vala, the lava-colored lower face, rumbled and grew quiet. The smallest, Wee, whistled one long note that echoed through the cavern. Sea, the top of the totem, lifted its long nose; sniffed the air; and focused its golden eyes on Penee and Gar.

"You wonder why you are here and with me. I spirited you away on the orders of the Sun Queen. Penesert, you are in danger. Garon, you, as her guardian, are here with me to protect her. I have told no one about our destination...not even Cadhōla or your friends. We will journey together for a short time, and then I will leave you in excellent hands."

Penee shook her head. "Why am I in more danger than Brie or the others?"

Sea squinted down at her. "Raiherr, who leads your enemies, has a particular desire to find you and to use you to achieve his personal goals. Not even his leader knows of his plans. That's all I have been told." He held up a hand and whispered, "Scytral."

Penee gasped.

"Wow!" Gar's already magnified eyes rounded even bigger.

The crystals' shimmering surfaces glowed. Their magnificent radiance changed the frequency of the cavern and opened a smooth, narrow tunnel. The trio shot down it. Their arrival at the end left Penee and Gar gasping for breath.

Gar yanked her hand. "Look!"

Sea Wee Vala's aura glowed brighter. The Spirit Totem grew taller. A shudder shook its frame. A deep moan later, Sea's features morphed into a face they both recognized.

Chealim gazed down at them, his essence throbbing with an attentiveness Penee had never felt before. The Galactic Guardian of the Fourth Galaxy knelt so she could see the seriousness with which he regarded her. "It is rare for the Council to interfere in the lives of mortals. Your importance to the destiny of the Fourth Galaxy and the Inner Universe is underscored by the fact that I am about to transport you to Shiór Ridu."

The cavern blurred. Inōni and her guardian, Xairā, materialized.

Chealim rose, his attention flashed from the new arrivals to Gar, who choked, double over, then straightened. The rims of his spectacles blazed with ember light; his eyes glowed fire-opal red splashed with blue. He groaned and rubbed his throat.

The Sun Queen's voice filled the space. "The Council of Deities sends a warning. Shiór Ridu is no longer safe for Inōni, Penee, and Gar. Hide them where no one can find them. I must go!"

Gar collapsed to his knees. Inōni gaped at Chealim. Xairā bowed her head, then stood at attention. At an acknowledgment from the Galactic Guardian, she relaxed.

Penee helped Gar to his feet, then put an arm around the astonished tribeswoman. "This is Chealim, Inōni. He will not hurt us. Do not be afraid."

Inōni swallowed her rising alarm and moved closer to Penee. Never had she seen such a magnificent being. As tall as the Totem Spirit Guardian, he gazed down at them with glistening blue eyes. Beside her, Penee's calm helped to cancel her growing apprehension. Even Gar faced the majestic being without a trace of fear.

Uncertain and anxious for her friends and her unborn child, Inōni hid her turbulent emotions and watched.

Chealim's serious demeanor eased, and a smile warmed those who awaited his response to the situation. "I am relocating you to a secure place where you will be well cared for. Please hold hands in a circle and do not let go of each other."

When Xairā hesitated, he addressed her with compassion. "I understand you are duty bound to serve the Sun Queen. Tell me why you hesitate."

Inōni saw her personal guardian struggling. "Xairā, if you feel that your place is with Abellona, I understand. Penee and Gar will take good care of me."

The Stannag Luna Moth landing on Penee's shoulder caught the attention of everyone. Even Chealim grew still.

Penee listened, then repeated the message from the Sun Queen. "Xairā, you are to remain with Inōni until she returns to her family and village. Guard her well."

La fluttered closer to the young guard. Her wing brushed Xairā's cheek before she faded from sight.

Inōni regarded her new friend with a hope-filled look.

Xairā joined the circle. "Please, Chealim, take us to safety."

The cave vanished, pitch-black wrapped them in an intense silence. A bird's call and a childish giggle penetrating the quiet changed the darkness to the misty, gold and salmon light of morning.

Inōni inhaled the scent of wildflowers and heard again the child's joyful laughter.

Penee expelled a whispery breath. "Look!"

Not far ahead was a beautiful cottage backed by a forest of deciduous trees that were covered with dark pink and purple leaves. On the porch a girl, who appeared to be a bit younger than Gar, held a rainbow striped jump rope that matched the ruffles on her puffy sleeves and short, full skirt. Her strawberry-red curls framed a face filled with so much joy and wisdom that Inōni could only stare.

Chealim herded his charges forward. "Glori, the Council thanks you for your willingness to help." He drew Penee forward.

Glori smiled. "Welcome to Rainbow Cottage, Penesert El Stroma. I am honored to host you and your friends."

Inōni listened to the maturity in the young voice and knew she was much more than a cute girl child.

Twinkling brown eyes turned to gaze at her. "Welcome, Inōni, daughter of the K'iin and host mother of Penee's child. Xairā, I am honored to meet a personal guardian of the Soputtan Sun Queen."

Throughout the introductions, Gar peered at the young girl through his spectacles. When she turned to him, he sent them into hiding and smiled. "I am Garon Anaru, and you are not what you seem." He glanced at Chealim who remained silent but attentive. "Who are you really?"

The Galactic Guardian responded. "This is Glori, a mystic of great power and wisdom. Learn everything you can from her, young Gar." His chin came up, his jaw tensed. "I must go. Glori, take them where your heart and your wisdom direct." His immediate disappearance left an intimidating emptiness in his place.

Glori motioned the group into the cottage. Stepping in after them, she uncoiled her jump rope and chanted as she used it.

> *"Cottage take us far away,*
> *Where evil cannot find us.*
> *Hide us from all searching eyes*
> *And those who wish to bind us."*

She paused, alert and watchful. Her rhythm quickened; her voice grew more urgent.

> *"Wrap us in a safe disguise,*
> *One they will not recognize.*
> *Warn us if they gather near,*
> *So we may quickly disappear."*

A cyclone of light lifted the cottage and its surroundings into the sky. Inōni clutched Penee's arm and held her breath.

13
Neul Isle

The Sanctuary Pod in the Bāoba Tree seemed too full of people. Brie moved closer to Esán. Torgin and Thorlu sat side-by-side, studying a map of Neul Isle. Den paced from one side of the pod to the other. The K'iin gathered at the table, their attention riveted to their wise woman.

The time to make plans had arrived, yet no one seemed confident enough to present one. Brie lifted her gaze to the rounded top of the pod. *How do we rid the K'iin's village of Raiherr's men?* An answer prowled at the edge of her overpowering fear for Penee and Gar.

Den stopped and sank into a seat next to her. "How could they just vanish? You didn't hear anything?" He scrubbed his dark hair with a hand and dropped it to his knee. "We don't have one clue—"

Brie touched his hand. "Den, we know they are with Sea Wee Vala. The Spirit Totem will not allow harm to come to them. Right now, you and Esán and I need a concrete plan to rid the K'iin village of the six Vasro who hold it." Her hand flew to mouth. She laughed. "Of course!"

In unison, Den and Esán faced her. Understanding lit Esán's expression. Den leaned closer. "Well?"

Brie straightened as she drew in a breath. "What if we put a spell of forgetting on the Vasro in the village? Not the Shaman or the Chief...just on the Vasro mercenaries."

Den frowned. "Then what do we do with them?"

Cadhōla joined them as he spoke. "You let the K'iin take care of them." She sat down. "We will separate them, so they cannot rekindle each other's memories, and teach them the ways of our people."

Torgin led Thorlu over to the group. "We're ready to leave for Raiherr's camp. Our plan is simple. Since we know little about the four men and their dynamic, we will spy for the rest of the turning and return later to rest and to share what we discover."

Brie pursed her lips, then studied the group. "I think we should do the same thing. It will be much easier to use a spell of forgetting on the Vasro if they are together and we know more about them." She looked from Den to Esán.

Den heaved a sigh of relief. "I agree with you. Let's do some knowledge gathering before we act."

Cadhōla chimed in. "I will alert our tribesmen to be ready when we need them." She stood. "Thank you for coming to our aid. I'll tell my people what you plan." She crossed to the table and rejoined her tribe's men and women.

Brie put her concern for Penee and Gar aside. "I believe shaping birds and flying to the village is the best way to spy without drawing attention to ourselves. Torgin, will you ask Ostradio to show us the best way to the K'iin's village?"

Torgin withdrew the compass. "Ostradio, please show us the way to the Valley of Tá Súil."

Den, Esán, and Brie moved closer. The compass needle blurred and stopped, pointing northwest. A map took shape; a course glowed between the valley and the Bāoba tree.

At a word from Torgin, the map vanished. He slipped the compass into its pouch and tucked it away. "Are you ready, Thorlu?"

The High DiMensioner nodded. "Let's go. Good luck to us all! See you tonight."

Shape shifting two fire eagles, Torgin and Thorlu took their leave.

Brie and Esán changed to mérlin kestrels and shot after Den, who shaped a larger sparrow hawk. Leaving distance between so they would not draw unwanted attention, they flew toward the K'iin village.

Brie embraced her love of flying and soared high above the Isle of Neul.

The opaque cyclonic light carrying Glori's cabin thinned to an iridescent haze. Gar, his spectacles in place, stared at a planet growing closer and closer. The wise woman chanted a soft verse.

"Leave this place of never ending
Settle down within time's bending."

With the field of flowers and forest surrounding the cottage intact, Rainbow Cottage landed, at the edge of a skeletal weaving of white branches. Through the front windows of the cottage only a parched, gray, rock-covered expanse could be seen, stretching all the way to the horizon.

Glori met their confused glances with a smile. "We are on the uninhabited planet of Chûrinne. Like Persow, where Relevart's cabin remains hidden, this planet is in the Spéire Solar System. Only a few know it exists, and they assume it cannot support life."

Gar wrinkled his nose. "But, Glori, there's no life here."

With a cheerful laugh, she picked up her skipping rope, and walked to the edge of the field of wildflowers. To the rhythm of her jumping, she chanted,

"Land of Chûrinne, show your light,
But only to those with unfettered sight.
Reveal your essence, your fertile ground.
Let your beauty come forth unbound."

A silence thick with anticipation settled over Penee, Inōni, Xairā, and Gar. Huddled together on the porch, they watched the harsh, colorless landscape ripple and blur. Flat-topped mountains emerged covered in green and gold foliage. White, barren branches of the dead forest clicked together like a band of percussionists. Tiny green buds sprouted and burst into shimmering blue-green leaves. A chorus of songbirds announced the appearance of a lush valley spreading out between the two mountain ranges. The distant gurgling roar of water grew louder. A waterfall appeared, cascading down the steep side of a flat mountain. From its bubbling plunge pool, a stream formed and flowed into a shimmering lake. Scents of flowers and damp earth permeated the freshened air. A large bird swooped low over the water's surface, caught a fish in its talons, and soared upwards.

Gar removed his glasses and sent them into hiding. "I woulda never guessed so much beauty could come from nothing." He walked over to Glori. "The bad guys can't see it, right?"

Glori coiled her skipping rope and smiled. "Only we can enjoy Chûrinne's magnificence. Of course, the Galactic Guardians and the VarTerels can always see it."

Her red curls bounced as she bound up the steps and gazed up at Penee and Inōni. "You need to rest. The cabin provides what we need. You may select to rest in one room together or in individual rooms. Just state your preference."

Xairā frowned and moved closer to Inōni. "What about me, Glori?"

The child-like wise woman regarded her with open respect. "A room will appear near your charges, Xairā."

"Thank you." The queen's guardswoman caught Inôni's eye and smiled.

Gar climbed onto the porch. "What about me, Glori? I'm not tired." He grinned.

The wise-woman placed her rope on a bench by the door. Her child-like persona bristled with excitement. "You and I will shape eagles and explore. I have not been to Chûrinne for many Persowan sun cycles." She descended to the field of flowers surrounding the cabin, and, lifting her arms to the sky, spun around like the child she resembled. A delighted giggle ended her spinning. "I had forgotten how beautiful this planet truly is."

Gar, his grin widening at her delight and at the thought of exploring the planet with her, turned to Xairā. "You'll take care of Penee and Inōni, right?"

Xairā snapped to attention and saluted. "I will, sir."

Gar sobered and returned her salute. "Thanks!"

Penee hugged him. "We will rest and look forward to hearing about what you discover."

Inōni's dark eyes sparkled. "Have fun!"

Satisfied his charges were safe and in good spirits, Gar joined Glori. Her shift to eagle triggered his, and soon they were soaring over the beautiful planet of Chûrinne.

Raiherr left the Vasro camp early and walked to the clearing where his jumper craft, *Toneer*, sat beneath the dome's dim grayness. *Today Callum will finish his modifications on the box, or I will... What will you do, idiot? If you throttle him, you'll be stuck beneath this dam'n dome for the rest of your existence.*

A fierce blast of wind hit him broadside and sent him stumbling backward; a second blast knocked him to the ground. Rolling onto his side, he watched a churning whirlwind of sand, dried leaves, and blazing orange light form in the clearing. Fear for *Toneer* brought him to his feet. A tall, muscular warrior bursting from the whirlwind's center, a shield in one hand and a wicked-looking sword in the other, froze him mid-sprint.

The warrior eyeballed the ship and faced Raiherr. Combatant's power thrumming around him added to the menace of his angry snarl roiling across the plains.

Raiherr suppressed his desire to cower, held his ground, and blanked his expression.

The warrior, a head taller than Raiherr, who stood taller them most men he knew, marched over the rough ground, his slate-gray eyes boring into him. Coming to a halt, he sheathed his sword and slung his shield over his back. "Is that your ship?"

The deep, rumbling voice forced Raiherr a step back. "It is, and it's a jumper craft. Who in Hades are you? And how did you breach my dome?"

Arrogance straightened the man's spine. "I am Carûtix, God of War of the Spéire Solar System." He glanced up at the dome and shrugged. "I offer you friendship for a ride in—" A hint of laughter erased the disdain from his features. "—your jumper craft."

Raiherr tipped his head and examined the hawkish features of the deeply tanned face. Dark, slanted brows accenting the young god's sable-colored eyes. A beak-like nose above a wide, thin-lipped mouth and a narrow chin were all framed by a close-cropped beard and mustache. Mink brown hair, shaved close from his temples to the back of his head, bordered longer hair on top that swept upward and back. His stance had eased; eager interest lit his expression.

"When my SorTech finishes his work..." Raiherr glanced upward. "...and we can penetrate the dome without destroying it, I would gladly take you for a ride. Until then, how about a tour?"

Carûtix pursed his lips, then shrugged. "I would like to see your craft."

Raiherr entered the frequency code. The door opened, and he ducked inside. "Come in and have a look around."

After a brief tour, Carûtix stood gazing at the instrument panel in the cockpit. "Let us sit and get acquainted."

Their conversation, at first stilted and uncomfortable, shifted to the ease of comrades sharing interests and desires. Raiherr soon realized this god would be a mighty ally. Strategic questions on both sides produced answers that left them each hatching ways to make use of the other.

When Raiherr recognized the animosity Carûtix felt for the Sun Queen, he went to work stoking the flames. At the mention of Inōni's possible residency at the queen's palace, the god shot to his feet and bellowed like a moose ready to charge.

"The Deities do not allow Humans in Shiór Ridu. What is Abellona thinking?" A malicious laugh echoed through the small craft. He exited into the clearing and turned to glare at Raiherr. "I will bring the human girl to you, but only if you allow me to help destroy this island."

Raiherr kept his voice steady. "Bring her to me, and we will consider our next move."

The young demi-god unsheathed his sword. Whirling wind surrounded him, lifting him into the air and up through the dome.

In the ensuing quiet, Raiherr inhaled a steadying breath and rubbed his hands together. *I have joined forces with this solar system's God of War! My goals grow closer!* He threw his head back and laughed with pernicious abandon.

Ari, Rethson, and Elf huddled at the center of *El Aperdisa's* Holographic Center's new entertainment section, exchanging information in low voices.

After sharing her encounter with Reedan and Nesen, Ari told them about Torlad and Equis. "Commander Odnamo hired them to help find our spies and asked Torlad to share his code name with us. It's Maskaid. We are to contact Torlad telepathically if we're in danger."

Elf frowned. "I'm pretty sure I'm being watched. There's this crewman in engineering who stays in the background but... Whenever I enter or leave, I can sense his eyes on me. The couple of times we made eye contact, he ducked out of sight."

Rethson joined in. "Vigilance is key when I'm in the cafeteria. Like Elf, I'm certain I'm being watched. So, I have nothing to report."

Voices in the Holo Center's main section ended their conversation. Elf touched his ear, then shifted to Zak.

Rily flashed into being beside Jem. "Better get gone." He vanished.

Zak moved close to Jem. "You go. I'll stay here. If they heard something, they may try to enter this section. They'll find me muttering about "stuff". Meet me at the Plantitarium in Elf's space after evening meal."

The voices grew louder. Jem shifted to a tiny fly and landed in the crack between viewing panels. Zak prowled the space, mumbling to himself.

"Well, well, look who's here." Reedan, his cruel mouth twisted into a grin, strode ahead of a man Zak had not seen before. "So, Zak, who were you talking to?"

Zak scowled. "Some idiot accused me of stealing his favorite knife. He got pretty nasty, so I thought I'd better find a place to vent my anger." He looked from one to the other. "You off duty?"

Reedan stepped closer, his hooded eyes unblinking. "I think you're lying, crewman." He glanced at his friend. "What do you think, Rozar?"

Scowling, Rozar circled behind Zak.

Reedan raised a fist. "Why don't you tell us who you really are and who you were talking to?"

A tiny insect landed behind Zak's ear. Jem buzzed. "I'm here. Help's on the way."

Reedan threw a punch. Zak blocked it with an arm. Another punch followed. This time, he dodged sideways, missing the flying fist by a whisper.

"Reedan," Zak's voice was steel-edged and level. "I suggest you consider whether this is a smart idea. We work together. Until now, I respected you as someone I could talk to who would give me a straight answer."

Behind him, Rozar crept closer. Zak spun around and jammed his palm under the man's chin, shoving his head back with all the strength he could muster. The startled crewman flew backward, fell, and did not move.

Zak, fists ready, executed an about face. "Shall we continue?"

Reedan's round face flooded with angry red. He growled low in his throat. "Tell me what I want to—"

Two guards marched into the space. The taller of the two took charge. "What is going on? Didn't you see the restricted sign? This area is closed."

Zak lowered his fists and sighed. "I needed to be by myself, so I hid in here. These guys came to find me." He looked from Reedan to his sidekick, who sat on the floor resting his forearms on his knees. "Sorry, I took my frustration out on you guys."

The guards escorted them into the main Holographic Center and locked the entrance to the new section. One stepped up beside Zak. "You come with us, Private Zakeron." He nodded at Reedan and Rozar. "You two are free to go."

With Zak between them, they left the center and marched him down the hall. Once they were out of range, the taller man spoke in an undertone. "For your own safety and to keep those two guessing, Commander Odnamo ordered us to detain you overnight,"

Jem's fly buzzed further down the passageway, assumed his human shape, and walked back toward the trio. He passed them with a nod and continued on his way. Since he was off duty, he headed to the cafeteria, ate a quick meal, and wandered to the T-lift. He exited at the entrance level of the Plantitarium. Aimless wandering along manicured paths brought him close enough to Elf's secret space that he teleported and shifted.

H‍eaving a relieved sigh, Ari sat down on the bench by the stream. *That was way too close. Hope Rethson gets here soon.* She tugged a long curl over her shoulder and sat counting the strands.

14
Shiór Ridu

The Sun Queen sat on her throne, her scepter in hand and her attention following the angry movements of Carûtix, the youngest son of the God of War. That he was raving at his superior, the Sun Queen of the Spéire Solar System, did not seem to phase him.

He came to a halt in front of her, his broad-shouldered, muscular body tense with anger and his slate-gray eyes filled with hatred. Arrogance and antagonism roiling, he took a step forward, brushed a stray hank of hair away from his face, and growled. "You have been sheltering a Human in your palace. You disgrace your position, Abellona. Where is she?"

Reining in the desire to teach him a lesson, the Sun Queen cradled her scepter and rose, the power of her rank and position a shining aura surrounding her. A subtle signal alerted her guards. Two marched forward; a third left the room.

Her steady gaze examined the young man's face. "I am, Carûtix, not some underling that you can rant at indiscriminately. Either calm down and provide an explanation, or my guards will escort you to your quarters until you can be civil. Do I make myself clear?"

An arrogant snarl distorted his features. "I am the God of War. Do not presume to underestimate me, or you will be sorry."

She raised her scepter. Four additional guards entered the room and positioned themselves behind and on either side of him. Choosing not to dignify him with a response, she inclined her head.

The Captain of the Guard turned. "Take him away."

Surrounded by equally strong and well-trained men, Carûtix shot her a venomous look and exited the room with his escort.

Abellona descended from the throne and paused.

Ferêlith emerged from the shadows, distaste written in every line of her body. She regarded her mistress and queen with respect. "What do you require of me?"

"See what you can discover about Carûtix. Why he is here? Did he come of his own volition? Is his father aware he is raging throughout the solar system? Also, have Aahana and Nimah report to me as soon as possible. You may go."

When the door closed behind Ferêlith, Abellona traversed the throne room to her private study. A focused thought opened the red-gold curtains on the black granite wall opposite her desk. She raised her scepter. "La Mòr Gisof."

A palatial door materialized and opened inward. A warm golden light drew her into the realm of Tismilú. At the whispered command, "Dù Intē", the door and the curtains closed.

Inside the mystical chamber, she took a moment to recover her equilibrium, breathed in the sweet scent of sacred oils, and, with slow, measured steps, crossed to an elegant tinewood table. With a reverent bow of the head, she uncovered a large crystal ball sitting at the table's center. *It's time to contact the Council of Deities.*

With her entire attention on the crystal, she recited:

> *"Galactic Deities hear my plea.*
> *Answer my call; come to me.*
> *Advice and counsel I require*
> *To put out a raging fire."*

Abellona drew a sacred symbol above the crystal and prepared to wait. A relieved smile formed as the features of Itarān Cirana, the Council leader, grew sharp and clear. His well-modulated voice greeted her.

"Dear Abellona, I answer your call. We are, like you, concerned by the actions and desires of the Demi-God, Carûtix, and his developing relationship with Karlsut Sorda's henchman, Raiherr Yencara. Our young god's desire to punish his father has led him down a path from which he may never return.

"Your role, honored Sun Queen, is to warn him of the results of his folly and step back. I fear Carûtix will pay you no mind. The choices he makes will dictate his end game.

"Please continue to assist those important to the successful conclusion of the CoaleScence. Our allies, Neul Isle's Incirrata and her Stannags, will help you in any way they can."

A rush of relief created a glowing red-orange aura around Abellona. "Thank you, Itarān Cirana, for coming to my aid. I know your duties require your immediate supervision. May I ask one question before you go?"

The deity in the crystal smiled. "I am at your service, dearest Sun Queen. What is your need?"

"Penee, Inōni, and Garon have disappeared from Neul Isle and Soputto. What is my role in their return to the game?"

Itarān Cirana's sea foam blue gaze gleamed iridescent. "Relevart has requested that you allow him to oversee their safety, while you help Brie and her companions rid Neul Isle of Raiherr and his gang. We both feel with Carûtix added to the list of players, you will indeed be busy." He began to fade. "Beware our demi-god's youth and arrogant rage."

After Itarān Cirana's departure, Abellona sat in the tranquil quiet of Tismilú contemplating the conversation. Her gaze lingered on the crystal ball. A grim smile vanished into a severe frown. *I remember the arrogance of youth, young Carûtix. Take care.*

Covering the crystal ball, she slipped from the hidden room and prepared to inform Aahana and Nimah of their newest challenge.

Torgin's fire eagle lifted into flight, shot up and over the enormous trees of the Bāoba Forest, and leveled off. Thorlu's eagle flew higher and to the east. Circumventing the K'iin village, they followed a river in a narrow gorge, bordered on both sides by steep mountain cliffs. Near the Plains of Cârthea, where the river curved toward the sea, they flew northwest.

Landing in a wooded area a distance from the Vasro camp, Torgin assumed his human form and scanned the curve of the dome for his fellow eagle. Worry nudged. His gaze focused upward, he rotated, searching the emptiness. *Where are you, Tangorra?*

A dark-skinned man stepping free of the trees sent a thrill of alarm up his spine. *What is the Sun Queen's son doing here?*

Nimah walked toward him. "I see you recognize me, Torgin Wilith Whalend. My mother, the Sun Queen, sent me to rendezvous with you. The High DiMensioner, Thorlu Tangorra, is now with her in Shiór Ridu, disguised as me. Mamai asked me to share with you a recent occurrence that endangers you and your friends and complicates our quest to rid the island of Raiherr and his men."

Torgin frowned. "How did you get beneath the dome, and how did Thorlu leave it?

"Ahhh. Mamai said your thought process is quicker than your consideration and polite questions. Please take the lead."

Releasing a breath, Torgin shifted. Beside him, the Sun Queen's son flashed into fire eagle form, and together they flew through a ravine to the river and back along the gorge to the grouping of spruce-like pines. Landing among the sturdy trunks, they searched for somewhere to sit and talk.

Nimah implied the need for silence with two fingers on his lips. Shields shot up around them. He knelt and drew two large circles on the ground. Lifting his hand, he made a swooping motion, closed his fist around the gathered energy, and touched his heart. The circles rounded into mounds of dirt covered in moss, providing a seat for each man.

The shields shimmered into nothing, and Nimah sank onto a mound. "Let us share."

Torgin sat down and rubbed a hand over his short, dark curls. "I suggest you take the lead, Nimah. Then I will answer your questions about what has occurred here."

Nimah nodded and began by describing the Demi-God Carûtix and his choice to join Raiherr and the Vasro rebels. Next, he share the unexpected appearance of the Galactic Guardian, and his departure with Penee, Gar, Inōni, and Xairā a short time later.

Ignoring his desire to know their location, Torgin studied the man across from him. "Since the Galactic Council set aside their directive to stay aloof and sent Chealim, the situation here must be more critical than I'd guessed. Tell me more about Carûtix. How much power does he wield? And what has motivated him to leave Shiór Ridu and mix with Humans?"

Nimah squeezed a piece of moss between his fingers and tossed it into the trees. "Mamai shared that Carûtix and his father, Bucānetis Marûs, the High Deity of War and Peace for our solar system, disagreed about Carûtix's position in the line of succession. When his father refused to give in, Carûtix left Shiór Ridu in a fit of rage, seeking vengeance against his sire."

Torgin's brain hummed with the ramifications of Nimah's words. "Do you possess the powers of a deity?"

Nimah's expression morphed from foreboding to regal. "I do. I am the heir to the Sun Queen's throne." He rubbed his chin with a finger, then gripped his knees. "Mamai sent me to join you in the battle to end the strife on Neul Isle. She has made it clear I am to follow your lead and to learn everything I can from you." Narrowed, opal-flecked eyes examined Torgin with intense interest. "Mamai is impressed by very few, yet she admires you and your friends." He looked harder. "You, Torgin Whalend, top her list. How smart are you, anyway?"

"Smart enough to know I have as much to learn from you as you have to learn from me. Your mother is providing us both with the opportunity to grow."

The Sun Queen's heir grinned. "Mamai said I would like you. She's right." He straightened. Seriousness cloaked him. "I require time to adjust my thought process. Please give me a moment."

Torgin waited in silence for him to speak. *I wonder, Nimah, where your thoughts will take you?*

At the Sun Queen's palace, Thorlu Tangorra gazed in the mirror at his new persona. Nimah's smooth, black skin, exquisite eyes, reminiscent of the queen's, and the power of a trained warrior rippling through his agile body made Thorlu smile. *I wonder what young Gar would say if he could see me?*

He paced the room, exploring the feel of his new, younger body and examining the personality of Nimah. Abellona had allowed him to keep his intellect and memories intact but had infused his mind with enough of her son's personality, knowledge, and instinctive tendencies to make the persona believable.

Memories mixed with the needs of the moment. The image of himself as a young man snapped into focus. *My longevity has led me on a journey from El Stroma, on the other side of the Outer Rim, to the Clenaba Rolas System and beyond.* He frowned. The only woman he had ever loved came to mind. *When I get back to El Aperdisa, I will declare my love, Healer De Dilliére. But now, I must focus on the present.*

A long stride ended in front of a floor to ceiling window, where he studied his new environment and reviewed his conversation with Abellona.

She had explained why she required his objective view of events as they unraveled. Her insights regarding Nimah and Torgin produced a nod of agreement. The appearance of Carûtix clearly concerned her more than her words conveyed. Potential disaster loomed on the horizon. Abellona ended the conversation as it began by emphasizing that Thorlu's knowledge of Brie and her companions and his instincts as a High DiMensioner were vital to a positive outcome.

A knock at his door interrupted his musings. He opened it to find Ferêlith, the Sun Queen's personal attendant, who waited with concern radiating from her like the rays of the Soputton sun.

"Nimah, your mother wishes you to join her. Please come with me." Without a backward glance, she hurried down the hallway.

Gathering his wits and his Nimah persona around him, he strode after her.

Torgin sat on a mound hidden among the trees, his mind busy with options for how best to work with the Sun Queen's son. Time was passing, and they needed to make a move.

Across from him, Nimah straightened. His opal-flecked gaze lifted to Torgin's face. "I believe, Torgin, it is best if I shape the Human, Thorlu. We do not want our enemies to discover the Sun Queen's heir is on Neul Isle." He scrunched his eyes into the beginnings of a squint, then relaxed his expression. "Do you agree?"

"I do." Torgin smiled. "We reached the same conclusion. I suggest we now resume our fire eagle forms and fly to Raiherr's camp." He climbed to his feet. "The dome glows brighter, so time is passing. Let's see what we can learn."

Nimah stretched and rose to his feet. "The next time I shape Human, it will be as Thorlu. What must I know to make his persona appear true to your companions?"

Torgin studied the young deity. "I will provide you with personality markers and memories. May I touch your temples?"

"You may, Torgin Whalend." Nimah's dark lids closed.

A short time later, Torgin lowered his hand. "Open your eyes and tell me how you feel."

Nimah blinked and took a breath. "I am amazed by the DiMensioner Thorlu Tangorra." He shivered. "I've so much to learn. How did you do that?"

Torgin stared at his hands. "I do not know. I opened my mind to Thorlu's thoughts and focused on transferring what I know of him to you." A crooked smile tugged at his mouth. "I learn something new about my gifts every turning. Shall we fly?"

Nimah shifted and flew to a high branch. Torgin changed to his favorite eagle and launched into flight. Soon, the two fire eagles perched on the sturdy branches of a tinewood tree, their keen raptor sight picking out their enemies and their keen minds, absorbing every detail of the activities, personalities, and rivalries of Raiherr and his men.

While Nimah concentrated on Raiherr, Torgin fixed his attention on Callum and the SorTechory Box. His quick intelligence soon jumped ahead of the SorTech's scramble to complete the changes. Torgin understood why the SorTech struggled to make his adjustments to The Box hold true.

Beside him, Nimah's fire eagle clicked his beak and fluffed up his feathers, a signal it was time to go.

At Torgin's answering click, both eagles shrunk to a smaller size. Taking the lead, Torgin flew between sturdy trunks until the canopy of branches overhead provided a safe exit. As he reached the openness beneath the dome, his eagle body resumed its original size. Nimah's full-size fire eagle glided to his side.

The river, gleaming in the late-turning sun, provided a direct path to the K'iin's village, which they circumvented. Dusk pursued them to the Sanctuary Pod, where they alighted and shifted to Human.

Torgin smiled as Thorlu appeared in Nimah's place. "You are good, my friend. Follow my lead." He tapped the oval, waited for the shimmering to cease, and stepped through the entryway. A soft gasp behind him made him glance back. Thorlu blinked and stepped in after him. The pod's wall reformed, and together they crossed the space to greet Cadhōla and their companions.

15
Neul Isle

In their shifted forms, Brie, Den, and Esán perched in the trees surrounding the K'iin's village and observed Raiherr's men stuffing themselves with food from the tribal stores, telling jokes, and having a good time.

Brie's kestrel flew closer and settled down to listen.

The apparent leader of the group, a Vasro named Relno, spoke up. "Taneg, take food to the prisoners, then get back here." He held up a pack of playing cards. "You owe me a rematch."

A short squat man scowled, climbed to his feet, and grabbed a couple of baskets filled with meager supplies. Mumbling to himself, he shuffled to the tribal shaman's hut. After setting a basket by the wooden door, he knocked, shuffled to a second hut, and delivered the second basket to the tribal leader. Seated once again with his comrades, he eyed his leader with misgiving.

Relno spread a blanket on the ground, and, sitting cross-legged, began to shuffle the cards. "Well, Taneg, are ya gonna play or are ya chicken?"

From her perch, Brie tipped her kestrel head. Impatience building on

Relno's bearded face presaged an angry confrontation. His jaw tightened; his muscular neck tensed.

Taneg, oblivious to the brewing tempest, yawned. "I don't got any money, Rel. You took it all yesterday. Get yourself another dupe." He stood up and ambled to the wooden bridge spanning the lake.

Kestrel wings unfurled and carried Brie to the far end of the footbridge. Heavy footsteps on the wooden tread induced her to settle in a nearby bush.

Relno halted and glared down at Taneg.

Taneg glanced up. "I told you I don't have no coin. Go, pick on someone—"

A yelp preceded the loud splash as he hit the water. Relno stood, fists on hips, watching the smaller man struggling to keep his head above the water.

Taneg disappeared, splashed to the surface, and sputtered, "Can't swim —" His bald head vanished.

A third Vasro ran to the shore, waded into the lake, and swam to the rescue of his comrade. When he had dumped Taneg, huffing and puffing, on dry ground, he left him to recover and marched up to Relno. "What're you trying to do? You appointed yourself leader, and now you trying to kill us off one by one?"

Relno tugged at his beard. "Don't test me, Oger, or you'll be next." Marching off the bridge, he crossed to a small hut and disappeared inside."

Brie landed beside Esán's kestrel in a tall tree a safe distance from the bridge. Den's sparrow hawk alighted on the next branch. Brie's feathers spiked around her neck, then smoothed. She unfurled her wings and bobbed her head.

The sparrow hawk launched into flight. Two kestrels flew after it, staying side-by-side. They landed on the stoop of the Bāoba Sanctuary, shaped Human, and moved to the entrance. Brie tapped the opaque oval and stepped into the pod as the side shimmered into nothing. Esán and Den followed. The entrance scintillated into a solid wall, leaving them facing Cadhōla and her companions.

The wise woman hurried forward, nodded to Den and Esán, and spoke to Brie. "Welcome back, VarTerel. Thorlu and Torgin are here. They have gone to clean up and will join us soon. Please come and enjoy the food my people have prepared. Then you can share what you have discovered with all of us."

The tribal women had arranged a table with tantalizing finger foods near the fireplace. Cadhōla hovered. Once they were all seated, she joined her tribesmen at the table across the pod.

Brie nibbled a piece of fruit covered with nuts. Her attention kept shifting to the door oval to the men's pods. When it finally opened, her eyes narrowed. *Who accompanies Torgin in the persona of Thorlu?*

A quick warning flitted across Torgin's face.

Brie resumed her nibbling and tucked her questions away for later.

Abellona paced her private suite of rooms, preparing for what she knew was to be a tumultuous interview. "The time to confront the raging Carûtix has arrived." She alerted the Captain of her Imperial Guard and sent Ferêlith to fetch Nimah/Thorlu.

Retrieving her scepter from its special case, the Sun Queen opened the door into the passageway, greeted her personal guards with a nod, and walked, with them in her wake, to the small throne room where she greeted guests in private.

Nimah met her at the door and escorted her to the throne.

The Captain of the Guard strode forward, bowed, and met her gaze. "Are you certain you wish to do this, My Lady? Our young demi-god is ready to do battle."

With the sovereignty of her role creating an aura of power, the Sun Queen of the Spéire Solar System lifted her chin and nodded. "Have your men escort him in. Please remain by the throne." She turned to Nimah. "Observe, my son, but do not interfere."

The Captain of the Guard gave his men their orders. Carûtix, surrounded by four guards, entered. The moment they were within the walls of the throne room, the Demi-God of War raged forward.

"How dare you confine me to my quarters. I am the *God of War*!" He sneered and bared his teeth. "I will make you sorry you ever stood in my way, Abellona. Where is the human girl, Inōni? I want her brought to me now."

"I'm sorry, Carûtix, I do not know this Inōni." The Sun Queen spoke with calm indifference. She came to her feet, her scepter in hand. "Please leave my palace and my realm and do not return unless invited. If you choose to ignore my orders, the Captain of the Guard will escort you back to your father's court in disgrace. Do you understand?"

An angry red flush tinted his cheeks, the skin beneath his shaved hair, and his neck. Outrage launched him forward. His hand instinctively reaching for his sword found only an empty sheath. A howl rolled like thunder through the throne room. A whirlwind spun up around him. "You will be sorry, Abellona. I will make you pay."

The Sun Queen raised her scepter. Her resonant voice filled the throne room. "Bannis Ements!"

Both the whirlwind and the man vanished. Abellona lowered her scepter. After dismissing the guards, she descended the three steps to the floor and faced Nimah. "Come with me."

She led him from the room through a nondescript door hidden by the throne. At the end of a short corridor, they entered a room with a panoramic view of the Drega Mountains. Placing her scepter on a long, narrow table, she guided Nimah to a chair. "You are safe to resume your true form, Thorlu.

With a sigh of relief, Thorlu materialized and sat opposite her. Gray-blue eyes studied her with concern. "What just happened? Where did you send him? Why did you allow him to leave at all? Please share your reasoning so I may understand."

Abellona pursed her lips. *Do I share my conversation with the Leader of the Council of Deities or—* An image of Itarān Cirana filled her mind's eye. Her uncertainty fled and she began.

"After my first confrontation with Carûtix, I contacted the Council of Deities. Their leader, Itarān Cirana, answered my call. He explained that the council already knew of the demi-god's rebellion and instructed me to let him follow his anger. Nimah has shared what's afoot with Torgin, so they are prepared to handle him. What are your concerns?"

She sat back and watched the High DiMensioner considering his response. "You can speak openly, Thorlu. You and I are partners in the quest to bring peace and calm to the sacred Isle of Neul. Raiherr and his Vasro will soon discover Carûtix is not interested in their desires, but only in paying back his father. What our young demi-god does not realize is that if he joins forces with Humans, he is negating his ability to return to his father's court and indeed to Shiór Ridu."

Thorlu's frown deepened. "Watching him reminded me of myself as a young man. I predict he will not realize his self-righteous anger is as much a danger to himself as to those he wishes to punish until he is much older. How do we assist my companions on Neul Isle if you cannot interfere?"

"With your help and your inside knowledge, Thorlu, we will provide information to Abarax and the Luna Moth. They will make certain it reaches the right players." She let herself relax. "For now, let us get better acquainted."

On the living ship, *El Aperdisa*, Ari sat by the pond in Elf's secret space. Impatience beat a steady rhythm with her booted foot. She pressed it against the ground, stared at the root-covered wall, and sighed. "Where are you, Rethson?" Her foot resumed its restless tapping.

"I'd say that foot would be an outstanding drummer." Rethson grinned down at her before sitting beside her on the bench.

Ari squirmed to see him better. "What took you so long? I was getting nervous, Rethson."

"Sorry to worry you, but I managed a private chat with Commander Odnamo. Zak's in the brig till tomorrow." Rethson chuckled. "That should be an eye-opener."

Ari punched his arm. "Don't be mean. It might be you next time. What else did the commander say?"

"Relevart joined us, and we discussed the Vasro spies and whether to toss them in the brig. The commander's view is that Karlsut will only plant more men. If the spies who are here feel secure, it will keep us in control of the information they share. The hope is that, since Elf took the blame for the situation in the Holographic Center, Reedan will try to recruit him."

Ari stared into the pond, her thoughts as active as the small fish darting back and forth beneath the flat, green leaves. "What is our next move?"

Rethson's brow creased. "We continue to play our roles. Just hope one of us doesn't get unmasked." He stood and stretched. "I'm off to bed. Meet you here tomorrow after evening meal."

Rily appeared in Rethson's place, listened intently, and stepped through the wall into the Plantitarium gardens.

Ari rested her forearms on her knees and watched the fish for some time before she straightened and shifted to Jem.

Jem frowned, stood up, and scanned the area beyond the wall. Once he felt certain the Plantitarium was empty of Humans, he teleported to a small waterfall closer to the entrance. Another mental scan, and he wandered down to the entrance and into the passageway. The T-lift deposited him at the crewmen's sleeping quarters. A yawn escorted him to his bunk. After gathering what he needed to prepare for bed, he made his way to the cleanse space.

While his uniform and personal items ran through their cycle in the sanitizer, he put his boots in the polisher and stepped into the cleanse stall. The feel of warm water spraying his body followed by warm jets of air drying him off left him refreshed. He dressed in the provided sleepwear and slippers and carried his clean clothes and boots to his locker.

"You're the new guy, right?"

Jem's instincts hummed. He faced Reedan's pal from the ship's Holographic Center. "That depends on how new. I've been on board for a few turnings." He yawned. "Names Jem Taisley. You?"

"Laris Rozar. Haven't been on the ship that long myself. How 'bout we meet for dinner tomorrow and get acquainted?"

Jem stifled another yawn. "Sounds good. I'm scheduled for the mid-turning watch, so I'll head right down to the mess hall afterward." He closed his locker and touched the lock pad. "Now, I'm off to my bunk. See you tomorrow."

Laris nodded. "Get some sleep."

Shuffling to his bunk, Jem gritted his teeth. The Vasro's eyes drilling holes in his back made him wish he could turn around and punch him. Self-discipline kicked in. He plumped his pillow and snuggled under the blanket on his narrow bunk.

Much to his surprise, sleep crept closer and closer and...

Raiherr, Zorin, and Dulno sat around the campfire squabbling about nothing in particular, while Callum worked on The Box. Bursts of frustration broadcast in guttural mutterings suggested the SorTech's changes were not going well.

The unexpected whirl-wind arrival of the Demi-God of War in the clearing's center froze all four men to the spot. Carûtix stepped free of the frenzied swirl of leaves and light and glared from one startled face to the next.

Raiherr scrambled to his feet. His narrowed gaze rested on the rage-filled face. "I didn't expect to see you again...at least not this soon."

Carûtix shook his head like a wild animal dodging a hornet. He reached for his sword. His empty hand clawed at the air. He threw his head back and howled. Bitterness and animosity roiled over the clearing.

Zorin and Dulno ducked behind Raiherr. Callum lowered the cover on The Box and stepped in front of it. No one spoke.

Raiherr's thoughts raced. The rage pouring from Carûtix did not bode well for him or his men. He breathed a stabilizing breath, squared his shoulders, and took a step forward. "Let's take a walk, Carûtix. When you've caught your breath, we can decide what's next.

The demi-god shuddered from head to foot. He clenched his teeth and puffed air in and out. Pivoting, he strode from the clearing toward the jumper craft.

Casting a warning look at his men, Raiherr followed. His thoughts jangled around in his head. Fear, anticipation, and resolve clashed. Mocendi training took over and ushered him into the Plains of Cârthea in the tumultuous wake of the demi-god.

16
Chûrinne

Two fire eagles soared a wide circle above the planet of Chûrinne. Glori in her shifted form had led the exploration beyond the flat top mountains, over a salmon sea, and back over amber adobe dunes that glittered with sparkles of ruby light.

Gar's astonishment grew as Glori's eagle swooped into a deep ravine and reappeared with a strange-looking plant dangling from her beak. The telepathic word *"Cottage"* filled his mind. His fellow eagle streaked over the flat top mountain and dropped into the valley where the cottage glistened in the pale peach rays of the afternoon sun.

As her taloned claws touched the ground, Glori materialized, cradling her collected bounty and grinning from ear to ear. She climbed the three steps and waved.

Gar landed beside her, his wonder overflowing. "What a beautiful planet. Thank you, Glori, for sharing it with me."

Her girlish giggle chimed. Then a cloak of seriousness matured her features. "Our sweet baby is eager to be born. Come, we must help her wait longer."

As the wise-woman turned to enter the cottage, Penee appeared in the doorway, her expression harried. "The baby wants to come too soon. What do we do?"

Glori followed Penee into the cottage and held up the plant she had collected from the ravine. "We make Inōni tea. It will relax both mother and baby. You help Xairā keep our patient calm. Gar will help me in the cookery. It won't take long."

Penee swallowed. "I'm so glad you heard my call for help. Inōni is afraid of a premature birth. I'll let her know you are back with a solution." She hurried toward the back of the cottage.

Gar watched her go, then turned to the wise-woman. "What do I need to do?"

"Come with me." She hurried to the cottage cookery and laid the plant on a large block of wood next to a deep stone sink with a pump at one end. After putting on a ruffle-edged apron, she stoked the fire in her wood-burning stove, pumped water into a kettle, and placed it on a burner.

She smiled at Gar. "While that's heating, you pump the water, and I'll rinse the plant." When they finished, she shook the water free of the leaves and roots and spread them on the wooden table block. "Similar plants are found on many planets. This variety is endemic to Chûrinne." She pointed to a bunch of red, bulbous berries nestled in the dark green leaves. "This berry plant is called rasmillo. Please pick the berries from the stalk while I collect additional herbs for the tea."

Gar went to work. When Glori returned with dried herbs tied in bunches, he had just finished. "I picked all the berries. What now?"

The mystic held up a dried herb. "This is melissa balm. A tea brewed from these leaves and the berries can help the mother and baby relax. Please bring me the flowered teapot from the right-hand cupboard while I prepare our ingredients."

Gar set the teapot on the wooden table block next to Glori. She put the smashed berries and crushed balm leaves in it and added boiling water. After stirring the contents of the teapot, she prepared a tray with it, three teacups, and a small strainer.

"I suggest while I take the tea to Inōni, you wait on the porch. Once our mother-to-be and the baby are calmer, you can join us."

Gar nodded. "I'll enjoy the sun."

Glori picked up the tray and flashed from view.

Gar strolled outside, inhaled the freshness of the air, and sat with his feet resting on the top step. His senses filled with the wondrous beauty spreading out before him. Thoughts of the old man who raised him in New York in 1969 made him smile. *You wouldn't believe all the great things I've seen and neat stuff I've done since you passed, Gin. Wish you were here to share. I miss making music with you. Wish...*

The screen door creaked, and Glori sat down beside him. Her childish features lit with a gentle light. "Your friend is not gone, Gar. You carry him in your heart."

Gar swallowed the lump in his throat and pressed a hand to his chest. "I bet you'd have liked Gin, Glori." He glanced over his shoulder. "How're Inōni and the baby?"

Glori plucked at the ruffles on her skirt. "The wee one has calmed its desire to be birthed too soon. Inōni and Penee are both resting, and Xairā is keeping watch."

"You helped the baby, right?" He twisted to see her better. "It wasn't just the tea?"

The mystic's girlish smile widened. "I sang a special lullaby."

Gar nodded and returned his gaze to the beautiful valley, which should have eased the anxiety creeping closer by the chron-circle. He sighed, glanced at Glori, and bit his lip. *Penee is my responsibility. I need to be right here.*

Brie's gaze wandered the Sanctuary Pod while she listened to her companions compare notes. She pursed her lips. *Who's using Thorlu's persona?* Torgin's acceptance and his warning glance kept her from asking while they were in the company of the K'iin.

Torgin listened to Den and Esán describe the behavior of the Vasro in the village. When they finished with the rescue of the man named Taneg from the lake, he shook his head. "It appears we have a group of misfits who don't get along."

Den's eyes narrowed. "I'd say divide and conquer is the key."

Thorlu cleared his throat. "We have one more thing to share. The Sun Queen got word to us that Carûtix, the Demi-God of War, has joined forces with Raiherr. He is a danger to us all."

Cadhōla joined the group. "Did I hear you say Carûtix is working with the Vasro leader?"

"You did," Torgin said. "He is angry at his father, so he is now our problem. La and Abarax will keep us abreast of what's happening."

The K'iin wise woman's gaze traveled from face to face and lingered on Thorlu. Keen intelligence gleamed. Her mouth pursed, then relaxed into a smile. "Please share information as you receive it so our warriors will be ready when you need them."

Thorlu smiled. "Please join us, Cadhōla. Your wisdom and knowledge of Neul Isle will be helpful as we consider our next move."

Torgin eyed Thorlu with interest, rose, and offered his chair.

From beneath lowered lids, Brie regarded the High DiMensioner with increasing interest. While Cadhōla and Torgin settled, she stifled the questions forming a long queue in her mind.

Esán touched her knee. Eyes full of knowing moved from her face to Thorlu. She reached for his hand and embraced his patient calm.

Torgin gripped his knees, his gaze fastened on Thorlu. "I suggest we adjourn to my pod for some private conversation."

Thorlu, standing in response, brought the group to their feet. "Please, Torgin, lead the way."

With his companions closing in behind him, Torgin moved to the exit leading to his pod. Thorlu's steady gazed following his every move made him realize how interested the Sun Queen's son was in everything outside Shiór Ridu. He touched the center of the rectangle outlined with symbols on the pod's wall. As they stepped onto the wooden platform and Cadhōla called forth the bridge, he noted the twinkle in Thorlu's eye.

In Torgin's sleeping pod, Thorlu helped Den arrange cots to create a meeting area. Everyone sat, their attention centered on Torgin. He focused on the High DiMensioner. "Would you care to start, Thorlu?"

"Thank you, Torgin." His gaze moved from one companion to the next until he rose to his full height. "For the safety of everyone involved, what I am about to share must remain our secret. If you feel ill at ease with that, please say so now." When no one spoke up, he inhaled a deep breath and shed the persona of Thorlu Tangorra.

Regal and in control, Nimah allowed his audience to assess the meaning of his presence.

In a silence weighted by curiosity rather than surprise, Torgin moved to his side. "Allow me to introduce Nimah, the Sun Queen's oldest son and heir. She asked him to join us here on Neul Isle. Thorlu remains at her side as an advisor and confidant in the shifted form of Nimah."

The young god smiled. "My mother recognized that Torgin and I have much to learn from each other and sent me to help rid Neul Isle of our enemies." Dark eyes glinting with fire-opal red and green, met the inquisitive gaze of each member of the group. "I am here as one of you, not as the heir to the Sun Queen's throne. To succeed, we must function together without reservation. Set aside my true identity. I am from this point forward your comrade, Thorlu Tangorra." His shift to the High DiMensioner was instantaneous. "Torgin and I will answer your questions."

Torgin sat down and released a relieved breath.

Before Thorlu could join him, Cadhōla rose and bowed her head. "The K'iin honor your—"

Thorlu's raised hand cut her short. "Only you may know the truth of who I am. Please, Cadhōla, honor me by accepting that, until destiny points the way, I am Thorlu. Treat me as you would treat him. If you find this too difficult, I sympathize and will erase your memories of Nimah."

The K'iin elder bowed her head. When she lifted her chin, she offered a question. "Thorlu, how much do you know of Carûtix—his god-power—his reason for seeking the Vasro leader?" She sank onto the edge of the cot, her determination to respect his wishes visible in her expression and the straightness of her spine.

Thorlu pursed his lips and joined Torgin on the cot. "Carûtix is a demi-god with aspirations to become the God of War. His father, Bucānetis Marûs, has other ideas. Abellona shared that his oldest brother is the true heir. Carûtix heard the news and went into a rage. He left Shiór Ridu and landed on Neul Isle near Raiherr's camp. The two men met by accident, and since like minds intuit like minds, they began talking. Raiherr shared Inōni was with the Sun Queen. What else transpired, I do not know, but Carûtix showed up at the queen's palace. His disrespect got him banned from her realm. As for his powers, they're still developing. He is a trained warrior and can move throughout the Spéire Solar System via his thoughts. Whether this will continue to be the case, only time will tell."

Brie studied the man opposite her. "You and Torgin visited the Vasro Camp. What did you learn that might help us deal with Carûtix and Raiherr?"

At a nod from Thorlu, Torgin took over the conversation. "The Box is key to Raiherr's power. It created the dome and is the means by which he monitors what is happening on the island.

"I studied SorTechory, so I could understand how The Box gives the SorTech his power. The most important thing I learned was the energy vibration of The Box must align with the SorTech's, or it will not work.

"Callum's changes have readjusted the dome's vibrational frequency, which is why he can't see outside it. If he makes one minor error, The Box will quit working altogether—a catastrophe for us all. Rather than have that happen and perhaps leave the dome forever over Neul Isle, Thorlu and I have devised a plan. I will make some of my own changes." He took a breath. "I'll require someone who has telekinesis in their arsenal and the ability to create holograms to come with me."

Esán sat up straighter. "Telekinesis is one of my gifts. The art of creating a hologram is one of Brielle's. Is your plan to remove the dome now or wait?"

Torgin tapped his lips with an index finger, then took a breath. "That's a good question, one I haven't yet answered. Let's talk about the ramifications of the dome, as it is this turning." He looked at his companions. "Den, tell us what you've observed."

Den frowned. "With the dome in place, no one can leave or enter without the special powers to do so. That traps all of us in a situation fraught with uncertainty. I, for one, would like to see the dome gone, rather than being trapped with Raiherr and his gang indefinitely."

Thorlu nodded. "I agree. With the dome gone, we will have the freedom to come and go and to move about the island."

Cadhōla clasped and unclasped her hands. "How will removing the dome help free Dri Adoh and Artānga and rid the village of the Vasro warriors?"

"Right now, the dome traps the Vasro and us." Thorlu paused. "If we remove the dome, before we have control of them—"

Torgin inserted, "They can escape and return in the future."

Den's wicked laugh snapped all eyes to his face. "Not if we gain control first and have them incarcerated on Soputto's ever-winter moon. TaSneach has a penal colony from Hades, one from which it is almost impossible to escape." He turned to Thorlu. "I suggest we contact the Sun Queen and ask her to ensure the head of the prison is someone she trusts."

Brie grinned. "Great idea! Ari and Elf were imprisoned there and told me all about it. It will be perfect. But right now, what do we do about the dome?"

Thorlu's eyes widened. "Look!"

Five heads turned. All gazes followed the Luna Moth's flight from the entryway to Brie's shoulder.

Torgin watched her expression grow more and more somber as La shared her news. When the Luna Moth finished, she fluttered from one person to the next and alighted on Thorlu's hand. His face lit up and then sobered as she took flight and vanished from sight.

Expectant gazes returned to Brie's face. She smoothed a curl behind her ear and took a moment, Torgin knew, to order her thoughts. Giving the curl a tug, she focused on the group.

"Carûtix and Raiherr joined forces. Penee and I are their primary targets, but all of us are in their sights. La says the Sun Queen has been in touch with Bucānetis Marûs. Although Carûtix does not yet know, he has crossed the line established by the Deities of the Spéire Solar System and faces banishment forever from Shiór Ridu. When he tries to return to the home of the Deities, he will learn the ramifications of his behavior. I shared our thoughts about the Penal Colony on TaSneach. La will inform the Queen of our plans."

Thorlu's expression hardened. "We must achieve our goals before Carûtix learns of his fate. You think he is dangerous now? Just wait." He smoothed his mustache. "Removing Dri Adoh and Artānga Fedâch from the village is vital, or we may lose the opportunity." He looked at Brie. "Tell us your plan, VarTerel."

Brie's eyes gleamed. She regarded Esán with a raised brow. He nodded.

"Tonight, we will rescue the K'iin Shaman and their leader. Den will accompany Esán and me to the village." She regarded the wise woman. "Cadhōla, our goal is to keep the Vasro believing their prisoners are in their huts. I have some thoughts on how to accomplish this, but I wanted to ask your advice first."

A knowing expression crept over the wise woman's face and grew stronger and more assured until she lifted her chin and made direct eye-contact. "Dri Adoh is a shaman of great power. I believe he will assist you in creating the illusion to keep the Vasro unaware he and Artānga are gone." For a long moment, she chewed her bottom lip. "Will you bring them here, VarTerel?"

"Can you guarantee you and your tribesman will not share their whereabouts with anyone else?"

The wise woman seemed to grow taller. "I will make it clear that all our lives depend on total secrecy."

Torgin's crooked smile caught everyone's attention. "I know I'm about to sound like Gar, but we need food before we embark on this venture." He noted Brie's raised brow. "Yes, I said we, Brielle. Thorlu and I will join you in case your plans unravel and help is required."

Cadhōla rose. "My kin have prepared a repast." She moved to the entryway. "I will see you in the Sanctuary Pod."

Torgin watched her cross the bridge, then turned to his companions. "Food and then…"

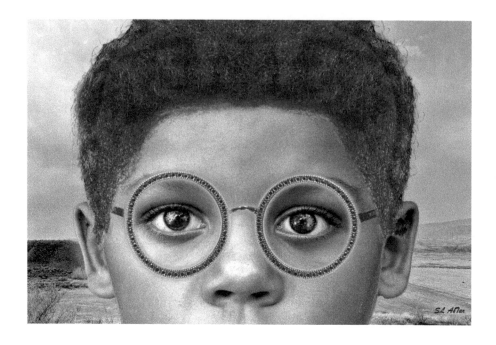

17
El Aperdisa

At the completion of Jem's watch schedule, Ari flashed into being in Penee's quarters, her throbbing thumb in her mouth. She removed it and allowed herself time to fully embrace her true form, felt the pain in her thumb ease, and sank down on the couch. The chronometer informed her the meal with Laris Rosar loomed. "Wish I could just stay here, but—"

Elf materialized near the entrance hatch, put a finger to his lips, and beckoned. As she reached his side, the Plantitarium's secret room took shape around them. His arms wrapped around her in a tight embrace. Their hearts beating in chorus made her want to stay with him forever. Instead, she took a step back, studied his solemn face, and pulled him down beside her on the bench by the pond.

"Are you alright? Why are we here?"

He rubbed his palms together, clasped them and lowered them to his lap, and let out a shaky breath. "Never get thrown into the brig. It's not a pleasant place, even half empty." Gritting his teeth, he shook himself and faced her.

"Reedan wants to meet and have lunch. I know you and Laris are lunching together, too. It wouldn't surprise me if we all end up at the same table. Remember, you are unaware of my background or my night in the brig."

Ari touched his hand. "Don't let Rethson's memories of Reedan get in the way. Zak has never met him or his men and you need to portray that."

Elf leaned over and kissed her cheek. "Don't worry. Circumspection is key." He stood up. "I'll leave from here. I love you, Arienh AsTar."

Zak's persona took over. With a nod, he stepped through the wall.

Ari teleported to Penee's quarters. A glance at the chronometer told her she'd better get going. With a heavy sigh, she used the cleanse space and shifted to Jem. His dark face in the mirror produced a crooked smile.

A short time later, Jem walked into the mess hall. Laris Rozar, Reedan's henchman, was waiting at a table off to one side. When Jem entered, Laris stood up and waved him over.

Jem ambled his direction, assessing the man as he approached. Pausing at an empty chair, he surveyed the mess hall. "Place is full. Sure glad you found a table."

"Me, too." Laris grinned. "Hey, look who's here. My friend Reedan and the new guy who works with him in engineering." He pushed back his chair. "I'll see if they'd like to join us. Alright with you?"

Jem nodded. "Sure enough. It'll be nice to meet some more people." His expression open and interested, he waited by the table.

Laris strolled up to Reedan and Zak, had a brief conversation, and led them to the table. "Jem, this Reedan and Zak. Reedan and I'll go do the chow line while you two get acquainted. When we get back, you can go fill your plates."

Jem smiled at Zak. "Have a seat. Reedan told me you're new. How long have you been aboard *El Aperdisa*?"

Zak returned the smile. "For several turnings. You?"

"Seems like forever, but maybe a quarter moon cycle." Jem noted the insignia on Zak's uniform. "Engineer. I'm an AeroTech. I work on the bridge. Commander Odnamo sure is sharp."

They continued their conversation, aware that listening ears were everywhere. When Reedan and Laris returned, Jem led the way to the chow line; grabbed a tray, plate, and utensils; and selected his favorites. He waited for Zak, and they strolled to the table and took their seats.

Reedan studied them as he chewed a bit of muffin and swallowed. "You arrived on the ship about the same time, right? I'm surprised you don't know each other."

Jem shrugged. "Different jobs and different schedules...whichever, we missed each other. Thank you for introducing us." He sipped his juice. "How long have you been on board?"

"Longer than you, but not by much. Laris and I met during orientation. It's been nice to know at least one person." Reedan stuffed the last of his muffin into his mouth and followed it with a gulp of juice. "Where are you from, Jem?"

"Thera."

Reedan nodded. "You must be familiar with Idronatti?"

"Actually, never been there." He shivered. "I was lucky and grew up in the Central Mountains." After sopping up the last drippings on his plate, he lifted his chin. "Where you from, Reedan?"

"My parents immigrated to a planet in the Clenaba Rolas System. Know anything about Tao Spirian?"

Jem shook his head. "Nope. Oh, wait. I remember... it's a planet beyond RewFaar that's mostly ocean and lots of islands." He produced a self-satisfied grin and an "I'm-proud-of-myself" nod.

Laris chimed in. "How about you, Zak? Where are you from?"

A dreamy look registered on Zak's face. "I grew up in a small village on the Von Baar Peninsula on DerTah." He sighed. "I miss it...my friends, my da's boat, the sun setting on the ocean..." Another sigh and he popped a piece of fruit in his mouth, chewed, and smiled at Laris. "How about you?"

"I was born on the planet of Persow in Baille, a village on the continent of Dast." Laris' eyes narrowed. "Bet you never heard of it..."

Jem noted the intense interest on Reedan's face. "Persow isn't in the Clenaba Rolas System, so..." He wrinkled his brow and let confusion seep into his expression. "...where is it?"

A server walked up to the table. "Excuse my interruption. Which one of you is AeroTech, First Class, Jem Taisley?"

Jem lifted a hand. "That's me."

"The Commander requires your presence on the Bridge, AeroTech Taisley. I'll clear your meal."

Pushing back his chair, Jem wiped his mouth with his napkin and rose. "Sorry to break up the party. It was nice meeting everyone."

Without a backward glance, he hurried from the cafeteria and strode with purposeful steps down the passageway. The doors to the T-lift opened, showing an empty car. He stepped in. A man moved from the shadows. Reedan's boss, Nesen, studied him with cold indifference and exited the lift.

The door closed. Jem frowned. *Sure hope Zak isn't in danger.*

◦ ◦

Gar sat on the steps of Rainbow Cottage fidgeting with his shirttail, while Penee and Inōni walked with Glori in the small vegetable garden. He listened to their soft voices and the occasional bursts of laughter and sighed. A glance over his shoulder showed him Xairā standing on the porch, her demeanor alert and watchful. *Why am I here on Chûrinne? Glori and Xairā can take care of the girls. I should be helping on Neul Isle...I know I'm needed there.*

His spectacles materialized on his nose. A hazy figure walked along the path toward him and stopped a short distance away. Gar peered closer. Chealim's blue eyes came into focus first, then his entire face framed with taffy-blond hair, and finally his tall, muscular frame.

Glori appeared on the porch beside a tense Xairā, her eyes fastened on his. "Have our enemies discovered us?"

The Galactic Guardian shook his head. "You are safe here. I have come for Garon and Xairā. Gar's presence is required on Neul Isle." His gazed switched to the guardswoman. "The Sun Queen requires your help, Xairā, to confuse our enemies."

Penee and Inōni rounded the end of the porch. Their eyes widened.

Chealim beamed. "Inōni, you are looking happier than the last time I saw you. Penee and Xairā must be taking good care of you."

The girls' tremulous smiles were fleeting. Penee slipped an arm around Inōni. "Why are you here? Are we in danger?" She glanced at Gar. "Why are Gar's spectacles glowing and his eyes the color of opals?"

Chealim gazed down at her. "The Sun Queen requires Xairā and Gar to return to Shiór Ridu. Glori will continue to watch over you. She will also help you hone your talents, Penee, to prepare for the end of the CoaleScence and your destiny's unfolding."

He focused on Inōni. "Your role, as the bearer of the child of Penesert El Stroma and Den Zironho, is to learn all you can, so you will be the best mother for your wee one."

Penee moved to Gar's side, tears glistening in her unique eyes. "Take care of yourself, Garon Anaru." She hugged him and joined Glori on the porch where Xairā and Inōni were bidding each other farewell.

Chealim reached for Gar's hand. "Xairā, it is time." With a final whispered word, the guardswoman hurried to join them. The Galactic Guardian nodded at Penee and Inōni and raised a hand. Chûrinne vanished.

Palatial rooms enclosed them. As Gar prepared to say goodbye to the Galactic Guardian, Chealim faded from view. Xairā hurried forward to greet the Sun Queen and her son. Eager to know why the Sun Queen had summoned them, Gar smiled up at Abellona. "Chealim said you need our help?"

Beside the queen, Nimah cleared his throat. Thorlu materialized in his place. "We require you, Gar, to return to Neul Isle and help our friends."

"Wow! Thorlu, I never expected you to be here." He grinned. "You make a pretty convincing Nimah." He looked at the Sun Queen. "Will Penee and Inōni be okay without Xairā?"

Abellona's presence seemed to hum with anticipation. "Glori and Den are watching over them." She inclined her head toward her personal guard. "Xairā is required here to help me appear uninvolved in our quest." She studied Gar for a long, serious moment. "Garon, as one of my chosen family, you hear me and understand my needs. Your friends are preparing to rescue Dri Adoh and the K'iin chief. To succeed, they require a connection to me, one no one will suspect. Are you prepared to be my go-between?"

Gar touched his heart. "I am, Your Majesty."

The palace blurred. A dimly lit space focused. The soft, frightened inhale of someone nearby held him motionless.

From beneath lowered lids, Zak watched Jem exit the crew's mess. Picking up a piece of bread, he nibbled the crust and waited for Laris or Reedan to make the next move.

Reedan's gaze darted beyond him. A questioning lift of a brow quickly replaced his frown. Zak forced himself to remain intent on enjoying the last of his meal.

The feeling he was in danger multiplied tenfold when Nesen entered the mess hall and made his way toward the table. A glance at the two men who occupied the table with him suggested surprise.

Zak patted his mouth with a napkin and pushed back his chair. "I'm scheduled for a review of my performance."

A hand on his shoulder held him still. "No, need to hurry away." Nesen did not remove his hand, but looked from Reedan to Laris. "Which one of you is Reedan?"

Reedan sat back. "That would be me. What's up?"

"You're required in engineering." He glanced at Laris and removed his hand from Zak's shoulder. "Names Specialist Nesen Trulvue. May I join you?"

Laris tried to hide his nervousness. "Sure."

Nesen sat down and rested his forearms on the table. His intense gaze rested on Zak. "I've met Laris. You are?"

"Name's Zakeron. Sorry to greet and run, but I've a meeting to attend." He stood up. "Enjoy your meal."

Nesen stood up, too. "I'll walk with you as far as the chow line."

Zak shrugged and headed for the exit. Again, Nesen Trulvue's hand gripped his shoulder. "Don't hurry away, son. I've got something to share. I'll meet you tonight at the Crew Bar for a drink." He let go. "See ya later."

Zak simply nodded and continued out into the passageway. When he reached the T-lift, he entered with two other crewmen. At the level of Engineering, he hurried to his station, checked in with Sergeant Teva Rivan, and followed her to a small cubicle.

Eyeing him with interest, she glanced at her notes. "I understand you just met Nesen Trulvue. He's a dangerous man. I suggest you don't meet him at the Crew Bar. Leave a message that you're ill. I've arranged for you to check into the infirmary for the night.

Zak studied the face opposite him. "Care to explain how you know about my encounters?"

"Your aunt asked me to look out for you. When Reedan asks me if you met with me today, I'll affirm our meeting. Be careful, Zak. You are being closely watched. Every move you make and every word you speak is reported up the line. Now, please go to the infirmary. Head Healer De Dilliére is waiting for you."

A knock on the hatch brought Zak to his feet. "Thank you for your time. It is a privilege working with you."

The Sergeant's expression, though bland at a glance, held a warning. "Please go directly to the infirmary. I'm sorry you aren't well. Let me know how you are tomorrow." She tapped the touch pad by the entrance.

Reedan waited in the passage. He looked Zak up and down. "You sick, Zakeron?"

Zak swallowed. "My stomach's—" He gulped. "Excuse me. I think I'm—" He made a choking sound and scurried toward the men's personal space. A short time later, he rested in a curtained cubicle in the infirmary, his thoughts in turmoil. *How do I get word to my pals?*

Healer De Dilliére stepped into the cubicle, a mini-comp tab in hand. "How are you feeling?" She held out the tab so he could see it. "A healer will check on you later. I suggest you get some rest. The anti-nausea meds should keep your stomach calm." She nodded and departed, closing the curtain behind her.

Zak sighed. The comp-tab showed a message to him. "Don't shift. Friends alerted. Beware of giving yourself away." Torgin's experience with having a tracking device planted on him by a med-tech not long ago came to mind. Zak closed his eyes. With an exhausted yawn, he let himself relax.

18
Neul Isle

While her friends finished their meal, Brie slipped away to her sleeping pod. Sitting on the edge of the stairs leading to the personal needs space, she quieted her mind and allowed an all-encompassing tranquility to flow through her. The K'iin village in turmoil focused in her mind. Urgency flooded her thoughts. She gripped her knees and gulped a breath. Her intent focused on her companions; she sent a telepathic message.

Esán, the first to cross the bridge from the Sanctuary Pod, stepped inside, scanned the space, and hurried to her. His warm hug helped her to anchor in the moment.

"We must leave for the village as soon as possible. While renewing myself with some quiet time, I received a vision. The Vasro have captured several K'iin children and imprisoned them in a hut close to Dri Adoh."

Den, Thorlu, and Torgin filed into the pod. Torgin's astute gaze fastened on her face. "What did you see? I felt you go from serene to anxious."

After her quick explanation, Thorlu suggested they make plans once they knew what they faced. The companions agreed and prepared to leave for the K'iin village. Brie and Esán shifted to their favorite kestrels and followed Den's sparrow hawk over the Bāoba Forest and headed for the Elgnat Range, which bordered the village closest to the eastern shoreline. Torgin and Thorlu changed to their fire eagle forms and soared overhead. Once the village came into view, they flew to a pre-selected spot and alighted in a group of full-leafed deciduous trees at the north end of the village.

Brie fluttered to the ground and shaped Human. A mental probe produced a nod of surprise. Her telepathic message brought Torgin into human form beside her.

"Gar is here." He scrubbed a hand over his hair. "Chealim or Relevart brought him. What do you want us to do?"

"Ask Den and Thorlu to keep watch. You find Gar and the K'iin children and explore our rescue options. Esán and I will find Dri Adoh and decide how best to remove him and Artānga from danger. Keep in touch with telepathy, but be subtle."

Torgin regarded her for a long moment before giving her a quick hug. "Be careful, VarTerel AsTar. Your talents are growing. If I sense it, so will others." He shifted to eagle and flew between tree trunks and up to land in the intertwining branches.

Brie smiled as Esán landed at her side. "Torgin said you needed me?" He brushed a curl away from her face. "I need you, too." He kissed her cheek then became all business. "So, what have you discovered?"

Her quick synopsis produced a nod.

"Let me make sure I am clear, Brielle. You and I will find Dri Adoh and follow his lead if it feels right. Torgin will find Gar." He shook his head. "What a life of adventure our young Garon is experiencing. Who do you think brought him back to Neul Isle?"

"Chealim is the most likely person, but it doesn't matter. He's here, and I'm glad." She clasped his hand. "Let's teleport to Dri Adoh's hut. We'll arrive but remain invisible until we are certain it is safe to materialize."

Esán nodded. "You're the boss." He squeezed her hand.

Glad she had visited his hut when she first met the K'iin shaman, Brie pictured it. They arrived in a dark corner to find Dri Adoh facing a man in the open doorway. The Vasro, whom Brie recognized as Taneg, radiated fear he attempted to hide with a nasty scowl. "Just makin' sure you're here and doin' as you're told, old man." The scowl grew more fierce. "Don't do anything stupid or…" Taneg slammed the door shut.

The shaman waited, wariness like a cloak around him. When the Vasro's footsteps faded, Dri Adoh turned, looked at the spot where Brie and Esán stood, and spoke in an undertone. "You may show yourselves."

Still holding hands, they materialized. Brie took the lead. "Dri Adoh, I am the VarTerel Brielle AsTar and this is Esán Efre. We are here to rescue you and Artānga."

The elder shaman smiled a toothless smile. "I remember you, Brielle and Esán. We have no time to waste. How can I help?"

"Our goal is to remove you from the village, but create the illusion that you're still in the hut. Cadhōla suggested you might know how to accomplish this."

He worked his lips, then nodded. "I know a spell which will obscure my absence and Artānga's." Narrowed eyes blinked wide. "Ahhh! Your young friend watches over the K'iin young ones."

Dri Adoh moved with precise intent, drew a symbol on the door, and repeated it at the hut's center. He then raised his arms to the heavens. As he spoke in the language of the K'iin, his words filled Brie's mind in her language.

> *"Let those who enter with evil intent*
> *See only what they perceive is meant*
> *Scrambled thoughts will hide what's real*
> *Behind a screen of perception's zeal."*

He lowered his arms and offered a hand. "Take us to the children."

Brie and Esán moved to his side. Brie focused on Gar. They arrived in the hut where five younger children cowered behind him. His spectacles glowed with fire-ember brightness, and his eyes flashed opal before returning to normal. He threw his arms around Brie. "So glad to see you, VarTerel. Can you get us outta here?"

Dri Adoh moved forward and spoke to the K'iin children. One by one, they nodded and managed a nervous smile. The shaman turned to Brie and Esán. "I have told them you are our friends who have come to help us." Alertness held him quiet. His astute gaze fastened on the corner opposite the children.

Torgin materialized behind Esán. Gar grinned. "Hey, Torg." He touched the bow of his specs. "Knew you were there."

Dri Adoh's dark eyes, alight with resolve, focused on Torgin and Gar. "I will place an image in your minds of where to take the young ones. Once they are safe, return to the Bāoba Sanctuary and alert Cadhōla to our arrival."

Torgin moved to stand next to Gar. At a nod from the shaman, the children gathered around them. Dri Adoh touched Gar's forehead and then Torgin's. Torgin and Gar locked eyes. The group shimmered and vanished.

The shaman moved to the center of the hut, drew his symbol, whispered the chant, and made the closing symbol.

Without warning, Den flashed into being. His harried gaze darted from Brie to Esán, to Dri Adoh. "Artānga is in trouble. The Vasro Relno is preparing to question him."

Brie's thoughts raced. "Den, take Dri Adoh to Thorlu, then return here. Esán and I will create a diversion. Be ready to grab Artānga as soon as chaos breaks out in the Vasro camp."

Den and the shaman vanished. Brie tugged her hair back from her face and knotted it into a low bun. "I have an idea, Esán." She shared. He smiled. They materialized behind a bank of huts, shaped two kestrels, and took flight.

Torgin and Gar delivered the children to their families in the Labyrinth Cavern, deep beneath the Elgnat Range. As Torgin finished explaining the situation in the village, a tug on his arm switched his attention to Gar. The dark frames of the spectacles resting on the bridge of the young boy's nose blazed. His eyes, exact replicas of the Sun Queen's, held an urgent warning.

With a brief farewell to the K'iin, Torgin clutched Gar's shoulder and focused his intent. Instincts taking the lead, they flashed to the cavern entrance of the labyrinth and stared with relief and surprise at the Totem Spirit of the K'iin.

Sea Wee Vala lifted its bear-like head and sniffed the air. "Trouble in the Village. We must hasten there and create a diversion." It stepped between them, rested a paw on each of their shoulders, and emitted a deep growl. The cavern disappeared. A grove of trees snapped into focus. Thorlu greeted them with a curious stare, while Den and Dri Adoh exchanged knowing smiles.

Creature, men, and boy gathered around Torgin. He glanced up at the Totem Spirit, received a nod, and took charge. "Dri Adoh, please stay with Sea Wee Vala. Den and Gar, you keep watch and alert me if more trouble approaches. Thorlu and I will shape fire eagles and prepare to help Brie and Esán rescue Artānga."

The Totem Spirit's three pairs of eyes gazed at them. "Go. We three guard those in our care."

Torgin embraced the fire eagle and flew dome-ward and, when Thorlu's eagle reached his side, circled high above the village. Far below, Artānga stood between two men. A third faced him, a whip in his hand, his expression conniving and filled with malice. The K'iin leader remained blank-faced and unmoving. The whip snapped in the air.

A kestrel launched from a hut's roof, extended its taloned-claws, and landed on the man's head. The whip flew from his hand and skittered over the ground. Arms thrashing and fists punching, he tried to send the kestrel flying. Leaving behind blood-filled scratches on the Vasro's scalp, the kestrel shot away and perched on the railing of the bridge.

Joining the fray, a fire eagle swooped in, caught up the whip, and dropped it in the pond. A second eagle chased Vasro warriors one way and then the other. Artānga sprang into action, sprinted away from the scrambling men, and disappeared into the trees. The two fire eagles landed on the ridge atop the roof of the K'iin leader's hut and screeched in chorus.

Winded and befuddled, the Vasro huddled on the walkway by the pond. A kestrel swooped over the bridge and alighted at its center. Brie materialized, red curls flaming around her face and her VarTerel's power filling her voice as she chanted.

> *"Vasro memories now take flight.*
> *Leave behind a wish for right.*
> *Erase this moment filled with strife,*
> *So all may find a better life."*

Six men, faces and minds blank, blinked as though blinded by the sun. Relno's gaze darted over the Valley of Tá Súil. He dropped to his knees and buried his face in his hands. The Vasro called Orge shook himself and stepped away from the group. The loss registering on his face changed to interest. He glanced at his cohorts. Total lack of recognition registering, he turned to meet Dri Adoh face to face. The K'iin shaman touched Orge's forehead. Intelligence and curiosity flooded the Vasro's flushed face.

Sea Wee Vala stepped into view. Except for Orge, the confused men gathered closer together, eyes rounded in awe rather than fear. Three pairs of totem eyes studied them.

Wee, the middle and smallest face, pursed its lips. Blue eyes fastened on Orge. "I see potential for good. Like."

From his low position on the totem of three faces, Vala's blue eyes came to rest on Taneg's chubby face. "I see a man thirsting to learn new ways…I like."

Sea lowered his bear-like head and fixed his gaze on Relno. "You, Relno, will soon discover who you truly are. Dig deep. Surprises await you."

One by one, the Totem Spirit touched the foreheads of the last three men. Humility and curiosity replaced sulky inscrutability.

Satisfied they were under his control, Sea Wee Vala turned to Torgin. "What are your needs, Torgin Whalend?"

"These men must appear as usual. It's important that Raiherr remains unaware of any changes in the village."

Sea's dark blue eyes surveyed the companions. "Den and Gar, please take our K'iin leaders to their tribe in the labyrinth. Once there, they must then decide whether to stay or go to Cadhōla at the Sanctuary."

Vala rumbled. "Tell tribe to stay in hiding until Sea Wee Vala alerts them it is safe to return to the village."

Gar and Den moved to stand with Dri Adoh and Artānga, their attention fixed on the Totem Trio.

Sea Wee Vala gazed down its long snout. "I'll put the image in your mind. Tell me when you are ready."

Den motioned the K'iin closer and spoke in Inik. "Please touch each other and one of us." He waited until he felt Dri Adoh's hand on his arm. "Good. We're ready, Sea Wee Vala."

Gar's spectacles glowed. The group faded, leaving only the fading memory of them behind.

The Totem Spirit examined the remaining companions. "Torgin, stay with me. Esán and Thorlu, please take our VarTerel and hide in the trees. We will assure the spell of perception remains solid in all three huts and make sure our Vasro players appear to be as normal. Go."

Brie disappeared into the village's deciduous forest with Esán and Thorlu.

The Spirit Totem spoke to Torgin. "Stand close to me and learn." He turned to tower over the former Vasro, lifted his arms, and spoke in his deep, bass voice.

"A dream of past embraces you.
Until it's time to be what's true,
Act out the story in your mind;
Reward will follow close behind."

A large paw gripped Torgin's shoulder. Artānga's hut enclosed them. While the Totem Spirit repeated the spell of perception, Torgin watched the Vasro shake their heads and shoot questioning looks at one another. Relno, the first to recover, took charge.

Torgin glanced up at Sea. "What now?"

Deciduous trees surrounded them. His companions, their attention fixed on La, the Luna Moth, watched her land on Brie's upraised palm.

Torgin moved closer. *I wonder what's happening now?*

※ ※

Den, Gar, and the K'iin leaders materialized next to the fire in the hidden cavern beneath the Elgnat Range. Excitement and relief rippled through the tribal members, who pressed forward to surround Dri Adoh and Artānga with their respect and love.

Several children ran up to Gar. Smiling and laughing, they led him away from the adults to an area set up for the younger members of the tribe.

Den stepped back into the shadows. Happy to observe from a distance, his thoughts turned to Penee and Inōni. *Where are you? Is someone taking care of you?* His first meeting with Penee in the penal colony on TaSneach surfaced. *I remember your distrust, and your courage. I know you can take care of yourself.* He smiled at his memory of the moment she recognized him. *Each new adventure has deepened my love for you, Penesert. And what a wonderful thing to have Inōni carrying our child.*

Riahtán, the mother of Inōni, approaching him ended his musing. She touched her heart and bowed her head. In the language of the K'iin, she invited him to join her family for a meal.

Den expressed his gratitude in her native language but explained that he and Gar would not be with the tribe much longer.

Riahtán nodded and withdrew two rose crystal hearts from beneath her woven shawl. "For Penee and for Inōni." She placed the hearts on his palm. When they were tucked in his pocket, she held up a finger. Slipping a hand once more under her long shawl, she withdrew it, her curled fingers hiding its contents, and offered it to him. "For you."

He raised his palm. She held her hand above it and released a warm, smooth object. Smiling shyly up at him, she lowered her hand to her side.

Den gazed in wonder at the sapphire cabochon, flecked with amethyst. He curled his fingers around it and pressed it to his heart. Meeting her timid gaze, he smiled. "I am honored. I thank you, Riahtán."

She blinked back a tear. "You take care of—" Shyness and emotion choked her.

"I promise to return Inōni to you soon." Den slipped the cabochon into his pocket and looked past the petite tribeswoman. Sea Wee Vala walked toward him with Gar at his side. Riahtán bowed to the Totem Spirit and hurried to join her friends.

Den felt Gar's hand on his arm. The cavern hideaway vanished.

19
Neul Isle

Brie lifted La to eye level and listened intently to the Sun Queen's message. "La is here to inform us that Hossela, the Pheet Adolan Klutarse, has returned and is near the clearing. Abellona warns us he is even more dangerous than Raiherr. She also shared the Council of Deities have banned Carûtix from Shiór Ridu." She glanced around the group. "We are to approach the Vasro camp with care."

Esán spoke up. "We could attempt to change the memories of Carûtix and Hossela, along with Raiherr and his men."

Torgin frowned. "We can't change the SorTech's memory until I have made some adjustments to The Box. That needs to be our priority." He squinted up at the dome high overhead. "Hossela isn't going anywhere, and even if the *Surgentin* arrives in Soputto's atmosphere, Karlsut will have to orbit the planet until Callum or I remove the dome. As for the God of War's son, I don't know enough to project what he will do." He shook his head and turned to Thorlu, who shifted to Nimah.

The young sun god's dark face expressed his distaste. "Despite banishment from the home of the deities, Carûtix's powers will persist for a time. He is strong, and he is enraged. When the time comes, it's my responsibility to neutralize him."

A rustling sound in the undergrowth deeper in the grove sent him into the shape of Thorlu. Everyone turned as soft muttering escorted Gar into the middle of the group. He glanced around, released a whooshed breath, and sighed.

"Every time I turn around, I'm somewhere else." He shook his head. "I was just with Den and Sea Wee Vala and the K'iin. Now, I'm here. What the—"

The Spirit Totem stepped from the trees. "Our sun, K'inich, races for the horizon. Return to the Sanctuary for the night. I will keep watch. When you have rested, make your plans for tomorrow."

Gar's hand flew to his throat. His specs flashed to his nose. Fire-opal eyes blazed. The queen's voice flowed from his mouth. "Beware! Carûtix and Raiherr head your way. Be gone!" Gar gripped his knees and gulped in long cleansing breaths. With a final huff, he straightened. "What now?"

Thorlu's facial features morphed into Nimah. "I must be gone or my presence will give you away. Torgin and Esán must create a diversion. Do not get caught. Brielle, take special care. Raiherr may be focused on Penee, but you are Carûtix's primary reason for being on Neul Isle. Go with Gar to the Sanctuary. We will meet you there when it is safe."

Brie resisted the urge to respond with Ari-like stubbornness and clasped Gar's hand. "Fooling Carûtix is important, so we will not go directly to the Bāoba Tree."

She took a breath, squeezed Gar's hand, and the tide pool at the end of the lagoon focused, then Rina Island, and finally the cavern at the edge of the Forest of Deora.

Gar looked up at her. "Holy Cow, Brie! You're amazing!"

Brie sat cross-legged on the floor. A small blue light flared on her palm. "We aren't safe yet, but we can rest. Thank you for your help, Garon."

"Wait, how did I help?"

"Your talents merged with mine. We're a great team."

Gar's bespectacled eyes scanned the area. "I don't recognize this cavern. Where are we?"

"We're in a cavern I discovered during my first adventure on Neul Isle." She glanced around and pointed. "There are several tunnels over that way. Better rest while we can."

Gar yawned and curled up on his side on a patch of blue-black sand.

Brie sat close by smiling at his soft snores and occasional sleep induced murmurs. She glanced around and hugged herself as memories surfaced: the Cavern of Feranni deep under the mountains; confronting Tura, the ghost of the wannabe shaman; and the violent death of Abarax inspired a full-bodied shiver. Tucking the difficult memories away, she rested her back against the wall. With a corner of her awareness alert to any changes, she closed her eyes and slept.

Swirling light obscured Den's vision, lifted him from Sea Wee Vala's side, and up through the dome. Awareness dimmed, leaving him suspended in a spatial nothingness. His feet touching solid ground, woke his senses and enlivened his brain. Blurred reality came into focus. Something throbbing against his thigh made him slip his hand into his pocket. Searching fingers wrapped around a flat object. He held it up in the light. Sapphire blue and amethyst gleaming in the sunlight mesmerized him. Recollections flooded his mind...reuniting the K'iin leaders with their tribe, Inōni's mother, her gifts for the girls and... His gaze fastened on the cabochon, he inhaled the scents of flowers and damp air. A slow rotation introduced him to a lush valley between two flat-topped mountain ranges. The distant sound of a waterfall, a wealth of rich colors, and a lake sparkling in the afternoon sun left him steeped in wonder.

Questions formed and spilled one by one into his consciousness. *Where am I? How did I get here? Why am I here?*

A childish giggle made him turn to discover he stood on a path leading to a cottage in the middle of a field of wildflowers. On the porch, a child in a dress of rainbow colors skipped rope. The cottage door opened and Penee stepped into the sunlight, her beautiful presence warming his heart. Exquisite, mismatched eyes blazing with recognition, she descended the steps and ran toward him.

Caught in the moment's delight, he sprinted to meet her, gathered her up in his arms, and buried his face in her hair. Laughter filled with love filtered through his euphoria. He set her down and held her close.

She trembled in his arms. "Den, is it really you? I have missed you so much." She gazed up at his face. "How did you get here?"

Before he could answer, Inōni stepped onto the porch with her hands resting on her rounded belly. Her lovely smile flew his direction. Penee clutched his hand and together they ran to the cottage and met her at the bottom of the porch steps.

Happiness flowered. Den hugged Inōni and placed the rose quartz heart in her hand. Her gaze widened. He smiled. "It is from your mother." He withdrew the second heart and presented it to Penee.

"It's beautiful." She smiled at the girl child who joined them.

Penee clasped his hand. "Den, this is Glori, our wise woman protector."

Den regarded the person in front of him. She looked younger than Gar, with her small, youthful stature and bouncy red curls.

A coy smile and the cock of her head suggested she understood his confusion. Stillness settled around her. Her brown-eyed gaze sought his. For a long, intense moment, they connected. Glori shook her curls and giggled with a delightful abandon.

Torn between the desire to show his respect for the powerful, wise woman and the lure of her infectious laughter, he shook his head and joined in. Penee and Inōni watched with amusement twinkling in their eyes.

Glori's child-like demeanor changed. She led the way into the cottage and faced the elated trio. "We must understand the reason you are here, Den Zironho. Who sent you and why?"

Den sat on the couch between Penee and Inōni and gripped his knees. "I'll share what I know, and perhaps you can help put the puzzle together."

After describing the rescue of the K'iin leaders and how he and Gar had taken them to join their tribesmen, he squeezed Penee's hand and smiled. "I remember standing to one side thinking about how much I missed you, Pen. Suddenly, Sea Wee Vala materialized, and he and Gar flashed to my side. The next thing I knew, a swirl of light picked me up and carried me through the dome. That's all I remember until my feet touched down here." He glanced out the window. "Where are we, anyway?"

Glori tipped head. "We are on the planet of Chûrinne, and we understand your confusion. What are your questions?"

"I grew up on Persow in the capital city of Reachti on Igran. Our teacher taught us that Chûrinne and Ainnē were uninhabitable dwarf planets. Please explain, if you can."

Her eyes narrowing, Glori fingered the ruffles on her skirt. A nod bounced her curls; a smile shaped her rosebud mouth. She relaxed in her chair. "I believe, Den, you are here for two reasons...your love for Penee and as an added layer of protection for her and Inōni. As for Chûrinne...The Deities of this solar system prepared it as a hideaway from our enemies. Only those humans we grant asylum here can see its true beauty. To anyone else, it is a cold, arid, unlivable planet." She bit her lip. "My question is, what danger heads our way?"

Den pinched the bridge of his nose and lowered his hand. His attention focused on the wise woman. "The gods know about Chûrinne, correct?"

She nodded. "They created it. What are your instincts telling you?"

Den could feel the intense emotions of the women on either side of him. "Would Carûtix, the youngest son of Bucānetis Marûs, know about this?"

He watched understanding burning in Glori's eyes.

She slid from her chair and paced to the window. When she faced her guests, her solemn expression and the absence of her child-like joy answered the question. "I need a moment." Her skipping rope in hand, she stepped onto the porch. Singing to herself, she began jumping. As her chant ended, she coiled up the rope and returned to her guests.

Inōni edged closer to Den. He put an arm around her, held Pen's hand, and waited.

Glori closed her eyes and chanted.

"I open to the truth of me,
But only for these three to see.
I share my secret and my trust;
I shed my guise because I must."

Den gulped a startled breath. Penee gasped. Inōni pressed a protective hand to her belly.

Glori's childish form morphed into an elegant and ethereal adult. Her acute honey-gold gaze studied the trio. "I am, as you can see, more than meets the eye. My true name is ShioCáni." A wistful smile appeared and vanished. "I am the Goddess of Harmony. Carûtix is my cousin, and the reason I left my home."

Den pulled the girls on either side of him closer and fought to manage the dread inspired by her words.

Zak stayed in *El Aperdisa's* infirmary for two turnings. When he emerged, he made his way to engineering and met with his boss, who sent him to rest and report for duty the next afternoon.

As he prepared to leave, Reedan approached him. "You look better. How are you feeling?"

"Tired. Still a bit woozy. Sorry I messed up our meal."

The older man positioned his back toward the room. "Better keep your wits about you. For some reason, Nesen's out to get you. Not sure why." He rubbed his chin. "Anyway, get some rest. See you tomorrow." He ambled back to his station.

Zak ignored his uneasiness and made his way to the T-lift. At the level of the Plantitarium, he exited and strolled to the entrance. Once inside, he assured himself he was alone, ducked behind the bushes by the secret room, stepped through the wall, and shifted to Elf.

Elf heaved a long sigh and sat down by the pond. After another mental scan of the Plantitarium, he messaged Ari, hoping she would have time to meet him. He didn't have to wait long.

Ari flashed into view, eagerness and curiosity churning as she joined him on the bench. "Are you alright?"

Elf pulled her closer, kissed her gently, and sat back. "I think our Vasro are making a play to get me to confide in them, or at least Reedan is. Nesen is acting like the bad guy, and Reedan and Laris are the one's protecting me. It's weird. Sure wish I knew what to expect—how to act—" He shrugged.

Ari's hand on his knee sent a current of calm through him that left him smiling.

"Thanks, Arienh. I needed that. What are you thinking?"

She pressed her lips into a thin line. "I think Jem needs to pay a visit to Aunt Henri." Her brow creased into fine lines. "Sure wish Relevart were here." Facing him, she reached out and touched his knee. "I want you safe, Elf. Nesen is sly and dangerous, an unsavory combination, and Reedan isn't much better.

Elf glanced up. His expression lit with surprised interest.

Ari turned to find Rethson standing a short distance away, his demeanor cautious. He put a finger to his lips and listened, his concentration complete. Tipping his head back, he exhaled and moved to sit by the pond. "That was close! I had duty in the mess hall when I recognized Reedan." He shivered. "He sat down at the table with Nesen, so I started cleaning up a mess a couple of tables away. When Reedan said he thought Zak would make a good snitch, I finished up." He shuddered. "After I passed their table on the way to the galley, Nesen left, but Reedan stayed. At the end of my shift, I signed out and found Reedan waiting in the passageway. Fortunately, my boss called me to come back."

Ari frowned. "Was Reedan there when you left?"

"I'm not sure, but when I arrived at the Plantitarium level, he was waiting at the entrance." Rethson clenched his teeth. "When he didn't notice me, I ducked into the herbal garden, moved away from the entryway, and teleported here. I hate that he knows I come here."

Elf leaned forward and stared into the pond. When he lifted his head, his gaze held Rethson's. "You can't let him see you're afraid, or we're all in trouble, so…I suggest you go back to the herb garden." He pulled out a comp tab and handed it to Rethson. "Take this. Add a list of herbs you know are in the garden. Stroll down the passageway to the T-lift. Bet he'll be waiting there. Rily's never met him, so he'll introduce himself and attempt to find where you've been. Casually, share that your boss sent you to inventory the herb garden. If you need to, show him your list."

Rethson slipped the mini comp tab in his uniform pocket. "Sure wish I didn't have to be alone with him."

Ari smiled. "Rethson, you can handle this. Besides, we'll be close, right Elf?"

Elf stood up. "We sure will. Now change to Rily and get going."

Rily appeared and then vanished.

Elf raised a brow. "And how will we be close by?"

Ari took his hand. "We are about to become invisible. Hold onto me, no matter what. If you let go..." She shook her head. "Just don't."

Elf took her hand. She whispered Brie's invisibility spell.

"You ready, Troms el Shiv?" A light kiss on her cheek made her smile.

The next instant they were across from the T-lift, where Reedan paced, his impatience palpable.

20
Neul Isle

Esán shaped a fire eagle and landed on the branch of a tree. *The Vasro leader cannot shift shape, so how will they travel to the village?* Launching into flight, his eagle wings outspread, he glided in a circular pattern over the Valley of Tá Súil, keen eyesight seeking Raiherr and the disowned demi-god.

At the far end of the valley, a high-pitched whistle echoed off the mountain peaks. A mammoth Spéire Condor with Raiherr on its back swooped over a high ridge. Torgin's fire eagle form shot from the village woods straight for them. As the condor's bald head, vicious beak primed, swung to meet it, the eagle shot upward and out of reach.

Fear for his friend propelled Esán's eagle into a serpentine swoop over the village. Its screeched warning scattered the Vasro in all directions. The condor dropped lower and landed at the edge of the pond. As Raiherr scrambled to the ground and ran for cover on the bridge, Esán's eagle flew into the woods and shifted to a kestrel. From its perch within the leaf covered branches, it watched Torgin's fire eagle streak straight for Raiherr. The Vasro yelled, stepped back, and toppled over the railing into the pond.

The Spéire Condor extended its neck and swept its ugly, bald head one way and then the other. Large eyes picking apart the landscape, it unfolded its wings. Its high-pitched whistle accompanied its launch into the air. The breadth of its enormous wingspan casting a shadow over the village sent Vasro warriors scrabbling for the nearest cover.

Eagle and condor performed an evasive dance. Torgin's eagle, the more agile of the two, dodged the bigger bird's powerful beak several times before swooping low over the village.

Esán shifted. Strong eagle wings carried him from the woods to join the fray. Whistles and screeches intermingled. The condor soared upward, focused on its prey, and dropped, talons extended. Two fire eagles shot opposite directions, one high overhead, the other along a narrow river-formed ravine. Wings pressing against the air, the condor rocketed higher and faster. Missing the elusive fire eagle, it slowed its ascent to land on a ledge at the summit of the tallest mountain overlooking the valley.

Esán's golden eagle eyes sought the enemy, gauged the condor's distance away, and streaked along the mountain river's ravine. Torgin's fire eagle shot ahead and landed in a shallow pool. High-pitched whistles sent both eagles into the shape of stone-brown river fish. A winged shadow passed overhead. Blending into rocks and crannies, the fish swam into deeper water. Around a curve in the river, they swam close to the shore and shifted. Two Neul Isle tinimunks darted from the water onto a forest-lined beach and scampered into the deepest part of the woods.

Certain the Spéire Condor was Carûtix's shifted form, Esán embraced Human, merged into the trunk of a large tree, and tuned his instincts to vigilance. When he sensed nothing to suggest anyone followed, he stepped free of the tree. Torgin materialized beside him. They clasped hands and teleported. The Orāk Cavern's dark tunnel enclosed them. Remaining motionless and blanking their minds, they waited.

Esán's awareness peaked and then relaxed. He slid down the wall, wrapped his arms around his bent knees, and rested his head on folded arms. Torgin's breathless panting grew calmer. He, too, sat in the dark stillness.

Esán lifted his head and met Torgin's eye. *"We are safe. I only hope Brie, Gar, and Nimah are as well."*

Torgin leaned his head against the coolness of the tunnel wall and stared straight ahead. "Gar and Brie reached the Sanctuary, but I'm unsure where they are exactly." His summer green eyes glinted. "I can't find Nimah. See what you can discover."

A relieved breath whispered from Esán's lungs. "Gar is with Brie in her sleeping pod. Nimah has not arrived at the Sanctuary yet." He stretched his legs in front of him, leaned forward, and grabbed his toes." Then scrambling to his feet, he grinned. "That felt great. We need to go. Shall we hike the stairs to the bridge or teleport? We can't shift and fly, or we put all of us in danger."

Torgin climbed to his feet. "Let's teleport beyond the wall to the bottom of the steps. If we're sure no one follows, then we teleport to the footbridge and decide what's next."

Esán touched Torgin's arm. When they arrived at the foot of the steep steps, Esán ran a hand through his hair. "I have an idea, but we will need Brie and Gar to help pull it off."

Torgin sat on the bottom step. "I'm betting we are thinking the same thing. Soon it will be dark. Raiherr and Carûtix are at the K'iin village—"

A gasp of surprise preceded Esán's appreciative smile.

Raiherr crawled from the pond, profanities flying in concert with glistening droplets as he shook his hair free of water. An angry glare sent his men cowering into a group at the end of the walkway. The condor's whistle and simultaneous landing produced a stoney silence laden with fear.

Carûtix flashed into view, peered at Raiherr and burst into laughter. "Well, well, you look bedraggled, my friend. Let me help." He moved closer, waved a hand, and muttered three indiscernible words.

A shudder roiled through Raiherr. He ran a hand over his dry hair and gazed down at his new, dry clothing. Grinning, he made a swooping bow to Carûtix. "Thank you, my friend!"

The demi-god inclined his head. "My payment is an introduction to our warriors."

Raiherr swallowed an egoic reply and walked over to his men. "I would like to introduce you to Carûtix, the Demi-God of War for the planet of Soputto. He's joining us in our search for the Girl with the Matriarch's Eyes and the youngest VarTerel in the Inner Universe. Prepare to introduce yourselves."

The men formed a military-straight line facing the arrogant man standing beside him. Relno stepped forward, stated his name, and stepped back into line. Taneg and Orge followed his example. One by one, the three remaining men stepped forward, introduced themselves, and stepped back.

Carûtix grinned. "Our men are well-trained! My compliments, Raiherr Yencara." He glanced around. "Is there someplace quiet where we can confer?"

Raiherr motioned Relno to join them. "Where can we rest and regroup?"

Relno's gaze darted over the village. "You can choose any hut you want, except the three where we keep our prisoners."

The demi-god raised a brow at Raiherr. "Prisoners? You said nothing about prisoners."

Raiherr shrugged. "I figured I'd share more about the K'iin when we got here. When we find a quiet hut, I'll tell you what I've discovered and the steps I've taken to locate the women." Crossing the footbridge over the pond, he made his way to the furthest hut. Behind him, the bristling anger of the demi-god pelted his back like a porpine's quills.

Once inside the hut, Raiherr faced Carûtix, hands on hips and his expression schooled to arrogance that matched the young god's. "Let's get something straight before we go any further along the path of working together. I am the Vasro leader. These men are *my* men, and they obey *me*. When I'm confident I can trust you, maybe things will change. Until then—"

A powerful hand gripped his throat. Air hissed from his lungs. Carûtix glared down at him. "Live or die… I don't care which." He squeezed harder and lifted Raiherr off the floor.

Gathering all the strength he could muster, Raiherr gripped the god's wrist with both hands, bent his knees up to his chest, and slammed his sturdy boots into the god's broad muscular chest.

Carûtix released him and scrambled to remain standing.

Raiherr hit the ground, shook himself, and stumbled to his feet. Protective shields shot up around him. "Keep your distance, Carûtix."

A bolt of lightning shot across the space between them. Raiherr's shields trembled, shimmered into nothing, and reformed. Carûtix shot Raiherr a scowl. Offering a hand, Raiherr said, "I don't want you as an enemy, Carûtix. Our combined skills will make us great partners."

The god pulled his hand away and glared. A wave of anger shook his person. With an abrupt about-face, he stared out the window, his stance rigid and his hands curled into tight fists.

Raiherr watched with his feet firmly planted on the ground, ready to fight if provoked.

Carûtix relaxed his fists, ran a hand over his hair, and faced him. "I recognize you are the leader. Perhaps knowledge of each other and our personal goals will provide the framework for a partnership." He yawned and lay down on a wooden cot. Sleep announced itself in soft snores.

Limp with relief, Raiherr sank onto a second cot and squeezed the bridge of his nose. A studied gaze rested on the sleeping god. *I'm not sure what brought you to Neul Isle.* He rubbed hands together. *But I'm sure glad you're here. Never imagined I'd be working with the God of War.*

Gar sat in the cavern, tapping his specs against a palm in an excellent imitation of Henrietta, while Brie sat tugging at long red tendrils of hair. With quick fingers, she wove her coppery curls into a single braid, tied a leather cord around the end, and cleared her throat.

Gar's gaze flicked from the spectacles to her face. "Can't help feelin' we need to be doin' something important. Just don't know what."

Brie jumped to her feet and held out a hand. "I agree. Let's find Torgin and Esán. Maybe they'll have an answer."

The spectacles flashed into hiding, and Gar clasped her hand. "Where to?"

Brie's chestnut eyes gleamed, a knowing smile flashed. "Orâk Cavern at the bottom of the steep stairs. Ready?"

"You bet!"

A breath later, Esán's surprised gasp turned to a soft laugh. "How'd you know we needed you?"

Gar grinned. "'Cause we're smart. Right, VarTerel AsTar?"

Brie accepted a quick hug from Esán and nodded at Torgin. "Gar and I keep sensing something is unfinished." She looked from one to the other. "What are your instincts telling you?"

Torgin stood up, his gazed fixed on Gar. After a concentrated pause, he rested a hand on his young cousin's shoulder. "What are you thinking, Garon?"

Gar tapped his lips with a finger. "If Raiherr and Carûtix stay at the village, you have a better chance of changing that Box thing."

Esán's soft laugh made Gar shoot him a perturbed glance. "You laughin' at me?"

"No, Gar. You never cease to amaze me. My laugh was one of delight and appreciation." He looked at Brie. "What do you think about our chances?"

She bit her bottom lip. "Even with them gone, we still have Hossela to deal with, and he's more dangerous than Raiherr." She blew out a breath. "Wish Nimah were here."

Emotions infused Torgin's face. He gasped and pressed his hands to his temples. His eyes rounded, then narrowed. Exhaled air hissed between clenched teeth. "Gar, call your spe—" A shudder left him sitting on the step, his face in his hands.

Gar moved to his side. "Repapa!" The spectacles shimmered into being, their rims' ember blaze highlighting the opalescence shining in his eyes. Gar's hand flew to his throat. The Sun Queen's voice filled the steep stairway.

"Nimah will appear when the time is right. Torgin, you must make the adjustments to The Box before Carûtix realizes his powers are fading. Do not shift to your birds of prey. They will attract our renegade demi-god to your side."

A flash of light filled the stairwell, spun around them, and left them blind and dazed beyond awareness.

Gar, the first to recover, groaned and crawled to kneel beside Brie, where she lay on a soft bed of forest mulch. He touched her arm and whispered, "Brielle, are you okay?"

Her eyes blinked open. Recognition brought her to sitting, her gaze darting from her companions to the dim forest surrounding them. "Where are we?"

Esán sat down next to her, his intense gaze on Torgin, who studied Ostradio's glowing face. "What have you discovered, Torg?"

"We are in the Cârthea Wood, close to Raiherr's jumper craft." He slipped the compass into its protective pouch and tucked it away.

Gar removed his specs and held them up. "Nehidd." They vanished. He lowered to sitting. "If we can't shape our birds, how do we explore and not get caught?"

Torgin sat cross-legged and gazed deeper into the forest. "What animals are endemic to Neul Isle?"

Brie tapped her chin. "As I recall from my research, besides rodents, the most prevalent larger mammals are foxes, eneti wolves, a type of lone coyote, and a small mountain cat called a yinyx. Wolves are the only ones that travel in packs."

Esán slid closer. "So what is safest...shaping individual animals or a pack?"

"No matter what we shape..." Torgin rubbed a hand over his short hair. "...Carûtix will know it is one of us." His brows bridged. "Unless we are all identical."

Brie touched the back of her neck. "The Star of Truth is warm and tingling when I imagine wolves, so Neul Isle's eneti wolf is our best bet. Each of us must choose a backup animal to shift to if we need to befuddle our enemies. Any other ideas?"

After a brief discussion, they reached a consensus. Brie scanned the dome overhead. "Darkness is creeping closer. We must prepare and be ready." She climbed to her feet, offered a hand to Gar, and pulled him to his feet. "I'm going to shape a wolf. I want you to study it and match it. Once you shape your wolf, Torgin and Esán will shape theirs."

Gar tipped his head. "I've only seen wolves in books, so..." He stood up. "I'll do my best."

Inhaling a deep breath, Brie embraced the form of the auburn-colored eneti wolf. Her friends shifted and gathered around her. She flashed back into human form and watched her friends materialize.

Gar grinned. "I like the wolf! Now, we'd better make plans." He noted Torgin's knowing look and grew serious. "You know I'm growin' up, right?"

The glint of white teeth against Torgin's brown skin suggested a smile. "I do, Garon. Now I need to think. Give me a few chron-clicks, and I'll be ready."

Gar's curious gaze followed his cousin as he strolled to the stand at the edge of the trees. *Wonder what you're seeing, Torgin Whalend?*

Thankful for Den's presence on Chûrinne, Penee listened to ShioCáni share her personal story. The description of her relationship with Carûtix made Penee shudder. His hunger for power had led him to propose. Her refusal had caused chaos in her parents' realm. When the goddess' harmonious tone faded, Penee asked, "Why did you assume the persona of Glori?"

ShioCáni sat down. "My parents and I decided that I must go into hiding, at least for a time. Before I left, I asked to meet with The Council of Deities of the Spéire Solar System. Galactic Guardian Chealim, whom you know, was attending a special meeting to decide how to deal with the growth of evil spreading throughout the Inner Universe. He listened to my story and consulted with Itarān Cirana, the head of the Council.

"Because of their meeting, Chealim offered me the opportunity to live among humans and be a protector when called upon to do so. He transported me to Rainbow Gulch on Persow and helped me create this cabin and its surroundings. Acting on his advice, I transformed into Glori, a persona that appears much less powerful than my own.

"Before Chealim brought Penee and Inōni to me, he shared concerns about Raiherr's desire to use them to thwart Karlsut Sorda's authority and to gain power. Carûtix had not yet joined the game." She shook her head. "My cousin's temper has always gotten him in trouble."

Quiet filled the cabin. Penee considered the beautiful woman across from her. ShioCáni's honey-gold eyes shimmering with a sheen like sunlight on water held a deep sadness. Dark, cherry brown hair falling in soft waves to her mid-back highlighted her oval face, refined features, and natural elegance. *It's no wonder the demi-god wanted to wed her.*

"He tried to hurt you, didn't he?" Inōni's soft voice quivered.

ShioCáni rose and paced with fluid grace to gaze out at Chûrinne's beauty. A long sigh accompanied the return to her seat. "When he asked me to be his life-partner and I refused, he threatened me. His mother contacted mine and warned her our family was at risk if I stayed. That's when I asked to meet with the Council."

A thoughtful silence settled around her. Her lovely eyes regarded Den with interest. "I believe you are here, Den, to help if Carûtix looks toward Chûrinne as a potential hiding place for Penee and Inōni." She rose. "I think it wise that I return to Glori's persona. She hides my power which, if my cousin casts his thoughts this direction, will be less of a magnet."

She picked up her skipping rope and walked out to the porch. A breath later, Glori jumped rope, her curls bouncing and her short, ruffled skirt flaring around her.

Penee leaned her head on Den's shoulder. *So many of us caught in the CoaleScence's currents…good and evil churning as one.*

21
Neul Isle

Torgin peered between sturdy tree trunks across the Plains of Cârthea. A glance at the opaqueness of the dome vibrating overhead switched his focus back to his friends. "I require some information and quickly, so we'll save our wolves for later. What small bird is commonplace on the island?"

Gar pointed. "How about the little bird up there? Inōni told me it's called a topaz warbler. She said it's quick and smart."

Torgin studied the small, beige bird and smiled. "Good job, Gar. I've seen flocks of them on the island, so I doubt Carûtix will notice us."

"Is it okay if I shift and listen from up there?"

His young cousin's unmistakable excitement eased Torgin's growing urgency. "Off you go."

Gar vanished, and a small, golden-beige warbler landed on a low branch, its feathers blending into bark and leaves.

Torgin turned to Brie. "Shape a warbler and go with Gar. Discover what Raiherr's men and his SorTech are up to. While you're at their camp, learn everything you need to create a hologram of The Box. Esán and I will find Hossela and see what we can do to distract him. Meet us back here in a quarter chron-circle."

Four warblers took flight and faded into the dusk-like dimness.

Two warblers flew to the Vasro camp and took cover in a deciduous tree. Below them, Raiherr's men sat around a small campfire. Zori and Dulno argued about the demi-god's appearance, and what it signified for them. Callum sat across from them, a look of disgust twisting his pudgy features.

While Gar's warbler kept watch, Brie's warbler alighted on a branch in the shadows near The Box. Absorbing every detail of its outer appearance, she fluttered to a higher branch.

"Done." Her telepathic message summoned Gar, and together the two tiny warblers flew back to the far side of the Plains of Cârthea.

Torgin changed to the tiny warbler and alighted in a tree to give himself time to adjust to his new form. Surprised by its quick intelligence and great eyesight, he flew a meandering route along the eastern side of the plains in search of Hossela. Esán's small bird form searched the shore of the lagoon near Rina Island and southern end of the plains.

The Pheet Adolan Klutarse remained illusive. No sign of him began to gnaw at Torgin's patience. Night's encroaching darkness inching over the dome, stole what light there was beneath. The question 'Where are you Hossela?' repeated, like the echoed refrain in one of his musical compositions. Landing in a small rocky crevice, he fluffed his beige feathers and peered at the landscape from first one tiny eye and then other.

A soft whistle floated through the night. After answering in kind, Torgin waited. A warbler fluttered to his side and landed. *"Found."*

Esán's wee bird flew toward a rugged cluster of hills bordering the end of the Vasro's clearing. Back toward the river, he spotted a ship well-hidden in a shallow gulch. The Klutarse, himself, sat at the top of a hill, his field-lenses focused on the clearing.

Both warblers fluttered to a bush near Hossela. Engaging the Seeds of Carsilem, Esán wove a curtain of sleep around him. Hossela yawned, lowered his lenses, and climbed to standing. Smothering another yawn, he turned his back on the Vasro camp and hiked down the rocky slope toward his spacecraft. Moments later, Esán's mental probe assured him the Klutarse was on board and slept.

A soft whistle alerted Torgin all was well. Esán's bird lifted into flight and led the way to the Vasro camp, where Torgin's warbler kept watch while the Seeds wove a web of sleep over the trio. Satisfied they would sleep until morning, Esán's warbler led the way to the other side of the plains, where their shift to Human was met by worried, question-filled glances from Brie and Gar.

Torgin updated them in a low voice. "The Vasro and Hossela are sleeping, but not forever. We need to bring The Box here and create a hologram there. I require half a chron-circle to make the adjustments to The Box. Then we'll return it to the clearing and remove the hologram." He looked at Esán. "Are you ready to teleport The Box here?"

"I am."

Brie clasped Esán's hand. "I'm all set to create the hologram. Just give us a countdown so we can act in sync."

"Will do." Torgin turned to Gar. "I need you to fly to the Vasro camp and land near The Box. Once you tell me you're set, I'll give the signal. The minute The Box vanishes and the hologram takes its place, send me a telepathic warbler whistle. When I'm finished making adjustments, I'll do the same for you. When The Box returns to its original position, get back here. Clear?"

Gar saluted. "Clear, sir." He shifted and in warbler form flew into the night.

Torgin stared after him, his thoughts racing. *What if he gets caught? What if...* He shook himself. *Don't bring trouble to your doorstep, Torgin Whalend.*

Rily glanced around the ships herbal garden, made a last check of his inventoried list of herbs, and ambled along the passageway, whistling a catchy tune. When he rounded the corner a short distance from the T-lift, Reedan waited. Wishing he were anyplace else, Rily continued his ambling pace and stopped beside him.

Reedan studied him for a moment, then smiled. "Hello, I don't remember seeing you around."

Returning the smile, Rily forced a calm he didn't feel. "I haven't been aboard that long."

"Guess I missed you in the Plantitarium?" The man's eyes gleamed with anticipation.

Rily shrugged. "I wasn't in the Plantitarium. My boss sent me down to inventory herbs in the herbal garden."

Reedan inched closer. "I love herbs, but I never visited the garden. Can I see the list?"

After a minor pause, Rily pulled out his mini-tab, scrolled to the list and prepared to show it as the T-lift arrived and several crewmen exited.

Reedan motioned him to enter first and followed. The entry closed, the T-lift shot upward and stopped. Three more crewmen entered.

Rily studied the herb list, moved closer to Reedan, and held it out for him to see. A female officer glanced over and smiled. "I love the herb garden. Did you find anything of interest?"

Happy to focus his attention on someone besides Reedan, Rily showed her the list.

She read it and smiled. "My favorite is rosemary. What's yours?"

Rily studied the list. "It depends on what they're used in, but I love mint and thyme." He showed the list to Reedan. "What's your favorite?"

The Vasro spy examined it and pointed at cumin. "That's good stuff. I didn't know there was an herb garden. You'll have to give me a tour sometime." He offered his hand. "I'm Reedan. Glad to meet you."

Rily smiled and slipped the mini-tab in his pocket. "Name's Rily."

"I'm Lt. Pallee Oranson." The officer smiled at both men. "It is nice to meet you."

The T-lift whooshed to a stop. With a nod at Reedan, Rily followed the Lieutenant into the passageway. Chatting like old friends, they strolled toward the mess hall.

Reedan followed a few steps behind. When Rily bid his new acquaintance goodbye and entered the walkway to the galley, the Vasro spy turned to meet Nesen.

From the shadowy side of the corridor, Rily observed the two men converse briefly and stroll back toward the T-lift.

With a sigh of relief, Rily entered the galley.

Gar's tiny warbler settled amidst leaves and dark shadows on the branch of a tree. From his position, he observed two men by the campfire snoring on their bedrolls. The SorTech stood next to his SorTechory Box fighting sleep, even as a series of yawns shook his stout body.

Muttering about needing to rest, Callum checked the box, stumbled to his bedroll, and collapsed onto it with a yawn. Soft snores proclaimed sleep's arrival. When the man's body relaxed and the snores grew louder, a warbler's telepathic whistle whispered from Gar to Torgin.

Moments later, The Box vanished, and a hologram shimmered into place.

Callum jerked to sitting. His bleary-eyed gaze fastened on The Box. A snorted yawn lowered him back onto his bedroll. Another ushered him into the land of dreams.

A second whistle from Gar's warbler to his cousin alerted Torgin that the hologram was in place. Stillness, but for the occasional chorus of snores, settled over the clearing. Fighting his increasing desire to nap, Gar ruffled his warbler feathers. *Gotta stay awake... Gotta keep...* A noise below woke him from a light doze. Wariness held him motionless but for his warbler eyes peering between leaves.

Faint light from the moon penetrating through the dome picked out the silhouetted figure of a tall, muscular man staring down at Callum. The figure walked over and stared down at The Box, raised his gaze, and searched the trees closest to it.

Nestling his warbler form further into the leafy darkness, Gar forced his human mind into a thoughtless void. His tiny heart slowed. Still as stone, he waited.

The man's gaze shifted to The Box and then to the forest canopy. He muttered under his breath, then turned to study the sleeping men. "Who put you to sleep...and why?" He strode to the edge of the trees and shifted. A condor launched into flight and flew toward Raiherr's ship.

Gar's warbler shuddered. *I have to warn the others.* Riotous thoughts pursued each other in quick succession. *Calm down and think.* The temptation to shape Human almost overwhelmed him. Skills learned on the back streets of New York, took over.

He assessed his options. Warn the others. He bobbed his tiny head, formed a concise message, and focused. One word flashed from his tiny bird brain to his cousin's.

⸺ 👁 👁 ⸺

Esán watched Torgin kneel in front of The Box, whisper a quiet word, and remove the control panel. With total concentration, he made one microscopic change after the other to the complex circuitry. Beside him, Brie, a ball of golden light on her palm, illuminated his work. Esán smiled to himself. *You never cease to surprise me, Torgin Whalend.*

A chill made him search the woods for the reason. His gaze darted to Brie as she stiffened and glanced over her shoulder. Her serious expression magnified his own mushrooming edginess. Words of warning remained unsaid as Torgin took a breath and sat back to study his work.

Eyes narrowed, he looked closer, then nodded. "One more and we're done." Attention refocused, he made a change and sat back. "I'm—" He froze with his hand reaching for the front panel.

Beside him, Brie gasped. The ball of light vanished. "Gar sent a message, didn't he?"

Torgin secured The Box before standing to face his friends. "He did. One word—Carûtix. It's vital that we replace the SorTech's Box before the demi-god finds us. Brie, can you tell where he is?"

Esán gripped her hand. "Careful, Brielle. Don't give yourself away."

She released his hand and walked to a nearby tree. Eyes closed, she took a breath, exhaled, and blinked. Her nostril flared as she returned. "He perches on Raiherr's ship in his condor form. Esán, can you move The Box without alerting him?"

"Yes. I must go to the Vasro camp." He frowned. "How about the hologram?"

"It will fade once The Box is in place. Go. Torgin will message Gar to stay put."

Esán's brow creased. "If Carûtix searches for us, he'll expect to find us in a bird form. I'll shape a tinimunk until I reach Thea Lake, then shift to warbler. Be careful, both of you!"

A quick shift later, he darted between trees and along the bank of the river, until he arrived at the small lake near Rina Island. From there, he shifted to a warbler and flew straight to the Vasro Camp. Landing on a branch close to Gar, he placed an image of The Box in his mind. The boy's warbler bobbed its head.

Esán focused on The SorTechory Box. Moments later, it flashed into being, and the hologram faded.

Across the clearing, a yawn and a stretch brought Callum upright. His quick scan of the clearing ended on The Box. Swiveling to face it squarely, he regarded it with a selfish possessiveness that made Esán's warbler shiver.

He touched Gar's beige wing with his beak and fluttered to a higher branch. Soon, both warblers perched high in the thickest part of the tree. Below them, Callum stood studying The Box, his expression a mix of confusion and frustration. He opened the doors, revealing the control panel, and examined every knob and switch. Shaking his head, he secured it and rested a hand on top. After a protective caress, he returned to his bedroll, yawned, and laid down.

As sleep overtook him, Esán's warbler lifted into flight with Gar's close behind. When they reached Thea Lake, they landed in human form beneath a large weeping tree's vine-like branches. Esán drew Gar closer, and explained that Brie and Torgin hid in Cârthea Wood, and Carûtix perched on Raiherr's jumper craft.

Gar cocked his head. "So, what do we do now?"

The condor's hissed whistle cut through the night.

Esán gripped Gar's arm. "Let's find out what caught the demi-god's attention." He shaped a kestrel streaked along the river to the forest and alighted in a tree next to Gar's warbler. Keen kestrel sight picked out Carûtix, climbing over tree roots to reach Torgin and Brie where they had stepped free of the trees to face him.

The demi-god halted, feet apart, fists on hips, and chin jutting forward. "Where are your friends? Are they afraid to face the God of War?"

Torgin moved in front of Brie and glanced beyond Carûtix. "Why should they be afraid? Your father isn't here."

Anger held the demi-god rigid, except for his flaring nostrils. Red crept up his neck and over his face. Sable brown eyes bulged. Panted breaths grew louder and louder. Without warning, he threw back his head, keening a chaotic mix of emotions.

Brie and Torgin vanished.

Carûtix's howls increased in volume as he lumbered over mulchy ground to the spot where they had been. His meaty fist met only emptiness. Angry growls bouncing from tree to tree, he pivoted and thrashed his way between sturdy trunks to the open plain. With an infuriated shriek, he shaped a condor and launched into flight.

In the depths of the trees, Esán and Gar landed in human form as Brie and Torgin materialized and stepped from behind a large tree to join them. With a wave of relief, Esán wrapped Brie in a hug, looked up at Torgin, and mouthed the words, "Thank you".

Gar tugged at his cousin's sleeve. "What if he comes backs? We don't want to be here."

Torgin's gaze darted upward before focusing on his friends. "We must leave, but what's the safest way?"

Brie grew still, her eyes narrowed. "The condor is circling the plains and forest. He hasn't seen us in warbler form, but...?"

Torgin pulled out the compass. A map of Neul Isle rose above the surface. He held it out. "We are close to the ocean. What about our seagulls?" He pointed at a spot on the map. If we get separated, we can meet here at the mouth of the river." The map faded and Ostradio disappeared beneath his shirt.

Branches crashing to the ground scattered the companions in four directions. From behind a stout trunk, Esán searched for Brie. Her gaze met his. She shifted to a Neul gull, flew further into the woods, and alighted behind a rough-barked tree. He followed her lead.

Moments later, four gulls watched a condor drop through the gapping hole in the forest canopy and land in the only clear area. Folding its wings and snapping its vicious beak, it planted one clawed foot and then other, rotating its mammoth body, its condor eyes searching for prey.

22
Neul Isle

Hidden close to Torgin, Esán, and Gar, Brie's gull gazed between low-hanging dark green leaves at their enemy's frustrated search and considered their next move. A quick mind touch alerted her friends to take flight on her signal.

The condor's unfurled wings struck the trees on either side of the small clearing. It stretched its neck and tilted its bald head to gaze up at the hole in the canopy. A long, hissed screech preceded the appearance of a red-faced Carûtix. He kicked a fallen branch aside and shouted, "I will find you, Brielle AsTar, and your friends as well." Muttering profanities under his breath, he tromped between close-packed trees and knee-high plant growth toward the plains.

Brie ruffled her white feathers. When he was midway to the jumper craft, she lifted into flight, her gull wings carrying her toward the sea. Her fellow seagulls followed their own course to rendezvous at the mouth of the river near the dome.

A gull's panicked squawk echoing over the plains launched her into a banked turn back the way she had come. Acute sight picked out a young gull trapped in the condor's talons. Swooping to a landing behind the spacecraft, she embraced her human form and prepared to step into the open.

A hand closed over her arm and drew her to the back of the craft. Esán turned her to face him. "Carûtix wants you. Stay here. When he releases Gar, you and Torgin take him to safety. If he captures me, I'll escape as soon as I can."

She shook her curls back from her face. "I can't let you do this." A quick kiss later, she strode from behind the jumper craft.

"Let the gull go, Carûtix. It has done nothing to you."

The demi-god flashed into being, the gull clamped in his hands. "But it means a lot to you, doesn't it, Brielle AsTar? So, now what do you do?"

Brie, her unwavering gaze riveted to the man's face, regarded him with a calm she did not feel.

With a panicked shout, Carûtix threw both arms up as a fire eagle swooped from the trees, talons extended, and flew straight for his head. In his haste to protect his face, he released the squirming gull. A quick dodge avoided the reaching talons. Wing-wind tossed his hair into tangles as the fire eagle swerved and streaked after the gull. Straightening to his full height, he searched for his escaped prisoner.

The young gull squawked and shot higher. Jinking one way and then the other, it streaked over a low ridge and dropped from sight.

Carûtix shaped the condor, hissed a long whistle, and gave chase. Powerful wings closing the gap awoke his ego. He pressed them harder. Focused only on his attacker, he missed the threat racing his way.

Knifelike claws gripped his back muscles. A sharp, hooked beak raked his head. Blood streaming down his face sent him spiraling downward. He slammed into the ground hard enough to knock him senseless and back into his natural form.

. . .

Awareness leaked drop by drop into his consciousness. A groan woke him to the distant glow of the sun rising beyond the dome and the realization Brielle AsTar and two of her friends had escaped.

Pushing himself to sitting, a diabolic smile contorted his mouth. You will be back, VarTerel! He turned his attention to the jumper craft's entry hatch. Another groan accompanied him to his feet. He bent forward clutched his knees and assessed the damage to his body. Arrogance produced a smile and stiffened his spine. He combed his fingers through his knotted, bloodied hair, and squared his shoulders. "I remain in control, Brielle AsTar." He laughed aloud. "It pays to be a deity!"

He searched the sky, then crossed to the hatch, where he entered the frequency code and stepped aboard. Narrowed eyes searched. A quick movement caused him to reach upward. Seconds later, he pressed a squirming gull to his chest. A sardonic laugh shook his chest. "My ruse worked." He looked down at the gull.

"Garon Anaru, you are my bargaining chip. With you in my control, the Sun Queen will give me anything I want, and your VarTerel pal will come begging for me to let you go. As for Raiherr and his silly Vasro..." A wad of spittle shot from the demi-god's mouth.

He studied the gull. "What I need is a cage, one not even the VarTerel can rescue you from." Freeing one hand, he pointed an index finger at the ground and recited:

> *"Spéirian iron, shape a prison cage.*
> *One a VarTerel can't break, even in a rage.*
> *Shape a door that opens, with a secret rhyme;*
> *Shape the cage so it will last 'til the end of time."*

Silence filled the plains. Air rushed from his lungs as a mirage-like illusion of a cage quivered into being and then melted into nothing. Startled disbelief left him gasping for air. He stared at his finger and then at the ground, barren of anything but grass and fallen leaves. A scream of denial vibrated over Neul Isle. His hands shook, his heart slammed against his ribs. The world around him blurred. Rage ignited. He flung his prisoner into the air. Senses reeling, he stared in confusion and defeat at the gull, his bargaining chip, disappearing into the trees.

Fighting for reason, he made himself breathe and repeat the verse. Still no cage appeared. He picked up a stick, whispered a phrase, and howled with angry indignation when it did not change to a sword at his command. The sudden realization his powers were fading hit with the force of a lightning bolt. "My father has banned me from returning to Shiór Ridu, the Home of the Deities of the Spéire Solar System. My father—"

Lifting his arms, he attempted to summon the cyclonic wind and light that transported him throughout the solar system. Only muted island sounds penetrated the overwhelming sense of outraged loss gushing through him. With a moan, he collapsed in a shivering heap of anguished, growl-like sobs.

Awareness gradually penetrated the web of loss. Sobs changed to hiccuped gulps. He sat with his elbows on his bent knees and his palms pressed to his temples. *A deity doesn't cry like a moronic child, Carûtix. Focus.* Shaking himself, he straightened his spine. *My powers will not all leave at once. The last to leave will be my ability to shift shape. As long as I can do that, I can find a way to reclaim myself.* He climbed to his feet. *I will find you, Brielle AsTar, and you will be my redemption.*

Torgin landed in the midst of a colony of Neul gulls on a sandbar at the mouth of the San Crúil River. Ruffling his white feathers, he waited impatiently for his companions. Two more gulls alighted a short distance away. Worry almost launched him into flight when a fourth swooped low over the river and landed in the shallow water along the pebble-strewn seashore.

High overhead, a condor circled, then plunged, beak extended toward the colony. En mass, the gulls lifted into flight. Their *ha-ha-ha* warning call changed to long, yelping cries as they jinked from one end of the shoreline beach to the other and back.

Careful to remain within the colony, Torgin summoned his friends with a telepathic whistle. When the gulls jinked low over the river's mouth for the second time, four warblers shot back along the river, flying low and close to the shoreline.

Black rust-streaked rock created steep inclines on both sides of the river. Up ahead, a landslide had deposited boulders and smaller rocks in chaotic heaps at the river's edge. Four warblers dropped into the crevices between rocks and merged their small bodies into the dark rusty browns, tans, and blacks of the tumbled stones.

Swooping low over the river, the great Spéire Condor glided, wings widespread and raptor eyes ripping apart every niche and cranny of the landscape. Long after it passed over their hiding place, the warblers kept their minds blank and their small bodies motionless.

Just as Torgin prepared to give the all clear, a dark, threatening shadow flowed over the shoreline, glided lower, then streaked upward. Wings pressing harder carried the condor over the rugged terrain north of the river and back toward the Plains of Cârthea. Its hissed shrieking gradually faded into the distance.

The river's rippling sounds embraced the warblers. Torgin's small bird form raised its beige and cream head. When his tiny warbler eyes had adjusted to the brighter light, he led the way up-river to the forest glade and landed in a tall, regal evergreen. One-by-one, his three fellow warblers arrived. Brie's warbler whistling "all-clear" sounded in his head. Torgin landed at the base of his tree in human form and inhaled a cleansing breath.

Brie appeared next to him. Esán and Gar materialized at the foot of their tree. Forest sounds embraced them. The scents of pine, forest foliage, and dark earth anchored them more firmly in their bodies.

Torgin motioned his friends into a huddle and spoke in an undertone. "Bāoba and rest?" He pulled out the compass, called up the map of the island, and pointed at the forest. "We're here. I believe we'll be safest if we stay in this valley and away from the river."

Brie nodded. "I agree."

Esán put an arm around Brie. "That route takes us straight to the Bāoba Forest without exposing us to the village. Good, Torg."

Gar's eyes glinted with anticipation. "Can we all shape eneti wolves until we're close to the trees?"

Torgin squinted and gazed into the distance. "What do you think, Brie?"

Esán spoke up. "It's a good way to blend into the scenery here."

All eyes turned to Brie. "Since I'm sure our demi-god hasn't given up the hunt, we need to see him before he sees us." She nibbled her bottom lip. "I'll remain in bird form as a lookout. You shift to wolves, and I'll warn you of trouble. Torgin, you take the lead. Esán, you bring up the rear. Keep Gar between you." Without giving them time to argue, she shot upwards.

Torgin put a hand on Esán's shoulder. "Let her go, Esán. She's a VarTerel and is well-equipped to take care of herself."

Esán's uneasy gaze followed the warbler circling above him. With a shake of his head, he shifted.

Torgin followed suit.

Gar flashed to a wolf cub and trotted to his side.

Alert for any energetic changes in his surroundings, Torgin trotted along the rusty black foothills bordering the valley on the side opposite to the river. Behind him, Gar scampered along, sniffing the ground. Esán followed, occasionally peering up through the dimness beneath the dome.

Torgin forced his focus to remain fixed on their destination. *Brie'll be fine, Esán. She has to be.*

• •

Brie's warbler circled, then swooped over the valley, blending into the low underbrush coated hills rolling toward the river. Nothing visual disturbed the valley's serenity, and, yet, fear weighting her tiny frame carried her into a banked circuit of the valley.

The startled flight of a flock of blackbirds turned her back the way she had come. Beneath her, a shadowy shape stalked her companions. With each stealthful scuttle, it closed the gap between itself and the trio of wolves. Alarmed, she sent a telepathic whistle into the minds of her friends.

Keeping her distance from the predatory figure, she tracked its progress. A woven web took shape around it. A shudder shook the shimmering threads, expanding the web to span the width of the valley. At its center, the dark shape exploded into an enormous red and black spider with a condor's head. Jumping to the ground, its long, red and black legs carried it with unexpected speed over the valley floor.

Recoiling in shock, Brie sent a mental message. *"Run!"*

Three wolves raced over bracken and ferns toward the scrub oaks and shrubbery at the valley's edge.

A silvery thread shot from the spider's spinneret and caught the hind leg of the smallest wolf. With masterful skill, the spider spun the thread around the scrambling cub, drug it closer, and fastened it to the gigantic web.

A second thread lassoed toward Brie's warbler. She darted into the foliage-covered area near the furthest side of the valley, slowed her tiny heart's frantic beating, and peeked between fern fronds. A shudder of fear sent her into her wolf shape. At full speed, she bolted toward the spider. Two adult wolves joined her. They raced to the rescue, a chorus of barking and snapping proclaiming their intent.

The spider snatched its squirming captive from the web and dropped it to the ground. Long, hairy legs formed a cage around it. A high, wheezed humming changed to a warning shriek.

The cub squirmed free of the silky threads, dodged the spider's pinchers, and zigzagged between its hairy legs. Not stopping to look back, it raced into the scrub oak and out of sight.

Brie's wolf barked a retreat signal. Three wolves scattered.

A long, red leg shot out and tripped the closest one. Pinchers snapped around its neck.

The wolf collapsed and lay still. Silken threads cocooned it. The massive web evaporated; the spider morphed into a condor. A huge, taloned foot anchored the silky bundle of dark auburn fur to the ground.

The condor's neck stretched to its full length. Its beak opened and closed with a thunderous clap. Unfolding its wings, it released the tangle of silky web and fur, lifted off the ground, and gripped its bounty with both taloned feet. Powerful and triumphant, it launched into the air and flew toward the Valley of Tá Súil and the village of the K'iin.

Brie embraced her human form and stared after the condor. Torgin stepped free of a patch of scrub oaks and walked toward her. A sharp yip accompanied Gar's wolf cub from the underbrush. He scampered toward her, shaped Human, and threw his arms around her.

Unable to speak, Brie gulped air and wiped tears from her cheeks. With Torgin and Gar huddled close, she tracked the vanishing dot in the sky. *Carûtix has Esán.* She sank to the ground, terrified for the man she loved.

23
El Aperdisa

After their work duties had ended, Ari and Elf met in Penee's quarters in a cubicle off her sleeping space. Now, they waited with growing worry-edged impatience for Rethson to join them.

Rocking back and forth on the edge of a padded bench, Ari sucked in her cheeks, blew out a breath, and yanked a long red curl over her shoulder. The sight of it reminded her of Brie. Doubt assailed her. *Wish I'd demanded to go with you, Brielle AsTar.*

Elf raised a brow. "You're worrying about Brie again, aren't you?" He slid closer and put an arm around her shoulders. "She's a VarTerel and has companions with her who are as powerful as she is." He inched her around to face him. "You know our role here is crucial to the Sun Queen's quest, and the safety and success of our friends." His gaze explored her face.

She leaned forward and accepted his kiss, then gripped the edge of the bench and glanced at the entrance. "I'm not good at doing nothing, and that's what this feels like to me." Straightening, she stroked her coppery curl. "How do we know Brie is safe?"

Rily materialized and shifted to Rethson. "If they had captured Brie, we'd know it by the behavior of the Vasro on board the ship." He sat down on a second bench and shared his adventures with Nesen and Reedan. "They are fishing. They're sure we aren't who we appear to be, but they can't prove it."

Elf nodded. "If they can recruit one of us, they think we'll give ourselves away by providing them with information they require. They could also use their recruit to plant invalid information with Relevart, Henrietta, or Commander Odnamo."

Ari lifted the curl, stared at it, and flipped it over her shoulder. She looked from one young conspirator to the other. "What if we play their game and provide them with the perfect catch?"

The trio sat in silence for some time. Ari studied the palm of her left hand, drew an infinity sign with an index finger, and switched her attention to her companions. "We're new crew members who arrived onboard about the same time. What if we hang out together for a few turnings and act like we are becoming good friends?"

Elf grinned his approval. "A disagreement turns two of us against one."

Ari grinned back. "They'll take advantage of the tension between us and cozy up to the ostracized crewman, and we both have a spy! What do you think, Rethson?"

Relevart's youngest son fingered the crease in his uniform pants. "It's a good plan." A shiver ran through him. His eyes filled with pleading. "Please don't ask me to be the spy. I can't guarantee what I'll do if I'm left alone with Reedan." He shuddered.

Elf spoke with soothing calm. "Of all of us, Reedan knows the least about me, so I should be the one to be banned from our little trio."

Rethson's obvious relief made Ari cross to his bench and sit beside him. "We understand, Rethson." She looked at Elf. "Don't we, Troms el Shiv?"

"We do." He glanced at the chronometer on the opposite wall. "It's time for evening meal. Shall we begin our charade?"

Ari tipped her head back. Ideas raced. One settled with the perfect clarity. "Rethson and I will leave first. We'll find a table in the mess hall. Elf, you are the obvious outsider right from the start. Come in alone. See us, but hesitate. I'll wave you over. Act unsure but relax as the meal progresses. Then we'll play it from there. Sound good to you?"

Elf nodded. "Let's meet back here after we eat and make plans for tomorrow." Zak materialized and grinned.

Rily appeared, a flush creeping over his freckled face.

Ari did a mental scan of the passageway, then shaped Jem and linked arms with Rily. "All clear. See you in a bit, Zak."

In an empty meeting room close to the mess hall, Jem nudged Rily toward the exit. "Go ahead. I'll be right behind you. Let's meet at the door, say hello, and decide to sit together. Ready?"

Rily rubbed a hand over his hair and squared his shoulders. A nod later, he stepped into the passageway and ambled toward the crew's mess hall.

Jem waited for a couple of chron-clicks and followed. He arrived to find Rily talking with a pretty, blonde crew member. Strolling over, he smiled. "Hello, I'm Jem."

The blonde grinned. "I'm Pallee. It's nice to meet you." She glanced into the mess hall. "I'm meeting friends for a meal. See you around."

Jem watched her cross the room and join a group of younger crewmen before smiling at Rily. "Nice! Hey, how about we share a table?"

"Great." Rily headed to the opposite side of the large mess hall, laid his cap on a table and sat down. "So, how're you liking your new assignment?"

"Not bad. I like my job, so that helps." Jem glanced up. "Look who's here. Isn't that Zak?"

Rily scowled. "I didn't really like him much when we met."

Jem studied the young man standing in the entrance. "I didn't either. Maybe we should give him a second chance. He's new, too, and seems pretty shy. If it's alright with you, I'll invite him to join us."

Rily pressed his lips into a thin line before nodding his agreement. "Go ahead."

Pushing his chair back, Jem stood and strolled across the hall.

Even though Zak's expression brightened at the sight of him, he moved uneasily from foot to foot and stuffed his hands in his pockets.

Jem stopped beside him and smiled. "Rily and I have a table. Want to join us?"

Zak bit his bottom lip, removed his hands from his pockets, and nodded. "I'd like that. Thanks for asking."

They chatted as they walked to the table and sat down. Rily said hello and suggested a trip to the chow line.

Jem relaxed in his chair. "You two go. I'll guard the table."

Chairs shuffled and the two crewmen made their way to the end of the chow line, grabbed trays, and began to fill them with the delicious food prepared in the ship's galley.

A released breath later, Jem shot a subtle sideways glance at a table where Reedan watched every move they made. *And so the game continues. Who will make the next move?*

The Neul condor's wing-wind stirring up currents of air battered Esán. Half conscious and disoriented, he clung to his wolf shape. Deep inside, the Seeds of Carsilem thrummed a warning. Mind blank and heart beating a slow and distant rhythm, he fought for strength and reason. The Seeds pulsed again. Clarity flowed through him. Drawing on their power, he transmuted the spider's numbing venom to a harmless fluid.

His captor swooped low, placed the wolf on the ground outside a K'iin hut, and shaped Human. Carûtix stripped away the silk threads and nudged the wolf's ribs with the toe of his boot. "Wake up, Brielle AsTar. There is someone waiting to meet you."

Motionless and barely breathing, Esán waited.

The demi-god bent, scooped up the limp wolf, and entered a small hut. After laying it on a sleeping pad, Carûtix nudged it again. "You'd better wake up soon, or I'll dump you in the lake."

A door slamming shut and calm quiet in the hut allowed Esán to relax. Alert to everything inside and out, he stretched his canid form and focused on his next move. *Do I escape, or do I stay, shape Brielle, and keep the Carûtix and Raiherr focused on me?*

Voices moving toward the hut grew louder. Mind blanked, the wolf's body went limp. The door opened. Two men entered and glared down at the motionless animal.

"You're positive this is Brielle AsTar?" Raiherr's tone dripped with disbelief.

Carûtix snarled. "I'm certain it is."

Raiherr moved to the door. "We won't know for sure until it wakes up and shapes Human. Until then, there are other matters we must address...like the dome."

The men departed, closing the door behind them.

Acute canid hearing tuned to their soft conversation, Esán listened. Raiherr explained he had left a window open in the hopes the wolf might try to escape. He also posted additional guards and threatened them with a beating if the wolf got away. A Vasro entered the hut and threw a sleeping mat on the floor beside the wolf. Grumbling about Raiherr's stupidity, he stretched out and stared up at the ceiling.

Soon, staccato snores alerted Esán he could safely relax. His furry form lengthened and scrambled to sitting. A sniff of the Vasro's face and a suggestion planted in his mind assured Esán of the man's prolonged sleep.

Esán stretched and embraced his human form. A crooked smile twisted his mouth. *Divide and—* He froze, his gazed fixed on a man materializing in the opposite corner. A relieved exhaled later, he acknowledged Nimah with a slight smile.

The Sun Queen's son put a finger to his lips, then beckoned.

Esán moved to his side.

Nimah pointed at Esán's empty pad. An identical dark-auburn eneti wolf took shape, shivered, and slept.

A hand on his arm kept Esán quiet. The word *"teleport"* and an image filled his mind. Nimah squeezed his arm. They materialized at the edge of the Bāoba forest where, at the foot of a giant tree, Torgin and Gar sat trying to help a distraught Brie calm her roiling emotions.

She brushed a tear from her cheek. "What happens when they find out—"

"That I've escaped?" Esán stepped from behind a tree and offered a hand.

Brie grabbed it and scrambled to her feet. His arms enclosed her. For several emotion-filled chron-clicks, they did not move. Then Esán held her at arm's length, brushed a tear from her cheek, and looked up to find Gar grinning and Nimah and Torgin deep in conversation. Drawing Brie with him, he moved to join the group.

Gar studied Nimah through his dark-rimmed specs. "You went home to Shiór Ridu, and the Sun Queen sent you back to save Esán, right?"

Nimah rested a hand on his shoulder. "She called me home because she and Thorlu have discovered something important to your safety and the positive end to our joint quest." He examined each member of the group. "I'll share what they've found when we've slept. We need to be rested and mentally sharp to develop a workable strategy for our next move."

Gar removed his specs and peered up at the Abellona's heir. "Do gods need to sleep?"

Laughter filled Nimah's eyes and rippled softly over the companions. "Gar Anaru, you always make me smile. Yes, like you, we need rest." He shaped Thorlu. "Gather around, and I will transport us to the Sanctuary."

They arrived at the entrance a breath later. Esán followed his friends into the sanctuary pod. *I wonder what you've learned, Nimah?* He yawned. *Sure could use some sleep.*

Torgin glanced up from his large, empty pottery bowl. Fresh bread, a dark slab of cooked meat, and vegetables baked over the fire filled the emptiness in his stomach and helped to reignite his thought process. Grateful for his returning energy, he noted the fatigue holding his friends silent was lifting, too.

Gar smiled up at the K'iin wise woman who sat by his side. "Achōsi Tu, Cadhōla." He rubbed his stomach. "This food is yummy. I feel better already."

"Tu Ōmthra, Gar. I am pleased you feel better." She smiled.

"Tu Ōmthra..." He pronounced the words with care and cocked his head. "What does this mean?"

"In the language of my people, it means I am blessed by your pleasure."

Gar nodded. "So it's kinda like you're welcome?"

Her smiled widened. "It is, young Gar." She looked around the table. "When you finish your repast, you must rest. My people and I will keep you safe." She stood. "I will call forth the bridges to your sleeping pods."

Torgin watched her cross the Sanctuary Pod, then looked at Thorlu. "I don't know about everyone else, Thorlu, but I'll sleep a lot better if I'm not fretting about your news. Can we meet in your pod, hear what you discovered, and then sleep?"

Thorlu smiled. "You might all dream solutions to the problem if you know why the queen sent me?" He rose to his feet. "Night embraces Soputto. Let us adjourn."

While the High DiMensioner bid a gracious goodnight to Cadhōla. Esán led the way to the pod he shared with Thorlu. He and Torgin arranged sleeping cots to form a conversing area and drew Brie down beside him on a cot. Gar sat on the floor at his cousin's feet and stared out the entry opening.

Thorlu stepped through. As the entrance shimmered into an opaque oval, he released the High DiMensioner's persona. Nimah crossed the pod and sat down across from Torgin.

Before he could speak, the exotic features of Sea Wee Vala's three totem faces blurred into being and solidified. Blue eyes in the bear-like uppermost head surveyed the group and came to rest on Gar. "Call forth your specs, young Garon. Confirm I am who I appear to be."

Gar clambered to his feet and held out his hand. "Repapa!" Ember glowing spectacles flashed from his hand to perch on the bridge of his nose. His magnified eyes glowed fire-opal red and gold. He seemed to grow taller.

Torgin stepped to his side. "Tell us what you see."

Gar opened his mouth. The queen's voice filled the pod. "You see my emissary, Sea Wee Vala. Please note the change in Wee's small eyes."

Torgin studied the three faces of the Totem spirit. Wee's once blue eyes gleamed emerald green in the tiny, central face. He looked at Nimah. "Carûtix can shape Sea Wee Vala. That's part of the reason you are here." He rested a protective hand on Gar's shoulder.

His cousin grinned. "He shapes the old Sea Wee Vala, right?"

"He does, young Gar." The queen's voice grew more serious. "Listen to Nimah. He has more to share. Heed his words and plan accordingly."

The fading of her voice coincided with the Spirit Totem's disappearance."

Gar's eyes resumed their rich brown, and his black-rimmed spectacles vanished. A shaky hand massaged his throat. "When she speaks through me…" He shook his head.

Torgin gave him a reassuring hug. "She knows your strength and the truth of your heart." He sat on a cot, tugged Gar down beside him, and put an arm around his shoulder. "Nimah, what else must we know to save Neul Isle?"

The Sun Queen's heir resumed sitting and inhaled. "As I believe you have guessed, Bucānetis Marûs, under a dictate from the Council of Deities, banned Carûtix from Shiór Ridu. Coupled with this, his followers at the court of the High King are rebelling and threatening to join forces with the banished demi-god." His gazed fastened on Torgin. "You made changes to the SorTechory Box, correct?"

Torgin nodded. "I did. The dome will not disintegrate until I engage the changes I made in it. No one may enter or leave unless we allow it." He frowned. "A god or goddess can pass through it, and..." Nodded toward Brie. "...of course, a VarTerel can access Mittkeer to move beyond it."

"The most important thing is that Karlsut Sorda cannot enter, and our enemies cannot leave. Thank you, Torgin Whalend." The queen's heir sat in a thoughtful silence."

Gar squirmed forward to rest his feet on the floor. "What will Carûtix use Sea Wee Vala for?"

Nimah's lips pursed, then relaxed. "We believe his plan is to shift to the Spirit Totem, gain the confidence of the K'iin and lead them against us to take over the island and to capture Brie and Esán." He almost smiled. "Neither Carûtix nor Raiherr realize how powerful you and your cousin are, Gar." He scrutinized the companions. "We all require sleep. Since I realize our conversation will haunt your dreams, please allow me to assist."

He stood up and gazed at each upturned face.

> *"Let sleep embrace each person here*
> *By clearing thoughts and ending fear.*
> *Let rest inspire deep within*
> *Ways to save the isle and K'iin."*

Yawns stretching mouths wide brought everyone to their feet. After hugs all around, Torgin led the way over the branch-created bridge to the platform of the Sanctuary Pod. When Brie was safely in her sleeping pod, he and Gar crossed the bridge to their's and closed the entryway.

Gar hugged him. "Sleep good, Torg." He yawned, curled up on his cot and fell into a deep sleep.

Torgin, his mind circling around a score of ideas, prepared for bed and lay down on his cot. Nimah's poem whispering through his mind was the last thing he remembered before dropping deep into a peaceful, dreamless sleep.

24
Shiór Ridu

Thorlu Tangorra gripped the back of a chair in his sitting room. *I'm feeling trapped. I know my role as Nimah is important, but—* He paced to the arched windows and stared out at the blistering terrain.

A soft knock turned him from the window. A mental scan of the corridor brought a whisper of hope. He shifted persona.

"Come in." Nimah noted the agitation rippling around Ferêlith the minute she entered and bobbed a curtsy.

"Your Mamai wishes you to join her, Nimah. Please allow me to take you to her."

Intrigued, Nimah followed his mother's attentant down the corridor, through a small courtyard and into the queen's palatial residence. At the elegant door to Abellona's suite, Ferêlith announced him, and scurried away.

He stepped across the threshold and paused, his expression blank and his mind racing. Standing with the queen, a tower of a man, whose regal bearing broadcast power and authority, regarded him with a steely gaze.

Abellona waved him forward. "Nimah, please embrace your true form."

Thorlu released Nimah's persona and gazed up at the statuesque figure.

"Thorlu Tangorra, I am Bucānetis Marûs, the Spéire System's High King of War and Peace. I have traveled to the Sun Queen's realm specifically to meet you and to ask that you return to Chirē Pâmit, the realm of my subjects. Let us sit, and I will explain."

Abellona escorted her guests to a sitting area, where her servants had placed a throne-like chair. The High King waited for the Sun Queen to take her seat, lowered his muscular girth onto the chair, and inclined his bearded chin to look at Thorlu. "Please, High DiMensioner, be seated."

Stilling his sprinting thoughts, Thorlu sat down next to the Sun Queen.

For a long moment, Bucānetis Marûs gazed at him over steepled hands. Eyes the color of polished ebony glinted with interest. A slight, gracious smile lifted his dark chestnut mustache, as his hands lowered.

"I have received word that Karlsut Sorda is preparing to destroy Neul Isle. He has no use for Raiherr and his men. First however, he wishes to gain control of your friends, Brielle, Esán, Penee, and, of course, Inōni. To date, he is ignorant of the power of Garon, Torgin, and Den. When he has the hostages he requires, he plans a takeover of the ship *El Aperdisa*. My informant tells me Karlsut placed Vasro spies on board the ship but does not realize a spy on *Surgentin* reports to Raiherr. Additionally, he appears to be unimpressed by the fact that the Universal VarTerels are overseeing the living ship's safety."

Once again, he rested his chin on his steepled fingertips. His expression shifted to one of determination. He clasped his hands and rested them in his lap. "I am joining Abellona in her quest to save Neul Isle. She, in turn, is aligning her desires with mine to rid our Solar System of Karlsut Sorda and the *Surgentin*. You know Sorda and his brother, Skultar Rados, better than anyone." The king stroked his short beard. "Abellona, please share your thoughts."

Thorlu's gaze swept from the High King to the Sun Queen.

Her nostrils flared. "My quest and the king's goals are in alignment. We value Neul Isle's sacred history and wish to see it safe once and for all. To assure this, we agree that Sorda and his ship must be removed from our solar system. We also agree that as long as *El Aperdisa* remains in the Des Pencoti Solar System, our closest neighbor, Karlsut will find a way back to this section of our galaxy. To free the *El Aperdisa* from its orbit, we must accomplish our joint goals and thus bring the CoaleScence to a successful conclusion." She raised an elegant hand. "Please, Bucānetis, continue."

The king's full lips curved into a thoughtful smile. "You, Thorlu, and your companions are vital to the success of our quests. The Sun Queen shared that your friends can create a time fold as well as travel through time. Although Abellona and I and our fellow deities can navigate throughout this solar system, we do not have the power to enter Mittkeer, nor to travel through time and dimension."

Thorlu frowned. "I can't do those things on my own either. So what do we gain by my accompanying you to your realm?"

Bucānetis smiled. "Your use of we suggests you have accepted our cause as yours. Am I correct?"

"Yes, you are correct. "Thorlu experienced a sense of belonging he did not expect.

The king rose to his full height. "Please stand, High DiMensioner."

An oval of pale azure light swirled into being beside him. Chealim stepped free, his expression solemn and his blue eyes scrutinizing Thorlu's face.

Thorlu met his gaze with steady openness.

The Galactic Guardian's lips curved into an appreciative smile. "Thorlu Tangorra, I bring greetings from the Galactic Council. If you are willing and feel ready, we would like to elevate you to the level of VarTerel. While I confer with their majesties, please take a few chron-clicks to discover your true feelings."

Escorted by Abellona, Chealim and the High King left the room.

Overwhelmed by emotions new to him and paralleling the self-doubt engendered by his infamous past, Thorlu crossed to the arched windows and stared out at the Sun Queen's realm. *Me, a VarTerel? How can that be? Will I serve with honesty and steadfastness or fall prey to the greed and anger of my former self?*

Chealim appeared at his side, his attention on the sizzling beauty of the fire-red and black landscape.

Thorlu inhaled a calming breath and faced the imposing representative of the Galactic Council. "I am afraid, Chealim. What if the angry, selfish man I was as The MasTer's Mocendi emerges to answer the call of power?"

A satisfied expression flitted across the Guardian's bold features. "I understand your predicament, Thorlu. If you had not admitted your doubts to me and more importantly to yourself, I would need to reconsider our offer. Knowing your weaknesses will serve you better than hiding from them. The Council members are confident of your strength of character and understanding of the former you, or they would not have made this offer."

He paused, then spoke with the authority of his position. "I ask you again, do you feel ready to accept your promotion to VarTerel, the highest level in the Order of Esprow?"

Wonder-inspired certainty flowed through Thorlu. Confidence lengthened his spine and raised his gaze to meet Chealim's. "I am ready to elevated to the level of VarTerel."

A dazzling blaze of golden light surrounded the Galactic Guardian and then dimmed, revealing a topaz crystal topping a carved rowan wood staff. Chealim held it out to him. "By accepting this staff, Thorlu Tangorra, you are stating your willingness to fight for right, to protect those less powerful than yourself, and to always be true to the oath you swore as a member of the Order of Esprow."

Thorlu wrapped his fingers around the staff's shaft and closed his eyes. Tingling energy began in his feet and flowed upward into every cell of his body. His senses responded with dancing, prismatic light, music induced ecstasy, and the enhancement of touch and smell. Coolness rushing through him calmed his emotions and prompted him to open his eye. He stared up at the topaz crystal. "Thank you, Marichi."

Chealim smiled. "Your crystal told you her name. You are indeed ready to embrace your new role and ready to align your allegiance with the Galactic Council. You will, from this turning forward, report to Relevart, the Universal VarTerel. Do you understand?"

Thorlu experienced a moment of relief. "I understand, and I am grateful to step beyond the Order of Esprow. Please thank the council for me."

The Galactic Guardian's wise smile warmed him. "I believe they are aware of our exchange, VarTerel. Before I leave you, the Council asked me to share one more thing. The son of Bucānetis Marûs is more powerful than even his father knows. Nimah is the key to neutralizing him. Now, I must go. Stand tall, Thorlu Tangorra. You are ready for the battles to come." He vanished in a flare of blue light.

Thorlu inhaled and, guided by new and dynamic instincts, thought his staff into hiding. He stared at his empty hand. *I am indeed a VarTerel!*

The Sun Queen dismissed her attendant and walked down the corridor. A response to her soft knock escorted her into the room where Thorlu waited. Her smile broadened as she entered and met his penetrating gaze.

"You have embraced your new position. I see it in your stance and in your eyes. Congratulations, VarTerel Thorlu Tangorra."

He bowed his head. "Thank you, Your Majesty. Is Bucānetis Marûs still here?"

She motioned him to join her in the sitting area. Once settled, she regarded the new VarTerel. "Bucānetis received word of trouble in his homeland. He has returned to Chirē Pâmit. Although he remains hopeful that you will join him there, he trusts us to devise the plans to address our immediate needs."

She paused and regarded him with a gracious smile. "The High King congratulates you on your advancement to VarTerel. As a High DiMensioner you were powerful. Now, as VarTerel, your powers have achieved new heights. Share your thoughts on what must be done."

Thorlu inhaled a long breath, exhaled, and allowed his magnified instincts to take charge. Ideas formed a queue. After rejecting several, he met the queen's gaze.

"First, Your Majesty, I wish to affirm that your quest is my quest, and I intend to help in any way I can. Bearing that in mind, I believe input from my fellow VarTerel, Brielle AsTar and our friends is vital. Esán is the bearer of Dual Seeds of Carsilem. Each time we meet, I can feel the Seeds' expanding their power. Torgin is one of the most talented young men I know." He smiled. "Garon is your apprentice and is growing by leaps and bounds." A flash of insight slowed his thought process.

Across from him, Abellona arched a brow. "What is it, Thorlu?"

"I believe I just experienced a premonition. Can the comrades of Carûtix travel to Chûrinne?"

The Sun Queen's fire-opal eyes glinted with urgency. She rose. "Come with me."

Thorlu followed her down the corridor to a wooden door opening into a second hallway. At the far end, an arched, obsidian door bearing the queen's royal insignia opened into a palatial room. A fire-opal throne sat at its center in front of lush red and black brocade curtains. Abellona circled behind the throne and faced him.

"You are the only Human ever to enter this space. I am allowing you to do so because you have stated my quest to save Neul Isle and the planet of Soputto is also your quest. What I am about to reveal must remain between us. Do I have your solemn pledge that you will share nothing of what you see or hear?"

Thorlu called forth his staff. "I swear as a VarTerel to keep what happens between us."

Marichi glowed a warm, vibrant orange.

The Sun Queen smiled. "Your crystal affirms the truth of your words." She turned. The curtain parted, revealing a palatial entryway. Lifting a hand, she whispered, "La Mòr Gisof." The door opened inward. A warm golden light drew them into the secret and sacred space. The queen whispered, "Dù Intē". The curtains swished together, and the door closed without a sound behind them.

Standing in the profound silence, Thorlu curbed his rush of questions and waited.

The queen surveyed the room with a serene smile. "Welcome, VarTerel Tangorra, to the Realm of Tismilú." She crossed to an elegant tinewood table and sat in its matching chair. A second seat materialized beside hers. "Please sit."

When he had settled, she reached forward, removed the blue cloth covering a large, clear, crystal ball, and laid it on the table. She inhaled the scent of sacred oils and absorbed the tranquility permeating the room. Beside her, Thorlu's new role cloaked him in a calm confidence she had not glimpsed previously.

She placed her palms on the table. "Please do as I do. We are about to begin. My goal is to reach out to the High King. It is my hope he will have new insights into what is occurring in Chirē Pâmit. She gazed into the crystal ball.

> *"Bucānetis Marûs, come to the fore;*
> *Help us prepare for what is in store.*
> *Guide us with knowledge to succeed in our quest*
> *To rid Spéire System of unwanted guests."*

The table vibrated beneath her palms. A spark of amber at the crystal's center expanded, filling it with a radiant glow. Abellona pursed her lips in thought and prepared to change her tactics when the king's visage took shape within the crystal.

Dark eyes met hers, then moved to Thorlu and back. "We must be quick. The banishment of my son has created chaos among my people. I am about to address the mob amassed in the courtyard." A frown underscored his next pronouncement. "Word has come to me that my brother's son, Chóc Tagoh, the cousin of Carûtix, and a group of young warriors are preparing to do my son's bidding. Although my brother, Tagoh Efarragi, and I have set up wards around our realms so no one may come or go, it would be wise to move The Girl with the Matriarch's Eyes and her companions. Glori knows the best place to hide." His eyes narrowed. "I must go." He faded, leaving the ball an empty, crystal quartz blue.

The Sun Queen met Thorlu's inquiring gaze. "I cannot leave my domain or our enemies will suspect something urgent is in the making. You must go to Chûrinne. Glori will assist you. Do not allow her youthful appearance to fool you, Thorlu. She is more powerful than you can imagine."

Thorlu smiled. "In my infamous past, I met Glori. Hopefully, she will discern the change in me."

Abellona laughed softly. "I can guarantee she will do so."

"May I ask a question?

"Of course, Thorlu. What is it you require?"

Thorlu stroked his short beard. "I am not versed in the Deities of Shiór Ridu. What is Tagoh Efarragi's role?"

The Sun Queen's eyes narrowed. "He is the High King of Wind and Sea. His son is the demi-god of Chinooks." She rose. "Now, I must secure Tismilú, and you must decide how you will travel to Chûrinne."

He followed her through doorway and paused behind the throne. "Do you wish me to share my plans?"

"I ask only that whatever you do is done with the utmost secrecy." She whispered the phrase to close the door and the curtains. "Your friends are resting in the K'iin's sanctuary. Alert them to what has occurred and, with their input, make your plans."

Thorlu nodded and flashed from view.

Abellona inhaled a long breath. Allowing herself a brief respite, she absorbed the silence and reveled in the knowledge that a new and powerful player joined her in her quest. *I trust you, Thorlu Tangorra, to help secure the future of Neul Isle and the K'iin.*

Thorlu stood at the center of Nimah's suite, awed by the Sun Queen's trust. Shaking himself free from the doubts tiptoeing ever closer, he calmed his overwrought nerves, walked to a mirror on the wall above a polished ebony table, and studied his reflection. *I did not see this coming. As much as I wished to be a VarTerel, I felt certain the position was beyond my reach.*

He called forth his staff, closed his eyes, and pictured himself in Mittkeer.

Coolness caressing his skin and a wave of nausea alerted him he had achieved his goal. The spectacular vista of stars and galaxies, constellations and unending night almost overwhelmed him. The Universal VarTerel materializing a short distance away brought a wave of relief that left his knees weak.

Relevart walked forward and smiled. "Congratulations, VarTerel! I thought you might require some guidance on the workings of Mittkeer."

Thorlu smiled. "Thank you, Relevart. I understand I am to report to you. Is this correct?"

"Yes, Thorlu. You now join the ranks of those who fill the vacancies left by the VarTerels The MasTer destroyed. I am now your mentor and leader." He took a step closer. "What is your most urgent need?"

Thorlu smiled and gazed at the globe-like field of universal vastness surrounding them. "How does one navigate all of this?"

Relevart smiled. "Your instincts will adapt and grow, but I will give you the information you require so you may draw upon it as you need it. "May I touch your forehead?"

"You may."

Relevart's intense gaze rested on his face. "Please hold my staff in your right hand and yours in your left. Do not let go of them until I tell you to do so."

The Universal VarTerel's staff warmed his palms. Glowing light from Froetise, the clear quartz crystal topping it, joined with Marichi's topaz light to form a cocoon of color around him. Thorlu closed his eyes. Cool hands touched his temples. Stars, galaxies, and solar systems flowed into his mind, carrying with them knowledge and understanding of Mittkeer. Constellations flashed into view. Their names and those of their adjoining planets filed themselves into his subconscious.

Relevart removed his hands. "Open your eyes, VarTerel."

Thorlu gazed at the man opposite him. "You gave me so much, Relevart." He returned his mentor's staff. "Thank you."

After a calming silence, Relevart stepped beside him and touched his arm. A fleeting moment of blurred stars snapped back into focus. The Universal VarTerel pointed at a cluster of stars overhead. "That is the Incirrata Constellation, the way-marker for Neul Isle. We are at the exit portal for the Bāoba Forest."

Thorlu shook his head. "All Time and No Time—"

"And you now have access." Relevart's amber eyes gleamed. "Meet with your friends. Develop a plan and proceed. Until you are confident that you can navigate Mittkeer, Torgin and the Compass of Ostradio will serve as excellent guides."

Froetise glowed brighter. Relevart lifted his staff higher. "The safety of Inōni and Penesert el Stroma rests on your shoulders. Trust Glori."

Thorlu stood alone in the vastness of the Land of Time staring at the emptiness left by Relevart's departure. A wave of doubt skittered up his spine. With a shiver, he forced himself to remain calm. Channeling his new knowledge, he visualized his destination and immediately experienced the unsettling symptoms of exiting Mittkeer. His slight dizziness and nausea faded, leaving him clear of mind and eye. He scanned the enormous Bāoba tree in front of him and laughed. *VarTerel Thorlu Tangorra, you did it!*

25
El Aperdisa

In Elf's hidden space between walls in the Plantitarium, Ari sat on the bench by the pond. *Today, Zak, Rily, and Jem will stage a disagreement and toss Zak to the Vasro spies.* She gripped her knees. *Wish I was sure Reedan won't hurt Zak.* She curled her hands into fists, then pressed palms down against her thighs. *If he does—"*

Elf materialized on the bench beside her. "Don't worry, Arienh. I can take care of myself." He faced her. "You'll need to keep Rethson calm, so he doesn't give us away. Speaking of Rethson—"

Relevart's youngest son stepped through the wall. A spark of amusement lit his eyes. "You two sure look cozy."

Elf pulled Ari to her feet. "We were just talking about you. Are you ready for the next step in our plan?"

Rethson inhaled, blew the breath out through his mouth, and shrugged. "As ready as I'll ever be. How about you? You're about to come under the scrutiny of Vasro spies."

Ari looked from one to the other. "No more speculating or anticipating.

It's time to go to the mess hall. I suggest we arrive together and go from there." She stared at the pond. "The conference room is empty. Let's go."

They arrived in an instant. Zak grinned. "Gotta love teleporting. Passage is clear." He tapped the exit icon. "Here we go."

Together, they ambled down the passageway. Jem and Rily gave Zak a sideways glance, shared a joke, and laughed. Zak scowled and walked ahead of them. Fuming, he glanced around the hall for an empty table.

Rily walked up behind him and smothered a laugh. "Can't take a joke, huh?"

Zak glared at his fellow crewman. "Leave me alone. I'm tired of your stupid jokes." Without a backward glance, he marched to the chow line, selected his favorite dishes, and turned with his loaded tray to survey the array of full tables. Annoyance infusing his expression and his stance, he crossed to a table with one seat left and was told that it was taken. A half turn brought him face to face with Reedan.

"Hey, Zak, you're looking lost. Wanna join us? Nesen is holding our table."

Zak's frustration flashed strong before mellowing to a subdued smile. "Sure. Thanks for asking."

Reedan led the way to a table where Nesen chatted with two crewmen. The Vasro leader looked up, glanced over at Rily and Jem sharing a laugh, and pulled out the chair next to him. "Looks like you and your friends had a squabble?"

Zak shrugged and slid onto the chair. "I just get tired of being the brunt of their jokes. Thought we were friends, but..." Another shrug and he focused on his tray of food.

Reedan sat down across from him. "Did you know them before you arrived on the ship?"

"Nope. Met them at orientation." He took a bite, chewed, and swallowed. "Thanks for letting me join you."

Nesen caught Reedan's eye and nodded. "Any time."

Zak concentrated on his meal. *And so it begins.* He suppressed a shiver and avoided thinking about what might happen next.

The quiet of the sleeping pod in the Bāoba tree, wrapped Esán in a deep sleep. Dreams of Thorlu Tangorra brought him to wakefulness. His eyes fluttered open and focused on his friend gazing down at him.

The Seeds of Carsilem hummed. His instinctive knowing informed him this was indeed Thorlu, although not the Thorlu he had last conferred with. He glanced over at Nimah, where he sat wide awake on his cot, dark eyes regarding Thorlu with heightened interest.

Thorlu acknowledged the Sun Queen's heir with a slight bow and sat on the end of Esán's sleeping cot. "We have a problem. Since Abellona cannot leave Shiór Ridu without alerting our enemies, she has sent me to confer with you. I require your input, Nimah, as well as Brie's and yours, Esán."

Throwing back the hand-woven blanket, Esán stood. "I'll wake Brie."

Thorlu smiled. "There's no need. She knows I'm here and will join us shortly.

Esán sat down and considered the man next to him. "I imagine she realizes the two of you share something you haven't shared until now, correct?"

Nimah moved his cot closer and eyed Thorlu with an appreciative smile.

Brie materialized, her astute gaze on Thorlu. "You come as an emissary of the Galactic Council and the Sun Queen. I welcome you, VarTerel Tangorra. Congratulations on your promotion!"

Thorlu rose. "Thank you, VarTerel AsTar. I am thrilled to walk at your side."

"And I'm delighted to walk at yours." Brie inclined her head and offered her hand, palm up.

The newly initiated VarTerel touched it with his palm, pressed his hand to his heart, and released a breath. "Before we begin, I will awaken Torgin and—" He laughed and shook his head as Gar materialized at the center of the pod and stared at him through his black-rimmed spectacles. "Hello, Garon Anaru."

Gar grinned. "I knew it! I told Torg you were here, and that you're different." His magnified gaze darted to Brie and back. Excitement filled his voice. "You're a VarTerel like Brie 'cause Relevart knew you were ready, right?"

"You are a very astute young man." Thorlu's amused chuckle widened the boy's grin.

"I knew it." Gar tipped his head. "Bet you'll be a great VarTerel, Thorlu." He glanced around. "Wonder where Torgin is? He was right beside me."

Esán grinned. "He went to inform Cadhōla we will need refreshments in a while."

Gar studied him more closely through his specs. "You're like a VarTerel, Esán, but different." His brow wrinkled, then he nodded. "That's because you have the Seeds, right?"

"It is, Garon." He glanced over at the pod's oval entryway shimmering into its open state.

Torgin stepped through and surveyed the group with interest. His summer green eyes narrowed as he lowered onto a cot. "Thorlu, I sense you are eager to share important information, but first... Congratulations on your new status."

As Gar sat on the floor at his cousin's feet, Nimah rose. Majestic and somber, he faced Thorlu and drew symbol in the air. A fire eagle's feather appeared in his hand. "VarTerel Tangorra, I offer this feather, the emblem of courage and bravery in Shiór Ridu, in honor of your new rank and as a symbol of my allegiance to you and our shared quest."

Thorlu accepted the feather with a gracious smile. "I am honored by your pledge and your gift, Nimah." He returned to his seat, stroked the feather, and whisper, "Nehidd". When it vanished into hiding, he smiled, then focused on the Sun Queen's heir.

Nimah inclined his head, then faced those waiting to hear Thorlu's news. "Based upon Thorlu's initiation, I believe our mission grows more complex." He took a seat opposite Thorlu. Please, VarTerel, share the reason Mamai and the Council have sent you to us."

"Thank you, Nimah." Thorlu leaned forward and rested his forearms on his thighs. "I have several things to share, and..." He straightened and looked at each member of the group. "...then I need your input."

After presenting a synopsis of his last interview with the Sun Queen and Chealim, he allowed his companions a moment to absorb the information, then continued. "We know Raiherr's focus is to find Penee and Inóni; Carûtix considers Brielle his ticket back to Shiór Ridu. By joining forces, they hope to increase their chances of achieving their goals."

Brie's chestnut eyes squinted into the distance, then came to rest on

Nimah. "Carûtix's father has banned him from the Land of the Deities. The longer he's away, the less powerful he becomes. Am I correct?"

The heir to the Sun Queen's throne nodded. "I believe Thorlu has more to share on that score." His gaze returned to the new VarTerel.

Thorlu regarded his audience for a moment. "Although Carûtix is losing his power, he retains the instincts of a demi-god and realizes Penee and Inōni are hiding on Chûrinne. His inability to leave Neul Isle has not stopped him from getting word to Cóch Tagoh, his cousin. Cóch has gathered a group of young warriors to travel with him to the planet. At this time, Carûtix's father, the High King of War and Peace, and his uncle, the High King of Wind and Sea, have joined forces. No one may enter or leave their realms." He frowned. "Of course, Cóch has all his powers intact, so he may slip away sooner than we expect."

Esán looked from Nimah to Thorlu. "Before Cóch and his warriors figure out a way to escape, we need to consider how to keep Raiherr and Carûtix—"

"Chasing their tails, right?" Gar grinned. "Kinda like Spyglass." He sighed.

Thorlu exchanged a confused glance with Nimah. "Chasing their tails?"

Esán grinned. "It's an Old Earth expression meaning to be busy doing a lot of things but achieving nothing."

Gar pressed a hand to his shirt's logo and nodded. "Yep. It's something Gin used to say." He sighed.

Thorlu's eyes twinkled. "I appreciate the vocabulary lesson. Now, let's list our goals, the best ways to achieve them, and how to keep our enemies 'chasing their tails.'" He caught Gar's eye and smiled.

Esán sniffed the air. "I believe we have something important to do first, Thorlu." He hurried to tap the opaqueness of the pod's side.

Cadhōla entered. Two trusted tribesmen bearing food-laden trays followed. At a sign from their wise woman, they placed them at the end of each cot and departed.

Surveying those gathered in the pod, Cadhōla said, "I understand you have many things to do to save Neul Isle and bring Inōni home. Please fuel your minds and bodies before you depart." With a gracious smile, she left, closing the entry behind her.

Thorlu cleared his throat. "Before we eat, I have one more thing to share." He regarded Nimah for a long moment. "Chealim informed me Carûtix is more dangerous than even his father knows. Since you are a demi-god, you are the only one with the power to neutralize him."

Nimah met his gaze. "I understand and will do so when the time is right."

Thorlu relaxed and reached for a bowl of delicious looking stew.

Esán squeezed Brie's hand and stood up. "I'll bring you a bowl." He walked to the end of the cot, selected two brown clay bowls and wooden spoons from the tray, and returned to his seat beside her. "Here you go. Enjoy."

She accepted her bowl and spooned up a sizable bite. "Yum. Thanks."

Esán tasted a bite and glanced around the pod. *I wonder what's next?* He chewed and swallowed another mouthful. *At least we'll be well-fed!*

In the K'iin village, Carûtix urged Raiherr across the bridge to one of the larger village huts. Once inside, he faced the Vasro leader. "We need more men if we are to find and capture Brielle's companions."

Raiherr scowled. "You said the wolf is the VarTerel's shifted form. Eventually, she has to change to Human or risk remaining a wolf forever. Once she does, we have our bargaining chip. So what's the problem?"

Carûtix raised a dark eyebrow. "Do you believe a VarTerel will sit in that hut and do nothing? She will escape unless someone she loves is under our control. Which means, Raiherr, that we require more men to help us search for her friends, and—"

The door burst open. Relno stepped through. Anxiety flashed like lightning around him. Fear filled his voice as he explained. "I went to check on the wolf. When I opened the door, it lunged at me, knocked me down, and ran into the trees. The men are searching for—"

Raiherr grabbed his shoulder and yanked him around. "You stupid—"

"Let him go, Raiherr. You and I have things to discuss."

Raiherr ignored him and slapped the cringing warrior across the face.

Carûtix jerked Relno from his grasp and shoved him outside. "Find the wolf." He slammed the door, faced Raiherr, and regarded him with a contemptuous glare. "When you've regained your common sense and your composure, I have something to show you." Arms folded, he watched the Vasro leader fight the desire to punch him in the face.

A shudder took Raiherr a step back. "How dare you make me look bad in front of my man. I am the Vasro leader—not you. Don't forget that." He smoothed his hair.

The demi-god pressed his lips together. His chin jutted out. Anger glinting in his eyes sent Raiherr back another step. A gulped breath appeared to steady him. Releasing his anger, Carûtix forced the appearance of calm.

Raiherr swallowed and tried a new tack. "You said we need more men. I agree. What are your ideas for getting this done?"

Looked him up and down, Carûtix stretched to his full height, and shifted shape.

"What the heck!" The Vasro's astonished gasp bounced off the walls.

A creature with three faces glared at him. Each face sneered. The bearish top face growled low in its throat. "I am Sea Wee Vala. Beware my anger."

Raiherr clenched his fists and did his best not to show how frightened he felt.

Carûtix reappeared. "I see you know nothing of Sea Wee Vala, the Totem Spirit Guardian of the K'iin. The tribal members will do anything their spirit totem tells them to do. I'll find the tribe's hiding place and bring their warriors back to the village. They will obey m—us. With their knowledge of the island, we'll find Brielle and her friends in no time."

"Great idea." Raiherr licked his lips.

Carûtix yanked open the door and stepped out into the dome-created dimness. His long stride carried him into the trees at the end of the village. He found a patch of grass beneath a tree and lowered onto it. For a time, he sat listening to nature's soft sounds. A hand twitched. Lifting both, he stared at his palms, whispered a word, and cringed when nothing happened. *I can't have lost all my powers so quickly.* Confidence leaking back into his mind calmed him. *I won't give up.* He inhaled a slow breath, held it until his lungs ached, and blew it out. Hands extended in front of him, he again whispered the lexeme of calling.

His palms tingled…his spine lengthened…his fingers curled around a carved knife handle. Relief flooded through him. He held the knife up in the dim light. I did it. Whispering the second lexeme, he lowered empty hands and leaned against the tree trunk. *All is not lost…yet.*

In the main pod at the Bāoba Sanctuary, Thorlu washed down the last bite of his stew with a cool drink of water and placed his empty bowl on a tray. Returning to his seat, he smiled at his companions. "Food helped. I'm ready to share a few thoughts about how to proceed."

Gar held up an almost empty bowl. "I gotta finish first, okay?" He slurped the last of his stew, placed the clay bowl on a tray, and plopped down on the floor. "I'm good."

Thorlu, who received affirming nods from the others and a smile from Nimah, cleared his throat and began. "The Sun Queen directed me to go to Chûrinne and, with Glori's help, remove Penee, Den, and Inōni to a safer location. Torgin, Relevart suggested I ask you to accompany me since I am new to Mittkeer." Continuing without a pause, he turned to the queen's son. "Nimah, we do not want to alert our enemies that you are abroad. How would you feel about remaining here to protect Neul Isle and the K'iin?"

"I agree with you. If I continue to adopt your persona while you are away, no one will miss you, and it will provide me with an excellent cover."

Thorlu smiled. "By all means, continue the charade, and if required, I'll do the same."

Nimah looked down at Gar. "Garon Anaru, as the special apprentice of my mamai, I consider you my brother. Would you be my partner and help me protect the K'iin and their island home?"

Gar's spectacles appeared in his hand. He placed the temples on his ears and peered through the lenses. Conviction cloaked him. "Thorlu and Torgin will take care of each other, and Nimah and me will do the same. It is good."

With a slight bow of his head, Thorlu focused on Brie and Esán. "Even though Torgin has adjusted The Box, Abellona asks that you and Nimah combine your power and your knowledge to make the dome impenetrable. It is vital none of our enemies enter or leave Neul Isle until the Council removes Karlsut Sorda and his ship from this solar system." He regarded his companions with a slight smile. "I wish us all luck."

Torgin stepped to his side. Thorlu called forth his staff and held it between them. As Torgin's fingers wrapped around the carved rowan wood shaft, they arrived in Mittkeer.

Amazement at his new powers made Thorlu almost as giddy as the wave of nausea washing over him.

Torgin swallowed, shivered, and turned to face him. "Ari taught me to think about something pleasant in the past to speed up my adaptation to entering or leaving Mittkeer."

Thorlu sucked in a breath, thought about his love for Healer De Dilliére, and sensed his discomfort melt away. "Thanks for the tip. Shall we discover the way to Chûrinne?"

26
Neul Isle

Quiet permeated the pod. Esán massaged his forehead and gasped. The power of the Seeds overtaking him left him half conscious and shaking.

Brie knelt in front of him. "Esán, are you alright?"

The urgency in her voice penetrated his dazed fog and nudged him back to full awareness. He smoothed his shoulder-length blond hair away from his face. His gaze darted to Nimah and Gar and back to her. "I am fine. I'm just not used to the Seeds being this active." Again, he rubbed his forehead. "Something on the island is changing. Are you sensing anything?"

Brie stood and held up a hand. Her staff flashed into being. "Mittkeer calls. All of us are being summoned. Please hold on to me."

Esán stood up, shook himself like a wet puppy, and touched her arm.

Nimah and Gar moved to her other side.

Stars in the night sky cloaked them. Esán gulped a settling breath and glanced over at Nimah whose creased brow highlighted his discomfort. "Think about a happy time, Nimah. It will help the dizziness."

The Sun Queen's progeny swallowed, shook himself, and exhaled. "Thank you, Esán. I do not believe I have ever experienced anything quite like that." His dark eyes scanned the universal night, stretching in every direction. Enraptured amazement lit his features. "Beauty abounds in the Land of the Deities, but nothing like the magnificence of The Land of All Time and No Time."

Esán shared a knowing smile. "I remember my first visit to Mittkeer. Its vast beauty never ceases to fill me with wonder." He shook his head. "Entry is easier now, but stirrings of nausea and dizziness still welcome me."

Between them, Brie took a breath. "Since we've all stabilized, I'm going to create a time window. Our goal is to uncover the reasons behind the changes on the island."

Esán watched her draw a large oval with the crystal topping her staff. As the ends met, the oval shimmered into a translucent window. He edged closer.

An image solidified. Carûtix sat beneath a tree, his hands before him. A knife materialized on his palm. At a word from him, it vanished. Satisfaction beamed as he climbed to his feet. Walking to a clear spot where the dome arched into visibility high overhead, he lifted his arms and spoke in the language of the deities. A slow, steady wind swirled up from the ground, engulfed him, and, picking up speed, carried him toward the dome.

Esán sensed the tension in his companions, each with their eyes riveted on the demi-god. Nimah's expression showed nothing of his feelings. Gar moved closer to Brie, whose steady gaze did not waver. Nimah touched Brie's arm. "He must not exit through the dome. Can we do anything from here?"

A howl of dismay snatched their attention back to the window, where Carûtix plummeted downward. Condor wings lifted him only moments before he and the ground would have become one.

Nimah's dark eyes glinted with fire-opal sparks. "His powers continue to come and go. What is important is that he cannot exit the dome."

The Seeds of Carsilem thrummed in Esán's chest. He slowed his breathing and focused inward. "His anger will lead him to find the K'iin and, by shaping Sea Wee Vala, bring them under his control." The Seeds calming left him clearer and more determined to stop him. "Nimah, take Gar and go to the K'iin's hide-away. Prepare them to resist the Spirit Totem."

Brie stared at the time window. "I can send you to the labyrinth from here.

Nimah, please assume Thorlu's shape. The K'iin must continue to think you have returned to Shiór Ridu."

Thorlu's persona replaced the demi-god's true form. He remained still for a long moment, then touched Gar's shoulder. "Are you ready, Garon?"

"Yes I am, Thorlu."

The crystal Musette shot a ray of rainbow colors through Mittkeer's eternal night. "Follow the rainbow light and be ready for your exit into the labyrinth."

Esán's gaze tracked the two figures striding over Mittkeer's tapestry of stars until they flashed from view. He shook his head. "It always amazes me how powerful you are, Brielle AsTar."

Her quiet laugh turned serious. She tapped the time window with the rainbow tourmaline tip of Musette. "Sure hope Torgin reminds Thorlu to use the time window. I'm certain he will need it." She shook her hair back from her face. "Our next step is to reinforce the spell of forgetting in the Vasro in the village. This time, we will not disguise it but allow their lack of memory to add to Raiherr's confusion."

"And after that, VarTerel AsTar?"

She touched his arm. "One step at a time..."

Their arrival at an empty hut in the village left Esán alert to any danger and awed by the woman he loved. After a subtle mental search of the village, he turned to Brie. "Since I know what we have both discovered, what's the next step?"

Brie smiled. "You gather Raiherr's men and use a simple forgetting charm to corral them. I'll see what Raiherr is up to and join you. Be careful, Esán, Carûtix continues to hold his power to him." She shaped a warbler and flew out the window.

He developed a plan and stepped from the hut. Shaping a fire eagle, he flew to an evergreen at the end of the pond.

Torgin stood beside Thorlu Tangorra in the Land of Time, his admiration for the man next to him growing exponentially the longer they worked together. He withdrew the pouch containing the Compass of

Ostradio from beneath his shirt, tipped the compass onto his hand, and held it out to Thorlu.

"Shall we find the way-maker for Chûrrine?"

The VarTerel pressed his lips together and studied first the endless night and then the topaz crystal topping his staff. "It is important we arrive unnoticed." He focused on the compass. "Show us the way, Ostradio."

Torgin recited,

> "Ostradio, our compass fine,
> Guide us to the portal line.
> Take us to our destination,
> Chûrinne's entry constellation."

The arrow spun into a blur of golden light above the glowing red icons and came to a quivering stop. A star chart floated above the face. A hushed silence pressed the men closer together, their attention on the chart, where a glowing circle of stars with a small galaxy at its central point took center stage.

Torgin felt a rush of excitement. He looked up and scanned the endless night. "We're looking for the Circlet Constellation." At his pronouncement, the star chart faded. Replacing the compass in its pouch, he tucked away.

"Over there." Thorlu pointed at a circle of stars, his excitement matching Torgin's.

Gazing at the distant constellation, Torgin experienced a shiver of anticipation. He faced Thorlu. "We need to know what we're up against. I suggest you create a time window to observe what's happening on Chûrinne."

Thorlu's brow furrowed. "Give me a chron-click. Relevart provided me with a wealth of information, so I'm betting I know how to—" Closed eyes blinked wide, a wonder-filled laugh floated through All Time and No Time.

"Show me, Thorlu." Torgin shivered again. "We need to move."

Worry cloaking him, the VarTerel drew a large oval with the tip of the crystal Marichi and whispered the secret lexeme. The oval's opaque center shimmered into a clear window.

Torgin moved to his side and studied the scene playing out below them.

. . .

Den stood on the porch of Glori's quaint little cottage, his nerves tingling. He rotated slowly, studying the forest behind, but sensed only the wildlife going about the business of living. He examined the field of wildflowers and the lake in the distance, shook his head, and faced the opposite direction, where a garden boasted row upon row of vegetables ripe for picking but nothing that suggested why he was so on edge.

The door swung open and a young girl in a rainbow-striped skirt and ruffly blouse hurried to his side. "Inōni is ready to give birth. Her wee one will be here before we know it." Beautiful chestnut eyes rounded and alert, she searched the landscape. "We are about to have company." She frowned. "Not who I expected, but…" Coppery curls bounced around her childish face as she whipped around to face him. "We have to remove Inōni from Chûrrine."

Den stared into the distance. "I can feel their power drawing closer. What do we need to do?"

Glori looked relieved. "We will go into Mittkeer."

"Wait, Glori, none of us has power to enter the Land of time."

She smiled. "No, we don't, but your friend does."

Den turned. "Thorlu! Torgin! Are we glad to see you?"

Thorlu and Torgin stopped at the foot of the porch steps, their attention on Glori, who was skipping rope a short distance from them. The childish persona flashed from view. An elegant, regal young woman materialized in her place and studied them with interest before speaking to Thorlu.

"Thank you, VarTerel, for hearing my call. You must take us into Mittkeer."

Thorlu regarded her with quiet interest. "And who, may I ask, are you?"

"We have little time to waste. I am ShioCáni, the Goddess of Harmony. You first met me as Glori." Her intense gaze hardened. "My cousin, Chóc, is about to land on Chûrinne with his men. Please come into the cottage. We can talk when we are safe."

Penee appeared in the doorway. "The baby may be coming." Her gazed darted over those gathered in front of the cottage. "Please, ShioCáni, I need help."

The goddess shot Thorlu an urgent glance and hurried inside after Penee.

Thorlu motioned Den and Torgin ahead of him and studied the cottage and its surroundings. Mounting the steps to the porch, he hurried inside. "Our best bet is to take the cottage into Mittkeer, but—" He turned as Inōni's high-pitched cry filled the cottage, surprised to find ShioCáni hurrying to his side.

"I like your plan, Thorlu. We leave immediately. Cóch is approaching the planet. When he arrives, he must see only desolation. I will create an illusion to obscure the landscape, then prepare the cottage to move. At my signal, take us all into Mittkeer."

Without waiting for a response, she opened her arms wide.

> "Illusion, keep this landscape hidden
> From all whose presence is forbidden."

Through the window, Thorlu glimpsed the field of wildflowers shimmer and vanish, and motioned Den and Torgin to his side.

The Goddess of Harmony raised her arms and chanted,

> "Rainbow Cottage, prepare to move,
> Leaving nothing behind to prove
> That our presence was ever here.
> Spin unbound into Mittkeer."

Cyclonic-like wind lifted the cottage into the air. At a nod from ShioCáni, Thorlu raised his staff. Mittkeer's endless night opened above it. The wind-propelled cottage rose into the Land of Time and settled beneath the Circlet Constellation. Timelessness enshrouded it and those within its walls.

The Goddess lowered her arms and touched her heart. "We are a good team, VarTerel Tangorra." She glanced toward Inōni's bedroom as her pain-filled cries grew less distressed and faded into the all-encompassing quiet.

ShioCáni reassured Den. "All Time and No Time... Inōni will not give birth until we depart Mittkeer." She inclined her head. "Thank you, Thorlu, for your quick response to our needs."

He glanced at Torgin and then returned his steady gaze to rest on her face. "With your permission, I will take a page from my good friend Torgin's play book and create a time window. It will allow us to observe your cousin and his men when they land on Chûrinne."

ShioCáni shifted to Glori and grabbed her skipping rope. "Please, VarTerel, work your magic."

He led them from the cottage into the cosmic beauty of Mittkeer and stopped at the bottom of the porch steps. Torgin and Glori stood on either side of him. Den remained on the porch. Lifting his staff, Thorlu accessed his new knowledge and drew the time window. The center cleared, and an image formed.

Beside him, Glori pranced from one foot to the other. "Can the time window take us back to the time before the cottage winds lifted us upward?"

Thorlu frowned. "I'm new to this, so I'm uncertain. Why do you ask?"

Glori's curls bounced around her face. "My instincts are shouting a warning, but I'm uncertain why."

Torgin stepped forward. "I have my time whistle, Thorlu. Check your memory. Together, I bet we can make it happen."

A search of the information Relevart shared provided a simple answer. Thorlu nodded. "I'll picture the moment we want to see and share it with you, Torg. At my signal, play a short low note, and I'll tap the window with Marichi."

Glori edged closer. Please hurry. Something is amiss."

Torgin pulled out the time whistle and raised it to his lips.

Thorlu projected an image and nodded. A low note vibrated the translucent surface. Marichi's topaz tip touched the window. The cottage appeared sitting in its Chûrinne landscape. The wind began to swirl. As the cottage lifted, a cyclone composed of leaves and dirt rose above the lake and shot toward it.

Glori grabbed his arm. "That is my cousin and his men."

As Mittkeer enshrouded the cottage, a giant Shiór gull lifted into flight above the demi-god's disintegrating whirlwind. The time window went dark. A malicious laugh echoed through Mittkeer.

Zak frowned as he made his way to the crew's mess hall on *El Aperdisa* to meet Reedan and Nesen for mid-turning meal. He had joined them for the past two turnings. This turning, his instincts prickled a warning. *Something's about to happen. Hope I can handle it.* He ran a hand over his military-short, blond hair, settled his cap on his head, and paused in the entrance to scan the crowded space.

Nesen sat at a small table by himself, a tray full of food in front of him. He glanced up, waved, and motioned him over.

Zak steadied his nerves and made his way to the table. He looked around. "Where's Reedan?"

"His schedule changed." Nesen jerked his thumb at the chow line. "Get some food, and we'll talk. I've got a proposition for you."

Zak removed his cap and left it on the table, glad for time to regroup. At the chow line, he filled a plate with a scrumptious-looking casserole, added fresh-baked bread and a tall glass of Fiz-Water. Back at the table, he set his tray down and slid onto a chair.

Nesen picked up a fork. "Hope this casserole's as good as it smells."

They ate in silence until their plates were empty. Nesen looked up, wiped his mouth with a hand cloth, and grinned. "Sure can't complain about the food. I've been on other ships where you couldn't tell the difference between the food served and the garbage." He took a sip of water and set the glass back on the tray. "Speaking of other ships, where were you posted before you joined the crew of *El Aperdisa*?"

Zak finished his Fiz-Water, reviewed the information Relevart had put in his memory, and scowled. "I was on *Corsango,* an older Space Corps military cruiser. Sure was glad for the transfer."

Nesen rested his forearms on the table and leaned forward. "You and Rily and Jem never met before, right?"

Zak tipped his head. "I already told you we met in orientation here on *El Aperdisa,* so what's up?"

"I'm looking for someone to help me with a job my boss assigned to me." He worked his mouth...puckered his lips, pressed them into a thin line, and puckered them again. "Question is, can I trust you?"

Zak straightened his fork. "Depends on what the job is. I ain't looking to get myself in trouble."

Narrowed eyes searched his face. Nesen licked his lips. "Meet me tonight on Observation Deck 3 after your shift. I'll tell you more then."

Appearing to hesitate, Zak pushed back his chair and stood up. His gaze never left Nesen's face. He pushed in his chair and bent forward to pick up his tray. "See ya tonight. Shift ends at nine." Without waiting for a reply, he turned and walked to the tray caddy.

Once outside in the passageway, he made his way to the T-Lift. The doors slid open, two crewmen exited. Zak stepped on board. The doors closed, leaving him the only occupant of the car. A rush of relief left him breathless. *Calm down, Zakeron. Don't want to give yourself away.* The T-lift reached his level. Whistling to himself, he made his way to engineering, logged in, and went about the business of doing his job.

After completing a busy shift, he grabbed a sandwich from the crew's snack bar and stowed it in his locker. Then he prepared himself for his meeting with the leader of the Vasro spies on board *El Aperdisa*. As he made his way to Observation Deck 3, the least busy one on the middle deck of the ship, he reminded himself he was both capable and ready to do this.

When he arrived at the entryway, he stopped. Two men arguing made him press against the passage wall.

"You plan to recruit one of the crew we think—"

"Reedan, I told you when the time was right, I'd decide. Now, is the right time."

"Leave before he gets here." Nesen's tone was icy.

His righthand man growled, "I'm not going anywhere, and you can't make me."

Zak tensed. A dull thud followed by Reedan's grunt of pain painted a clear image in his mind's eye. The temptation to not show up dissolved. *I have to do this.* He glanced around for a hiding place. When none came to his attention, he headed back to the T-lift, steadied his nerves, and returned to the observation deck entrance. Stepping inside, he stopped.

Nesen raised a hand. "Give us a minute. Reedan isn't feel well."

Zak retreated down the passage and leaned against the wall. Tuning his acute hearing to listen, he waited.

Reedan sworn. "How dare you—"

"Go to your quarters." Nesen's low tone was steel-hard. "I'll find you later.

Don't forget, Reedan Coegi, who's the boss. If you cross me one more time, you'll never do so again. Understand?"

Heavy footsteps thudded across the observation deck. Reedan stepped into the passageway, caught sight of Zak, and shuffled off in the opposite direction.

Nesen appeared in the entryway and waved him forward. "Thanks, Zak, for understanding. Let's find a quiet corner in case someone else visits."

He led the way to a padded bench seat and lowered onto it. While Zak settled opposite him, he maintained a quiet, sympathetic demeanor. "Poor Reedan. He must have some kind of stomach bug. I'm glad he didn't throw up here." He shook his head.

Zak nodded. "Reedan did seem pretty sick when he left." He looked Nesen in the eye. "Sure hope you don't catch it."

The Vasro spy flashed a slight smile. "Have no intention of doing so. Now let's get down to business, shall we?"

Zak folded his hands in his lap and waited.

27
Neul Isle

Gar and Nimah, as Thorlu, listened while the K'iin leaders explained Carûtix's plan to shape Sea Wee Vala and to fool them into following his lead. After instructing the tribe to pretend to believe the fake Totem Spirit was real, they appointed several tribesmen to stand guard at the various entrances to the Labyrinth.

Thorlu's hand on his shoulder alerted Gar to follow him to their alcove, where he shifted to the Sun Queen's heir and lowered onto a sleeping mat. Concentration narrowing his dark opal-specked eyes, he stared unblinking at the opposite wall.

Gar, sensing Nimah's need for uninterrupted time to reach a decision about something, placed his spectacles on his nose. He studied the demi-god's handsome black face and smiled. *We could really be brothers.*

A nod broke Nimah's thought-filled trance and brought his gaze to rest on Gar's face. "I have a plan and will need your help, Garon Anaru." He paused, then smiled. "As I have said, I consider you my brother. Let me explain my plan."

. . .

A short explanation later, they stood at the entrance to the Labyrinth Cavern. The soft whisper of the Deities' Wind surrounded them, carried them up through the dome, and set them down on Áfini Plains. The lush green acres bordered the Bāoba Forest on the inside and outside of the dome, stretching all the way to the sea.

As per their plan, they shaped fire eagles and flew to the lake near Áfini Sacu, alighted in a tree next to the dome, and peered down at a silver-gray spacecraft. While Gar kept watch in eagle form, Nimah's eagle landed on the ground beneath him, shifted, and walked into the open.

Gar tipped his eagle head, one golden eye scrutinizing the ship. Silence, but for the occasional shriek of a Neul Gull, enshrouded the clearing. Nimah remained unmoving, his dark eyes fixed on the entry hatch, his muscular arms relaxed at his sides.

The silence ceased as the hatch slid open and a man of medium build with intelligent, jade-colored eyes stepped down from the ship and faced Nimah. Neither moved, nor spoke. The man Gar felt certain was Pakdon regarded Nimah with curiosity rather than fear.

"Gar, come." The demi-god's telepathic words propelled Gar's eagle into the air. Swooping to Nimah's side, he shifted to Human.

The man shook his shoulder length, brown-blond hair back from his face. "I knew there were shape-shifters on the island." He looked from Gar to Nimah. "Why are you here?"

Nimah touched his chest with a flattened palm. "I am Nimah, the heir to the Sun Queen's throne." He rested a hand on Gar's shoulder. "This is Garon Anaru, my comrade and adopted brother." His steady gaze did not waver. "You are the Haptic Holo Controller named Pakdon, correct?"

The HHC did not hesitate. "I am Pakdon. I repeat, why are you here?"

Gar's spectacles materialized in his hand. He perched them on the bridge of his nose and adjusted the temples, then nudged Nimah. "I sense a listening device."

Pakdon studied him more closely, then beckoned and led them to the lake shore. "We can talk in private here." His gaze scanned the lake, then focused on Nimah. "Please answer my question?"

Maintaining his cloak of calm seriousness, Nimah nodded. "I come with a proposal that I hope you will find interesting. My mother, in her role as the Sun Queen of this solar system and galaxy, has gathered a group of people to help her achieve her goal of ridding Neul Isle of its enemies. Gar and I are here to ask for your help in this quest."

Jade-green eyes searched Nimah's face. "How do you know I am not your enemy?"

"I know of you from two of our companions. Because of their knowledge of you and your Seeker-Rangers, I performed a discreet mental assessment to confirm whether we could trust you. That's when I discovered how unhappy you are in Raiherr's employ."

Gar watched Pakdon digest what he had been told and saw him flinch.

"You invaded my privacy and read my mind? How dare you?"

Nimah straightened. "I apologize for the intrusion into your thoughts, Pakdon. Had I not done so, I would be here for an entirely different reason." His regal bearing and the understanding in his expression highlighted the honesty in his formal apology.

Turning away, the HHC stared into the distance, released a long breath, and faced Nimah. "I accept your apology. Raiherr is your enemy and is about to become mine. Please share your proposal."

"Garon and I are here to ask you to help us remove Raiherr's Vasro warriors from the K'iin village."

Pakdon's brow shot up. "You want me to remove six men—"

Nimah shook his head. "Let me explain. The men are under a permanent spell of forgetting. As we speak, they are discovering who they are afresh. We would ask you to take them to a specific place and leave them. The Council of Deities will obscure your departure, making it impossible for Raiherr to track you.

"What about Karlsut Sorda and the *Surgentin*?"

Gar peered up at him. "Carûtix's father is making sure they are gone from here for good."

Pakdon ran a finger over his droopy mustache and smiled for the first time. "If you can promise I'll be free of Raiherr Yencara, I'm your man."

Gar felt a surge of excitement and grinned.

Nimah tipped his head and gave him a 'be-careful' glance. "What are you thinking, Gar?"

"Maybe Pakdon should come to El Stroma with me."

"El Stroma!" Pakdon stooped, his eyes level with Gar's. "My ancestors are from the planet of El Stroma. Are you, by chance, from the ship *El Aperdisa*?"

Gar nodded. "I am."

Pakdon smiled and straightened. "Nimah, I'm ready to help you remove Raiherr's men. I have one request. When they are off on their own, may I return to *El Aperdisa*?"

Before Nimah could reply, Relevart materialized beside Gar, his staff in hand.

Pakdon gaped. "Who are *you*?"

A brief introduction later, the Universal VarTerel said, "I am here at the request of Commander Odnamo. He requires the services of an HHC and asked me to offer you the position."

"Please tell the Commander I accept his offer." Pakdon's delight lit up his smile and his eyes. "What now?"

Relevart walked over to the spacecraft, tapped it with the crystal tip of his staff, and motioned them to join him. "I've disabled the listening device, and I am about to transport us and your ship to the plains bordering the Bāoba Forest on this side of the dome. Nimah will then bring the Vasro warriors to you. Once they are on board, we will once more travel through Mittkeer to Persow, where you will leave your human cargo."

The Land of Time embraced them. Gar looked at Pakdon. "Think pleasant thoughts and you'll feel better faster." When the HHC straightened, Gar grinned. "You look good. Hey, will you teach me to fly a Quest-Seeker?"

Pakdon laughed. "I'll definitely teach you what I know."

Gar saw the look of satisfaction Nimah and Relevart exchanged. He removed his spectacles and sent them into hiding. *I wonder if this was all planned?*

Relevart's satisfied smile provided the answer.

In the K'iin village, Raiherr kicked over a basket full of children's shoes, plopped down on a wooden bench, gripped the rounded edge, and stared at the wall. Anger, uncertainty, ego all fought for supremacy. Conceit rose to the top of the pile. *I am the Vasro leader.* Memories of his Mocendi mentor surfaced. *What would you do in my place, Thorlu Tangorra?* He sat up straight and sneered. *Of course, you turned traitor. You left Karlsut to pick up the reins. Dam'n you. I hate you as much as I hate Carûtix.*

He lunged to his feet and walked to the window. Creases laddered his brow. Muttering to himself, he peered through the dimness. "What's going on out there?"

On the far side of the bridge, his men sat huddled together, staring straight ahead. A fire eagle perched in a tree nearby. *Bet that's the VarTerel or one of her friends.*

Creeping to the door, he eased it open, jumped to the ground, and caught his breath. A silence so profound he thought he would simply melt into it cloaked the village. A sudden chill made him shiver. His eyeballs rolled back in his head.

Soft words whispered through his mind.

> *"A dream erases who your are,*
> *Fills your heart, and leaves no scar.*
> *Act out the story in your mind—"*

Raiherr's hands flew up to cover his ears. He screamed a horrified denial as memories fled. A frantic about-face sent him stumbling into the trees; a fallen branch pitched him face first on the ground, stunned and unmoving. His own jumbled thoughts and heavy panting prodded him upright with his hands once more pressed to his ears.

A stranger walked from the trees. "What are you doing, Raiherr Yencara?"

The voice penetrating his confusion brought vague memories to the surface. He stared up at the man's arrogant face, examining it with lethargic interest.

A powerful hand jerked him to his feet. Frigid dark eyes bored into him. "Wake up, Vasro. We've got work to do."

Recognition—one drop, two drops— Raiherr shook his head. "Who are you?"

The man gripped his shoulders and shook him. "Tell me your name."

"All I recall is the voice—" He jerked away. "What's going on?"

Realization registered on the man's face. "Tell me what you remember, word for word."

Raiherr licked his lips, sniffed, and shook his head. "Something about a dream that erases and a story to..." A shudder overtook him. "That's all. Please help me." He heard the pleading in his voice and swallowed.

Half-stumbling, half-dragged, he arrived at the far side of the copse of trees. Strong hands gripped him by his shoulders. The cold, demanding gaze riveted on his face kept him from looking away. Words enunciated with measured precision penetrated his befuddled mind.

"I am going to shape shift a Spéire Condor. You are to climb onto my back and hold on." The voice paused then continued. "You've done it before, Yencara, and loved it. When we're safe, I will explain what I believe is going on. Are you ready?"

Raiherr glanced around, rubbed his forehead, and shuddered. Trust flirted with him. He clenched his teeth and hissed. "I'm ready."

The man flashed from view. In his place, a giant condor materialized, swung its mighty head to look at him, and lowered its wing.

Fighting his rising panic, Raiherr scrabbled up onto the broad, feathered back. The condor's launch into flight left him sobbing with fright. Confusion filled with misgiving, he hugged the bird's back with his knees and clung to its feathers with white-knuckled fists.

Air slapped his face and tugged at his hair. His clothing plastered to his chest felt like a restraining-jacket. A frantic desire to jump, to be anywhere but flying high above Neul Isle, rushed through him. A glimpse of the land below squelched the dam of feelings and left him hunched over and rigid with dread.

Brie, in her warbler form, hid in a wide-leafed deciduous tree. Raiherr's panicked response to her charm of forgetting didn't surprise her. *I wish I'd finished the last line.* She ruffled her feathers. *The charm will hold, but I'm not sure how long.*

Below her, she witnessed Carûtix arrive and depart with the Vasro leader. *I'm certain he will take Raiherr to his ship. The demi-god is no fool and continues to retain more power than I expected.*

A short flight later, she landed beside Esán's fire eagle. After sharing what had occurred with Raiherr, he took flight and soared toward Cârthea Plain to confirm their destination. She remained on her perch, her tiny warbler eye peeking between the prickles on the evergreen branch.

Raiherr's men sat huddled together, looking lost and forlorn. Esán's charm of total forgetting lingered. *It's time to return their recent memories of who they wished to be.* A fluttered landing beside the group and her shift to Human went unnoticed by the confused men.

She gazed at each one and recited:

> *"No Vasro memories fill your mind*
> *For you have left them all behind.*
> *Embrace the man you wish to be.*
> *Let him guide you and be free*
> *To choose your path, the one you sow*
> *That fills your heart and frees your soul."*

Once again she shaped the warbler and flew to a tree to witness the men emerge from forgetting. Wonder-filled smiles lit their faces. They stood and surveyed the village.

Relno climbed to his feet and stared. "Anyone know where we are?"

Nimah stepped from behind a tree. "You are on the Isle of Neul on the planet of Soputto. I am here to help you reach your true destinies."

He glanced up at Brie's hiding place. "First, I have something I must do. Please stay close by."

He walked over the bridge to Dri Adoh's hut and held the door open.

Brie flew through and landed in Human form. "I didn't expect to see you here. Has something happened?"

Nimah nodded. "I have several things to share. Gar is with the K'iin. He and I conferred with Dri Adoh and Artānga. They are ready for Carûtix to appear as imitation Sea Wee Vala. I met with them as the Sun Queen's heir. They are men of honor, Brielle, and will not give my secret away."

He stroked his smooth chin. "After our meeting, Gar and I returned to my sleep space for some quiet reflection. Thorlu's shared memories surfaced. When he and Torgin arrived on the island, they discovered a Haptic Holo Controller and his small spacecraft. The HHC's name is Pakdon. A distance probe of his mind suggested he disliked Raiherr and Sorda and had no desire to become a Vasro. His dedication to remaining independent intrigued me, so Gar and I went to see him. He was, of course, suspicious, but our desire to rid

Neul Isle of its enemies appealed to his sense of right. I told him my ideas for removing the Vasro warriors."

A pause brought a satisfied expression to his dark, aristocratic features. "He is a good man, Brielle. You will have the opportunity to meet him soon."

Images flared and faded in Brie's mind. Based on the new developments they presented, she controlled her own racing ideas and nodded. "Relevart has revealed his thoughts to me. I imagine Gar is most excited. Please Nimah, share your plan."

The Sun Queen's son glanced up at the dome, then met her interest with an explanation. "Since I am able to exit the dome without disturbing its energy frequency, I will remove the men from the village through it and deliver them to Pakdon's spacecraft at the far side of the dome. From there, Relevart will transport them using Mittkeer. When they are safely deposited at the spaceport on Persow, he will return to *El Aperdisa* with Pakdon."

Brie bit her lip, then smiled. "I like your plan. How will the Vasro manage after you leave them. We don't want them to become confused and end up in trouble."

Nimah smiled. "From there, I have provided them with the funds to travel anywhere they wish. I have also promised to obscure Pakdon's departure from Neul Isle and to cover his energy signature and that of his spacecraft until he is safe aboard *El Aperdisa*. What do you think, VarTerel?"

"Your plan is excellent. When do you wish to execute it?"

Nimah smiled. "Since Carûtix and Raiherr are absent and the men are ready to be gone, now would be the best time. I will alert you when the spacecraft leaves the island."

Brie nodded. "As soon as you've departed, I'll join Esán. We believe Carûtix took Raiherr to his ship."

With a nod, Nimah crossed to the door. He glanced back and smiled. "I am honored to work with you, VarTerel AsTar. Take care. Carûtix and Raiherr are dangerous, especially working together. I will return to Garon and the K'iin when my errand is complete." He strode over the bridge and joined the six men.

A raised hand and a lexeme of calm stilled the group. Brie watched them gather closer to the Sun Queen's heir and listen intently. Rounded eyes lit with excitement accompanied their departure as an atmospheric whirlwind lifted them and carried them up through the dome.

Brie allowed the peace-filled stillness to replenish her energy. Shaping a fire eagle, she soared above the empty village toward Rina Island.

Fiendish laughter echoing through the Land of Time held the occupants of Rainbow Cottage still. A finger to his lips, Thorlu motioned Den toward the bedroom, then bent down to look Glori in the eye. "Remain as you are. Be ready if I require your help."

Another fanatical laugh amplified the tension in the room. Den hurrying in from the hall to the bedroom, his face alive with worry, multiplied it.

"Penee and Inōni are gone." He scrubbed his hair. "I've looked everywhere, and I can't find them." Distress melded with fear saturated each word.

Glori uncoiled her skipping rope and moved to the side. Curls bouncing, she jumped and whispered soft words. When she stopped, her expression broadcast only confusion. She returned to the group. "All I can tell is that they are unharmed."

Thorlu turned to Torgin. "Can you create a time-fold?"

Tapping his temple, Torgin whispered, "I have previous experience and the Sun Queen's book in my memory if I require further information. Don't worry, I know how. If we need to create one, just give me a sign."

Glori moved closer. "I can help." Her gaze darted to the door. "Before we move the cottage, we must discover what happened to the girls."

Heavy footsteps on the wooden porch drew the group into a tight huddle. Thorlu took charge.

"Torgin, stay with me, but stay out of sight. Den and Glori hide. Don't come out unless I call you."

As soon as Glori had led Den from the room, Thorlu pulled open the door and stepped onto the porch. "Hello, Cóch. Welcome to Mittkeer." He regarded the four men huddled at the bottom of the steps. "You realize you and your friends could be stuck here for All Time?" He pursed his lips. "Unless, of course, one of you is a VarTerel."

The Demi-God of Sea Squalls sneered. "You won't be going anywhere without us, Thorlu Tangorra."

Thorlu's brow arched. "And why is that?"

His men spread out around the cottage. "Because we have you surrounded, and..." Contempt etched his bold features. "I am much more powerful than a mere VarTerel. Give me the Girl with the Matriarch's eyes and the K'iin woman who carries her child."

"I wish I could help you." Thorlu shrugged. "But neither of those women are here. Now, if you'll excuse me—"

"Stay—where—you—are. If you so much as blink, I will end your existence."

Thorlu narrowed his eyes. "Really? You would end the life of the only person who can return you to your world? I doubt you are that stupid." He turned, entered the cottage and shut the door in his enemy's face. Wards shot up around the cottage. He turned to Torgin. "Get us out of here."

"Den slipped into the room. "What about the girls?"

"We'll find them, but not until we have dealt with the rabble outside. Get Glori. We have work to do."

The child-like wise woman entered. "I still cannot find the girls, but my instincts tell me they are safe. Do what you must do, Thorlu."

He regarded Torgin with a firm smile. "Tell us what you need and be as quick as you can."

Torgin pulled out the time whistle. "Stay close to me. We will not take the cottage. I'll visualize the four of us in a fold in the space-time continuum." He played a single note. "Hold on. Now!" A series of three notes trilled.

The cottage flickered and grew distant. The time fold embraced them.

Glori laughed softly. Thorlu grinned. Den exhaled. "What just happened?"

Torgin pointed. Below them, Cóch, stood on the cottage porch, his hand on the door. Four men gathered in a tight group behind him. The demi-god entered and froze. His growl of disappointment echoed through the empty cottage.

Thorlu thumped Torgin on the back. "You are a miracle, Torgin Whalend."

"Thanks, VarTerel." A broad smile brought a twinkle to his eye. "We are all miracles in our own right. All of us created the time-fold together." He regarded Glori. "Your cousin and his men are now stuck in Mittkeer. What shall we do about them?"

Den chimed in. "Can we take them back to their arrival in Chûrinne in their dimension?

Thorlu joined in. "The cottage is no longer on Chûrinne. It's still in Mittkeer, correct?"

Torgin pressed the time whistle against his chest where it hung on its lanyard. "You're correct. Rainbow Cottage is not on the planet. Going back to before it arrived—." He studied Glori. "We require ShioCáni's knowledge to make the best decision."

All eyes focused on the goddess as she materialized in front of them. "Redoing the past never benefits the present. Let us consider returning Cóch and his men to his father's realm; then we can return to the cottage. I am certain, his father, Tagoh Efarragi, will apply the strict code of behavior demanded by the deities. The Council will decide his future."

Thorlu studied the Goddess of Harmony and nodded. "Thank you for your insight, ShioCáni. Are you able to place an image of Tagoh Efarragi's realm in Shiór Ridu in our minds?"

"I am. We will all work together to transport them. The way-marker for Shiór Ridu is Dia Nōrtara. Torgin will show it to us on the Compass of Ostradio."

Thorlu's head began to thrum. "I understand! We move them to the waypoint and release them from Mittkeer." He moved to Torgin's side and motioned Den and the Goddess of Harmony to join them.

Den spoke up. "Can we remain in the fold, or do we return to their dimension to transport them?"

Torgin grinned. "Because we don't need to release them from Mittkeer and then teleport them to their homeland, we can stay in the fold. Whew! Thank you, ShioCáni." He pulled out the compass and nodded at Thorlu. "Shall we begin?"

Thorlu inhaled. "Ostradio, show us the constellation Dia Nōrtara.

28
El Aperdisa

Relieved that Observation Deck 3 remained deserted but for Nesen and himself, Zak ignored his edginess and prepared to listen to the older man.

Nesen's penetrating, unblinking gaze fastened on his face. "I am about to share critical information, Zak. My boss has given me permission to offer you a part in an important enterprise." He pursed his lips and lifted his chin. "There are enemy spies on board—spies who do not want *El Aperdisa* to leave orbit around TreBlaya. My assignment is to learn who they are and report them. You and your two friends top the list of suspects." His cold pale-gray eyes underscored the hard edge in his voice and expression.

Zak let his brow crease in a question and allowed shocked surprise to register. "Are you kidding me?" He shook his head and blew a clipped exhale from his nose. Narrowed eyes examined the man opposite him. "I assume, if you believed I was a spy, we would not be having this conversation, so what do you want from me?"

Nesen studied him with a hint of surprise. "You are perceptive for one so young."

"First, Sergeant Nesen, I may appear young, but I am an experienced member of this crew. If you are looking for a snitch, I'm not your man." He paused, his expression open, but cautious. "If you are looking for someone to help with your investigation, I might consider your offer."

The man opposite him stroked his clean-shaven chin. "Do you think your friends could be spies?"

Zak let his thought-filled gaze wander to an oval view-portal and back to Nesen. "Rily and Jem are two crew members I met when I arrived on *El Aperdisa*. I do not consider them my friends, rather acquaintances I am getting to know. The more time I spend with them, the less I like them. Are they spies?" He shrugged.

The Vasro leader regarded him with a glint in his eye. "How about we do this? You continue to do things with Jem and Rily. If something happens that makes you suspicious, you can share the information if you choose."

Zak pursed his lips and nodded. "Alright. What am I looking for in the event they are the spies?"

"See if you can discover who they report to on board the ship. Also, keep your eyes open. If they meet with other crew members who appear suspicious to you, let me know. For now, we'll keep this casual, but, Zak, if you are playing games with me, I promise to make your life miserable."

Coming to his feet, Zak looked down at the older man. "That goes both ways." Head high, he walked away, fully aware of Nesen's knife-sharp gaze boring into his departing figure.

He stepped into the passageway as Reedan rounded the corner, nodded, and entered the observation deck. A glance over his shoulder sent a shiver up his spine. Reedan sat down next to Nesen and the two men began an intense conversation. *I don't trust either of you.*

Eyes straight ahead, he ambled down the passageway and made his way to the T-Lift. A wave of relief almost made him stumble when the doors slid opened, revealing an empty car. Once inside, he leaned against the wall, exhaled, and shook his head. **Glad that's over with.** His nostrils flare. *Talking one-on-one with Nesen has made it clear he's even more dangerous than we thought.*

At the ship's Plantitarium level, he exited the car and strolled to the entrance. Once inside Garden Level 1, he wandered aimlessly up a manicured path. *I hope Jem and Rily are waiting for me.*

When he reached the patch of taller plants obscuring the wall to his secret hide-away, he dodged behind a large bush. A search of his clothes assured him Nesen had not planted a mini-trans on him; a mental probe confirmed no one followed him. Quickly shifting to a black-tailed butterfly, he flew through the wall into his special place.

Cóch and his men huddled on the porch of the cottage in Mittkeer. One man swore and sank to his knees, another hugged himself, stared at the never-ending night, and shuddered.

A third man turned on Cóch. "We're trapped in Mittkeer." Fear rang like a bell in his vociferous voice. "You're not a VarTerel, Cóch Tagoh. How are we going to escape?"

The Demi-God of Sea Squalls scanned the universal heavens. "They will not leave us here. Carûtix will see that Thorlu Tangorra releases us."

The man shot him a disgusted look and hissed through bared teeth. "Bucānetis Marûs banned Carûtix. If we don't find him and take him back to Shiór Ridu, our demi-god will lose everything." He sat down on a porch step and covered his face with his hands.

Cóch turned to examine his fourth comrade. "You don't seem upset, Raifō."

He shrugged. "I don't believe the VarTerel will leave us to wander around Mittkeer. He'll figure out a way to remove us." Sitting on the edge of the porch, he surveyed the vastness spreading in all directions. "It's just a matter of 'time'."

Sighing, Cóch joined him. "Suppose you're right." He shook his head. "Guess I was foolish to chase after Carûtix. He'd never had done so for me."

Raifō gave him a sideways glance. "He's less likely to do so now. We'd better hope the VarTerel releases us from Mittkeer, or we'll finish our lives in this cottage." Sliding off the porch, he stared up at a sudden change in the constancy of Mittkeer.

Cóch jumped to the ground beside him. "What in the solar system is that?"

The other men joined them in a tight group, attention riveted to the rippling stars in the universal vastness.

In the time fold, Torgin held the Compass of Ostradio steady while the golden needle spun, and the star chart floated into being.

Thorlu touched the tip of his finger to the constellation Dia Nōrtara.

Den gasped and pointed. "Look!"

Hovering above the cottage, the most spectacular constellation Torgin had ever seen left him breathless with amazement. A fiery-red haze framed a pattern of stars forming a six-pointed star. At the center, a single, larger star's corona glowed brighter than all the rest, demanding both attention and awe.

ShioCáni's honey-gold eyes sparkled, and her aura glowed warm and bright around her. "I have never seen the constellation this close. It is more beautiful than I imagined. Dia is the central Deity star, and the six pointed outer star represents the harmony of the heavens." She switched her gaze to Thorlu. "VarTerel, what is required next?"

Thorlu's attention moved to Cóch and his men. "Let's get this done so we can return to the cottage. Everyone focus on removing the men from the porch to Dia Nōrtara. When I open Mittkeer, ShioCáni, please send them to the High King of Wind and Sea. Den, your power is required to help Torgin hold the time fold steady. Torgin, keep the time whistle handy."

Below them, Cóch pointed at the glowing grouping of stars within the fiery mist. He started to move toward the door. A shaft of topaz light from Marichi caught him mid-stride, enveloped the rest of the men, and transported them all through the Land of Time to the foot of the constellation.

The Goddess of Harmony sang a high note that filled the time fold. A ball of lapis-blue light engulfed Cóch and his men, and, as the fabric of Mittkeer's star-spangle endlessness thinned, carried them through, and deposited them at the feet of Tagoh Efarragi.

The Land of All Time and No Time reknit, sending a zigzagging of blazing gold light through the universal vastness. Torgin played a long, low note followed by three shorter ones. A steady hum vibrated through the time fold, dissolving it and leaving him, Den, Thorlu, and ShioCáni in front of Rainbow Cottage.

At first, no one moved. Then as though the conductor had given the down beat to begin, their held breath whispered out into universal space. Den, the first to reanimate, turned to Thorlu. "What's our next move?"

Thorlu gazed at Marichi and faced his companions. "Penee and Inōni vanished from the cottage while in Mittkeer. Is it best to begin searching here or return the cottage to Chûrinne and start there?" He addressed the goddess. "Your thoughts, ShioCáni?"

"I believe we return to the planet. If our friends were in danger, we would know. Release Rainbow Cottage from Mittkeer, VarTerel, and we will begin our search."

Torgin, Den, and the goddess formed a tight grouping around him. He raised his staff and ShioCáni lifted the cottage on the currents of her astral wind. Mittkeer opened and the cottage settled into its place in the Chûrinne's landscape. The Land of All Time and No Time closed. Blue sky, singing birds, and the touch of a cool breeze took its place.

Torgin scanned the landscape...the field of flowers, the garden, the grouping of trees now covered in tiny blue flowers behind the cottage, and the trail leading between the flattop mountains to the lake.

He felt the tension in the group ease and smiled at Thorlu. "Good work, VarTerel!"

In his fire eagle form, Esán soared high over Neul Isle's San Crúil River toward the Plains of Cârthea and Raiherr Yencara's jumper craft *Toneer*. The sudden appearance of the condor not far ahead sent him swooping low over the water. A short distance downriver, the immense bird with Raiherr on its back disappeared into the gully leading to the plains.

Careful not to draw attention to himself, Esán banked toward the island's central lagoon, Bolcán Murloch, and Rina Island, and followed the river bordering the north side of the plains. After shifting to a warbler, he alighted on the branch of a tall, leafy tree near the spacecraft.

The Spéire Condor swooped in for a landing. Golden eyes glinting, it stretched its long neck and swung its enormous head around to peer up at its passenger. The sharp beak snapped open. A screech echoed over the plains.

Raiherr scooted on his bottom over the condor's sleek feathers and climbed down its wing to the ground. Confusion vibrated around him. He shook his head, rubbed his eyes, and stared from the lush landscape of the plains to the jumper craft to the enormous bird with no sign of recognition.

Carûtix flashed into being and eyed the flustered Human with disgust, somewhat diluted by curiosity. Planting himself in front of the disoriented Vasro, he barked, "Look at me, Raiherr Yencara."

Dark rapidly blinking eyes froze wide open before making a tentative switch to his face. Puzzlement produced a frown. "I—know—you?" He cocked his head.

The demi-god reached toward him.

Raiherr jumped back, panting. "Who—" He licked his lips and waited.

"I am Carûtix, heir to the throne of the High King of War and Peace. You have had your memories tampered with. Let me touch your temples, and I can restore them."

Short, panted breaths expanded and contracted the Vasro's broad chest. He pressed a trembling hand to his heart and stared hard at the man in front of him. "P-p-please."

From his perch, Esán's warbler eyes noted the full-body shudder that ran through the Vasro as Carûtix pressed firm hands to his temples. When the demi-god stepped away, the tautness in Raiherr's body intensified. Darting eyeballs beneath closed lids created a ripple-like effect on their surfaces. His lips scrunched into a pouty line, and his head jerked right, then left, then right. Gradually, the staccato movements ceased, and the tension eased. Bending forward, he gripped his knees and gulped deep, cleansing breaths.

A soft rustling in the leaves beside Esán pulled his attention from Raiherr to Brie's warbler form, landing on a small branch next to him. She tipped her head from side-to-side, her tiny eyes glinting in the dim light.

Below them, Raiherr scrubbed a shaking hand through his hair and glared. "What did you do to me? Who in sedah are you?" Not waiting, he crossed to the jumper craft, reached for the touchpad, and frowned. "Whose craft is this?"

Carûtix, his expression bemused, stared at the hands he held up in front of his face. Joint by joint the fingers fisted. He lowered them and turned to stare at Raiherr. "What did you do to me?"

Raiherr, who seemed not to hear, shuddered. "My memories are all mixed up. I remember a place called Chirē Pâmit as home, and yet I also recall a spaceship. Everything is in a jumble." He stared hard at Carûtix. "Are you as baffled as I am?"

The demi-god's befuddled expression morphed to fear engendered agitation. "I...we..." He winced. "We are one. I share your memories and you share mine. How did you do that?" Carûtix shook himself. "How do we undo it?"

Total confusion lowered both men to the ground. Shaky hands covered their faces; soft muttering and moans floated between trembling lips.

From his perch, Esán's warbler bobbed its head and launched into flight. Brie's small bird shot to his side. Flying over the river bordering the plains, they landed in human form in a copse of sturdy dwarf elms.

Esán experienced a wave of sympathy for the confused men. "Do you know what blended their memories, Brie?"

"All I can think of is the demi-god's powers short-circuited, causing a shared flow of memories between the men. My question is, how do we untangle the mess? Leaving them tied together mentally could make them more dangerous than they were as individuals."

The Seeds of Carsilem vibrating held Esán still. Information flooded his mind. A shake of his head slowed the flow; a series of controlled inhales and exhales brought clarity. He gripped Brie's hand. "I know—"

Sea Wee Vala stepped from the trees. Emerald eyes gleaming in Wee's small face confirmed it was the true Spirit Totem. When Esán opened his mouth to speak, a shake of Sea's head kept him still. Its large paw-like hand reached for him.

With Brie clinging to one hand, Esán gripped the Totem's paw with the other. The copse of trees disappeared, replaced by oppressive darkness.

29
Chûrinne

Thorlu entered Rainbow cottage, his highly developed senses seeking any clue to where Penee and Inōni might have gone.

The door creaked open. Den stepped across the threshold and hurried to his side. "Are you sensing anything?"

Thorlu shook his head. "Nothing to suggest our enemies abducted them, nor what might have happened. Do you notice anything that worries you?"

Den's absolute concentration sent a rush of power pulsing through the cottage interior. Controlled, even breaths propelled him in a slow, steady rotation that ended facing Thorlu. "I'm not finding anything, either." He frowned. "What's happened to them?"

Fully focused on Relevart's oldest son, Thorlu examined him with fresh interest. "I misjudged you, Den. Your talent is extraordinary. I apologize for not realizing it sooner."

Den Zironho's worried expression eased into a slight smile. "The woman who raised me in Reachti taught me to mask my gifts so my enemies wouldn't turn my direction. I continue to mask for a variety of reasons. Your VarTerel's power is increasing, Thorlu." His smiled widened before concern replaced it. "How do we find the girls?"

Thorlu led him from the cottage to rejoin Torgin and ShioCáni. "Can either of you tell if Penee and Inōni's disappearance has put them in danger?"

Torgin's perceptive gaze scanned the landscape, stopped on the cottage, and moved back to his companions. "Maybe I should be worried, but I'm not." He eyed Den for a long moment. "Your connection to both girls is deep and instinctive, Den. Tune in to their energy signatures again and see if anything else triggers and alarm."

ShioCáni's beautiful eyes widened. "I understand you are concerned about Penee and Inōni but, right now, there is a crisis on Neul Isle. We are needed there." She glanced at Rainbow Cottage. "The cottage will be safe here." Her attention switched. "Thorlu, we are to meet your friends at a safe place you are familiar with." She tipped her head in a movement reminiscent of Glori. "You know where, right?"

Beside him, Torgin released a clipped hiss. "The Sanctuary of Nûsini in the Bāoba Forest." He moved closer to Thorlu. "Take us into Mittkeer, VarTerel."

Den also stepped closer, his sense of urgency washing over the group. "The threat to the island and our safety is escalating. We need to go!"

Thorlu's staff, with Marichi glowing bright topaz, appeared. "Everyone, touch me or the staff. Be ready!"

Mittkeer enclosed them. A shooting star shot across the immenseness of universal night and flashed into nothingness as the Incirrata Constellation took shape overhead.

Gazing at the constellation, Thorlu raised his staff. "I will put the image of our destination in your minds. At my signal, we arrive."

Three pairs of eyes fastened on his face. Stars and night disappeared. The smooth, curved walls of a pod embraced them. A soft gasp whispered through the total quiet.

◉ ◉

With his back against the stone wall, Gar sat cross-legged on the cool ground in the Labyrinth Cavern on Neul Isle. Around him, the K'iin worked with quiet speed to pack their few belongings for the trip back to their village. The true Sea Wee Vala had visited the Labyrinth on behalf of the Sun Queen to confer with Dri Adoh and Artānga. La, the luna moth, followed with the message that although the Vasro camped near the plains and the dome remained over the island, the village itself was free of the enemy. When Dri Adoh gave the word, they could return to their homes.

He shivered. All of his senses screamed a warning. *Something dangerous is still on the island. Sure wish Nimah would get back here, so we can find out what's happening before the K'iin go home.*

A shadow spilling its darkness over his knees alerted him to Thorlu's persona gazing down at him. "Come with me, Garon."

Scrabbling to his feet, Gar trotted after the VarTerel. In the private alcove they shared, Nimah materialized in Thorlu's place. "I have told Dri Adoh to keep his tribe here until I give them the word it is safe to go home. You and I have things to accomplish. First, we must meet with your friends." He held out his hand. "Please hold my hand, and I will take you to them."

Gar stared up at the Sun Queen's heir. *Why am I hesitating?*

Nimah smiled. "Please trust me, Gar. You are correct that danger continues to lurk on the island. Our goal is to end it for all time. Esán and Brielle await our arrival." He offered his hand again.

Gar licked his lips and clasped it. Darkness embraced them. A faint, cool blue glow appeared and grew brighter, highlighting the faces of his friends. Releasing a breath, Gar whispered, "Repapa." His spectacles appeared on his nose, glowing ember rims ablaze. He tipped his head and stared up at the figure of Nimah.

White teeth flashed in the handsome, black face of Abellona's son. "You were correct to be cautious." Opal-flecked black eyes glinted in the blue light. Stepping away from Gar, Nimah raised his arms. Fiery light blazed and faded, leaving in its place the Sun Queen of the Spéire Solar System.

Gar shook his head. "Ya coulda told me."

Abellona smiled. "But, Garon, in your heart you knew." She drew him to her side. "I can't stay long, but we have a serious problem to deal with." Her attention fixed on Brie and Esán, who watched with attentive interest. "Although Carûtix and Raiherr appear as separate individuals, they are, in fact, one in thought, word, and deed. Neither of them has the power to undo the linking of their two personalities. The Goddess of Harmony, with the help of a VarTerel or the dual Seeds of Carsilem, is the only one who can remedy the problem. My overriding concern is that once the two men are individuals again, chaos may ensue. We must contain both of them, and along with Raiherr's three companions and his SorTech, and remove the dome before the island will be safe. Gather your companions. All of your talents are required to accomplish our goals and to bring the CoaleScence to a positive conclusion."

Brie, who appeared unsurprised by the turn of events, brushed a tendril of red hair back from her face. "What of Karlsut Sorda and the *Surgentin*? When the dome no longer exists, won't he have full access to the island? Is he our responsibility, too?"

The Sun Queen's fire-opal eyes glinted brighter. "The Galactic Council has requested that Bucānetis Marûs, our High King of War and Peace, take the lead on removing Karlsut and his spaceship and crew from the solar system." Her chin lifted, and she held up a hand. "I must go. Gather your friends at the Sanctuary Pod." She vanished. Nimah stood in her place.

Gar removed his spectacles and sent them into hiding. "So, how do we get everyone to the Bāoba Forest?"

Nimah spoke up. "I have alerted ShioCáni. The Deities in Shiór Ridu have a close connection to one another, so she is aware of the new danger on Neul Isle."

Brie's VarTerel staff appeared in her hand. Musette's glowing rainbow light pooled around her. "We will enter Mittkeer, our safest means of travel to the Bāoba tree and Thorlu's sleeping pod. Gather around."

Esán and Nimah moved closer. Gar touched Brie's staff and gulped a breath.

⚬ ⚬

A wave of relief washed over Brie as Mittkeer withdrew, leaving her, Esán, Nimah, and Gar in the sleeping pod at the Sanctuary of Nûsini. Musette's rainbow light faded, but not before highlighting the face of a beautiful woman standing at Thorlu's side. Behind them, Den's edginess alerted her to the fact the Penee and Inōni were not with them. Questions piled up.

Nimah stepping forward to greet Thorlu's companion put them on pause. "Cousin, I am delighted to see you!" He drew the woman to his side. "Brie, this is my cousin, the Goddess of Harmony. ShioCáni, this is VarTerel Brielle AsTar."

Brie smiled. "I believe I met you as Glori in Rainbow Gulch?"

ShioCáni returned her smile of recognition. "We have indeed shared other adventures."

Nimah turned to Esán. "ShioCáni, Esán Efre."

The Goddess met Esán's gaze with a nod. "You are the only bearer of Dual Seeds of Carsilem in our galaxy. I am honored to meet you, Esán."

Den cleared his throat. Impatience stark in his stance and in his expression, he faced Nimah. "Let's sit down and focus on Carûtix and Raiherr before they realize we're back on Neul Isle."

Responding to the urgency in his voice, Esán helped him to arrange the sleeping cots into a meeting area. Once everyone was seated, Brie beckoned him to join her.

Den sat opposite them and immediately picked up where he left off. "The combined minds of our dangerous-duo will home in on us faster now that they are mind-fellows. How do we stop them, so we can search for Penee and Inōni?"

Brie's questions stampeded. "Wait. Before we jump to organizing our strategy for retaking Neul Isle, please tell us what happened to Penee and Inōni."

Den tipped his head back and inhaled. An exhale later, he provided a quick summary of events on Chûrinne, from the girls disappearing to Cóch and his men arriving, and their adventures in Mittkeer. He finished with another puffed exhale. "Since none of us feel the girls are unsafe, we decided the emergency here took precedence over our search."

ShioCáni regarded each member of the group before nodding her agreement. "We would know if they were in danger." She paused then continued. "Carûtix and Raiherr have a plan. We need to get ours underway."

Nimah, his expression urgent, spoke up. "First, we must scatter over the island, so our energy signatures are less of a beacon." He pressed his lips into a line, his dark eyes half closed. "I suggest Thorlu and Den find Karlsut's spy, Hossela, and either convince him to join us or remove him from the equation. We can't have him interfering. Brielle and Esán take ShioCáni and find out what our..." He almost smiled. "...mind-fellows are planning. If they are moving too fast, you can slow them down. Torgin, your job is to oversee The

Box. Make certain you know everything there is to know about it. Gar, and I will return to the K'iin's village, make certain it is still safe, and go to the Labyrinth Cavern to update Dri Adoh and Artānga. Have I missed anything?"

A muffled hum filtering through the Bāobas' over-arching crown of dense leaves and into the pod, prompted everyone's attention to fix on Brie.

She came to her feet. "The Vasro's jumper craft is on the move." Wards shimmered into place around the group. "Blank your minds. Thorlu, help me shield the K'iin in the main pod."

Total silence cloaked the Sanctuary of Nûsini. The hum grew faint, increased in volume again, remained stationary overhead, and then faded altogether. Brie relaxed but maintained the shields until Thorlu nodded and released those he had created. Raising her hand, she lowered the ones protecting the group gathered in the sleeping pod.

Nimah frowned. "I didn't expect the use of the jumper craft. It's the last thing we need that duo to have the use of."

Esán cleared his throat. "I believe I can help with that." His attention focused on Torgin. "Remember when you created a time-fold and sent me to *Surgentin*'s bridge?"

A spark if interest lit Torgin's expression. "Of course, I do. You memorized the ship's charts and intended trajectory." He laughed low in his throat. "What else did that eidetic memory of yours record?"

"I also unloaded into memory the circuitry and plans of not only the *Surgentin*, but several small crafts, including *Toneer*."

Torgin tapped his lips with steepled index fingers. "You can share your memory of *Toneer* with me, correct?"

Esán smiled. "I can do better than that. I will upload the plans to your memory so you can access them yourself." He stood and looked down at Torgin. "Are you ready?"

Torgin straightened and rested his hands on his thighs. "I am."

Esán placed his hands on Torgin's temples. When he lowered them and stepped back, Torgin opened eyes overflowing with enthusiasm. "You are good, Esán Efre. Give me a minute." A nod later, he regarded the group. "I can create a block in the jumper craft's propulsion thruster, which will keep it grounded until our mind-fellows discover what's up. I'll need access to the ship with them gone or placed in a deep sleep."

Brie listened, her VarTerel's mind devising a new approach to ridding the island of the Vasro and his men.

A gentle knock on the entry oval snapped everyone's attention in that direction. Cadhōla's face appeared in the opening at the entry's center and withdrew. La fluttered through and landed on Brie's shoulder. Her telepathic message filled Brie's mind.

"Rina, send me. Ship land. Men exit. They go camp. Meet SorTech. Me go." As the Luna Moth exited through it, the opening returned to its smooth opaqueness.

Brie responded to the curiosity buzzing around her and shared the message. "It appears we are all needed at the Plains of Cârthea." She faced the Sun Queen's heir. "May I reorganize your suggested plan, Nimah?"

A serious, open expression molded his handsome features. "Please, do what is best."

Brie's staff materialized. She motioned everyone closer. A whisper later, they all stood in Mittkeer. Thorlu caught her eye and nodded his approval.

Allowing time for everyone to stabilize, she reviewed what needed to be accomplished and prepared to put her plans into action.

Penee woke up slowly. Heavy eyelids lifted only enough for her to glimpse the blurred colors of a painting on the cottage wall. Sleep-weighted limbs refused to move. Her pillow kissing her cheek sent her into a deep sleep. Dreams came and went, leaving a momentary memory that slipped silently away. Hunger growling nudged her to awaken. Like a swimmer rising from the depth of the sea, she swam upwards. Her eyes flickered open, she gulped a breath, turned on her side and slipped into light, restful sleep.

A cool breezed whispering around her lifted the weight of her fatigue and carried it away. She rolled onto her back, yawned, and stared at the sunlit curtains fluttering in the breeze. Disoriented yet unafraid, she gazed up at the ceiling, scooched to a sitting position, and surveyed her surroundings.

Across from her, Inōni's dark eyes blinked open. Exerting the extra effort needed to hoist her pregnant body to sitting, she fixed her gaze on Penee, rubbed her eyes, and smiled. "We're still in Rainbow Cottage." She looked puzzled. "But I thought we were somewhere else." Bare feet pressed to the floor, she hugged her unborn child. "I thought..." Bewilderment cloaked her. A trembling brown hand tugged at her tangled black hair. She stared down at her belly, then lifted pleading eyes to meet Penee's. "What do you remember?"

Penee pursed her lips. "Men's voices arguing...a flash of golden light... that's all. The next thing I recall is waking up." She stood and slipped on her shoes. "You stay here. I'm going to look around."

Inōni leveraged her body upright. "I'm going with you. Please don't leave me alone."

Penee nodded and tiptoed to the door. Easing it ajar, she peered up and down the hall and listened intently. "I don't see or hear anything. Stay close to me."

She opened the bedroom door, walked into the hall, and led Inōni to the front room. When nothing set off an alarm in her head, she smiled. "We're truly in Rainbow Cottage, just like you said." After settling the mother-to-be on the couch, Penee stepped onto the porch.

Chûrrine's beauty flowed in all directions, yet something felt different. Her gaze roamed the landscape—the field of flowers, the flat-topped mountains, the shimmering lake in the distance—and stopped unblinking on a tall, willowy woman with long silver-blonde hair and a raven perched on her shoulder walking toward her up the trail.

Surprise and relief left Penee weak in the knees. She dropped onto the edge of the porch with her feet on the wooden step and forced herself to breathe.

Almiralyn Nadrugia stopped a short distance from the cottage, turned her head to see her companion, and nodded as Karrew lifted into flight and soared over the cottage. Her beautiful sapphire eyes glistening, she walked closer and smiled. "I didn't mean to startle you, but—" She glanced beyond Penee. "Hello, Inōni. We have not met, but I know of you from Relevart, the Universal VarTerel. My name is Almiralyn, and he sent me here to find you."

Penee looked over her shoulder. "Almiralyn is a VarTerel and our friend, Inōni, and the raven is called Karrew." She stood. "I am so glad to see you, Mira. Please come in. Inōni needs to be resting."

Inside Rainbow Cottage, Penee helped Inōni to settle on the sofa and sat down at her feet. Across from her, Almiralyn lowered her lithe body into an overstuffed chair.

"I know you have questions, Penee. I will do my best to answer them, but first, as soon as Karrew returns from his reconnaissance flight, we must leave Chûrrine. We'll need your help."

Penee tipped her head. "How can I help? I'm not a VarTerel."

Almiralyn smiled. "You always underestimate your talents, Penesert." Almiralyn turned her gaze to study Inōni. "Relevart suspended you in time, so your baby girl would not be born too soon. We must select the safest place for her birth. It must be somewhere your enemies will not consider. Sadly, now is not the time to return you to Neul Isle."

Karrew landed on the porch, shifted to Corvus Castylim, and stepped inside. His steady gaze studied the three women. He moved to stand beside Almiralyn, smiled at Inōni, then focused his raven-dark eyes on Penee. "Have you decided where we must take you, Penesert?"

Penee ran a finger from the tip of her nose down over her mouth to her chin and smiled. "I know just the place.

30
El Aperdisa

Ari and Rethson sat staring at the vine-covered walls of Elf's hideaway. Neither spoke. Rethson's fear of Reedan permeating the space nudged Ari's uneasiness a notch higher. She tugged a long curl over her shoulder and slid her fingers down its coppery length. *Where are you, Elf?*

A black butterfly with dots of emerald green on its wings fluttered around the space and landed on the bench opposite them. Elf materialized, a finger to his lips and his gaze riveted to the wall. Ari knew he felt safe when he lowered the hand and his gaze moved to rest on her face.

"Sure am glad you're here, Troms el Shiv!" She moved to sit next to him. "Tell us what happened in your meeting with Nesen."

A detailed explanation later, Rethson licked his lips and shivered. "So, you're in with the Vasro spies. Sure am glad it's you and not me." Another shiver left him sitting with his arms folded across his chest and his eyes fixed on the ground.

Ari slid an arm around Elf's shoulders. "You did great. I'll inform Aunt Henri of your success and get her advice on what our next step is." She stood up. "Rethson, I think you should share everything you know about Reedan with Elf. I'll meet you at the Snack Station on the mid-deck in a chron-circle." She did a mental scan of the Plantitarium's first and second levels, shaped a black butterfly identical to Elf's, and flew through the wall.

Voices at the entrance alerted her to company. Landing in a leafy bush with bright red flowers, she tuned her hearing to eavesdrop.

Reedan's tone, although low, carried the weight of annoyance. "I'm telling you, Zak and his friends meet here regularly. They must have a secret place where they can talk in private. We need to find it."

Nesen walked up the path. "Haven't been here before. What an accomplishment this is! The Eleo Predans had to gather all the flora and fauna from El Stroma and bring it on board the ship. When Sorda takes control of *El Aperdisa*, he'll make a fortune off this."

"If we don't find the Universal VarTerel's spies, he won't get the opportunity to take over anything." Impatience coloring each syllable of each word, Reedan faced his boss. "What's wrong, Nesen? You getting sof—"

The sound of a gut punch echoed through the Plantitarium. Reedan's gasp of pain changed to an angry snarl. "How dare you—"

"Do not tempt me to finish the job, Reedan, or you'll be spending the next few moon cycles in the infirmary. Understood?"

A groan was Reedan's only response.

"Never forget who's the boss, Reedan Coegi. I would hate to remove you permanently from the crew. Now, I want each of our spies tailed. You take our snitch, Zak. Have Rozar cover Rily, and I'll take Jem. I want a full report at the end of each turning. We'll meet on Observation Deck 3."

A single set of footsteps moved down the path and stopped. "Don't just stand there, Reedan. Get your backside in gear. I want confirmation that our three crewmen are Ari, Rethson, and Troms el Shiv by tomorrow's ending." His footsteps continued down the passageway.

Ari fluttered to a flower closer to Reedan.

The Vasro spy pulled out his hand cloth, wiped saliva from the corners of his mouth, and stuffed it back into his pocket. After straightening his uniform shirt, he headed down the path and out into the passage.

Ari flew to a bush near the hide-away, confirmed Elf and Rethson were still there, and sent Elf a telepathic message to wait. Flying to a tall tree, she watched Reedan sneak back into the Plantitarium and begin a stealthful climb up the central path. Aware that patience was the key to her safety and the boys', she waited.

A grumbled string of profanities accompanied Reedan's descent from level two. At the entryway, he turned, his frustrated gaze scanning the Plantitarium from top to bottom. "I know you three meet here. Question is where?" He left, shaking his head and muttering his frustration.

Ari mentally followed his progress until he reached the T-lift, then flew to the wall and, at ground level, passed into the hide-away and shifted. Taking a breath, she prepared to share what she had learned with Elf and Rethson.

○○

On the Plains of Cârthea, Raiherr sat next to Carûtix in *Toneer*, scrambling to find a balance between himself and his mental partner. The longer their competitive minds remain entangled, the harder Raiherr found it to separate himself from the demi-god.

A tense silence in the small spacecraft's control center made Raiherr's nostrils flare. Why did I ever agree to take *Toneer* on a recon flight? The answer came as a mental jerk that left his head throbbing. Raiherr scowled and regarded the being next to him. "Don't play mind games with me, Carûtix. We almost crashed because you tried to take control of the ship. Either we agree I'm the captain, or I will never take you up again."

The demi-god growled, unfastened his seat restraints, and came to his feet, dragging Raiherr with him. "I need some fresh air."

They stood outside in the dome-dim light, their thoughts intermingling and their nervous systems fighting for cohesion and control. The most disturbing thing was their inability to move as individuals. If one moved, so did the other. Raiherr fought to keep his thoughts under control. Beside him, he could feel his mental partner dealing with the same desire.

The demi-god frowned. "Until we figure out a way to unlink our mental bonding, we'd better make it work for us." Inspiration flickered into doubt on his expressive face. "Don't suppose your SorTech could break the bond?"

Raiherr didn't bother to speak; just let his thoughts answer.

Carûtix growled. "Talk to me! I can't unravel the threads of conversation in our combined thoughts."

"Sure, all powerful god, I'll talk out loud." His brain burned. He let out a yelp. "What the—" An attempt to look his partner in the eye brought him up short, his gaze fixed on the demi-god's broad back. Gritting his teeth, he faced forward. From the corner of his eye, he glimpsed the scowl twisting Carûtix's mouth. "Guess we have to face the same direction."

An angry response vibrated through his mind. "Answer the question, Vasro."

Raiherr shrugged. "I don't know if the SorTechory Box can undo what a VarTerel may have done. All we can do is ask Callum to try. Shall we walk to camp?"

"You set the pace, Raiherr. My body will follow your mental instructions."

"It's not that far from here." He focused straight ahead and walked toward the clearing.

Carûtix walked beside him, his body matching him step for step. Midway across the plain, the demi-god heaved a heavy sigh and came to a stop. "I hate this!"

Raiherr tipped his head and almost laughed when demi-god's head tipped at the same angle. Ego flared. Jerking his head straight, he ran a step and crashed to the ground.

A powerful hand on his shoulder kept him from standing. Carûtix pressed harder, then yanked him to his feet and jerked him around to face him. "Do not forget, Vasro, I'm a deity, and you're a mere human. Either we work together, or I will end our mental tangle permanently."

Raiherr stood motionless, his entire focus on his mental race to stay ahead of his mind-fellow. A slap across the face caught him by surprise. He opened his mouth to speak and snapped it shut.

Carûtix held up a hand. Raiherr's hand mirrored it. When the demi-god made a fist. Raiherr's fingers mimicked each movement. The god's muscular hand lowered. Raiherr's attempt not to lower his failed.

"Do you understand, Raiherr, that I can make you do as I want? I am a Deity."

A mind-shattering tremor quaked through Raiherr's mind. Opposite him, Carûtix's eyes bulged; a shudder shook him from head to foot. A smile of understanding curved Raiherr's mouth when his body remained unmoving.

"It appears, demi-god, that your powers are waning. I suggest we call a truce and work together. We are mind-fellows, after all. Let's make good use of our combined knowledge and our combined strength while we can. Come on, let's find Callum. Who knows…The Box might undo what binds us together."

Carûtix's non-verbal affirmative navigated the mind meld. Raiherr set the pace for their hike to the campsite.

※

Brie stared into Mittkeer's endless night, plans like a map in her mind. She turned to Nimah and ShioCáni. "I believe it is best that your presence on the island remains a secret until you're needed. Gar will go with you to the Labyrinth Cavern. We will communicate through him. Thorlu and Den, please prepare to find Hossela. Tell him the *Surgentin* is no longer in this solar system. If you can, persuade him to join the Queen's Quest. Torgin and Esán, you will come with me to ground Raiherr's jumper craft. Once that is done, we will begin the job of neutralizing Carûtix and the remaining Vasro."

ShioCáni's honey-gold eyes studied her. "You will require my help to unbind that which has been mentally bonded together. Nimah is the only one who can control Carûtix. We will join you when the time is right."

As the Goddess of Harmony clasped Gar's hand, Nimah touched the boy's shoulder. He nodded at Brie. "Please, VarTerel AsTar, release us from Mittkeer into the Labyrinth Cavern."

Musette's tourmaline glow surrounded them, Mittkeer's night sky opened, and they vanished. Stars and universal darkness reformed, enclosing those remaining in a globe of silent beauty.

Thorlu's gaze moved from the starlit vista to rest on her face. "Den and I need to go. We will find Hossela. I'll keep you informed." He held out his staff.

Den clasped it and nodded.

The two men vanished.

Esán moved to her side. "Are you ready?"

She raised her staff. "Torgin, we will arrive on Neul Isle in the forest near *Toneer*. If our mind-fellows are absent, enter the ship and do what must be done. Esán will go with you in case you require assistance. I'll keep watch."

Looking relieved, Torgin moved closer. "Thanks for anticipating my needs. I already know I'll want Esán's help." He touched her arm. "I'm ready when you are."

Trees and mossy ground took the place of Mittkeer's timelessness. After a brief mental scan, Brie sent her staff into hiding and looked at Torgin. "All clear. I'll be watching from the treetops. Our duo is at the Vasro camp. If they head back this way, I'll let you know." A quick shift to a warbler and she alighted on a leafy branch. Below her, Torgin and Esán talked in low voices and then walked to the edge of the forest. A moment later, they teleported into the ship.

Alert for any changes on the plains, Brie's wee warbler waited.

Thorlu and Den materialized in the small, wooded area bordering the San Crúil River. Shifting to fire eagles, they followed the river to the rocky ridge at the far end of the Vasro campsite. In a gully at the bottom of the ridge, Hossela's small craft, camouflaged by tree branches, cut and placed over and around it, sat in the dimness, its beacon off and entry hatch closed.

After a brief telepathic discussion, Den kept watch while Thorlu shaped a warbler and flew closer. A subtle mental scan found Hossela pacing in the confined space. His thoughts, though jumbled, provided a glimpse of his growing frustration.

Landing beneath a rocky outcropping, Thorlu shaped his human form. Den's fire eagle alighted on the ground close by and also shifted to Human. Together, they approached the spacecraft.

Before they had covered half the distance, the entry hatch opened and the Pheet Adolan Klutarse stepped out, a weapon leveled at them. Steel-hard eyes moved from Thorlu to Den and back. "I suggest you retreat faster than you arrived."

Thorlu studied him with interest. "You and I met as much younger men, Hossela. Then, you worked for Skultar Rados. Now his brother, Karlsut Sorda, is you controller. I bring news of him and the *Surgentin*. I am happy to share it..." He glanced around. "...but not out here."

Hossela examined both men as though he viewed them through a magnifying lens. "Am I correct that you are neither one a Vasro?"

Again, Thorlu took the lead. "I am Thorlu Tangorra, and this is Den Zironho. We are neither one Vasro."

Hossela lowered the weapon. "Thorlu Tangorra..." His dark eyes burned with curiosity. "You and your companion may enter my spacecraft—but only if you swear not to destroy it or me."

"Destroying you is not our goal. We desire to share information and make you an offer."

The Klutarse slipped his weapon into a side-holster. "Wait here." He entered the ship, and after a brief absence, returned to the entry hatch. "Please join me."

Inside the craft, Hossela led them to the control bridge, where three seats swiveled to face one another. Suspicion glinted in hard, steel-black eyes. "Share what you came to share." The clipped words were sharp with tension.

Den caught Thorlu's eye and began. "We are here to inform you the *Surgentin* is being removed from this solar system and will not be returning, which, I believe, frees you from your obligation to Karlsut Sorda. Correct?"

Hossela's jaw tightened. A tattooed hand fisted and then relaxed. "How do I know you aren't lying?"

Thorlu spoke up. "You won't know until we remove the dome. We've never trusted each other, Hossela, but I'm willing to remedy that if you'll trust me."

"What will I gain by playing your game?"

Counting on his fingers, Thorlu provided him with a list. "You will be rid of Sorda and his Vasro. You will gain my respect and that of Den and our powerful companions. Most important...you'll be free to choose your own destiny, not one handed to you by another."

Curiosity slowly replaced suspicion in the face of the Pheet Adolan Klutarse. "What power do you hold I do not, Thorlu Tangorra?"

Thorlu smiled. "I am a VarTerel."

Hossela's eye widened. "A VarTerel! How can that be? You are a MasTer's Mocendi, a traitor to the Order of Esprow."

"I grew up and followed my heart rather than the greed and destructive nature of others. The Mocendi League is dissolving into groups of wanna-be DiMensioner's like the Vasro...not my destiny. Is it yours?"

A slight shake of his head brought Hossela's gaze to rest on Den. "And you, Den Zironho? You worked for Skultar Rados at the penal colony on TaSneach. You helped the Girl with the Matriarch's Eyes escape his control. Why would I trust you?"

Den shrugged. "Perhaps because, like you, I removed myself from his ironclad grip. As a result, I discovered who I truly am. If you choose to join us in our battle against Raiherr and his Vasro, perhaps you, too, will be free to pursue your own destiny."

Hossela glanced from Thorlu to Den. "Who are you, really?"

"I am the oldest son of Rayn and Relevart. From them, I have inherited many talents to help us defeat our enemies and free Neul Isle."

"Why do you care about Neul Isle? It's just a tiny place on an insignificant planet."

"We are here with our companions at the request of the Sun Queen of the Spéire Solar System to assist in her personal quest to rid Neul Isle of its enemies and their dome." Den cocked his head. "I believe you know of her power?"

"I do. But why would I help her, or you, for that matter?"

Thorlu pursed his lips. "You are an intelligent man. I would hope, Hossela, you understand that by joining the Queen's Quest, you will claim the freedom to be the man you have the potential of becoming—the freedom to choose what you do and where you go. Karlsut will no longer own you. Give it some thought. Den and I will await your decision outside."

"And if I choose to remain faithful to my controller, what then?"

Thorlu and Den rose. "We'll decide if that time comes." Thorlu touched Den's shoulder and teleported, accompanied by Hossela's gasp of surprise.

31
El Aperdisa

Jem waited outside Henrietta's quarters, hat in hand. The Commander had sent him with information for the Universal VarTerel. When the entry hatch opened, Henrietta studied him through her amethyst-rimmed spectacles.

"Aero Technician Taisley, how nice to see you. Please come in."

Once inside, she lead him to her sitting area, placed a hand on his arm, and with a wave of her other hand created holograms of them sitting with Gar's terrier, Spyglass, between them. The instant the image solidified, they teleported to the restricted area in the ship's Holographic Center.

In an undertone, she said. "Remain Jem." Her magnified eyes squinted into the distance. "I have important news to share. You are to pass this information along to Zak and Rily. Tell Zak he is to leak it to Nesen and share that the supposed source is Laris Rosar, whom we have discovered is Raiherr's spy on board *El Aperdisa*. Commander Odnamo has him under surveillance."

Jem inhaled. "What's the news?"

She removed her spectacles and tapped them against her palm. Tap, tap...tap, tap... The specs vanished and her focus switched to him. "We have received word that the High God of War and Peace in the Spéire Solar System has corralled Karlsut and his ship, *Surgentin*. The spacecraft is being escorted from the solar system with the warning that should it ever return, the High King's troops will confiscate the craft and imprison the crew for life. Nesen and Reedan are Karlsut's men. I look forward to hearing how they take the news. Tell Zak to be careful." She handed him a small, flesh-colored disc. "Give this to him. It will alert us if he is in trouble." She pursed her lips. "You need to return to the bridge."

Jem shook his head as they arrived in her quarters, and the holograms vanished. Henrietta escorted him to the entry hatch and bid him good turning. A few chron-clicks later, he arrived on the bridge, reported to the commander, and logged out for mid-turning meal.

Rily and Zak awaited him at the mess hall. Soon they all sat, eating the excellent meal prepared by *El Aperdisa*'s chef and his staff. Small talk accompanying the meal was light and filled with jokes and laughter until, on cue, Rily made a snide remark about Zak.

Taking a calming breath, Zak rose. "I have work to do, so if you'll excuse me." He picked up his tray, deposited it at the dish cleaning unit, and left. In the passageway, he encountered Reedan, who scowled his dislike and dodged past him.

Zak continued to the T-lift. Riley and Jem would meet him in the Plantitarium following evening meal. Via their conversation, Jem had let them know he had things to share. Zak smiled. What he knew sounded like a light-hearted conversation was filled with code words and metaphors.

Zak frowned. "Hope his news is good news."

At the end of his watch, Zak logged out and left engineering by a side entrance. A hand on his shoulder brought him up short.

Reedan stepped in front of him. "Going to meet your fellow spies?"

Zak raised a pale brow. "No, are you?"

The man's expression froze. "What you talking about?"

"Takes a spy to know one, right?" Zak kept his expression serious.

Reedan sputtered and raised a fist.

Zak started to laugh. "Can't take a joke, Reed." He gave him a gentle punch on the arm. "Hey, you hungry? I was just headed to the mess hall."

Suspicion registered on the man's sharp, swarthy features. His high brow knit into tight lines; his hooded, brown eyes squinted above a puckered mouth. A full body shake brought with it a soft laugh. "Well, Zak, you got me! Let's go get a meal." Laughing softly, he started down the passageway.

Zak fell in beside him. "Did you hear the gossip going around engineering?"

Reedan stuck the tip of his tongue through the space left by a missing front tooth. "You mean the stuff about the Head Engineer? She's one smart lady. All said and done, the rumors are just that." He chuckled.

They strolled along, sharing jokes and more rumors until they reached the mess hall. Reedan clapped him on the back. "You're alright, Zak! I forgot. I gotta meeting. How about mid-turning meal tomorrow?"

Zak grinned. "Sounds good. See you at work in the morning."

Reedan waved and trotted off down the passageway as Nesen round the slight curve from the T-lift and strolled to his side.

"Hi there, Zak. Was that Reedan hurrying away?"

"Yep. Said he had a meeting."

Nesen raised a brow. "Busy man. Would you like to join me for a bite?"

Zak swallowed an excuse and smiled. "Sure thing."

Nesen returned the smile and led the way to the chow line.

Zak followed, filled his plate and carried his loaded tray to the table. Out of the corner of his eye, he saw Rily organizing colorful desserts on the chow line. Jem was nowhere in sight. *Can't wait to learn what's up.*

The mind-fellows entered the Vasro camp, side-by-side in matched step. Raiherr braked to an abrupt halt. Carûtix shouted and stumbled to his knees, pulling Raiherr with him. The demi-god's muttered profanities chimed in Raiherr's mind as they both clambered to their feet.

Carûtix bent to brush off his dirt-covered knees.

Raiherr scowled while his mind directed his body to brush the filth from his pant legs. A tangle of thoughts in his mind steadied into the demi-god's frustrated words. "You ever do that again, Raiherr, and you'll regret it."

Ignoring his mind-fellow, Raiherr surveyed the camp, and frowned. Two men lounged on their sleeping mats. The only one doing anything useful was Callum, who bent over The Box, his concentration total.

"Lazy bunch." Carûtix's mental sneer felt like a gut punch.

"It's a waiting game, Carûtix. The one who counts is at work." He walked toward the SorTech, the demi-god matching him step for step. Raiherr's sideways glance alerted Carûtix to stop.

Callum turned. His bushy gray brows shot up. "What's going on?" He tipped his head back and looked closer. "Why are you two in a mental trap together?"

Raiherr explained what had happened and took a breath. "Can The Box undo what a VarTerel and a demi-god have done?"

The SorTech studied The Box, reached out to touch a switch, lowered his hand, and shook his head. "I believe anything I try will only compound the problem. You must find the VarTerel and force her to undo the bonding."

A verbal growl followed by an angry step forward took Raiherr off guard and left him stumbling. Carûtix threw a punch that sent Callum plunging backward and the mind-fellows fighting to stay upright. The SorTech collided with The Box and sent it crashing to the ground. He landed in an unconscious heap beside it.

Above the clearing, the dome sizzled into nothing. An ozone-scented breeze wafted around the campsite. The Vasro scrambled to their feet, hands protecting their eyes from the blazing glare of the sun's light. A bird's startled whistle shrilled. Small rodents scurried over the ground to hide in the tall grass.

Raiherr started toward Callum. Carûtix's solid stance and alarmed shout stopped him. Swinging around, he stared in horror at the sparks igniting around The Box. Flames crackled behind the broken front panel, producing an explosion. Overhead, the dome reformed, its shimmery opaqueness gleaming, and then, like paint from a detonated container, splotches of black covered the dome's interior surface and flowed one into the other. A shadow-filled dimness settled over the camp and the island trapped beneath the dome.

Raiherr shouted. "Zorin, light the fire." He focused his thoughts. "Carûtix, you have just caused the destruction of the only thing that can free us from lifelong captivity on this island. Now, help me with Callum."

The sound of a faint sizzling snap switched his attention to the pile of wood and wires—all that remained of the SorTechory Box. He groaned and looked down at Callum, the only man who could fix it—if it was fixable at all.

◉ ◉

On *Toneer*, Torgin secured the safety panel over the jumper craft's engine compartment while Esán returned the borrowed tools to their locker. A mental review of the completed job made him smile. *The detailed schematics Esán uploaded to my memory provided a simple yet effective way to ground the jumper craft, one Raiherr will not suspect.*

Esán joined him. "Good work, Torg. When it's time to reverse it, it will only take a couple of chron-clicks."

Torgin grinned. "We're a good team. Time to—"

Brie flashed into being, her chestnut-brown eyes wide with alarm. "Something's happened to The Box. Look outside." She licked her lips and clutched Esán's hand while Torgin opened the entrance hatch.

Blue sky and sunshine met them as they stepped from the craft onto the moss covered ground. The dome reforming, the sound of an explosion, and black splotches covering the underside of the dome froze them in place. The splatters merging and the ensuing darkness casting deep shadows over the island urged them back inside.

Torgin secured the hatch. "We need to know what has happened at Raiherr's campsite." He pressed his lips into a firm line, gave a slight shake of the head, and faced his friends. "Do we stay together or..." He looked at Brie.

"We definitely stay together." She tapped her lips and turned to Esán. "You know this area the best. Shape your kestrel and take the lead. We'll follow in our fire eagle forms. When we reach the camp, Torgin and I will land to see what we can discover. You continue to Hossela's spacecraft, Esán. It's still behind the rocky ridge. Thorlu and Den are there. Find them. If Hossela is giving them trouble, put him into a sound sleep and bring Den and Thorlu back here.

Esán frowned. "And if Hossela is accepting the Queen's Quest as his?"

"Trust your instincts. Torgin, open the hatch. "We need to move."

Shifting, they flew one by one into the eerie murkiness enshrouding the land beneath the dome. Esán's kestrel, its keen sight helping to navigate the way over the grassy plains to the Vasro camp, led the way. Two fire eagles followed. When they reached the Vasro camp, the kestrel flew high overhead while the fire eagles landed in a tall, thickly leafed tree.

Fixing a golden eagle eye on the chaos highlighted by the flickering campfire caused Torgin's reddish neck feathers to spike. On the ground below, Callum lay unconscious next to the mangled wood and wiring that had once been The Box.

Torgin's senses scrambled. His youthful insecurity raised its head. *We could be trapped here forever.* Fire-brown feathers ruffled. *Can I fix it? Rebuild it?*

Brie's beak clicked. A telepathic message whispered in his mind. *"Remember how far you've come, Torgin Whalend. You will fix it."*

Confidence took the place of his growing panic. *We've got a lot to accomplish. Sure wish Esán, Den, and Thorlu were here.*

Next to him, Brie's eagle changed into a warbler. *"Let's go to them."*

Following her lead, he shifted to the tiny, creamy beige bird. Both lifted into flight. Sharp eyes peering through deep shadows, Torgin followed her between the trees bordering the end of the clearing and landed beside her on a rock-covered ridge. Shaping Human, they joined Esán where he stood, his gaze darting from the flat, black denseness of the dome to Hossela's shadowed spacecraft in the gully below.

Torgin experienced a wave anticipation. *Will the Klutarse join the quest to save Neul Isle?*

༺ ༻

Thorlu and Den exchanged startled glances as the dome shimmered into nothing and a sea breeze rustled through the nearby bushes.

Hossela exited his spacecraft and stared up at the dome. "It's gone!" He laughed. "I can leave!" He started back toward entry hatch, looked up, and swore. "Now what's happening?" He winced. "It's reforming. What the—"

An explosion splattered black splotches over the dome's curved underside. The three men gaped as they merged together into a murky blackness.

Den broke the stunned silence. "Something's happened to the SorTechory Box. What do we do now?"

Thorlu urged both men into the spacecraft and faced Hossela. "Either you are with us or against us. Which is it?"

The Pheet Adolan Klutarse moved to the open hatch and peered into the encroaching shadows. When he turned, he regarded Den. "I can go it alone…" His brow furrowed. "…a bad idea in this situation." He refocused on Thorlu. "Or I can join the Queen's Quest." After a pause to take another look outside, he faced Thorlu. "I have one question. Once we rid Neul Isle of its enemies, will I be free to go my own way?"

Thorlu met Hossela's direct gaze with a steady, open gaze of his own. "You will have complete autonomy to do as you choose. I should warn you, however, that returning to Karlsut Sorda as his spy and Klutarse may not be the best idea."

The tension in Hossela's homely features relaxed. "I have no desire to rejoin Sorda or his brother. When the quest is complete, you and I will talk further about my options. Right now, I am yours to command. I wish to help free Neul Isle and Soputto from Raiherr and his DiMensioner wannabes."

Thorlu offered his hand, palm up. "I welcome you as a comrade-in-arms."

Hossela touched his palm to it and turned to Den. "I am honored to work with you both. What's first?"

The whisper of small wings preceded the appearance of Brie. Hossela gasped. Den grinned his relief.

Thorlu nodded. "Good to see you, Brie. May I present Hossela, our new comrade? Hossela, this is Brielle AsTar, my fellow VarTerel."

Brie gazed up at the Klutarse. Hossela's direct gaze received a smile. "Welcome to the Queen's Quest. We require all the help we can get."

He glanced toward the hatch. "Any idea what's happened to the dome?"

Brie told him what she and her friends had experienced and described the damage to the SorTechory Box.

A surge of concern brought a frown to Thorlu's face. "Is the damage to The Box permanent?"

Torgin stepped into the crowded craft. "It's not. I can fix it, but we have things to accomplish first. He regarded Hossela with interest. "I understand you've joined the quest. Welcome. I'm Torgin."

"Hello, Torgin." Hossela scanned the group. "Can we go somewhere else to make plans? This spacecraft is ill-equipped to handle so many people."

Thorlu glanced at Brie, received a nod and called his staff into being. "Gather around." He looked at Hossela. "We are about to ascend into Mittkeer. Be prepared to feel nauseous on entry."

The spacecraft blurred into stars, planets, and galaxies, glistening in the endless night. Hossela gulped and gripped his knees.

Torgin swallowed. "Think of something pleasant. It helps."

The Klutarse straightened and wiped his mouth with the back of his hand. Wide-eyed, he scanned the unending universal beauty surrounding them. He shook his head. "I never expected to visit Mittkeer."

Thorlu chuckled. "Neither did I. It is beautiful, isn't it?" Seriousness cloaked him. "Before we make plans, Brie, where is Esán?"

"He's keeping watch at the Vasro camp." She squinted into the distance. "Right now, the mind-fellows are arguing. Esán says the Vasro are panicking. Callum regained consciousness for only a moment and is out again. Torgin, please share your ideas, so we can return to Neul Isle."

Without hesitation, Torgin began. "First, we neutralize the Vasro and the demi-god. To do so, we'll require help from the Goddess of Harmony." After a quick explanation for Hossela's benefit, he continued. "Neutralizing Raiherr's men is next on our list." He looked from Hossela to Thorlu. "I think you are the best to accomplish this. Since Callum may not be able to reconstruct The Box, we'll collect the pieces and take them some place safe. Since I have worked on it before, I believe I can fix it."

Hossela frowned. "And if you can't...?"

Torgin cocked his head and smiled. "If I can't fix it, I'll build a new one, or at least something similar that will accomplish our task."

Thorlu listened to Torgin with a slight smile. *You continually amaze me, Torgin Whalend.*

32
Neul Isle

Esán's kestrel perched on a sturdy branch, peering through shadows that seemed almost alive. Rising and falling, lengthening and shortening, they created an eerily dramatic backdrop for the panicked-fear permeating the Vasro camp.

Zorin Sedrin, Raiherr's second in command, stood in front of the mind-fellows, his expression unbelieving. "Stop playing around. We need to help Callum, or we will never leave this island."

Carûtix sneered and started to step forward. Raiherr appeared to resist, gave up, and moved with the demi-god.

Sedrin scowled at one man and then the other. "I said—stop—playing around." He shoved Carûtix backward.

The mind-fellows both stumbled, fought for footing, and steadied. As though rehearsed, they snarled in unison, "Don't touch us again. Understand?"

The Vasro lieutenant gawked. "Are you for real? Holy Sedah!" He shuffled backward, turned, and scurried to stand with Dulno, who gaped wide-eye with shocked fear.

Raiherr touched the demi-god's muscular forearm.

Carûtix pressed his lips into a tense line, nodded, and stared straight ahead.

The Vasro leader spoke in his solo voice. "Zorin and Dulno, when Carûtix and I return, we expect to find Callum working on The Box with you at his side." His voice grew hard. "No more sitting by the fire complaining. If Callum doesn't fix The Box, none of us are ever leaving this island."

Raiherr gave his mind-fellow a sign. They turned in unison and walked from the clearing onto the plains. Neither looked left nor right, but stared straight ahead at what Esán knew was their goal, the jumper craft, *Toneer*.

Torn between leaving The Box unattended and following the mind-fellows, Esán forced a moment of mental stillness. Bobbing his kestrel head, he ruffled his feathers and gripped the branch more firmly.

Below him, Dulno knelt beside Callum. Zorin joined him and gave the SorTech a shake. A faint moan and the slight twitch of a hand were the only signs the man lived.

Zorin slipped a hand under Callum's head, withdrew it, and stared at his blood-soaked palm. "He's hurt bad, Dulno. What are we gonna do?"

While the men debated, Esán tuned his mental acuteness to Mittkeer. Satisfaction ruffled his neck feathers when the branch next to him dipped and steadied under the weight of a fire eagle. Torgin's telepathic *"hello"* filled his mind. A message from Thorlu alerted him that he and Hossela were in place and ready to deal with the Vasro.

Esán affirmed he'd received their message and took flight. Kestrel wings carried him high overhead. Wing-stroke by wing-stroke, he circle the plains, monitoring the mind-fellows steady march. A breeze as soft as a baby's sigh wafted high above the plains. Carûtix signaled Raiherr to stop. The demi-god scanned the arched top of the dome, shook his head, and motioned the Vasro toward the jumper craft.

Another circle brought Esán to the ground in human form next to Brie, where she stood well back in the forest glade. She clasped his hand and pulled him even deeper into shadowy trees. With her head leaning against his shoulder, she whispered. "Gar and Nimah will arrive soon. Stay here and wait for them. I will keep watch near *Toneer*."

He released her hand and wrapped his arms around her. "Take care, VarTerel." He kissed the top of her head before stepping back as she shaped a warbler and flew up through the forest canopy. Shaking away his desire to be at Brie's side, he shifted to the kestrel and flew to a high branch to await Nimah and Gar.

Gar sat on his sleep-mat in the alcove he shared with Nimah deep in the Labyrinth Cavern. Glowing ember spectacles perched on his nose magnified his narrowed eyes. *Something has changed on Neul Isle.* A frown tugged at the corners of his mouth. *I gotta find out what.*

A man's silhouetted figure blocked the opening to the alcove. Nimah squatted down to look him in the eye. "I see the queen is alerting you, too. ShioCáni has already departed for the Plains of Cârthea." He stood and offered a hand.

Gar took it and climbed to his feet. His eyes rounded. "Nimah, it's La."

The Luna Moth landed on Nimah's shoulder. Moments later, she fluttered to Gar's, brushed her wing against his dark skin, and vanished.

He caressed his cheek. "Something's wrong, right?"

Nimah nodded. "Someone damaged The Box. Come, you and I are to meet ShioCáni at the Vasro jumper craft. I have informed Dri Adoh we are leaving. He will wait to hear from us before he allows the K'iin to return to their village."

Gar sent his specs into hiding. "I'm ready."

The Sun Queen's heir took his hand. "Hold on tight. I will take us first to the mouth of the cavern. Then, we must travel on Thēago, the Deities' Wind."

The cavern's mouth opened wide. They landed and stepped into the dark shadows covering the land.

Gar gasped. "The dome is black. Let's hurry!"

Nimah placed his hands on Gar's shoulder.

> *"Thēago Winds, I call you forth*
> *To carry us higher and further north.*
> *Lift us up on your currents of air*
> *And carry us to the ship, Toneer."*

Whispers of moving air swirled around them, growing stronger by the moment. It scooped them up, and, following the curved side of the murky black dome, carried them toward the Plains of Cârthea.

Gar glanced up at the Sun Queen's heir and grinned. "You sure are good, Nimah."

He returned the grin. "We are almost there."

Shadowy terrain flowed beneath them. The absence of birds and the thick hush sent a chill up Gar's spine. His spectacles appeared on his nose. He settled the temples over his ears and swallowed. Below them, Raiherr and Carûtix marched toward the jumper craft. The demi-god yanked the Vasro to a stop and put a finger to his lips. Dark eyes searched the plains, then lifted to the dome.

Nimah squeezed Gar's hand. The whisper of Thēago's wind ceased. Solid ground under his feet and a forest of tall trees surrounding him released a wave of relief that almost made Gar dizzy. Squinting through his lenses, he peered between tree trunks and over bushes.

Not far away, the shadowed form of *Toneer* took shape. The murmur of kestrel wings stopped nearby. Esán materialized. Silent footsteps carried him to stand beside Nimah.

A startled shout cut through the hushed silence like a scythe swung in anger. Nimah urged Gar and Esán to the edge of the forest. Carûtix and Raiherr, fists flying, tried to hit each other. Their loud voices blaming the other for their predicament.

Beside Gar, Esán stiffened. Only Nimah's hand on his arm kept him from dashing into the open.

Gar's dark frames glowed like embers. His eyes gleamed with fire-opal light. The queen's heir knelt. Gar's throat contracted.

Abellona spoke through him, her words soft but clear. "Prepare for the ultimate battle to begin. I shield your hearts and minds and those who fight alongside you. Stand tall and true to our quest."

Gar pressed a hand to his heart. His specs vanished into hiding.

Nimah rose to his feet and faced Esán. "The Seeds call, Esán Efre. You will know when the time is right." He drew Gar to his side. "Mamai has asked that you join Torgin at the Vasro Camp. It is important that you are by his side. Let us know when you are safely there."

A through-the-mouth exhale puffed Gar's cheeks. "Be safe." He shaped his fire eagle and flew to the bank of the river, followed it to Rina Island, then banked inland. When the trees surrounding the Vasro camp came into view, he circled around to the far side and landed in a tree close to the clearing. Taking stock of his surroundings, he picked out Thorlu and Hossela's hiding place, pinpointed Torgin's position, and alighted by his side.

"Hi, Torg. The Sun Queen sent me."

One golden eagle eye focused his direction. "Glad to see you, cousin. Stay close."

Gar bobbed his eagle head in reply and surveyed the Vasro camp. The sight of The Box, broken and battered beneath them, made his blood run cold.

The Sun Queen stood in the Holographic Laboratory studying the three-dimensional hologram of Neul Isle. The magnifying lens hovered over the murky blackness of the dome covering most of the island. Across the way, her holographic specialist worked with total concentration on refining the hologram.

The memory of their first meeting surfaced. Her assistant entered her personal suite with an orphaned boy of nine sun cycles in tow. He stood in front of her, his pale blond curls tumbling over his forehead and his intense aqua eyes shining with defiance. Their brief conversation confirmed her instinctual desire to help him. *I liked you right from the start, Shācor. Your acute intelligence and divergent mindset intrigued me.*

She beckoned the holographic specialist to join her. "Shācor, please adjust the control sensors so I can see through the dome."

"Of course, My Lady." He crossed to a paneled area containing his tactile station, tapped several glowing lights, and returned. Swiveling the huge lens to a new position, he touched the controls on its obsidian frame. The dome's murky darkness shimmered into crystal clarity.

With a smile, the specialist said, "The lens is adjusted to respond to your thoughts, My Queen."

Abellona smiled. "Thank you, Shācor. Please remain by my side."

A moment of consideration and a clear thought focused the lens on the Plains of Cârthea, where her nephew, Carûtix, and Raiherr Yencara hiked toward the jumper craft. She scanned the surrounding area and discovered Nimah and Esán hiding in the trees near *Toneer*.

At the Vasro camp, Brie exercised her power in Mittkeer to release Torgin in fire eagle form to guard The Box. Thorlu and Hossela now hid close by. Brie shaped a warbler, exited the Land of Time on Rina Island, and flew along the river to the forest. Shifting to Human, she met with Esán. At her request, he joined Nimah and her warbler flew nearer the jumper craft, where ShioCáni, also in warbler form awaited her arrival.

Abellona studied each member of the group. Her attention fixed on Gar's fire eagle as he flew to join Torgin. She pursed her lips, then nodded. *I have a special job for you, Garon Anaru.*

She prepared to leave. "Shācor, I must go, but I will check with you later. Please remain here. If anything changes, summon me at once."

"As you wish, My Lady." The tall, lean specialist escorted her to the door and returned to the holographic platform.

Hurrying to her private suite, Abellona summoned Ferêlith, her personal assistant, who arrived almost immediately and greeted her mistress with a curtsy. "You have need of me?"

"I require Aahana to join me. Tell her I have a special assignment for her."

Abellona smiled as Ferêlith hurried away. *I am lucky to have such an excellent assistant.* She moved to the balcony windows and stared out at her realm of Chadēta Apól, her fire-opal eyes narrowed in thought. Plans formed and faded until she settled on one she knew was perfect.

A soft knock announced her daughter's arrival. Aahana entered and joined her by the window. "You have need of me, Mamai?"

A wave of concern kept the Sun Queen quiet. A long moment passed.

Aahana touched her arm. "Mamai, are you alright?"

Abellona drew her daughter down beside her on an elegant brocade sofa. "I have a dangerous errand for you, one that I would prefer to do myself, but I cannot leave Shió Ridu. I am watched closely and almost got caught a short time ago when I snuck away." She touched the fire opal broach hanging on a black and gold chain and inhaled. "I have let it be known you are visiting the Council of Deities, so no one will miss you." Again, she grew quiet.

Aahana clasped her hand. "Mamai, I am your daughter. I can and will accomplish any task you set forth. Please tell me what you need."

Abellona released her fears and said, "I require you to summon Kat, the

Goddess of Small Creatures. The SorTechory Box on Neul Isle is broken..." She frowned. "...literally shattered. Torgin is our only hope of removing the dome. He has the knowledge to fix it but cannot do so on the island. You and Kat are to bring him and his young cousin, Garon, here. Our holographic lab has everything required to fix The Box, or, indeed, to build a new one." She pointed at a black tourmaline and ruby chest known as a Deity's Coffer sitting next to the side table. "Tell Torgin he must bring all the pieces with him in this chest. It is known as *Cónra*, and the word to call it forth is "Parepā".

Aahana's gaze held a question.

"What is making you uneasy, daughter?"

"I understand the dome has undergone several changes. What if we cannot penetrate it?"

Abellona came to her feet. "Come, let us go to the Laboratory, so you can see the lay of the land. Also, we will ask Shācor if the Deities' Wind will navigate the changes."

When they arrived, Shācor met them at the door and ushered them inside. He nodded at Aahana and bowed to his queen.

Abellona explained the reason for their visit and drew her daughter forward. "Please answer Aahana's questions so she is well-prepared for the work ahead."

Aahana studied the island covered by the crystal clear dome, then looked up at Shācor. "Please show me the dome now and what it is like underneath."

The holographic specialist moved to the control panel. The dome glinted muddy black. Another adjustment showed the shadowy world beneath it.

"Thank you, Shācor. That helps." Aahana glanced at the door. "I called for Kat to join us, Mamai. She arrived in our shielded space and will be here any moment."

Abellona felt a surge of pride. Her youngest daughter's talent for leadership was proving to be stronger than she realized. A knock ushered Kat into the Laboratory. The queen stepped back to observe her daughter and niece.

Aahana introduced Kat to Shācor and explained the situation on Neul Isle. When Kat nodded her understanding, Aahana asked the specialist about the Deities' Wind."

He smiled. "I have already made certain the winds will carry you through the darkened dome." His gaze moved from one demi-goddess to the other.

"Please take care of each other." He bowed, moved to the panel, and turned his back to give them privacy.

Abellona spoke with quiet authority. "Aahana and Kat, it is time. Please put up personal wards and leave from the shielded space so your departure goes unnoticed. *Cónra* will be with you, though invisible until you call it forth." She walked with them to the door. "Alert me when you are ready to leave, and please, Aahana, beware. The mental crossover between Carûtix and the Vasro leader makes them both far more dangerous."

"Do not fear, Mamai. Kat and I will return as soon as we can with Torgin, Gar, and the pieces of The Box." Ward's shot up around them both. Aahana touched Kat's arm, and they vanished.

The Sun Queen returned to the holographic display and stared at the object of her quest draped in darkness and shadow.

33
El Aperdisa

Zak stood in the locker room next to the crew's quarters, pressing his broad shoulders against the wall. Two men hidden by a central panel spoke in soft, urgent tones. Zak recognized Reedan's raspy voice. The second, softer voice was strange to him. He shivered. *If they find me eavesdropping, it won't be pleasant.*

The tension between the men escalated as a third man joined them. Nesen's accented voice demanded answers. "What is so important you would summon me to the crew's locker room?"

The unknown man spoke up. "I have a message for you. It's too important to wait. I just—"

"Don't move and keep quiet," Nesen ordered. "I'll make sure we are alone."

Zak tiptoed to the men's personal space and stepped into a stall. When Nesen entered, he pushed the flusher, opened the stall door, and walked to the hand cleanser.

Nesen stopped next to him. "How long have you been hiding in there?"

Zak looked confused. "I'm not hiding anywhere, Nesen. I came in to use the space before I start my second watch. What's up?"

Nesen shrugged. "It's been a weird day. You seen Reedan anywhere?"

"I thought I recognized his voice on the other side of the partition, but...I had to go, so I came straight here. Have you looked around?"

"Listen, something's happened. I need to find out what. Stay here, and be quiet. In fact, hide in a stall. I'll let you know when it's safe."

Before Zak could answer, the Vasro spy left. Zak took a breath, stepped into the locker room, and tuned his hearing to listen.

"So, you ready to find out what's up?" Reedan's annoyance grated in every word.

Nesen appeared to ignore him and spoke to the third man. "Alright, Andro, what's so important you've risked discovery to come and share it?"

Gruffness edged the soft voice. "*Surgentin* is no longer in the Spéire Solar System, and all communications have stopped. Also, Raiherr has gone silent. One more thing...I discovered Laris is Raiherr's man. He's been trying to radio him. I heard him swearing at the transmitter when he thought he was alone."

Zak's quick intellect jumped into action. He sent a telepathic message to Torlan, his contact on the bridge, to alert Commander Odnamo.

Reedan's raised voice yanked him back to the situation at hand. "I warned you something was up. Now, what? If they got to Karlsut—"

"Shut your mouth. I can't think when you're yelling." Nesen's tone, more than his words, produced a tense silence. "Andro, get back to your post and—" Narrowed eyes and a sharp 'sh,' produced immediate silence. "We're about to have visitors. Act natural."

Zak slipped back into the stall in the personal space and held his breath.

Nesen entered, turned on a hand cleanser, and spoke in an undertone. "Zak, you there?"

Zak stuck his head out of the stall. "I'm here, sir."

"You been anywhere else?" The Vasro demanded.

"How could I leave without you knowing?" Zak stepped into the open and allowed puzzled curiosity to tint his features.

The door opened. A guard eyeballed them both. "Get out here. You're wanted for questioning. Come peacefully, and you can wait in the receiving room. Resist, and you can wait in a cell.

Nesen shrugged and led the way from the space. Andro and Reedan stood amidst a trio of guards. Reedan, rage apparent in his expression and his body language, looked ready to fight. Andro's pale face remained blank; his tight muscled body stiffened.

The leader of the six-man unit stepped into the passageway. Nesen and his guard followed. Reedan, with a guard on either side, went next. Andro and his guard stepped into the passage, with Zak and his guard bringing up the rear.

As they neared the T-lift, Reedan launched his full body weight into one guard, shoving him into the unit leader. Dodging around them both, while they scrambled to regain their balance, he sprinted along the passage. Two guards gave chase."

The leader turned a razor-sharp gaze on the remaining prisoners. "Your friend will be put in a cell. Your choice—join him or cooperate." When no one moved or spoke, he marched into the waiting T-lift, motioned them inside, and touched the sensor light.

Zak swallowed, glanced at his fellow spies, and stared at the floor. *Sure hope Reedan gets caught.*

Thorlu and Hossela hid in the dense trees bordering the Vasro campsite. A second fire eagle landing nearby alerted them it was time to move. A quick conference and Hossela slipped between trees and high brushes to hide on the opposite side of the camp. When he was in place, Thorlu teleported behind the two men, attempting to revive Callum.

Zorin Sedrin straightened and turned. Round eyes the color of a dry autumn leaf reflected surprise with a touch of fear. "Who in sedah are you?" A hand inched toward his holstered weapon.

Thorlu's don't-fool-around-with-me gaze flashed from Zorin's face to his hand. "I wouldn't touch that if I were you."

The Vasro's nostrils flared. "You gonna stop me?"

Dulno jumped to his feet. "Don't be an idiot, Zorin! Can't you see he's a VarTerel!"

Sedrin sneered. "Yah, right. I'll believe it when he takes my weapon from me."

Hossela stepped from the trees and walked to stand behind the Vasro lieutenant. "I believe, Zorin Sedrin, you would be wise to give me your weapon before the VarTerel loses his patience."

The Vasro jerked around. "How'd you get here?" He scowled. "You're spying for Karlsut Sorda, right? Too bad you got stuck here." He yanked his weapon from its holster and pointed it straight at Hossela's head.

Dulno edged backward, tripped over Callum's legs, and, with a stifled shriek, sprawled on the ground.

Thorlu cleared his throat. "Enough, Sedrin, give Hossela the weapon."

The Vasro laughed. "Not on your life. You get any closer, and he's dead."

Thorlu visualized his intent and narrowed his eyes.

Sedrin yelped as his weapon moved from aiming at the Klutarse to pointing straight at his own forehead. An attempt to move his arm wiped the anger from his thin-lipped mouth. Fear rose like a high tide, peaking in his bulging autumn-brown eyes. He spoke out of the side of his mouth. "I'll give it to you. Just let go of my arm."

Thorlu caught Hossela's eye. The Klutarse moved to stand by Dulno. Thorlu walked around to face Sedrin. "I will unfreeze your arm when and only when I have your weapon in my hand. If you so much as twitch, I'll put you to sleep for a very long time."

Sedrin spoke between clenched teeth. "I won't move."

Thorlu step forward and removed the weapon from his hand. After handing it to the Klutarse, he allowed Sedrin's arm to lower.

The Vasro glared. "You got my weapon. Now, let me move."

Thorlu grinned. "I'm sorry, Zorin, I don't have the power to release you."

Hossela chuckled, pulled Dulno to his feet, and marched him to stand back to back with his fellow Vasro. "I believe tying their hands behind them and lashing their wrists together will keep them occupied while we see what we can do for Callum."

While Hossela checked on the SorTech, Thorlu used his VarTerel's power to do as the Klutarse suggested. He then sat the two Vasro next to a tree, summoned a sturdy rope, and commanded it to bind the men to the trunk with a strong knot.

After putting them into a deep sleep, he gave himself a mental pat on the back and joined Hossela, where he knelt beside the unconscious SorTech. A quick check for any broken bones or life-threatening injuries showed nothing that concerned him. He held up a large rough rock. "Must have hit his head pretty hard on this. SorTech's lucky he didn't fracture his skull." Thorlu tossed the rock aside. "It left a nasty gash above his ear."

Hossela regarded him over the prone body. "Did you find anything that suggests why he is still unconscious?"

The sound of eagle wings filled the campsite. Thorlu mouthed the word "company". His gaze darted dome-ward.

A fire eagle landed beside them. Torgin materialized and studied the unmoving man. "Carûtix purposely shoved him and put him under a sleeping charm." He shook his head. "The demi-god doesn't want the dome lifted. I'm not sure why."

Thorlu stared into the distance. Torgin's statement prodded something illusive that had been bothering him. When it didn't jump to the forefront of his thoughts, he drew in a breath and let it go. *Whatever it is, it will surface at the right time.* He glanced beyond Torgin. "Where's Gar?"

"He's keeping watch. Something is bothering him as well. I'll check The Box. If you need me, call me."

Thorlu nodded, leaned closer to the SorTech, and touched his temple. Callum's eyes rolled beneath closed lids and then blinked open. He stared up through the shadowy darkness, then gulped several panted breaths. A portrait of tumultuous confusion, he curled into a ball and whimpered. Thorlu again leaned closer and touched his temple.

Sleep enfolded him. His body relaxed, and his panted breaths became regular.

Thorlu studied the prone SorTech. *I may not like you, but I'd never wish this for you.* A wave of sympathy washed over him as he climbed to his feet and crossed to where Torgin sorted through broken bits of the SorTechory Box.

From her perch near *Toneer*, Brie watched the mind-fellows hike across the grassy Plains of Cârthea in match-step, looking neither right nor left. The expression on their individual faces presented a striking contrast to the exact sameness of their stride, posture, and swing of the arms.

Raiherr's features broadcast a mix of emotions ranging from fear to desolation. In contrast, the demi-god wore a self-satisfied half-smile. Realization dawned. *Carûtix destroyed The Box on purpose.* Needing confirmation, Brie performed a stealthful mind probe. What she discovered made her leave her perch and land beside Nimah as Esán landed and shaped Human.

Nimah and Esán exchanged glances. Both men faced her, their expression mirroring her fears.

Nimah drew them further into the trees, took a breath, and shared what he had learned in an undertone. "My esteemed cousin believes as long as the dome remains in place, Neul Isle is his to claim as his domain. Raiherr's life depends on whether he does as my cousin directs. Carûtix does not want their memories untangled because the Vasro has information vital to his success as the Deity King of Neul Isle. We must separate them, but leave their knowledge intact."

The rustle of leaves preceded the appearance of ShioCáni. Urgency cloaked her. Her honey-gold gaze embraced the trio, then focused on the far side of the forest glade. A quick shift to warbler and she led the way between trees to a shadowy beach by the river. Shaping her true form, she waited for them to join her.

Covered by the sounds of water rushing to the sea, a quick conference took place. They conceived a solid plan. Nimah, who would play his role once the mind-fellows were again individuals, returned to warbler shape and flew back to keep watch.

A brief silence later, Brie, Esán, and ShioCáni flew back to the plains. As they approach *Toneer*, Esán and the Goddess of Harmony remained in warbler form and alighted at the top of a tree. Brie landed in human form at the edge of the woods behind the jumper craft. Key to their plan was her success at putting the mind-fellows into a deep sleep without their knowledge.

An angry shout interrupted her thoughts. In warbler form once again, she flew to a low-hanging branch and trained her warbler eyes on the fight taking place below her.

Carûtix, his muscular hand entangled in Raiherr's muddy-brown hair, drug the Vasro toward the ship and slammed his back against the fuselage. "You will do as I say, Yencara. Don't fight me or—"

Pain ripped across the Vasro's face. His mouth opened, then snapped shut. His fingers gripped the longish hair on the top of the demi-god's head. As his other fist came up under his mind-fellow's chin, Carûtix's elbow hit his jaw with a loud crack.

Anger raged, and fists flew.

Brie materialized a short distance away and recited:

> *Sleep, wrap these two within your depths*
> *Hold them firmly til a time—*

"What are you doing here, VarTerel?" Carûtix caught Raiherr by the arm and yanked him around to face Brie. "Don't say another word, or I will make certain you never speak—." A yawn tugged. He ground his teeth.

Beside him, Raiherr gulped a yawn-inspired breath and dropped to his knees.

While the sleep drunk demi-god jerked him to his feet, Brie intoned:

> *"Sleep, diffuse each warrior's rage;*
> *Place them in a timeless cage,*
> *Where they will dream of their returning*
> *As memories cease their tangled churning."*

A yawn stretched Raiherr's mouth wide.

Carûtix blinked and loosed a rage-filled howl that morphed into a full-blown yawn. Eyes tearing and another yawn tugging, he sank to the ground beside Raiherr.

Both bodies twitched and contorted as they fought to stay awake. Carûtix pushed himself to sitting, his teary gaze darting one way and then the other. Raiherr, his thoughts still entwined with his mind-fellow, followed suit. A joint whimper whispered as in unison, their eyes squeezed shut; their mouths stretched wide; and limp as wet sheets, they sank to the ground and slept.

With the last whimper, ShioCáni stepped from the trees and joined Brielle. "We must work quickly. I will take Carûtix; you work on Raiherr." She held out her hands. "Let us link our minds."

Brie clasped her hands and closed her eyes. ShioCáni spoke a series of words in the language of the Deities. Brie felt a rush of wonder as the Goddess of Harmony opened her mind and shared her knowledge. In return, Brie allowed her knowledge to flow into the goddess' mind.

ShioCáni laughed. "We are wondrous women, Brielle AsTar. Let's go to work." She knelt beside Carûtix.

Brie moved to kneel in front of Raiherr. "I'm ready. Please begin."

Her hands resting lightly on her cousin's head, ShioCáni spoke. "Carûtix, hear my words and absorb them into your being." She inhaled and recited:

> *"Carûtix, your goal's the dome*
> *And to restore this island home,*
> *Your yearning is once more to be*
> *In Shiór Ridu, standing free.*

ShioCáni looked up and nodded.
Brie placed her hands and chanted,

> *"Raiherr, your world must open wide,*
> *So you may face yourself with pride.*
> *Focus on your goals and dreams*
> *Life is more fluid than it seems.*

When she finished, Esán's warbler alighted, shifted, and joined her and ShioCáni in a circle around the sleeping men.

At a signal from the Goddess of Harmony, the power of the Seeds of Carsilem produced a glistening sheen around him. His powerful voice intoned the last command.

> *"Memories untwist, unwind;*
> *Form two separate, single minds.*
> *Leave the fellows standing free*
> *To follow their own destiny."*

The trio shifted to warblers, flew to the trees and landed to keep watch while the men surfaced from their deep sleep.

At the Vasro campsite, Torgin examined the pile of broken wood and electronic debris, his frown growing. He glanced at Thorlu, who watched with interest. "I can fix this, but I'll require specific tools the K'iin don't have."

Hossela walked over. "I have some tools in my ship." He surveyed the mess. "I'm not sure they're what you need—" A current of wing-wind interrupted. His eyes widened.

Gar materialized beside him, glanced up, and nodded. "I'm Gar. Torgin's my cousin. You're Hossela, right?" Without waiting, he called forth his specs and studied the shattered pile. "Wow! Carûtix sure did a good job, huh?" He raised magnified eyes to his cousin's face. "You can fix it, right?"

Torgin frowned, fingered the time whistle beneath his shirt, and stared up at the black dome arching overhead. "I doubt the time whistle and Tumu Noci can remove it. If I don't fix it, the K'iin will have to live in shadowy darkness beneath it forever. My question is, how do I acquire the right the tools?"

"Torg, up there!" Gar pointed.

Hossela stared upward, his expression nonplused. "I'll go guard our prisoners." He strode to the other side of the campsite and leaned against a tree, his attention split between the Vasro and the trio by The Box.

Overhead, the soft gray light penetrating the dome melted into the shadows. Whispery wind rustled the leaves at the top of the trees, swirled around the campsite, and deposited Aahana and Kat next to Thorlu.

The Sun Queen's daughter took the lead. "Mamai has sent us to transport you, Torgin, and Garon to Shiór Ridu."

Torgin frowned. "What about The Box? I can't leave it."

Aahana smiled and said, "Parepā." A blurred glow solidified into a black tourmaline chest with a top made of glistening, red rubies. "This is a Deity's Coffer. It is called *Cónra*. Mamai sent it, so you can transport all the pieces to her palace."

Torgin's gaze tracked the distance from the coffer to the shatter SorTechory Box. He frowned. "If I leave one piece behind—" He turned to Thorlu. "Can you teleport everything from the ground into the chest?"

The VarTerel tilted his head and tapped his pursed lips with a fingertip. Assurance cloaked him. "If Gar will lend me his spectacles and stand with me while I work, I am certain I can collect and move all the pieces."

Gar removed his specs and handed them to Thorlu. "Since you've used 'em before, I'm happy for you to use 'em now."

While Thorlu placed the spectacles on the bridge of his nose, Aahana addressed Torgin. "Only you have the key to opening *Cónra*."

Torgin smiled and withdrew the time whistle. "What notes must I play?"

Kat and Aahana exchanged glances. Aahana's eyes twinkled. "Kat assured me you would know the whistle is the key. Mamai told me your highly tuned instincts will inform you which notes to play."

Torgin walked over to the chest and placed a hand on it. A slight vibration moved from his palm up his arm and settled around his heart. Raising the time whistle to his lips, he played three notes and repeated them three times. The first repetition produced a line of glistening red light around the coffer's rectangular top; the second sent a flow of color over the lid. On the third, the coffer's ruby-studded surface sparkled into nothing. Torgin lowered the whistle. "Your turn, Thorlu."

Thorlu focused his magnified eyes on the broken fragments of The Box and marveled at the clarity the spectacles provided. Embracing his VarTerel's power, he methodically teleported the scattered wood, wires, discs, and switches into the Deity Coffer.

When he finished, he handed the spectacles to Gar. "Garon, please look over the area where The Box was and make certain I left nothing behind."

Gar settled the temples over his ears and walked to the site where the shattered SorTechory Box had lain. "I found three small pieces. Shall I point them out to you?"

Thorlu shook his head. "Please teleport them into the coffer."

Gar started to speak, then pursed his lips. Concentration closed his eyes. Moments later, one eye squinted open. A grin filled his face. "I did it!" He faced Thorlu, his fists on his hips. "How'd you know I could teleport? I sure didn't."

The VarTerel simply smiled. "Abellona told me to trust you. Take one last look before Torgin closes the top."

Gar walked around the area, teleported one more small piece, and removed his specs. "I can't see any more."

Torgin raised the whistle and played the three notes in reverse. Red sparkles rose above the black tourmaline coffer and fused together to form the ruby red top. After tucking the whistle beneath his shirt, he beckoned his cousin to his side. "You did great, Gar."

The young boy's white teeth flashed. "So did you. We make a good team, huh?"

Torgin grinned. "We sure do."

After a quick conference with Thorlu, Kat and Aahana moved to stand with Torgin and Gar. The VarTerel regarded each member of the group. "Events are escalating on Neul Isle. Torgin, work as quickly and efficiently as you are able. We need The Box back and functioning as soon as possible." He placed a hand on Gar's shoulder. "You will keep me posted."

Uncertainty infused Gar's features. "Ah, how, Thorlu?"

"The Sun Queen will help you." He stepped away. "Aahana and Kat, go!"

The Deities Wind swirled dry dirt and leaves up around them. A gray haze obscured their presence as they floated up to the dome and vanished.

A soft cough behind him made Thorlu turn to find Hossela, observing him with interest. The Klutarse tipped his head. "I never expected you to become a VarTerel. What's it feel like to wield that kinda power?"

Thorlu rubbed his short beard. "It's like nothing I ever imagined, Hossela. The power is only part of it. What I find the most amazing is my desire to be an agent for positive change instead of a self-centered coward defined by evil intent, scrambling for wealth and power." He paused, his senses on high alert. "We have trouble brewing on the plains. Let's decide what to do with Callun and the two Vasro.

34
El Aperdisa

Zak waited in the outer office of Ship Security. Nesen, the first to be interrogated, departed in the company of two guards. He stared straight ahead, his expression blank. Andro soon followed. Stooped shoulders and a shuffled walk, his faded brown eyes, and the constant twitching of his mouth all broadcast his fear."

A uniformed guard entered the office. "Private Zakeron, please come with me."

Zak followed him to a cubicle where an officer sat, paperwork spread out in front of him. He motioned Zak to take a seat.

As the guard exited, a slight shimmer encircled the cubicle. The officer's features transformed. Relevart's serious gaze rested on his face. "You have done well, Zakeron. Unfortunately, the job isn't complete. Reedan got away and Laris Rozar has disappeared. We expect Reedan to contact you. Rumors are already spreading they released you. If anyone asks you about Nesen and Andro, you're not sure why they were incarcerated."

Zak leaned back in his chair. "I realized the game of hide and seek was still in play, but I'd hoped—"

Relevart rapped his knuckles on the desktop. "The game will be complete when we have all the Vasro spies, whether Raiherr's or Karlsut's. Your job, Zak, is to let Reedan contact you. See if you can discover where Laris Rozar disappeared to. I also expect Reedan to keep prodding you until you slip-up and give yourself away along with Rily and Jem. Do not let your attention wander. Stay focused, or you will play right into his hands."

The officer's face reformed, and the shields shimmered into nothing. "You may go, Private. I don't expect to see you at my desk again. Understood?"

Zak rose and saluted. "Yes, sir, I understand. Thank you, sir."

A guard stepped into view and escorted him from the security office. Eyes focused straight ahead, he walked to the T-lift. Greeted by an empty car, he stepped inside and tapped the touch pad for the crew's residential deck. When the entry hatch closed, he gave himself permission to breathe.

Two stops later, he exited and collected a clean uniform from his locker. A glance at the chronometer told him he'd better hurry, or he'd arrive late to his duty station. He scurried toward the cleanse area, stripped, and stepped into the stall. Hot water sprayed; hot drying air followed. Clean, dry, and refreshed, he dressed, put his dirty uniform in the clothes cleanser, and turned to leave.

Reedan blocked his way. "So, they let you go." He took a menacing step. His cruel mouth twitched. "I'm betting it's 'cause you're their spy."

Zak did not retreat nor bother to reply. Instead, he reached for his uniform hat, tucked it under his arm, and walked out of the cleanse area.

Behind him, Reedan sputtered but did not follow. Zak took the T-lift to the engineering level and logged in. Aware Reedan would not give up, he focused on work.

Five chron-circles later when the watch bell rang, Zak slipped out a little used exit and ducked into an electronics bay. After double checking he was alone and unobserved, he teleported to the Holographic Center and then to Elf's secret space in the Plantitarium. Much to his delight, Ari sat on the bench by the pond.

. . .

His shift to Elf focused her attention in his direction. Relief flooded her features. She jumped to her feet. "I was so afraid for you!" She studied his face. "You know I love you, right?"

He kissed her gently. "And, Arienh, you know I love you."

She drew him down on the bench beside her. "Tell me what happened."

He clasped her hand and provided a brief description. "I'm bait for Reedan, and I'm so tired—" A yawn highlighted his fatigue. "I need sleep, but I wanted to see you first. Tell Rethson that Reedan is on the warpath and to be extra careful. Also, tell Henrietta what's up." He stifled a yawn. "You leave first. I need a couple of chron-clicks before I return to the crews' quarters."

She held out a tiny, round black disc. "This is from Aunt Henri. It will alert her if you are in trouble." She stood up. "I'll meet you in the mess hall for morning meal. Be careful, Elf." With a nod, she shifted and flashed from sight.

With a relieved sigh, Elf tucked the disc in his pocket. *At least Henrietta is tracking me.* He remained in the safety and silence of his secret space until his nerves calmed and his head cleared.

Coming to his feet, he shifted to Zak and ran a hand over his short military haircut. *Keep your wits about you, Tezeeni Zakeron. Reedan is not someone you want to cross.*

His hand sought Henri's disc. Confidence stiffened his spine. Head high, he teleported to an empty conference room, walked across the hall to the T-lift, and exited at the level of the crew's deck. A yawn escorted him to his locker; another accompanied him to his sleeping cot. Crossing his fingers that Reedan wouldn't dare to risk a visit to this area of the ship, he curled up and slept.

Thorlu gazed down at the two sleeping Vasro tied to the tree. "What am I going to do with you?" He rubbed his beard-covered chin and let his thoughts play chase. A slow smile tugged. *Brielle AsTar, you are my role model, something I would never have dreamed possible.* Gray-green eyes narrowed, he turned and stared between broad trunks at the Plains of Cârthea. A soft laugh escaped as a charm whispered in his mind. *Thank you, Brie!*

Still smiling, he untied the Vasro and recited the charm she had shared.

> *"Vasro memories now take flight;*
> *Leave behind a wish for right.*
> *Erase this moment filled with strife,*
> *So you may find a better life."*

He looked up to find Hossela watching him with a hard set jaw and arrow-like uncertainty darting from his eyes. "What did you do?"

"I removed their memories to ensure they can live better lives elsewhere. It was that or the Penal Colony on TaSneach. Which would you choose?"

The Klutarse licked his lips. "Just don't do it to me, Thorlu, or I'll—" He shook himself. "Don't do it me, alright?"

Thorlu studied him for a long moment. "Hossela, I sense you are a good man, searching to rediscover himself and to find happiness. I have no intention of taking your right to seek a new destiny away."

Hossela's narrow chin dropped to rest on his chest. A shudder ran through his entire length before he lifted it. "Thank you, VarTerel. I will strive to live up to your belief in me." He glanced over his shoulder. "What do we do with the SorTech? I think the demi-god did something to him."

A warbler landed next to Callum. ShioCáni materialized. "The Sun Queen has requested that I bring the SorTech to her palace. She and Torgin feel if they help him return to full consciousness, he can help rebuild The Box. Nimah will deal with the two Vasro, but not until Carûtix is neutralized."

Thorlu's brow creased. "What is happening with the mind-fellows?"

ShioCáni stepped closer to Callum. "Brie and I untangled their memories, so they are individuals once more. Nimah, Brie, and Esán will require your help once they awaken." A wave of her hand called forth the Deities' Wind.

A swirl of leaves and grass surrounded her and the unconscious man at her feet and lifted them up toward the dome. The closer they got to the black energy field, the faster the cyclonic wind swirled. With sudden loss of speed, the wind returned the Goddess of Harmony and her passenger to the clearing.

"The dome has changed again. I could not exit through it. How do I get Callun to the Sun Queen?"

"I'll take you both through Mittkeer." Thorlu glanced at Hossela. "Please remain on guard until I return."

He moved to ShioCáni's side, called forth his staff, and touched Callun with his foot. Mittkeer embraced them.

As silent calm replaced the tension and sense of potential disaster looming over Neul Isle, Thorlu release a breath and gazed at the Goddess. "I know the way-marker for Shiór Ridu, so when you're ready, I'll place an image of where I wish to arrive in the Sun Queen's palace."

"Good. Let me check the SorTech." ShioCáni knelt, touched Callum's forehead, and stood. "He will remain unconscious until we leave Mittkeer. I am ready, VarTerel."

Thorlu inhaled, let the image of their destination form in his mind, and shared it with the goddess.

When she nodded, he raised his staff. Stars and planets and galaxies blurred. The constellation of Dia Nōrtara beamed a short distance ahead. Moments later, the Land of Time withdrew, leaving the trio in Nimah's quarters in the palace.

A soft knock brought a smile to ShioCáni's face. The door opened and Torgin ushered Abellona into the room.

The Sun Queen acknowledged her niece and Thorlu with a slight dip of her chin. Her fire-opal gaze flicked to Callum and back to Thorlu. "Please move him to the bed. ShioCáni and I can do our best to revive him."

Thorlu teleported the SorTech to the bed and joined Torgin by the window. "How's the rebuild coming?"

Torgin pursed his lips. "I'm making slow, steady progress. Hopefully, having Callum's input will speed up the process." He glanced over at the two Deities working their special kind of healing. "If he comes to and is coherent, do you think he will help?"

Thorlu's lips twitched between a smile and a frown. The smile won. "I believe Abellona can convince him to assist you." He stared out at the Sun Queen's realm…the blazing heavens, the red and black terrain, the ember glow of the mountain range in the distance—

The view dimmed and refocused. He stood in the Vasro camp on Neul Isle.

Hossela gaped and holstered his weapon. "Don't scare me like that, Thorlu. I almost shot you." He shook his head. "Our Vasro are waking."

Thorlu barely heard him. A telepathic message flooded his mind. He faced the Klutarse. "You stay here. Something is brewing on the other side of the plains."

Shaping a fire eagle, he soared upward.

Brie peered between branches at the Vasro and the demi-god swimming toward wakefulness. Raiherr, the first to reach the surface, leveraged his body to sitting. A bleary-eyed stare roamed the plains. When his gaze fastened on *Toneer*, his breath hissed between clinched teeth. Like clay in an artist's hands, puzzlement sculpted his features.

Beside him, Carûtix yawned, rolled onto his back, and stared up at the blackened dome. Scrambling to his feet, he made a slow rotation. His gaze darted over the terrain, his expression a wrestling match between confusion and frustration. He examined Raiherr with a knife-edged stare. His brow creased. A slight turn brought *Toneer* into his line of vision. Pursed lips thinned into a firm line.

Ignoring Raiherr, he crossed to the spacecraft and studied it from every angle. A determined stride carried him onto the plains. Dark eyes scanned its breadth and width. An about-face brought him around, his dark eyes fixed on the Vasro leader. "Who are you..." His gaze darted over the terrain. "...and where am I?"

Raiherr's eyes dulled. His expression blanked. "I don't know where we are. Who are you?"

Carûtix marched further onto the plains. He shook himself, clenched his fists, and tensed his broad shoulders. His jaw worked. His nostrils flared. "Something is not right." He closed his eyes and calmed uneven, panted breaths. "You and I were connected. Our memories...our thoughts..." Again, he shook himself. "I just don't remember how." He stared up at the dome, then at *Toneer*.

From her vantage point, Brie cocked her warbler head and projected a telepathic message into the demi-god's mind.

"Your memories remain unfound.
Your past—"

Carûtix clapped his hands over his ears, rounded on Raiherr, and strode closer. A powerful punch sent the Vasro stumbling backward. "Never do that again or—"

"What in sedah are you talking about?" Raiherr growled and took a threatening step. "Well?"

The demi-god scanned the plains. A flash of understanding appeared and flickered into uncertainty. "I—we—" He threw his hands in the air. After a silence saturated with ambivalence, he tapped his temple. "The answer's right here." He jerked his fisted hand down, uncurled his fingers, and stared at the empty palm. "Can't grab it." His gaze darted to *Toneer*. "Wonder if there's anything to eat in the jumper craft?"

Raiherr wandered over to the entry hatch and studied the tactile frequency pad. "Wonder whose ship it is? Wish I knew the code." He reached out and tapped several symbols. When nothing happened, he tried again. On the third try, the entry shield slid from sight. The Vasro looked surprised. "How'd I do that?"

Carûtix grinned. "Don't know how, but you did! Let's find some food." He climbed aboard.

For a long moment, Raiherr simply stared at the opening. A shrug and a shake of the head later, he followed the demi-god.

Brie tipped her warbler head, chirped, and alighted at the bottom of the tree in her human form. A flutter of wings and Esán materialized beside her. His stormy blue eyes scanned the plains, then fixed on her face.

Before he could speak, ShioCáni appeared. "Carûtix retains enough power to realize something is not right. I cannot guarantee his memory won't feed him the information he is seeking. What do we need to do—"

A howl preceded the demi-god's emergence from the ship. His dark eyes searched; his muscular body twitched with rage. The tattoos bordering his long top-hair blazed red, blue, and gold. "Whoever has been messing with us, show yourselves."

Three tiny warblers took flight and landed deep in a leaf-covered tree. Brie's bird form perched closest to the jumper craft. She ruffled her feathers and cocked her tiny head to watch the men below.

Carûtix flung his arms wide and trounced in a zigzagged path, his enraged gaze darting one way and then the other. "I said show yourselves. If you cower in hiding, I will find you and tear your limbs from your bodies one at a time."

When no one came forward, he fought to manage his mounting rage. A measured march from the jumper craft onto the plains slowed his heart rate. The retracing of his steps cleared his mind. He stopped in front of Raiherr and examined him from head to toe. Closing his eyes, he took three deep cleansing breaths, opened them, and, once more, scrutinized his companion.

A faint memory presented itself. Absolute calm rewarded him with a clearer picture. "You are the Vasro Leader, Raiherr Yencara." Again, he closed his eyes. Three even breaths later, he felt his spine lengthen and his chin lift. Power flowed through him. "I am Carûtix, the God of War."

A vague memory rippled through his mind. He squinted and scrunched his forehead into laddered creases. His head tipped back. Eyes focused on the blackness overhead. A maniacal laugh shook him from head to foot.

He swung around and fixed his attention on Raiherr. "I am the King of Neul Isle. This is my realm!" Consternation flashed. He froze as a wall of forgetting formed, then gripped Raiherr's arm. "The Box... I can't remember. What is a SorTechory Box? Why is it so important?"

The Vasro's lost expression intensified Carûtix's growing concern. Gripping his shoulders, he shook him. "Answer me, Raiherr! I must understand The Box. I must—"

The Vasro pushed him away. "Leave me alone. I do not know this box. I have no memory of the name Raiherr or you." He turned, entered the ship, and closed the entry hatch.

Carûtix gaped. "How dare you?" Sudden quiet gripped him. Faint memories prodded him. He turned and stared across the plains. Trees in the distance triggered more hazy memories. Determination propelled him forward, his focus—find The Box and destroy it.

Abellona sat at the bedside of the unconscious SorTech and pondered the best way to bring him back to himself. *Do I change his memories?* Her long, elegant fingers wrapped around the fire opal on its ebony chain around her neck. Warmth flowed into her palm. She touched the opal to her forehead and resettled it over her heart.

Her regal gaze rested on the sleeping man's pudgy face. "You must choose your destiny, Callum. I will not interfere." A long finger tapped his forehead. "The time has come to leave your dreaming behind."

A squarish hand lifted to smother a yawn, short legs bent at the knees and then straightened to their full, stubby length. Pale blue eyes flickered open, drifted shut, and widened with confused alarm. Callum pushed up to sitting and scooched to the edge of the bed. His bulgy eyes almost popped out of his head as they focused on the Sun Queen. Panic painted his round face a variety of swarthy colors. He glanced from the queen to the room's elegance and back.

"You are the Sun Queen." He swung his short legs like a child and licked his lips. "How'd I get to your palace? That's where I am, right?"

Abellona smiled. "You are in Shiór Ridu, in my palace at Chadēta Apól. How do you feel?"

He touched the side of his head and frowned. Stubby fingers examined the left side. "You healed my wound. Why? And why bring me here?" Understanding pursed his lips around a breathy "ooooohhh". "The Box... I smashed into The Box. It fell. That's all I remember."

"We transported you and all the broken pieces of the SorTechory Box to my palace. I have removed the charm placed on you by my nephew and healed the wound to your head. Would you like to see The Box?"

He crossed his short arms over his chest and stared at the floor. "If you expect me to help, I can't."

"I understand." Abellona rose. "Although we do not require your help to rebuild it...yours is beyond repair...we thought you might like to help build a new one. That is your choice, Callum. I will leave you to consider your options. When you are ready to talk further, pull that golden cord by the fireplace. One of my assistants will alert me." With a gracious nod, she left.

Callum sat on the bed, his mouth working. Thoughts cartwheeling with confusion prompted him to jump to the floor and prowl the elegant room. A pause at the arched floor-to-ceiling windows produced a gasp of wonder. *I never imagined I'd visit the Sun Queen's realm.*

Further exploration only increased the awed response to his surroundings. His wandering stopped by the fireplace. Thought-filled eyes focused on the golden cord. *Do I betray Raiherr?* His eyes narrowed. *I do not doubt he would betray me if it benefitted him.* He tipped his head back, looked up at the origin of the cord, and followed its woven length down to the level of his outstretched hand. Short, stubby fingers wrapped around it. He licked his lips. *Raiherr can't provide what I want in life.* He swallowed and voiced his desire aloud. "I want to be free."

The bell chimed. Releasing the cord, he exhaled a long, easing breath and returned to sit on the edge of the bed.

35
El Aperdisa

Jem woke with a start and swung his feet to the floor. A telepathic message from Henrietta left him wide awake and on edge. Throwing back the cover, he slid his feet into steel-gray slippers and tiptoed to his locker. Dressing quickly, he exited the crew's quarters. Halfway to the T-lift, he turned into a side passage and ducked into the crew's study space. A glance around confirmed he was alone. Relieved, he selected a study cubicle near the back and teleported.

His arrival in Elf's secret space brought him face to face with Henrietta. Without waiting for her to speak, he shifted.

Ari studied her aunt's face with growing alarm. "What's going on, Aunt Henri?"

"Sit down and I will share what I know." She folded her hands in her lap and waited.

Ari sat and faced her. "I'm sitting, Aunt Henri." When her aunt remained silent, she tapped an impatient rhythm on the stone beneath her foot.

Henrietta withdrew her spectacles, and, with her usual unruffled calm, placed them on her nose. Her magnified violet eyes, glinting with the amethyst gleam from the rims, regarded Ari with concern. "We have a crisis brewing. If I am to share what's happening, I require you to keep your temper in check and your intelligence in the forefront. Am I clear?"

Ari's nostrils flared. "Brie's alright, isn't she?"

"Brie is fine and so are her companions on Soputto." A momentary pause projected a message of calm. "Commander Odnamo has alerted us that Reedan and Laris have stolen a jumper craft. Zak is aboard as well, but we don't know whether he is there by choice or if Reedan kidnapped him."

Ari's hand flew to her heart. She heard her own hyperventilating breaths but could not make herself speak. Fighting to remain even-tempered and under control, she gripped her aunt's hand and took several long, easy breaths. As her mind cleared and her aunt came into focus, she tried to speak. "Elf isn't on *El Aperdisa*? How…when?"

Rethson's sudden appearance made her jump. What the—"

"Father sent me. He told me—" Rethson's gaze darted from Ari to Henrietta. "Reedan has Elf. What do we do?"

Ari managed a breath. "No, he has Zak, and he thinks Zak is his man." She turned to her aunt. "How do we track the ship and rescue Zak before the Vasro discover his true nature?"

Henrietta squeezed Ari's hand and flashed her an appreciative smile. "First, Ari, you gave Zak a tracker disc from me, correct? That's how we knew he was aboard just after the jumper launched. Relevart is working with Commander Odnamo. All jumpers, shuttles, and fighter crafts on *El Aperdisa* also have tracker units embedded within their engines. Once the ship is located, Relevart and Elf will confer in a time fold."

Rethson licked his lips. "If Reedan discovers Zak is Elf, there is no telling what he might do. Please, Henrietta, remind Relevart that Reedan is more dangerous than anyone on board this ship realizes. He pulled up his uniform shirt and turned.

Ari gaped at the raised scars striping his back. "Did Reedan do that to you?"

Relevart's youngest son, tucked in his shirt. "He did that and more. The fact I am still alive is amazing. Only Roween's interference saved me. If Reedan discovers Zak's true identity..." He sank onto the end of the bench and stared at the glistening surface of the small pond.

Ari sat next to him and put an arm around his shoulders. "Elf's smart, Rethson, and he knows what Reedan did to you. Relevant won't let anything happen to him." She tilted her head to look at her aunt. "Right, Aunt Henri?"

👁 👁

In the Sun Queen's Holographic Laboratory, Torgin and Shācro combined their knowledge to build a new SorTechory Box. Torgin smiled to himself. *I'm glad we couldn't revamp Callum's box. Building a new one is a challenge I am loving.*

He focused on the Chadēta emberwood substructure he and Shācor had built. The black wood with its streaks of red was harder than any wood beyond the boundaries of the Land of Deities. They had also constructed emberwood activator frames to house the latticework of filament-fine wiring required for the delicate work of the new Box.

He glanced over at the Holographic Specialist, who worked opposite him at the long table. "I am so lucky to be working with you, Shācor. Where did you learn so much about holographics, electronics, and engineering? Do you have schools in Shiór Ridu?"

The queen's specialist nodded. "The Deity realms are composed of communities scattered throughout the land. Each one has schools to accommodate the unique talents of the inhabitants. I grew up near Chadēta Apól."

Shācor smiled and inhaled a contented breath. "I was presented to Abellona as a young, orphaned boy. Because I was unlike the other children in my school, my fellow students teased and berated me. My unique mind would rebel. I'd pitch a tantrum and refuse to do what the staff asked. The only reason they allowed me to stay at the school at all was my high intelligence rating.

"Finally, the headmaster decided he'd had enough and sent me to a proxy placement center. One of the queen's inspectors discovered me locked in a dark room, took pity on me, and brought me here.

"Abellona arranged for me to attend a specialized school for children with divergent minds and high intellectual capacity. From there, she sent me to the Universal Polytechnic Institution at the Supreme Center of Shiór Ridu. When I graduated, she offered me this position. I have never regretted my decision to remain with the Sun Queen. I am honored to collaborate with you to help fulfill her quest."

A soft knock on the door ended their conversation. Abellona entered, turned and offered her hand. "Please enter, Callum."

The hesitant SorTech stepped into the Lab and paused. Eyes bulging with astonishment, he surveyed the expansive space and the technology represented. A hesitant but interested smile formed as he moved closer to the worktable.

Abellona stepped up beside him. "I believe, Callum, that you know of Torgin Whalend. With him is my Holographic Specialist, Shācor." She refocused her attention. "Gentlemen, Callum is joining us in our quest to save Neul Isle. He would like to work with you to build a new SorTechory Box."

Torgin studied the short, sturdy man who gazed up at him with a mix of uncertainty and curiosity. "Welcome, Callum, we're glad to have you. Your knowledge of The Box and how it was built will be most helpful." He placed a high stool beside him. "Join us, and we'll explain what we've done so far."

The SorTech climbed up and gazed in awe at everything laid out on the table. While Shācor showed him an activator frame and explained the technology, Torgin accompanied the Sun Queen to the door. "Thank you, Abellona, for having him brought here. We'll keep you informed of our progress."

"The sooner you succeed, the sooner we can remove the dome from the island. Please return to your work."

He watched her walk from the Laboratory. *I'm sure lucky.* With a smile of appreciation, he returned to the wooden workbench.

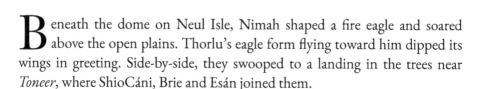

Beneath the dome on Neul Isle, Nimah shaped a fire eagle and soared above the open plains. Thorlu's eagle form flying toward him dipped its wings in greeting. Side-by-side, they swooped to a landing in the trees near *Toneer*, where ShioCáni, Brie and Esán joined them.

The Sun Queen's heir made eye contact with each of his companions. "Carûtix is regaining his memory, and, although I am not certain how, his deity power is returning. His inability to accept responsibility for his actions and his desire to be a king make him unpredictable. Bringing him under control must be our top priority. Until the dome is removed, he is a danger to Neul Isle and its residents."

ShioCáni regarded her cousin. "You are the only one who can gain control of him. We can help you corral him. What else must we do to protect Neul Isle?"

Nimah signaled for silence and squinted at the shadows deepening over the plains. "Something is happening."

Thorlu's gaze angled upward. "The dome's energetics are vacillating. He squinted. "And its surface is getting darker."

Nimah motioned his companions into a circle. "This is not the work of Carûtix. He is unaware the pieces of The Box and the SorTech are no longer on Neul Isle. However, when he reaches the campsite and discovers they're missing—" He shook his head.

Thorlu continued the thought. "And finds Hossela alone with the two Vasro, his anger will take over. We need to get them to safety before our 'king' focuses his returning power their direction. I suggest we bring them back here and secret them aboard *Toneer*. It housed all Raiherr's Vasro warriors on the way here, so there is plenty of space for the three of them."

The Goddess of Harmony nodded her approval. "Brie and I will remain here on guard while you, Thorlu, work with Nimah and Esán to rescue the Klutarse and the Vasro." She shaped a warbler and, followed by Brie's tiny bird, flew into the trees.

Nimah took the lead. "I suggest we fly to the campsite. Once we're there, we can decide what must be done."

At a nod from the Sun Queen's heir, Esán's kestrel lifted into flight. Thorlu shaped his fire eagle and soared upward.

Nimah focused on the jumper craft. A mental probe showed him Raiherr in a bunk sound asleep. Satisfied, he embraced his fire eagle form and flew toward the Vasro camp. Part way there, he landed in a tall tree and scanned the terrain. The dancing shadows visible a short time ago had merged into a murky darkness that grew more dense as he watched.

Cocking his head, he listened. Only silence pressed against his eardrums. Nothing moved. Already the air carried a stagnant tinge. *We have little time.*

He launched into flight, grateful for the fire eagle's exceptional sight and power of its wings.

<hr />

Gar perched on a high stool next to Shācor's hologram of Neul Isle. His instincts tingling a warning made him sit up straighter. Ember glowing spectacles appearing in his hand increased his alert edginess. Settling them on his nose and adjusting the temples, he fixed his enhanced gaze, first on the parts of the island unaffected by the dome. Nothing triggered an alarm.

He took a breath, focused on the dome, and cocked his head. Lips pursed, he examined it from its curved top to the bottom edge where it rested on the ground or in the water. *What's different?* He leaned closer.

His spectacles humming alerted him to their shift to magnifying lenses. He gasped. But for an occasional glint, the slight shimmer of the energy particles comprising the dome weren't visible. His thoughts raced as he jumped down from the stool. A final look at the dome sent him scurrying toward the laboratory work area.

Forcing a calm he did not feel, he stepped into the intense quiet where Torgin and Shācor worked with total concentration on assembling the black, filament-filled frames into the cabinet substructure. Carefully observing each movement, Callum sat on his stool, his expressive face a rainbow of changing emotions.

Gar cleared his throat. "Sorry to interrupt—"

Torgin glanced over his shoulder, then turned. "Your rims are glowing. What's happened?"

"The dome is changing. You need to come see."

Shācor carefully latched a frame into place and came around the table to join them. "Lead the way, young Gar."

When they reached the hologram of Neul Isle. Callum gave a squeak of dismay. "It is solidifying. Once it reaches its maximum density—" He shook his head.

Torgin and Shācor turned questioning gazes his direction. "Tell us what you know that we don't."

The short, stocky SorTech seemed to shrink. "If it solidifies, no one will ever enter or leave again." He licked his protruding front teeth. "I'm unsure if

VarTerels will gain access to Mittkeer, but nothing else will work." A shaking hand rubbed his balding head. "And—" A gulped breath made a hissed exit. "It will be as black as pitch beneath the dome forever."

Shācor's expression remained calm, though thoughtful. Torgin's summer green eyes glinted with intensity as he studied the dome. He turned to Gar. "May I look through your specs, Garon?"

Gar's throat tightened. Abellona's voice filled the Holographic Laboratory. "Torgin Whalend, your gifts will show you what you must know. Shācor's training will add more information when you require it." Gar's opal-eyed focus shifted to Callum, whose eyes bulged in a face filled with adoration when the Sun Queen's voice addressed him. "Callum, you carry the history of The Box in your memory. Please share it with Torgin. He will inform you how to proceed."

Gar rubbed his throat and blinked repeatedly. His spectacles lost their ember glow, and his eyes ceased to flicker with fire-opal sparks. "Wow! She always takes me by surprise." He wiped beads of sweat from his brow with the back of his hand. "Now what?"

Shācor spoke up. "I'll check my holographic settings to confirm what we are seeing is accurate." He moved away toward the instrument pad.

Torgin faced Callum. "If you are willing, I will help you share your memories of The SorTechory Box's history. I promise, I will only accept those memories and nothing more."

Callum chewed the bottom lip before answering. "Since Abellona wishes me to share, I will. One thing is making me nervous."

"Please tell me, so I can put your mind at ease." Torgin lowered to one knee and gazed at the SorTech eye to eye.

"If I share my memories, will I still have them?"

"You will." Torgin's steady gaze did not waver. "By sharing with me, I will gain the knowledge you carry. I will *not* remove your memories. You and I will be able to work together more efficiently. We'll also be able to explain things to Shācor as we continue our work on the new box."

Callum let out a relieved sigh. "Thanks. That helps. Tell me what to do."

Torgin rose. "Gar, please stand by Callum, and give him your support."

Gar moved to the SorTech's side. "I'm right here, Callum."

Torgin knelt and held his hands out, palms up. "Please rest your palms on mine and listen closely." When Callum's square palms rested on Torgin's long-fingered hands, Torgin spoke to him with calming clarity. "I am going to do a gentle mental scan. You can help me by picturing what you know of The Box and allowing it to flow freely in my direction. Again, I promise I am only seeking memories of The Box and its origins. Are you ready?"

Callum nodded and closed his eyes. Gar sensed him tense, then relax. A short time later, Torgin placed his hands on either side of Callum's and pressed the SorTech's palms together. "Open your eyes."

Bulgy eyes blinked open. A smile tugged. "That was easy." His brows bridged over his bulbous nose. "Did you get what you need?"

Torgin smiled and released his hands. "I did. Thank you, Callum. Your willingness to help made it easy for me to assimilate your amazing knowledge." He stood up. "Let's see what Shācor has discovered."

Gar followed the two very different figures, one short and squat and one tall and lean, across the lab, and smiled to himself. *Sure am glad you brought me with you from New York, Torgin Whalend.*

36
Jumper Craft

Zak lounged on a bench across from Reedan and Laris, his attention divided between them. Both men eyed him with suspicion and a hint of disbelief.

Reedan leaned forward. "You expect me to swallow your story that you stowed away because you were afraid Odnamo might discover you were working with us?"

Zak forced himself to maintain a relaxed, innocent demeanor. "It's the truth. Why don't you believe me?"

Laris sneered. "You turned on your friends." He shook his head.

"I told you before, Rily and Jem aren't my friends. They bully and tease me every chance they get. Reedan, you and Nesen were the only ones on the ship who treated me good. Why would I stay where I'm not wanted?"

Reedan glared. "Did you give Nesen and Andro away to the guards?"

"Why would I do that when Nesen tried to protect me?" Zak allowed desolation to seep into his tone. "Just drop me off at your first stop for supplies. I can fend for myself."

Laris broke his unbelieving silence. "You're liar, Zakeron. You're one of the VarTerel's spies. I'm betting if we lock you up and watch you like a hawk, we'll get to see you shift shape."

Befuddlement playing like a comp-tab viewer on repeat, Zak said, "What are you talking about? Shift shape? I can't shift shape any more than you can." He stared down at the floor. "Sorry I stowed away. I misjudged the situation and imagined I could work with you, and…" He peeked from beneath his lashes. "…maybe get some training as a Vasro."

Reedan shot Laris a startled glance and focused a hard-edged gaze on Zak. "Where'd you hear about Vasro?"

Zak shrugged. "A guy in engineering asked me if you were a Vasro. I didn't know what that was. He explained a Vasro was someone in training to be a DiMensioner." Zak frowned. "I know very little about DiMensioners…just that one lives on DerTah."

"You say you grew up on DerTah, right? So, tell us where." Laris didn't bother to hide his suspicion.

Zak noted Reedan's hungry gaze. *Good thing I chose a place I know well.* He tipped his head. "Grew up on the island of Aksala. Used to sail over to the village of Atkis to sell Ma's homemade jam. Met a kid there who dreamt of becoming a DiMensioner. Said he really hoped he had the talent for it."

Laris sneered. "You think you got the talent?"

Zak laughed. "How should I know? It'd be kinda thrilling, right? I mean, bet it's fun to shift shape, or use—" He scrunched his mouth into an almost pucker. "What's it called when you can talk in someone's head?"

Reedan started to relax. "You mean telepathy." His brows arched. "So, why'd the guy in engineering confide in you?"

Zak shrugged. "He saw you and me together and imagined you told me stuff."

The Vasro sat back. "We're headed for Soputto. When we get there, we'll decide if you stay or leave. Until then, you work with Laris. He'll teach you how to fly this jumper."

Laris coughed to cover up a choke of disgust. "I'm not interested in teaching this kid anything."

"I'm not a kid." Zak glared at the man opposite him. "Why would I wanna work with you?"

Reedan's growl filled the bridge area of the jumper. "Both of you will do what I say, or I'll dump you. Now get busy while I set the navigational course for Soputto."

Zak came slowly to his feet, with a tiny spark of hope igniting. It hadn't dawned on either Vasro that not only had they stolen the jumper craft, but he was AWOL. He wondered how long it would take Odnamo's men to track them. Slipping a hand in his pocket, he touched a tiny black disc-tracker. *Henrietta knows exactly where I am.*

Putting aside his dislike of Laris, he joined him at the jumper's control panel and eagerly embraced the training he'd always wanted to do.

Thorlu pressed his powerful fire eagle wings against the still, stagnant air trapped beneath the dome. Nimah followed a short distance behind him. Unable to see far in the gloominess, Thorlu used a mental scan to search for Esán's kestrel and discovered it had landed in the Vasro camp. A short time later, the faint flicker of a campfire shone like a beacon through the thickening darkness.

Nimah's eagle alighted in a tree overlooking the camp. Thorlu landed and shaped Human beside the fire, where Esán and Hossela stood and the two ex-Vasro huddled.

The high-pitched shriek of a condor ripping through the deep silence raised tension in the camp to a fever pitch. Leaves rustling and branches thrashing announced the arrival of the enormous bird of prey.

Carûtix flashed into being. With rage creating a radiant aura around him, he searched the campsite. A deep growl exploded between bared teeth as he marched to the spot where The Box had been. His booted feet shuffling around the area kicked up nothing but dust. Facing the group by the fire, he spoke in a low, controlled voice. "Where are the pieces of The Box?"

Raiherr's two men looked lost. Thorlu, Esán, and Hossela maintained a joint silence.

The demi-god closed the distance between him and them with a military-like march. "I want the pieces, and I want them now." A glance around diluted his fragile control. "Where's my SorTech? I want him here, beside me." When no one answered, control fled. He growled and took a threatening step toward Thorlu.

Wards shot up around the VarTerel and his fireside companions. Carûtix howled his disappointment and slammed a fist into the shimmering shield. A yelp of pain accompanied his staggered step backward. He caught his balance and glared from the Klutarse to Esán to Thorlu. "How dare you, Tangorra? Do Not forget who I am and the power I wield." He thrust his chin forward. "Unless you wish me to destroy your wards and you with them, tell me where Callum and The Box are."

Thorlu exited the shielded area and nodded at Esán. He, the Klutarse, and the two men disappeared, and the shields vanished. Carûtix snorted like a bull and charged. Thorlu stepped aside at the last second and watched the demi-god scrabbling to remain upright.

The demi-god rounded on him, eyes blazing and fists ready.

Thorlu stood, unruffled and unmoving. "I'll reveal where The Box and SorTech are, but not if you continue your threats."

Carûtix stopped mid-stride and clenched his fists tighter before slowly lowering them. His mouth worked around one reply and then another. An exhale snorted from his nostrils; a single word hissed between his barred teeth. "Where?"

Thorlu met the demi-god's fiery gaze. "Shiór Ridu."

A guttural laugh roiled over the small clearing. "Of course, Abellona would choose to interfere. And the boy with the spectacles and his cousin?"

Thorlu simply tipped his head and allowed his lips to twitch toward a smile and then relax.

Carûtix raised a tattooed hand. A weak whirlwind gathered a semblance of speed. Dust and leaves swirled upward, lifted the demi-god off the ground, then disintegrated, leaving him scrambling in the dirt at the camp's center. He stared up at the blackness overhead, moved closer to the campfire, and peered at Thorlu through the flickering light. "Why can't I use the Deity's Wind?" He pressed a hand to his forehead. When he lowered it, confusion replaced his rage. "She tried to steal my memories—she robbed me of my power—she helped the Sun Queen steal The Box!" He wheeled around and faced the plains. "You will pay, VarTerel AsTar."

The condor took his place. Wing-wind blew out the campfire. Total darkness robbed Thorlu of sight. He dropped to the ground as the condor's wing flashed over his head and the gigantic bird launched into flight.

Nimah appeared at his side. "I have warned Brie and ShioCáni. Let's go." His fire eagle embraced him and lifted into flight.

Thorlu shifted and followed.

Torgin put the final touches on the control panel of the new SorTechory Box. Satisfied he had done everything he could, he stepped back to allow Shācor to review his work.

A glance at the door produced a frown. Earlier, Ferêlith had taken his cousin to meet with the Sun Queen. *Where are you, Garon? I don't want to do the trial run without you.*

Shācor finished his inspection and smiled. "I believe we are ready to give it a try. What do you think, Callum?"

The SorTech peered at The Box and returned the smile. "It is time. Who's going to operate the controls?"

"You!" Torgin and Shācor answered in unison and grinned.

Callum glanced around the lab. "Where's your cousin, Torgin? He won't want to miss the test run."

"He's with Abellona, so I suggest we do our test run and then invite them both to join us."

The SorTech nodded and turned to review the new control panel.

Torgin joined the Sun Queen's Holographic Specialist to watch as Callum prepared to create a miniature dome on the holographic platform. The SorTech's knowledge of the original SorTechory Box had cut the building time in half. Both Torgin and Shācor agreed earlier that he should run the first test.

Awe in every line of his weathered features, Callum regarded the black cabinet with its glinting red streaks. He stood for a moment in silence, his eyes lowered, and both squarish hands pressed to his chest.

Determination giving him the illusion of height, he lifted his eyes, touched several glowing tabs, then ran a finger down a vertical relay line. The Box hummed. A clear dome formed on the platform. Another series of taps and a relay realignment and its energetic vibration stabilized. Clarity changed to semi-opaque. Callum grinned. "I did it!"

Torgin's appreciation beamed. "Your help has really sped up the process. Thank you, Callum. Now, dissolve the dome."

The SorTech pursed his full lips into a pucker and studied the array of tap pads. Looking defeated, he shook his head. "Don't know the new programing. Will you show me?"

"Of course." Torgin moved to his side in front of the cabinet. "Let's do this together." One tap, two taps, three taps, and a programing line later, the dome scintillated into nothing."

Shācor mimed applause and joined them. "I suggest we summon Abellona and Gar to show them what we have accomplished." He pulled a rope by the door and returned to the platform.

A soft knock announced Ferêlith. She entered and gazed at The Box. "Does it work?

Shācor smiled. "It does. Please let Abellona and Torgin's young cousin know it is ready for them to see."

Ferêlith hurried from the lab, her long skirt rustling with each eager step.

A serious-faced Callum looked up at Torgin. "Thank you for allowing me to help. I don't deserve your respect after what I have done for Karlsut Sorda and Raiherr Yencara." He hung his head.

Torgin placed a gentle hand on his shoulder. "All of us do things we're not proud of, Callum. That doesn't mean we are incapable of changing or embracing the best parts of who we are. Shācor and I are grateful you stepped beyond your loyalty to Karlsut and Raiherr to join us in the Queen's Quest." He removed his hand and faced the door.

Gar entered first, his spectacles in place and his expectation radiating around him. He looked up at Torgin. "The Sun Queen is right behind me."

Abellona glided with elegant grace into the Laboratory, her face alight with expectation. After acknowledging those present, she turned her attention to the SorTechory Box. "Please share what you have accomplished."

Torgin looked at Callum, who shook his head and stepped back. After explaining the workings of The Box to Abellona, Torgin created a dome, then stepped aside to allow Shācor to demonstrate its removal from the platform.

As it faded, Gar didn't try to control his excitement. "Wow, you did it!"

Abellona expressed her pleasure in a more dignified manner and stepped closer to the platform. "Please, Shācor, show us Neul Isle as it is now."

The Holographic Specialist moved to his cypher pad and programmed the parameters for a three-dimensional hologram of the island. After a quick double check, he entered the activator code and moved to the edge of the platform.

The flow of energy flickered upwards in glistening incandescent lines. Diamond sparkles rained down from overhead. The island took shape beneath the blackened density of the dome.

No one spoke. Attention remained fixed on the dome covered isle. Gar's magnified eyes flashed to Torgin's face. "Can you remove it from here?"

"We can try," Shācor answered and looked at Torgin. "You are the best qualified to attempt the dome's removal. Callum and I will stand by in the event you require help."

Torgin turned to the queen. "Is this what you wish, My Lady?"

Abellona studied the hologram, then said, "Shācor, what have you discovered about the dome besides its change to black?"

"My calculations suggest—" He faced his queen. "The dome's new density and composition make it impossible for anyone, Human or Deity, to exit or enter through it. Everything below it is now in total darkness. Oxygen grows thinner with each breath taken by island residents. We won't know if it is removable from here until we try."

Abellona's fire-opal gaze rested on the hologram, then lifted to Torgin's face. "Torgin Whalend, do your best."

Torgin inclined his head, inhaled a breath, and faced The Box. Forcing his uncertainty into the back of his mind, he set the program for the removal of the dome. At a nod from Shācor, he touched the activator pad.

All gazes riveted to the black dome; no one spoke, no one seemed to breathe. Nothing about the dome changed. It held steady, solid, and blacker than the lava stone at the base of Bholcáno, the island's volcano.

The first to move was Gar. He took off his glasses, wiped his eyes with his hand and replaced them on his nose. Magnified opal flecked eyes moved from one adult to the other. "What do we do now?"

Shācor's hand pressed to his heart and gazed at his queen. "If I am correct, and I believe I am, we might be able to remove it if we can take The Box back to where it created the original dome."

Callum, whose round face had become a mask of fear, spoke up in a husky voice. "Your calculations show the dome is impenetrable, so how can we return to the Vasro campsite with The Box?"

Torgin's dismay melted into a spark of hope. "Mittkeer! I bet a VarTerel can help us."

Gar groaned. "But there is no VarTerel in Shió Ridu."

Torgin met Abellona's knowing look with a nod. "No but, we know where one is. What's the best way to alert him he's needed?"

On the Plains of Cârthea, Esán settled the two men in narrow bunks in *Toneer*'s crew quarters and put them into a deep sleep. Close by, Raiherr, his mouth wide open, snored the story of his dreams.

Back in the ship's main area, Esán sat with Hossela and enjoyed a quick snack.

The Klutarse swallowed the last of a thick protein drink and tossed the empty packet in the disintegrator chute. "You realize Carûtix will come back here. How do we protect the ship?"

Esán rubbed his chin while solutions ordered themselves in his mind. "I could make the ship invisible." His eyes narrowed. "Not the right approach, but, for sure, I can put up wards to keep him from damaging or entering the ship." He sat up straighter and listened intently.

Hossela leaned forward. "What's happening?"

"Thorlu just informed me Carûtix is on the way here, and he is after Brie."

From her perch above *Toneer*, Brie sensed Esán's arrival on the ship. His close proximity helped her restlessness to ease. Beside her, ShioCáni's tiny head tilted. A single eye glinted in the darkness. In unison, they flew to the ground deeper in the forest glade and shifted.

Brie held out her arms to balance herself in the dark. Fingers brushing the rough bark of a tree trunk helped her reorient.

ShioCáni landed. Her hand clasped Brie's arm. She spoke in a quiet undertone. "We need to shape a bird with night sight. I suggest a Neul eagle owl. They are smart and powerful. Eventide is their preferred time to be abroad."

Brie whispered, "Put an image and what I must know in my mind."

The image of a large red, black, and gold owl with fire-red eyes, the beak of an eagle, and large pointed ear tufts took shape. More details flowed into her mind. The eagle owl was the largest owl on the planet of Soputto and competed with the eagle in size, intelligence, and predatory hunting skills.

ShioCáni's grip tightened on her arm. "Carûtix heads this way. Esán may need our help. Let's return to *Toneer*." Her instantaneous shift triggered Brie's. Two eagle owls flew up through the canopy, soared over the trees, and alighted, each on her own branch close to the jumper craft.

Brie's owl eyes skimmed the plains. Extraordinary night sight picked out every detail. Acute hearing picked up the sound of a condor's wing stroke, and its fast approach. The flutter of moth wings drew her attention away from the plains to La, hovering beside her.

A telepathic message whispered through her mind. *"Thorlu required in Shiór Ridu. Important. Needed now. You tell."* The soft flutter faded into the darkness.

Above her in an adjacent tree, a branch lowered to her level with ShioCáni's owl's careful sidestep along it. *"La's message was clear."*

Brie's beak clicked. Her ear tufts twitched. *"Yes. I must find Thorlu."*

ShioCáni's owl head swiveled in her direction. *"Nimah and I are in touch. He and the VarTerel are on the way. I will help Nimah create a distraction, while you inform Thorlu the Sun Queen has immediate need of him."*

"I'll inform Esán." She focused on creating the message, warned him of Carûtix's approach, and provided the details of the queen's request through La.

"Got it." His response came within moments.

Both eagle owls launched into flight. Soaring high above the plains, they soon caught sight of the condor's shadowy form about halfway across. The rhythmic press and lift of its massive wings carried it toward the jumper craft. Keeping above and a safe distance behind it, the two fire eagles followed.

ShioCáni's owl circled to fly in pursuit of the condor. The eagles separated, one swooping low and landing in a treetop and the other flying to the goddess' side.

Brie, her owl eyes fixed on the eagle below, swooped to the ground and alighted in human form beneath its tree. Branches moved in the eagle's wing-wind as it flew upward and then glided to a landing beside her.

Thorlu materialized, his expression questioning. "I understand you have a message for me from Abellona?"

"The queen requires your presence at the palace. La's message was urgent."

Thorlu frowned. "I have an urgent message for you, Brielle. Carûtix is focusing his hatred and fear on you. You cannot stay on the island." His staff appeared in his hand. He touched her shoulder.

Before she could decline, they stood in Mittkeer. A surge of Ari-like rebellion rushed through her. Her staff flashed into being. Beside her, Thorlu waited without interfering. A wave of calm washed over her. She took a breath and sent her staff into hiding.

"I apologize. Esán is on Neul Isle and in danger. I want to be there to fight by his side." She looked away from the silent VarTerel, allowed herself time to absorb more of his calm, and then met his understanding gaze. "You made the right decision. Thank you, Thorlu. Esán has both Nimah and ShioCáni to protect and fight with him. Abellona is waiting. Take us to Shiór Ridu."

Thorlu lifted his staff. Marichi's topaz light glowed. "Take us to the constellation of Dia Nōrtra."

Brie's gaze darted over the ever-night sky. Nothing changed. She glanced up at her fellow VarTerel, called her staff into being, and stepped closer to him. "Let's try it again, together."

He nodded. "On three…one—two—three.

"Dia Nōrtra." Their voices rang out in chorus and faded. Again, nothing happened.

"Perhaps I can help?" They both turned to face the Universal VarTerel.

37
Jumper Craft

Zak woke from a fitful sleep with a splitting headache and the sound of murmuring voices close by. Maneuvering to the edge of the narrow bunk, he sat with his head in his hands and his thoughts slogging through brain fog. *I'm betting Laris drugged me. Wonder if Reedan put him up to it?* He massaged his throbbing temples. *What did I think I was doing stowing away?* Bile rising in his throat sent him scurrying to the personal space, his hands over his mouth.

Once in the privacy of the stall, he vomited, wiped his mouth off, and shifted to Elf.

"Hey, Zak, where are ya?" Laris' voice held a touch of self-satisfaction. "You alright?"

Pushing the e-vac button, Elf shifted to Zak. Coughed several times and exited the personal space, wiping his mouth with the back of his hand. Scowling at Laris, he stumbled back to his bunk. "You didn't have to drug me. I'm here because I choose to be. Now leave me alone. I need to sleep."

Laris listened with a sly grin on his face. "How do you know it was me? Reedan coulda done it?"

"But I didn't, did I?"

Reedan's tone churned Zak's stomach upside down. He saw Laris turn pale and hurried past him to the personal space. After being sick again, he stumbled back to his bunk to find Laris gone and Reedan waiting for him.

The Vasro eyed him up and down. "You don't look so good." His crooked nose wrinkled. "For the record, I did not tell Laris to drug you." Again, his hooded eyes examined him. "Get some sleep. We'll decide what to do with you when you're feelin' better."

Zak groaned and rolled onto his side, facing the wall.

Footsteps retreated. The hatch slid closed. Although the low hum of the jumper craft's propulsion system blending with his quiet breathing nudged him toward sleep, his mind would not shut down.

Yawning, he stared at the bulkhead. *I need to escape, but*—He jerked to sitting, his wide-eyed stare fixed on the Universal VarTerel Henrietta sitting at the end of his bunk, her staff in hand. Zak's gazed dart to the hatchway.

Henrietta smiled. "We are safe." She touched the crystal topping her staff to Zak's forehead. As his nausea fled and realization dawned, Zak almost smiled. "A time-fold, right?"

The Universal VarTerel, nodded. "I suggest you shape Elf while we make plans. When we're finished, I will return you to your own dimension."

• • •

Brie wanted to hug Relevart, but she contained the urge and spoke instead. "Thank you for coming to help, Relevart. Do you think Mittkeer can remove us from beneath the dome?"

The Universal VarTerel looked from Brie to Thorlu. "All Time and No Time has no boundaries. However, the dome's new state is complicating things. It will be interesting to see if Torgin can remove it. Until then, we're suspended beneath it. Fortunately, Thorlu's quick thinking and desire to get you to safety have provided us with what we need. Our combined power will take us to Shiór Ridu."

"How did you get here?" Brie ignored her Ari-like tone.

Relevart responded with a slight twinkle in his eye. "I had help and will share more later. Right now, we must get you to safety, Brielle, and Thorlu to the Sun Queen's palace. Please summon your staff, Brie, and place it here next to mine. Thorlu, join us."

They stood in a circle with their trio of staffs forming a pillar at its center. With the combined light of the crystals Marichi, Musette, and Froetise pooling around them, Relevart recited,

"Mittkeer, the Land of All and No time,
Carry us forth on a journey sublime.
To the Sun Queen's palace in Shiór Ridu
And release us beside her, her quest to pursue."

The Constellation Dia Nōrtra snapped into view. Relevart lifted his staff higher. Stars blurred and they found themselves in the central living area of the Sun Queen's private suite.

Abellona walked from her study and greeted them with a gracious smile. "Thorlu, thank you for answering my call and for removing Brielle from my nephew's wrath." She switched her fire-opal gazed to regard Brie. "Relevart will take you to safety once Torgin, Gar, and the new SorTechory Box are back at the Vasro campsite on Neul Isle."

Relevart joined the conversation. "We may require Brie's help if the dome continues to harden. The sooner Torgin removes it, the better."

Ferêlith entered and curtsied to her queen. "I am here, my lady."

Abellona, seriousness cloaking her, addressed those gathered. "Let us dispense with the formalities. We have a crisis to avert. Ferêlith, go to the Holographic Laboratory. Tell Shācor to please have the hologram of Neul Isle established and ready for us."

Ferêlith bobbed a quick curtsy, gave her mistress a contrite smile, and hurried from the room.

The Sun Queen drew Relevart aside. After a brief conversation, they crossed to the door. "It is time to take matters into our own hands. Come." She swept from the room, and, with Relevart by her side, preceded down the corridor to the Lab.

Brie, anticipation making her giddy, brought up the rear. *Torgin told me about the queen's Laboratory. I just never expected to see it.*

When they reached the open door, Relevart escorted the Sun Queen to a chair by the holographic platform, and Thorlu ushered Brie in ahead of him. A thrill of amazement brought her to a standstill. Awe-filled eyes studied the magnificent hologram.

Gar grinned and hurried to her side. "Pretty cool, huh, Brie? Come and see it up close." He greeted Thorlu with a nod, then clasped Brie's hand and led her to the platform.

Thorlu joined them. "Where's your cousin, Garon?"

"I'm here." Torgin crossed to Brie's side and smiled down at her. "I didn't expect to see you, Brielle. Welcome to Shiór Ridu." He turned to Thorlu. "Shācor and I just put some finishing touches on the new box. It is now complete. Before we leave, he'll familiarize you with what's happening with the dome over Neul Isle in real time."

Brie looked from the hologram to Torgin. "It is an exact replica. I'm sensing it changes as the island changes. Am I correct?"

"You are."

A man approached from the work area. Blond curls framed a handsome face with intelligence etched in every feature. Large aqua eyes came to rest on her. "I am Shācor, the queen's Holographic Specialist." His smile widened. "You are Torgin's friend, VarTerel Brielle AsTar. He has told me so much about you. Welcome to the Sun Queen's Laboratory."

He nodded to Thorlu and walked over to greet Abellona and Relevart. "We need to remove the dome as soon as possible. If we wait much longer, it may not respond to The Box or anything else. Allow me to show you what we have discovered."

He moved to his panel and touched several pads. The dome appeared solid and blacker than night. Around its bottom edges where it touched the ground or the water, dark shadows crept toward the sea.

Abellona and Relevart rose. The queen's voice rang out. "Universal VarTerel, please put your plan into operation. There is no time to spare."

Esán stood on the bridge of *Toneer*, a frown twisting his mouth. He faced the opposite direction and concentrated his mental search over the plains. *Brielle, where are you?* The frown deepened.

Hossela stepped into his line of vision. "What are you doing?"

"I can't find Brie. The last time we communicated, she told me Carûtix was headed this way." Esán ran a hand over his head, curled his fingers around his low ponytail and tugged. "His condor is about to land."

The Klutarse hissed, "So, what are we going to do?"

Esán pressed his lips into a thin line. "Nimah and ShioCáni are pursuing him at a distance, but I still cannot find Brie or Thorlu."

"So the VarTerels aren't close by?"

"Shhh!" He put a finger to his lips. "Carûtix has landed. Let me create safety wards around the ship."

With efficient speed, he raised a shield encircling it, from end to end and top to bottom. He then erected another ward around the crew's quarters. "I've shielded the ship and the Vasro. You stay here, Hossela. I'll see if I can assist our demi-gods."

He shifted to his favorite kestrel and teleported to a treetop in the forest beyond the jumper craft.

Carûtix swooped low over the plain and landed close to Raiherr's spacecraft. His massive condor wings lifted parallel to each other. A shiver shook the wing feathers as they lowered and folded against his sides. He swung his condor head right and left, fixed his attention on the entry hatch, and extended his beak toward the tactile frequency pad. With a startled shriek, he pranced backward, unfurled his wings, and lifted into flight.

A wide circle above the plains and woods surrounding the jumper craft showed him the dim shimmer of wards protecting the ship. Nothing else suggested trouble awaited him. A swooped glide to prepare for landing placed him on the ground in his natural form. Wary of the shields, he stepped closer. "Brielle AsTar, make your presence known, or I will destroy the ship and everyone on it."

Esán walked from the woods and stopped a safe distance away. "Brielle is not aboard *Toneer*, Carûtix, nor is she on Neul Isle. I thought perhaps you might solve the mystery for me."

"I don't believe you, Esán Efre. Take me to her, or I will hold you hostage, and she will come to your aid." A snarl cut his self-satisfied laugh short. "Tell me where she is, or—"

Esán vanished. A kestrel exited the forest canopy and flew toward the island's central lagoon. Embracing his condor form, Carûtix shot upwards. The power of his massive wings closed the gap. The kestrel made a sudden course change and disappeared. A wide, banked curve brought the condor around to his prey's last known line of direction. The kestrel was nowhere in sight.

A cackled ha-ha-ha alerted him to a large colony of gulls nearby. His aggressive approach startled them into flight. Squawking and jinking one way and then the other, they flew en mass into the thickening darkness covering the Bolcán Murloch.

Carûtix landed on the shore and shed his condor form. Anger blazing, he scanned the lagoon and surrounding shoreline. Darkness camouflaging the kestrel and silent gulls produced a deep, rage-filled growl. "I will find you, Esán Efre, and I *will* make you wish you'd never returned to Neul Isle."

In the clearing by the tidal pool at the island's south end, an oppressive silence sent chills skittering over Esán's skin. He hugged himself and squinted across the ink-black lagoon. *Better get back to Toneer.*

With a shiver he shifted and a fire eagle launched into a low glide. Keen eagle sight picked out the lagoon's western shore. Following its shadow-patterned dimness, he landed opposite Rina Island, shaped Human, and considered his options.

The whisper of moth wings announced the Stannag Luna Moth's faintly glowing wings in the air in front of him. Her telepathic messaged filtered into his mind. *"Sun Queen send message. Torgin and Box return. VarTerels help. Go Vasro camp."* Growing fainter and fainter, La flew toward the shore. A pause and one telepathic word, *"Hurry"*, whispered, before the ghostly moth touched the water's surface and vanished.

Esán closed his eyes, established his trajectory, and flew toward the Vasro campsite. *I'm on the way, Brielle.*

In the Sun Queen's Laboratory, Torgin checked his inventory of 'to dos' and joined the group gathered around the new SorTechory box. To one side, Relevart conferred with Abellona and Shācor.

Gar's spectacle-magnified eyes darted from the Universal VarTerel to Torgin. "We gotta go. Is Relevart coming with us?"

The Universal VarTerel, staff in hand, walked to his side. "Shācor will remain here with the Sun Queen and keep watch over the hologram of Neul Isle. Brie and I will accompany you but will not exit Mittkeer." He scanned the group. "Thorlu and Gar, you will choose your favorite shifted form and stand guard in the trees around the camp. Torgin, Callum will help you prepare The Box to remove the dome. La has alerted Esán to join you at the Vasro campsite."

Brie's expression messaged her distress. "I want to be a part of—" She gulped and wiped a tear from her cheek. "I understand, Relevart."

Gar hugged her. "We all want you to be safe, Brielle."

She returned his hug then looked up at Relevart. "What about the Demi-God of War? Will he know The Box is back?"

Relevart's lips thinned. "Be prepared for that eventuality."

Torgin, his impatience growing, spoke up. "Shācor just checked the dome. If we wait, we may never get back on the island."

Brie responded to the news by lifting her hand. Her staff materialized. Next to her, Thorlu's staff, with Marichi glowing, appeared. The companions closed the gaps in the circle. At Relevart's signal, the three VarTerels lifted their staves to form a tent of crystal light over the SorTechory Box.

Abellona's voice rang out. "The end to the Queen's Quest is drawing near. May success be your champion."

Mittkeer surrounded the group, leaving behind the Sun Queen and her Holographic Specialist. Shooting stars streaked across the universal sky. The Incirrata Constellation took shape. Relevart, with Brie at his side, stepped away from the companions.

"The time has come to remove the dome and our enemies from Neul Isle. The CoaleScence speeds toward its conclusion. You, the Sun Queen's warriors, must bring it to a successful end and open the door for the finale of this Universal Cycle to begin."

. . .

Neul Isle's forest trees replaced the majesty of Mittkeer. Darkness, sticky, stagnant, and cold plastered itself over everything. Thorlu pointed Marichi at the ground. Sticks and dried leaves cycloned into the Vasro's fire pit and burst into flames. The flickering light painted strips of color over the dome-created black canvas.

The rustle of leaves turned four heads. Esán emerged from the clammy darkness into the warmth of the campfire's light. A quick look around produced a frown and a worried gaze. "Thorlu, where's Brie? I thought she was with you."

"She is no longer on the island, Esán. Relevart has pledged to take her to safety." Thorlu glanced at Torgin. "Prepare to remove the dome, or we may be stuck on Neul Isle forever."

Torgin straightened from performing a final check on a relay panel and faced his friend. "Please don't worry about Brie, Esán. She's safe." He rested his hand on the top of The Box. "Since we arrived, the dome has changed again. I may require you and the Seeds of Carsilem to help achieve its successful removal." The increasing urgency, left Torgin shivering. "Thorlu and Gar, please stand guard. And Thorlu, use your connection to Nimah to inform him we're back. Tell him to be ready for Carûtix to react."

Thorlu shaped his fire eagle and flew up to a high branch above the camp. Gar's spectacles vanished, and he shifted. Flying to the top of a Neul cedar on the side nearest the plains, he signaled his arrival with a low, eagle whistle.

Torgin inhaled a calming breath. "Callum, it's time for us to work together. Are you ready?"

The SorTech hung his head. A tremor shook his short stature. Lifting his gaze to Torgin's face, he stammered, "A-a-are y-you sure you t-t-trust me?"

"There is no one I trust more, Callum. You helped to create the new box. You are a SorTech. Stand with me, and we will remove the dome and free Neul Isle from its darkened existence."

"Esán, please be prepared to help. I'll signal—" Torgin froze.

"Carûtix comes." Gar's telepathic message sounded the alarm.

Torgin repeated the message. He and Callum moved in front of The Box. Esán stepped out of sight. A rush of wind shook the trees; a shriek sliced the stagnant air into pieces and riveted their attention upward.

Taloned feet first, a condor dropped through a gap in the forest canopy and landed, its deadly beak snapping first at Callum and then Torgin.

Within the trees bordering the campsite, Torgin sensed Nimah and ShioCáni arrive and shift shape. A VarTerel's shield shot up around The Box. Grateful for Thorlu's quick action, Torgin motioned Callum behind the emberwood cabinet. "Show yourself, Carûtix."

Total attention fixed on Torgin, the condor dug its talons into the dirt. The demi-god materialized, a sword in his hand. He scanned the forest and laughed. "Tell your friends to join us." His gaze as sharp-edged as the sword he held raked Torgin from head to foot. "Get away from my box, now! You, too, Callum." When neither moved, he raised the sword.

Esán walked to stand by the fire. "Drop the sword, or I will take it from you."

Carûtix threw back his head and howled. "Really? You truly believe you can challenge the King of Neul Isle."

Esán's demeanor changed. Power created an aura of pale blue light around his increasing height.

Carûtix lifted the sword higher. Rage distorted his reddening face.

Thorlu flashed into being. "You are outnumbered, Carûtix. Put the sword down, and we will discuss our options."

Narrow nostrils flared wider. "You have no options, VarTerel. I am a deity. You are nothing." He lunged toward The Box, lashed out at the shields, and shouted as the sword rebounded and flew from his fumbling fingers.

Nimah stepped free of the trees and strode into the light, the weapon glinting in his hand. "I believe, cousin, the time has come for us to confer."

Carûtix sneered. "Give me my sword and leave. You are no match for a king."

Lifting the sword, Nimah gazed at it for a long moment before it vanished.

Pure hatred shaped the demi-god's hawkish features. The condor flashed into being. Its wicked beak snapped open then shut. Unfurling its wings, Carûtix rose high on stocky condor legs, stretched his neck to its full length, and, fanning his wings, lumbered toward Nimah.

Torgin held his breath. A second condor, far bigger than Carûtix's shifted form, materialize and prepared for battle. Carûtix's shrieked, launched into the air and took flight up through the gap in the canopy and disappeared.

Nimah's condor squawked, and, wafting massive wings, followed his cousin into the deepening blackness.

Callum peeked around the box and joined Thorlu, Gar, and Esán as ShioCáni stepped into the fire's light.

The Goddess of Harmony studied each of those gathered, then turned to Torgin. "The Sun Queen's triumph depends on you taking the first step to remove the dome."

38
El Aperdisa

Ari paced the grassy floor of Elf's secret space between the walls in the Plantitarium. Three turnings had passed since he disappeared. More desolate than she could ever remember, except when The MasTer's gene took over Brie, she sank onto the bench by the pond. Burying her face in her hands, she let the tears come.

"I've never seen you cry, Arienh AsTar." Rethson sat at the opposite end of the bench, sympathy mingling with concern. "I guess we don't know anything more about Elf's disappearance?"

She sniffed and looked up. "Not one word." Pulling a handkerchief from her uniform pocket, she dabbed tears from her eyes and cheeks and blew her nose.

Rethson slid closer. "Did you know Relevart isn't on board?"

Ari frowned. "Where is he?"

Relevart's youngest son shook his head. "I think you ought to check in with Henrietta. She'll tell us what's up." He stood. "Gotta get back to the galley. Meet you here later." Rily appeared, gave her a quick hug, and vanished.

Smoothing her long red curls back from her face, Ari sighed. Duty calls.

She folded her handkerchief, tucked it in a pocket, and shaped Aero Technician Jem Taisley.

After teleporting to three different spots on the ship, Jem made his way to the T-lift and within a couple chron-clicks stepped onto the bridge. After logging in for his watch, he took his seat next to the communications officer and studied the ledger on his comp-screen.

A quiet voice addressed him. "AeroTech Taisley, Commander Odnamo requests that you meet him in his office."

Jem stood and smiled. "Thank you, Private. I'm on the way."

A short walk later, he tapped in his security code on the touch pad outside the Commander's office. The entry hatch opened. "Come in, Taisley."

He straightened to his full and impressive height, removed his hat, and stepped inside. Surprise made him hesitate.

From behind the desk, Brielle smiled at him. "It is good to see you, Jem. Sit down and let's catch up."

With a finger to her lips, she rose and came around the desk. Holograms formed of them, sitting across from each other. Her hand touched his arm. The restricted section of the ship's Holographic Center surrounded them. She grinned. "We're safe here."

Jem met her happy gaze. "Make me believe you are you? Tell me something—" She shrugged.

"Paisley James Tobinette loves to play chess with CheeTrann." Brie grinned.

Jem's deep laugh morphed into Ari's alto chuckle. "I have missed you, Brielle AsTar! Why are you here? What's happening on Neul—" Ari paused. "Are you alright?"

"I'm fine...just sad to have left Esán and Torgin and Gar behind. I have no idea where Inōni is or Den or Penee." She sniffed and studied her twin. "I understand Elf is missing. Do you know any—"

"Brielle, why are you here?" Ari's eyes narrowed. "And who told you about Elf?"

Brie inhaled. "I've supposedly returned from Neul Isle. After Inōni's baby is born, I'll bring Penee and Den back to the ship. You, Elf, and Rethson are continuing your studies with Wolloh Espyro."

"So why bring you back to *El Aperdisa*?

Henrietta materialized beside them. "To help us flush out the last of the Vasro spies." She smiled. "It is good to see you together, my dear nieces."

Ari felt her temper rising. In an attempt not to lose it, she put her hands on her hips and spoke with calm precision. "I will not let you use Brie as bait, Aunt Henri."

Brie linked an arm through hers. "You and I will work as a team." She smiled. "I'll let Aunt Henri explain."

Henrietta held up her hand. Amethyst rimmed spectacles flashed into being. With her customary tap, tap, tap on her palm, she looked from one twin to the other before perching the spectacles on the bridge of her nose. "We believe there are two more spies on the ship. One is Raiherr's spy and the other is Karlsut Sorda's. Since both our Vasro leader and his boss have been neutralized and communication is cut off, we believe their informants will be seeking a way to escape *El Aperdisa*. To do so they will require a ship or, in the case of Sorda's man, a way down to TreBlaya. We know a jumper craft from the *Surgentin* is hidden on the planet's surface.

"Ari, you as Jem, will meet Brie for the first time at evening meal tonight. You've heard all about the youngest VarTerel in the Universe from crew gossip and can't wait to meet her. Rily joins you and the three of you strike up a friendship.

She peered at Brie through her spectacles. "You are, as Ari noted, the bait. Jem and Rily will be nearby unless you are with me. We're certain one or both will attempt to befriend you."

Ari's mouth twisted into an almost frown. "What about Nesen and Laris?"

Henrietta removed her spectacles. "They are no longer on *El Aperdisa*. Anything else before we put our plan into play?"

Brie, who had listened without comment, broke her silence. "When I'm approached, what then? Do I play their game?"

"Your instincts are exceptional. Follow their lead, but do not leave the ship." Her spectacles vanished. "It is time." She studied them for a long moment before disappearing.

Ari grinned. "Well, sis, the fun begins. Remember, we are a team. Don't do anything without including me."

Brie gave her a hug. "I promise. Meet you at evening meal."

Ari stared at the spot where her twin had been standing moments before. *You'd better keep that promise, Brielle AsTar.*

Torgin knelt next to Callum, in front of the SorTechory Box, performing a last minute check. It's hum, which sounded far too loud in the intense quiet of Neul Isle, made Torgin uneasy. *Sure hope Carûtix doesn't hear it.* He tapped another relay tab and glanced over at the SorTech. "Do you think we're ready, Callum?"

The short man bit his bottom lip, puffed out his pudgy cheeks, and cocked his head. "Won't know unless we try. Shall I tell the others?"

Esán, who had been watching in silence, smiled. "I'll alert Thorlu, and he can tell Gar and ShioCáni."

Torgin climbed to his feet, ran a hand over his curly hair, and squinted up toward the dome. "Alright. Let's do this, Callum. You prepare to create the link between the activator frames and relays. Esán, tell me when you're ready."

He turned to find the SorTech trembling. "Are you alright?"

A repeated shake of his head ended with a hands pressed to his cheeks. "Raiherr and Karlsut will kill me. I c-c-can't."

Torgin knelt to look him in the eye. "Karlsut is no longer in this solar system, and Raiherr has no memory of you or The Box. Besides, you have all of us, including the Sun Queen, to protect you."

Callum snorted to clear his nose. "You're right." He faced the emberwood cabinet. "You're certain we have the right vibrational frequency programmed?"

Rising, Torgin brushed off his pant legs and straightened. "As certain as I can be. If it's not, we'll keep trying."

Esán took a step closer. "Everyone's ready."

Confidence ringing in his voice, Torgin said, "Do your magic, Master SorTech."

Callum took a breath and touched the tab.

The inky blackness enshrouding the island remained intact. Torgin frowned and examined the circuitry. The ground trembled and rolled. Callum let out a squeak and jumped backward.

Fingers crossed for luck, like Gar had taught him, Torgin peered up toward the dome. A shimmering streak zigzagged through the murky black. The muffled sounds of crackle and pop echoed like distant thunder. As suddenly as the change had begun, it ended and silence returned.

Torgin pulled his attention from the still shimmering streak to the interior of the emberwood cabinet, his mind racing. Beside him, Callum stared, unseeing, his shoulders weighted with disappointment.

"Why didn't it work?" Esán joined them.

Frowning, Torgin's analytical gaze darted to the jagged streak of light and back to The Box. "A slight smile curved. "It did work. That was step one...the dome is now connected to The Box. What we need to discover is the dome's new frequency and how to align it with the SorTechory Box and its operator." He tapped a long, musician's finger against his chin, then removed the time whistle from beneath his shirt. "I've got this and, Esán, you've got Tumu Noci. Our problem now is how to make the best use of them."

Esán slipped a hand in his pocket and curled his fingers around the key to the space-time continuum. "I have an idea, Torgin. What if Callum and I stay here with The Box, and you fly or teleport to the mouth of the San Crúil River. It's the closest place where you can analyze the dome close up, plus you know the area."

Thorlu landed in their midst. "You need to hurry. Nimah can only control his cousin for a finite amount of time." He shaped a fire eagle and soared upward.

Torgin gripped the whistle. "I'm going. Track me. As soon as I have the correct vibrational frequency, I'll share it with you." He turned to Callum. "Be ready to assist Esán." Stepping away from The Box, he vanished.

Nimah's condor flew in silent haste after Carûtix. A change in the air currents ahead of him warned him his cousin's condor banked back toward the Plains of Cârthea. Accelerating, Nimah cut across the smaller condor's path and sent his cousin swooping lower. Talons reaching, the queen's heir dropped and gripped Carûtix by the heart saddle at the back of his neck. With weight and balance as his allies, Nimah forced the smaller condor to land in the tall grass at the plain's center.

Nimah embodied his true persona, his gaze fixed on his cousin's materializing form. Neither spoke.

Carûtix glared, the nostrils in his crooked nose pulsing open and closed. Malice-tensed lips pressed into a firm line. Fisted hands shook. "How dare you —" His mouth worked. The muscles of his chest and arms steeled, ready to fight.

Nimah remained relaxed. "If you choose to fight me, you will not like the end result. Your sire and the Sun Queen sent me to negotiate with you. Help us remove the dome and return the K'iin to their village, and I will take you back to your father's realm in Shió Ridu."

Carûtix spoke through snarl-twisted lips. "I am the King of Neul Isle. Bow to me, and I will let you live to return to grovel at the feet of your ma—"

Without warning, a tremor shook the ground. Above them, a streak of light formed on the under surface of the dome.

Carûtix's howl of dismay joined the thunder-like rumble rolling over the island. He ran toward the Vasro camp, stopped, and glared at up at the dome. A quick about face brought him around to face Nimah. "Do Not touch me again." His brow creased with effort. He shook his head and held out his arms. A slow change began.

Nimah watched his cousin struggle to shift shape. Midway through his transition to a condor, he froze. The gray and orange skin covering his head, framed his terror-filled face; arms lengthening to form wings sported layers of pinions; and his legs shortening ended with the talon of the longer middle toes poking through the tips of leather boots.

A screeched whine preceded a low growl. Carûtix worked his mouth. Spit flew as he fought to form two words. "Help me."

The fear and pleading pouring from his cousin's entire being made Nimah cringe. He took a step closer. "I cannot help you, Carûtix. Your powers are fighting not to fade away, but they're losing the battle. Your anger at your father has kept you on Neul Isle too long."

"Please..." Tears streamed down his cousin's cheeks.

Nimah tipped his head back and stared up at the dome. *Who is the best to help us?* A thought surface. He looked down at Carûtix. *Can I trust you not to do more harm to yourself and others?*

Zak woke up from a deep sleep to find Loris glaring down at him. "What's up?"

The Vasro stepped back. "Get up. Reedan has something to show you." He scowled and left.

A yawn and a stretch later, Zak quickly donned his uniform, hurried to the jumper craft's flight deck, and stopped short. Eyes wide, he gawked through the ship's window at a solid black dome covering the majority of Neul Isle.

Reedan looked over at him and raised a brow. "You ever been to Soputto?"

"Nope." Zak shook his head. "What's that thing hiding the island?"

Reedan eyeballed him. A pinkish gray tongue poked through the gap in his front teeth and retreated. "Sure you don't know this island?"

Zak let impatience creep into his voice. "I told you...I've never been to this planet." He stared hard at Reedan. "You still don't trust me, even after I left *El Aperdisa* 'cause I trusted you."

Reedan studied him for a long time before he responded. "You still interested in studying to be a Vasro?"

Arms folded, Zak blew out a frustrated breath. "Why do you think I stowed away?" He frowned, his attention straying toward the flight deck's window. "Why Soputto? Is there something special here?"

The Vasro pursed his full lips, then inhaled. "What would you say if I told you the man who will oversee your training as a Vasro is on that island?"

Zak gaped. "Is he under that black thing?"

Reedan nodded at Laris, who sat at the controls. "We're about to find out. I suggest you buckle up."

Seated next to Laris, Zak fastened his safety harness and cast a sideways glance at the pilot.

Determination lifted the man's narrow chin. The ship swooped into a long glide circumventing the dome's outer edge. Rounding the northern end of the island, it flew along the eastern shore and landed on a patch of land, bordered by the sea on one side and the dome on the other.

My friends are under that. Zak stared at the wall of black and shuddered. *How do I get to them? Good thing Relevart had me memorize the map of the island.*

Reedan unbuckled and stood up. "Laris, you deal with the ship. Zak, come with me. We'll check this out." He descended to the ground and waited. When Zak jumped down beside him, the Vasro gripped his arm and shoved him ahead of him. "Touch the dome and see if it's safe."

Zak rubbed his arm. "Please don't do that again, Reedan. I may be young, but I am every bit as strong as you."

Reedan took a menacing step forward and stopped dead in his tracks as the island quaked. Distant rumbling followed by a thunder-like crackling sound sent him hurrying into the spacecraft.

Zak did not move. Narrowed eyes scrutinized every bit of the dome within his line of vision. Instinct tingled through him. He glanced at the jumper and then at the sea a short distance away.

Reedan stuck his head out of the hatch. "Are you coming, boy?"

Zak's only response was a mad dash toward the shore. Once out of sight of the spacecraft, he slid down the sloped bank and plunged into the sea. Water washing over him sent a chill of expectation over his entire body. Swimming deeper, he allowed the shape shift to happen. The sea creature Marji had created to save his life on DerTah once more embraced him and carried him further out on the currents of high tide.

Webbed feet and hands propelled him through the cool water. Luxuriating in a sense of freedom he hadn't experienced since he'd shaped Human on the Senndis' sailboat, SeaBella, he focused on putting as much distance between him and the jumper craft as possible.

The steady hum of the ship zooming low over the sea propelled him into a deep dive. Cool water wrapped him like a baby in a blanket, nurtured his very being, and made him wish, for one lone moment, that he could remain the creature forever.

39
Neul Isle

Esán withdrew Tumu Noci from his pocket and watched the key grow to span his hand from wrist to fingertips. His brow creased. *It's never grown this large before.* He scanned the camp.

ShioCáni strode from the woods. "Nimah controls our cousin, but not for long." She grew still. "I've never seen Tumu Noci grow to that size. Do you know what's happening?"

Esán experienced a rush of energy. He caught his breath and whispered, "Torgin has reached the mouth of the river."

His mind opened to a flood of information. Tumu Noci glowed bronze and gold. He pressed it to his heart, then touched it to the emberwood cabinet. His gaze darted to the side of the camp nearest the plains, where a ruckus erupted.

Nimah's voice rang out. "Carûtix, stop. I can't help you if you run away from me."

Feathered arms waving, the would-be king half-hopped, half-lunged into the clearing. Bulging eyes searched the camp and came to rest on The Box. Waving his arms faster, he fought his way closer.

Nimah flashed ahead of him. "Stop, cousin, or I will help you do so."

When the half condor-half man did not slow his awkward pace, the Sun Queen's heir chanted,

> *"Time ensnare this bird plus man.*
> *Keep it still right where it stands.*
> *Weave your threads of time to be*
> *Solid till I set them free."*

Carûtix jerked to a stop. His expression froze. Extended arm-wings ceased their frantic waving. His fear-filled eyes darted from Nimah to Esán to The Box then rolled back in his head.

Tumu Noci's demanding vibration pulled Esán's attention back to the emberwood cabinet. Background noise faded. The key and The Box flooded his consciousness. His increasing heart rate stimulated the dual Seeds of Carsilem. Pulsing energy spread down to his feet, up to his head, and beyond. Hands pressed to the top of the cabinet transferred the vibrational information from Torgin into the interior circuitry. The faint hum throbbing against his palms grew more insistent. He inhaled. Images of the dome flooded his mind. Pitch black, murky, and solid, it arched over the island. Exhaling, he pictured the blackness transitioning back to paint-like splotches accompanied by the explosion of the original box. Another inhale and he erased the splotches, leaving the dome an opaque gray.

Distantly, he heard the gasps of his companions. Gar's voice penetrated his trance state. "Look, he's floating above The Box and he's glowing and—"

Tumu Noci trembling refocused his attention. An image of Torgin, his whistle raised to his lips, shimmered and focused. One soft high note floated upward, followed by a series of notes that accelerated the throbbing of the key to the space-time continuum.

Brightness surrounding him lifted Esán higher. Up through the canopy, he floated with Torgin's music flowing around him. The dome arching overhead grew closer and closer. With Tumu Noci extended above, he touched its tip to the shimmering grayness.

The energetic structure of the dome sparkled and faded into nothing.

Sunshine warmed his upraised face. A breeze rustled through his hair and caressed his cheeks. Conscious only of the golden glow around him, he floated higher.

Esán's awareness broadened and journeyed with Torgin's melody throughout Neul Isle and beyond. In the lagoon, Rina, the Incirrata, surfaced, her Stannags, La and Abarax, floating above her. Cadhōla and the members of the K'iin and her tribesmen in the Bāoba Forest Sanctuary Pod cheered and sang their thanksgiving. And in Shiór Ridu, the Sun Queen and Shācor shared smiles of delight.

Everywhere he went, Esán swept up the negativity that had collected beneath the dome and neutralized it. From high above Neul Isle, he observed the jumper ship stolen by Reedan and Laris hovering over the Plains of Cârthea. He floated closer, pointed Tumu Noci, and wrapped the spacecraft in a time fold, one that would carry it into a new dimension.

Focusing on Torgin's position at the mouth of the river, he arrived in the sky high above him in time to observe Elf's sea creature scrambling through shallow water toward the shore. Kelp green eyes the size of fists focused on Torgin, who watched with surprise that quickly became delight.

The creature's fang-lined mouth opened in a cry of wonder. Water droplets flew around it as it reached firm ground and shook its seaweed draped head. Strong, scaly legs carried it over the sand. Midway to Torgin, it stopped, howled one last time, and shifted.

Elf met Torgin's gaze and strode to meet him. "Am I glad to see you!"

Torgin smiled and pointed upward at a figure cocooned in glowing golden light. He raised the time whistle to his lips and blew a series of notes.

Esán pointed the key at the two men, floated to the beach beside them, and stepped free of the fading light. He inhaled the fresh sea air and shared a smile with Torgin. "We did it. Neul Isle is free of the dome." A slight turn brought him around to face Elf. "Your arrival added to our energy reserve. Thank you for stowing away on the ship."

Torgin rotated. His summer green eyes glinting with pleasure, he stopped facing Elf and tucked the whistle beneath his shirt. "How did you know we needed you?"

Elf shrugged. "Instinct and the desire to see the dome removed." His curious gaze rested on Esán. "I've never encountered anything like the energy flowing from you, Esán Efre."

Still dazed, Esán slipped the now small key into his pocket and touched his chest. Wonder and gratitude infused his expression. "The Seeds have blossomed into maturity." He smiled. "And so have I."

Torgin studied him with a touch of awe. "I knew when the right time arrived, the Seeds would mature, but I didn't know how breathtaking your shift would be. Congratulations, Esán!"

"Thank you, Torgin Whalend!" Esán inhaled and looked up at the sky. Clarity replaced his astonished daze. "Gar's getting worried. Let's go set his mind at rest and decide what our next step is. We still have work to do before the Queen's Quest is complete."

He linked arms with Elf, who rested a hand on Torgin's arm. The trio flashed from the beach to the campsite, where Gar, Thorlu, and Callum stood by the SorTechory Box. Nimah stood next to ShioCáni, their faces alight with wonder tinted with surprise. Next to them, Carûtix, still trapped halfway to condor, did not move.

👀

Brie scanned the crew's mess hall. She had never liked crowds and found the room full of *El Aperdisa's* crew intimidating. Jem's appearance, a tray full of food in hand, produced a wave of relief.

After placing his tray on a nearby table, he walked over to her. "You look a bit lost. I'm Jem. Would you like to share my table?"

Relief brightened her smile. "Thank you, I'd like that. I'm Brie. My friends aren't on board so…" She shrugged. "I'll get my meal."

"Good. See you in a few." He returned to the table.

At the chow line, Brie placed a plate and eating ware on a tray and selected an assortment of delicious looking foods. Stomach growling, she turned and gasped. The sound of her tray hitting the floor and the coolness of her drink soaking through her blouse brought her up short.

A young crewman stared at her, aghast. "Oh no, I'm so sorry. I didn't see you until it was too late. My names Private Rojond. What if I wait for you, and we can eat together?"

Brie looked down at the food and drink splattered on her front. "You go ahead. I think I'll eat in my quarters." She turned to leave.

"Wait. What's your name?"

"I'm Brielle. Now, if you'll excuse me."

The crewman touched her arm. "I'd like to make it up to you. Could we meet tomorrow for mid-turning meal?"

Shaking her red curls back from her face, she forced a smile. "I'll see you then."

She walked from the mess hall and made her way down the passageway to the T-lift where several crew members waited. Relieved Rily that stood among them, she joined the group.

A female petty officer glanced at her food splattered clothing. "I saw the private bump into you. Are you alright?"

Brie sighed. "I'm fine. I just want to get clean."

When the T-lift arrived, the crewmen filed in. Brie hesitated, but a petty officer nudged her forward. A turn to face the entry spurred a tingle from the Star of Truth. Rily and the Head Chef were conversing. With a stab of alarm, she watched the entry close.

The petty officer edged over to stand beside her. "I'm Chief Sorela. Are you sure you're alright?"

Brie looked at her food covered hands and laughed. "Just starving." Her senses heightened. "What's your assignment on the ship?"

"I'm in communications with AeroTech Taisley." The chief raised a brow and smiled at Brie.

"I don't believe I've met AeroTech Taisley." Brie shrugged.

"Actually, you have. He's the man who spoke to you when you entered the mess hall."

"You mean Jem?" The Star pinched.

The chief's brow remained arched. "You're Brielle AsTar, correct?" She didn't wait for a reply. "Why don't you know him? You've been on the ship longer than me."

Brie prepared to exit the T-lift. "I don't know all the crew members. Do you?" She followed an older crewman into the passageway.

Once inside her quarters, she stripped off her food-covered clothes, tossed them into the clothes cleaner, and stepped into the body cleanse. A short time later, she entered the living space to find a note from Ari on her personal message tab.

"Cross your fingers." Their code for 'meet in the secret space' activated the Star of Truth, again.

Rubbing her neck, she almost smiled. *The Star is truly coming back.* She touched it and frowned. *Why react to Ari's message? Unless—"*

Her arrival behind a screen of trees in the Plantitarium was instantaneous. Down the path near the entrance, Sorela and Rojond conversed. A change to a butterfly allowed Brie to fly closer.

Annoyance colored the private's face. "I told you—I didn't mean to bump into her." He chewed his bottom lip. "It did get us talking, though."

Sorela frowned. "If I were her, I'd be suspicious. She's a VarTerel—she's smart." Sorela looked up the path. "We need her to take us down to the ship on TreBlaya." Her gaze traveled upward and returned to his face. "Reedan told me he felt certain Jem, Rily, and Zak met somewhere in here. He is also sure the trio are her sister and her friends, so she's bound to meet up with them here, too."

"This place is enormous." The crewman scowled. "I've been watching Jem and Rily since Zak vanished. They haven't done anything to suggest they aren't who they say they are. Brie's back, right? I'm bettin' the others will be back on board soon."

Sorela stared him down. "Then let's be waiting for them in their meeting place. Get a move on."

Rojond lifted his chin. "You're not my boss. I work for Yencara." He turned to leave.

"And I work for Yencara's boss, so..." Her brittle tone stopped him. "One more thing, we'd better be careful. I'm pretty sure Commander Odnamo knows there are still spies on the ship."

Rojond's dislike of her left him panting. "You find their secret spot. I'm going to—"

The chief's expression held a warning. He turned.

A guard stood in the entryway. Behind him, four more sturdy men made escape impossible. The leader's stern gaze sent a warning. "Chief Sorela and Private Rojond, fall in. You are both headed for the brig." With guards on either side of them, the Vasro spies marched down the passageway.

Brie's butterfly flew to the wall of the secret room, passed through, and shifted.

Seconds later, Ari materialized. "Whew! Glad you pinpointed those two."

After a relieved hug, they sat down on the bench by the pond. Brie smiled at her twin. "Guess what!"

"What?"

Brie touched her neck. "The Star of Truth is coming back."

Her twin patted the scabbard hidden beneath her clothes. "Efillaeh's healing powers did the trick."

Brie touched her arm. They teleported to Henrietta's and Relevart's quarters.

The aunt smiled. "A job well done, my dear nieces."

Ari twisted a red curl around her finger. "I have a question, Aunt Henri. How did we accomplish this so fast?"

Henrietta answered without reservation. "Relevart asked Commander Odnamo to have the word leaked that Brie was back. His informant also started a rumor that the commander continued to look for Vasro spies on board *El Aperdisa*. This put pressure on the two remaining spies to act quickly and get off the ship. With Brie back, they had her, as required by their bosses, and a way to reach their spacecraft on TreBlaya."

Ari released the curl and nodded. "And Brie and I did our part by just acting natural."

Brie smiled at her aunt. "Tell Relevart thank you for the help." After giving her aunt a quick hug, she touched her twin's arm. "I'm starving. Let's go prepare a feast."

Arriving in their quarters, they shared a chuckle and a hug and then Ari headed for their private dining area. "You are so good at teleporting, Brielle AsTar." She looked back at her sister. "Well, are you coming? I'm starving, too!"

More relaxed than they had been in a long time, they prepared their feast, sat down, and enjoyed every mouthful.

Still dazed by the maturing of the Seeds, Esán remained on the sidelines while Torgin and Gar greeted Elf. Laughter filled what had once been the

Vasro campsite. Splashes of sunlight bathing their smiling faces and splattering the ground around them added to the joy of the moment.

Esán inhaled and savored the sweet aroma of wildflowers and moss and fresh air. Exhaling a contented breath, he walked over to Nimah, ShioCáni, and Thorlu, who eyed him with keen interest.

The VarTerel's gray-green eyes gleamed in the sunlight. "You never cease to amaze me, Esán Efre. Not only did you remove the dome, but you arrived back here with my son at your side. Where did you find him?"

Esán smiled and described Elf's appearance on the shore where Torgin had accessed the dome. "Although I don't believe he realizes it, the Universal VarTerels sent him to help Carûtix release his condor form."

Thorlu glanced over at The Box, where Gar and Torgin questioned Elf about events on *El Aperdisa*, and a lost-looking Callum stared wistfully at the emberwood cabinet. "I have a question for Torgin, so I'll bring Elf—" He chuckled as his son caught his eye and walked over.

"Hello, Father. You look surprised to see me." Elf grinned.

"I am. We'll catch up later." Thorlu's return smile held a touch of humor. "Nimah and ShioCáni, may I present my son, Troms el Shiv, known to friends and family as Elf?"

ShioCáni held out her hand, palm up. "It is a pleasure to meet you, Troms el Shiv. Please tell me of the happenings on *El Aperdisa*."

Elf touched her palm with his, and said, "You are the Goddess of Harmony, correct? I'm so happy to meet you."

Thorlu, pride shining in his eyes, stepped away to observe his son before crossing the clearing to engage Torgin in conversation.

While ShioCáni and Elf talked, Nimah regarded Esán with a warm smile. "Did you know the Seeds were maturing when you sent Torgin to investigate the dome?"

Esán shook his head. "I had no idea. It wasn't until Tumu Noci touched the emberwood cabinet that I became aware something different was happening. By then, I was totally immersed. Until the dome faded and sunshine and fresh air surrounded me, I had only a vague awareness of what was occurring."

He glanced over at Carûtix, whose half man-half bird remained rigid. Panic-filled human eyes darted one way and then the other. His mustached upper lip quivered. Esán experienced a moment of sympathy. "I believe it is time for Elf and me to help your cousin."

Torgin and Thorlu joined them. "Before you release him back to himself, we need to remove The Box."

ShioCáni nodded her agreement. "If Carûtix sees the SorTechory Box, it will reactivate his desire to be King of Neul Isle. Where's the best place to hide it?"

Gar hurried over, his spectacles in place. Glowing ember rims highlighted the fire-opal glint in his eyes. He touched his throat. "The Sun Queen wishes to speak."

Abellona's voice filled the clearing. "Relevart and I discussed the safest place for the SorTechory Box. I will transport it to Shiór Ridu and keep it here until it is required elsewhere." She grew silent, then spoke once more. "Callum, you have a choice...remain on Neul Isle or return here with The Box. If you choose my palace, please touch the cabinet."

The SorTech, his bulging eyes bright with tears, reached out. The instant his hand touched it, streaks of red in the black wood cabinet shimmered brighter. Joy filled Callum's round face. The Box and SorTech both vanished.

Gar rubbed his throat, removed his specs, and sent them into hiding. "She says we are to complete the job at hand."

Nimah examined the bird-man's frozen immobile figure and turned to Esán. "Although I stopped him from reaching the box, it is his loss of power that trapped him halfway between bird and man, I believe you are the one who must bring him back to his full beingness. ShioCáni and I will stand on one side." He motioned the Goddess of Harmony to join him, and then added, "Torgin and Gar, please stand opposite us."

Torgin nudged Gar ahead of him and stepped up beside him.

The Sun Queen's heir conferred with ShioCáni before returning his attention to Esán and Elf. "Once Carûtix has returned to himself, be prepared to help us call forth the Deity Wind to carry us all home to Shiór Ridu."

"We'll be ready." Esán stepped behind Carûtix. "It's time, Troms El Shiv. Please combine your knowledge with mine to release the condor and bring Carûtix back to himself."

Elf moved to stand in front of the demi-god and solemnly examined the half-bird-half man. "Let's get this done."

Esán opened to the Seeds of Carsilem and allowed their pulsing vibration to fill him. At his signal, Elf placed his hands on either side of the wrinkled crown of skin topping the bird-man's head. Esán rested his hands on Elf's, fixed his gaze on Carûtix, and tuned into the demi-god's core being.

Pulsing vibration increased. The energy of the Seeds of Carsilem combined with Elf's creating an aura of golden light that wove a web of cognizance through the bird-man's psyche. Carûtix's distorted body began to quiver. Awareness flickered.

Esán removed his hands and pressed them to his chest.

Elf remained still, his hands in place. "Be ready, Nimah. He is pretty confused." He raised his hands and stepped away.

Carûtix quaked from head to foot. The dark crown topping his gray and orange head quivered. White feathers covering his neck and shoulders separated into fluffy clumps of white and floated upward on the breeze. Winged arms shook and lifted. Pinions fell to the ground in a pile around his short legs. Again, he quaked. The tremor moved from his feet upward, lengthening his legs and freeing him of what remained of the condor.

No one moved or spoke. Carûtix shuddered, shook his head, and raised clenched fists to eye level. His fingers uncurled. He pressed his palms to his cheeks, opened his mouth and howled. Gulping air, he lowered his arms and let his confused gaze travel over those surrounding him.

His slate-gray eyes rounded. The narrow nostrils in his hawkish nose flared. He stared at the spot where the SorTechory Box had stood. Repeated shakes of his head and fists pounding his chest stopped as suddenly as they began. He panted, his chest rising and falling as clarity dawned.

The Sun Queen's heir stepped to his cousin's side. A soft whispered phrase calmed the building agitation. Carûtix covered his face with his hands.

At Nimah's signal, Esán drew on the power of the Seeds to help ShioCáni call forth the Deity Winds. Leaves and grass swirled around the three cousins, lifting them upward. A ray of pale blue light shot down from the heavens, surrounded them, and carried them higher and higher until they disappeared.

Elf let out a breath and rubbed his hands on his pant legs. "That was close. His rage was boiling. Thank goodness for Nimah."

The companions moved closer together. A bird chirped, a tinimunk scurried across the clearing, and high above them, the leaves rustling in the breeze sang a song of freedom and hope.

40
El Aperdisa

On the living ship, *El Aperdisa*, Brie and Ari came to their feet, their attention fixed on the Universal VarTerel, Henrietta Avetlire. A soft lavender glow shone around her. The shimmering amethyst rims of her spectacles accentuated her wise and ethereal expression.

Brie released a breath and squeezed Ari's hand. "The dome is gone from Neul Isle." She looked at her aunt for confirmation.

Henrietta's violet eyes gleamed. "The CoaleScence nears its conclusion. You each have destinies to fulfill." The amethyst rims glowed brighter. "Ariehn, Relevart awaits you in Mittkeer. Prepare to join your true love." She raised her hand.

Ari gasped as Mittkeer embraced her.

Brie's heartbeat quickened. Anticipation propelled her a step closer to her aunt. "It's time for Inōni to return to her home and family, isn't it?"

"Almost. You must collect her and Penee and Den and take them to Neul Isle, but not until I give you the word." Again, Henrietta lifted a hand.

Brie caught her breath as The Land of All Time and No Time wrapped her in its starry night. Her staff materialized, and Musette's rainbow light pooled around her. A raven's call held her quiet. Another caw inspired a suspense-filled shiver. Mittkeer withdrew and left her staring at a place filled with so many memories it almost overwhelmed her. Rotating slowly, she absorbed the beauty of the sunlit cottage, where a smokey gray cat with eyes to match Aunt Henri's, reclined on the front step. Behind it, the Terces Wood formed the background for the beautiful garden, a red barn, and a pond. She hugged herself and wiped the tears from her eyes.

An excited bark announced the arrival of Buster. Tail wagging, the big, shaggy, brown dog, jumped up, rested his paws on her shoulders, and licked her cheek. She scratched his ears and laughed as his panted breath tickled her nose. With a happy yip, he dropped to the ground and pranced around behind her.

"Welcome, my dear. It has been some time since you visited us in Myrrh."

Brie turned to find Almiralyn smiling at her. "Aunt Henri sent me. You brought Inóni, Den, and Penee here, right?"

Almiralyn smiled. "We did, and they are eager to see you. However, I must clarify their situation first. Come in, and we'll enjoy a cup of tea while we chat."

When they reached the back steps to the cottage, Buster gave a sharp bark, licked Brie's hand, and trotted off toward the red barn. Brie smiled at her aunt. "I am so glad Chealim brought Buster back to you."

Almiralyn beamed. "So am I!" She led the way onto the back porch.

Brie followed, stepped into the kitchen, and smiled as the walls change from pale blue to a warm, sunny yellow. She sat down at the table, her memories flickering by, one image after the other. Squeezing her eyes shut, she calmed her mind and prepared to listen to Almiralyn.

Footsteps crossing the back porch stopped in the kitchen doorway. "What a pleasure it is to see, Brielle AsTar." Corvus took a seat across from her.

"You were in Mittkeer." Brie smiled.

"I was there to make sure you arrived at your destination." He studied her for a long moment. "Henrietta shared that Commander Odnamo has removed all Vasro spies from *El Aperdisa*. She is most relieved. More than that, she is proud of you, Ari, Rethson, and Elf."

Almiralyn set a fragrant cup of tea in front of her. "Why are you looking so sad, Brie?"

"I wanted to be on Neul Isle when they removed the dome. Even more important...the Seeds of Carsilem matured, and I wasn't there to support Esán." Struggling not to give in to a wave of emotions, she lifted her cup, inhaled the scents of dojanberries and ginger, and took a sip. The rich flavors made her smile. "My favorite tea! Thank you, Aunt Mira."

"You are welcome. Enjoy it while Corvus and I share a couple of things with you."

Brie pictured her yearning to be with Esán, dispersing with the steam from her tea, and took another sip. Setting the delicate porcelain cup in its saucer, she prepared to listen.

Almiralyn's sapphire blue eyes softened. "When we brought Inōni and your friends here, she was close to giving birth. Because her desire to be on Neul Isle with her family when her daughter is born aligns with the resolution of the Queen's Quest and completion of this universal cycle, Relevart devised a plan. Den and Penee are with Inōni in a pocket of Mittkeer, safe from time's passing. It is vital that we wait until everything is resolved on the island before you return with them. Henrietta will notify us when the job is done. Until then, you and I and Corvus will enjoy time together."

Corvus smiled. "Your visit, Brielle, is an unexpected treat."

Brie returned his smile, finished her tea, and sat back in her chair. "Is it possible for me to visit with Inōni?"

Almiralyn set her cup in its saucer. "Although we are all VarTerels, Relevart has asked us to maintain our distance. Isolation assures Inōni will not give birth until she is on Neul Isle. When it is time, we will enter Mittkeer and you will escort her, Penee, and Den to the K'iin village." She stood. "Come. I will show you to your room, so you can get some rest."

Corvus pushed back his chair. "It's time for me to make my rounds. I will see you both later." He shaped the raven Karrew and flew out the open window.

Brie watched his change with a slight smile. *So many memories! How lucky am I to be here in this moment in this place!*

Esán watched the demi-gods rise above Neul Isle and disappear into the heavens with mixed feelings. Their presence and their power, added to his and his companions, had helped to rid Neul Isle of the dome and its makers. He lowered his gaze and smiled at Gar, who stared up at him, a question in his ever-curious dark eyes.

"What's next, Esán? We've still got stuff to do."

Torgin moved to rest his hands on his young cousin's shoulders and studied Esán with curiosity aligned with Gar's. "We still have Raiherr, his ship, and his Vasro to remove permanently from Neul Isle before we can allow the K'iin to return home. Also, what about Hossela?"

The VarTerel and his son joined them. "Elf and I will work with Hossela to decide what he desires to do. He has already admitted Sorda and Rados are not on his list of potential employers. There's a good man hidden beneath the cloak of the Klutarse. We'll see if we might help him emerge."

Esán sensed the growing connection between Thorlu and Elf with a touch of envy. *Sure wish you were here, Father.* A slight shake of the head brought his attention back to the clearing. "That sounds good, Thorlu."

Gar's bottled-up impatience burst forth in a loud clearing of his throat. "What about Torgin and me?"

Unsuccessfully, trying to hide a grin, Esán chuckled. "You will take your cousin and go to the Bāoba Sanctuary. Inform Cadhōla about what's happening." He looked up at the beginning of the first sunset he had seen since arriving on Neul Isle. "I will do a final flight over the island and meet you there. Tomorrow, when we are sure all the Vasro are gone, we will go to the Labyrinth Cavern and share our news with Dri Adoh and Artānga."

"Great." Gar's white teeth flashed as his dark features lit up with delight. He peered up at Torgin. "I say we shape fire eagles and enjoy soaring in the open. Whatda *you* say?"

Torgin looked up at the blue overhead and back at his cousin. "Great idea, hold on." He turned to Thorlu. "Will you meet us at the Sanctuary Pod when you have removed Raiherr and his men?"

"Sure will."

Torgin smiled. "We will see you in the village. Please use telepathy, so we know what's—" He looked toward the plains where a Luna Moth perched on the Astican's shoulder. "Looks like we have visitors."

Abarax and La teleported to the group. The Astican gazed down from his magnificent height. "The Incirrata asked us to express to you her gratitude for removal of the dome and the return of the sun's light. As the sacred island's guardian, she asks how long before you remove the last of the enemies?"

Esán held out his hand. La alighted. He held her up at eye level. "Tell Rina that Thorlu and Elf are about to deal with the last Vasro and will remove them from the island as soon as possible." He looked up at Abarax. "I will tell her when we have completed the Queen's Quest."

The Incirrata's Stannags took flight and faded into the blue of the sky.

Gar watched them. "They are ghosts, right?"

Torgin nodded. "Yes, they are."

Gar pursed his lips. "Can ghosts be in love?"

Esán laughed. "Yes, they can. La and Abarax are in love and sealed to each other. Now, Garon Anaru, off you go!"

He started to run, then looked back at Torgin. "Beat ya up to the sky!" The exuberant boy vanished into a fire eagle already in flight.

Torgin shifted shape and flew after him.

Elf grinned. "They are definitely related. Kinda like me and you, huh Thorlu?"

His father laughed. "Bet I can beat you to the Vasro jumper craft." His fire eagle shot upward."

Elf caught Esán's eye and laughed when he mentally shared an image of the craft, "See you soon!"

He shaped an eagle familiar to him and soared upward, leaving Esán alone in the clearing.

Allowing himself time to absorb the peacefulness of the moment, Esán shaped his favorite kestrel and soared up into the soft glow of evening's colors starting to tint the sky.

Torgin and Gar arrived in the Bāoba Forest as the sun began its elegant glide to the horizon. Landing side by side on a porch platform, they shaped Human and stared in awe at the beauty of the trees and the pods in the late afternoon light.

Gar blew out a breath and hugged his cousin. "Thanks, Torg. I never expected to have a cousin or the adventures we're sharing."

A wave of closeness he had not experienced before left Torgin gazing at his young cousin with a bemused smile. "Nor did I, Gar. Shall we let Cadhōla know we're here?"

Soft laughter made them turn. The tribal wise woman stood in the open oval entry. "We have been hoping all turning that you would come to us." She gazed up through the forest canopy and brushed a tear from her cheek. "The dome is gone." Her glistening brown eyes lowered to meet Torgin steady gaze. "Will it come back?"

Drawing Gar to his side, Torgin answered with all the sincerity he could muster. "It will not be coming back. May we join you and your tribesmen? We have many things to share."

Cadhōla stepped aside and waved them into the Sanctuary Pod, where the small group of K'iin huddled, their eager expressions combined with the tension of not knowing. At a sign from their wise woman, they moved to one side, revealing a food laden table and a grouping of chairs near the fire center.

Leading them to the chairs, the wise woman sat down, her eyes sparkling, and a smile twitching. "Young Gar, I thought you might be hungry. We will eat soon. Now, share what has occurred."

Gar's smile flashed. "Glad you knew 'cause my stomach's growling. Torgin will tell you everything." He looked over at his cousin. "Won't you, Torg?"

The wise woman and those K'iin who understood his language prepared to listen with total concentration.

Reassurance filling his voice, Torgin summarized what had occurred over the past several turnings. "The Sun Queen removed the SorTechory Box and the man to controlled it to her palace in Chadēta Apól. Neither will be returning to Neul Isle. Esán is doing a final flight over the island, while Thorlu and his son, Elf, prepare to remove the last of the Vasro. The Deity Council, with the help of the Galactic Council, has removed everyone else beyond the Spéire Solar System and is prepared to deal with them, should they dare to return. They will also help with the three who Thorlu and Elf are removing should they remember Neul Isle."

When he finished, Cadhōla's eyes were shining. "We are truly free of the dome. Our sacred isle lays once more beneath the open sky and we, its guardians, are once more free to roam its shores."

Sitting back, Cadhōla stared up at the curved top of the pod. She straightened, rose to standing, and faced her tribal members. In their language, she summarized Torgin's words, endind with a sacred pronouncement.

Her people came together in a semi-circle, their gaze fixed on Torgin and Gar. As one, they lower to one knee and touched their hearts. Together they recited in their beautiful language.

*"You are the heroes of our hearts.
We praise your courage and your arts.
You will remain in memory,
From now through all eternity."*

Two eagles alighted near the jumper craft, *Toneer*. Appreciative laughter burst forth as Thorlu and Elf shaped Human. "You are good, my son. What type of eagle did you shape? It seems vaguely familiar."

"It is a DerTahan Sea Eagle. I learned to shape it when I lived with the Senndis at their cottage outside Atkis."

Thorlu's smooth brow creased. "That's why it seems familiar. I've visited the nearby Isle of Temecrya in the province of Tringue." A shiver dispersed his negative memories. "It was not a pleasant experience." A twinge of sadness made him sigh. "I was a different person then. Perhaps I'll share the story another time. Right now, Hossela knows we're here."

A man of medium height with the prominent musculature to support his training as an assassin jumped from the open entry hatch and strode to meet them. "Good thing you're here, Tangorra. Raiherr is waking up, and his men will soon follow." He regarded Elf with interest. "Who's your sidekick?"

"This is my son, Elf. He'll stay out here while we decide our next move."

Hossela's wide mouth curved. "Nice ta meet ya, Elf." He turned and climbed aboard the jumper.

Thorlu rested a hand on his son's shoulder. "Thanks for standing guard. I think we're safe, but you never know what surprises might await us. I'll see what's up, then fill you in."

"Be careful, Father. Once an assassin, always an assassin." Elf glanced around, shifted, and flew to a nearby tree."

Sure hope you're wrong. Thorlu climbed into the jumper craft, took a moment to analyze the situation and joined Hossela in the crew's quarters, where he kept watch over Raiherr and his sidekicks, Zorin and Dulno."

The Klutarse made space for him on the narrow bench across from the slowly waking ex-Vasro. "How do we remove 'em from the island?"

Thorlu studied the man next to him. "More to the point...what about you? Do you wish to be removed from this solar system or—" He waited for Hossela to fill in the blanks."

"I'm hoping I can return to *El Aperdisa* with you. Since my ancestors are from El Stroma, I thought the commander might consider allowing me to join his crew. My diverse skills might prove to be useful." Uncertainty edged his words and his expression. "I haven't met your ship's commander, but you could introduce us, right?"

Thorlu remained non-committal. "Odnamo is an astute and demanding commander. You won't find him easy to fool."

Hossela edged around to face him. "Neul Island and witnessing your transformation have altered my self-perception. I'm ready to leave my assassin's life behind me and discover who I truly am."

Thorlu listened with his instincts and his new VarTerel's ear. Nothing in Hossela's voice or demeanor suggested deceit. His direct gaze remained on the man next to him. "I will trust you to work with me. First, let's get Elf in here, so he's part of our decision-making process."

"I'm on the way." Whispered through Thorlu's mind in answer to his summons. Elf's eagle form landed at the foot of laddered steps to the entry hatch. His shift to Human was immediate.

Thorlu nodded a welcome as he climbed aboard. "Join us. We have plans to make."

Over the course of the next quarter chron-circle, they discussed and discarded several plans. Finally, Hossela exhaled a frustrated breath and glanced at the three men. "Maybe we should ask 'em where they want to go."

Raiherr sat up on the edge of his low bunk, his bewildered gaze seeking something familiar. He rubbed his high, protruding cheekbones and shot a searching gaze at the three men opposite him. "Who am I? Where am I? Who are you?"

"Your name is Raiherr." Thorlu smiled. "You are the pilot of this jumper craft. I am Thorlu Tangorra. My friends and I are here to help you."

The ex-Vasro stood up and walked from the crew's quarters to the flight deck.

Hossela nudged Thorlu. "I'll stay here. You and Elf look after him."

Leaving Hossela to guard Zorin and Dulno, Thorlu led Elf on to the craft's flight deck, where Raiherr sat in the captain's seat, lost in thought, staring at the controls.

Thorlu slid into the copilot's seat. "May I touch your temple, Raiherr?"

Pursed lips and narrowed eyes suggested reluctance, then relaxed. "I guess. What will that do?"

"It might help you remember."

"Ah, alright."

Thorlu's touch stimulated a few memories, but none that would help him recall who he once was. "If you could choose any planet in the Inner Universe, where would you go?"

Raiherr raised his gaze to Thorlu's face. "Anywhere?"

A nod from the VarTerel brought a smile. Raiherr tapped his chin. "I visited the planet of Roahymn once and loved it. There's a small rural town with a space museum. I've always wished I could study astrology and the museum offers courses and the town's people are welcoming and—" He grinned. "I'd love to live there."

Hossela stuck his head into the space. "I have two men ready to talk."

Thorlu stood. "Raiherr, tell my friend about your favorite planet while Elf and I see to your companions." With his son at his heels, he crossed to the crew's quarters. "Let's help—"

A swirl of light depositing Relevart made him pause.

Hossela sprang to his feet. Raiherr gripped the back of his seat and gawked.

Thorlu smiled. "What good timing you have, Universal VarTerel." He flashed Hossela a knowing look.

The Klutarse licked his lips and swallowed.

Relevart surveyed the situation. "I will take it from here. Hossela, you and I will transport the men to their new homes while we get acquainted. Thorlu and Elf, you are required at the Bāoba Sanctuary." A mischievous smile lit his eyes as he looked in Elf's direction. "But before you go, there is someone waiting for you outside."

Thorlu and Elf exited *Toneer*. Standing outside the jumper craft, he observed his son eagerly scanning the area and stifled a smile.

After looking all directions, Elf faced him. "Father, do you think Relevart was teasing?"

"You know Relevart never teases, Troms El Shiv."

The deep laughter-filled voice made him whip around. Ari walked from the trees, her beautiful red curls tumbling down her back and her chestnut eyes sparkling.

He started forward. "I can't believe you're here!" She met him part way, threw her arms around him and kissed him, took a breath, and kissed him again.

Thorlu cleared his throat. "When you two are finished getting...ah... reacquainted, we'd better move. *Toneer* is about to leave, and I for one would rather not end up in Mittkeer in her wake."

Giggling like a couple of children, Elf grabbed Ari's hand and pulled her further from the jumper craft. Thorlu strode to their side as it rose into the air a short distance and vanished.

Ari snuggled closer to Elf. "And into Mittkeer they go." She stepped away, but kept her hand in his, while she smiled up at his father. "It's good to see you, VarTerel Thorlu Tangorra. What's next?"

Thorlu let out a long, relieved exhale. "Our job with the Vasro on Neul Isle is complete. Now it's time to go to the Bāoba Sanctuary and see what's next." He smiled at Elf. "Shall we teleport or fly."

Elf's happy gaze sought Ari's. "Do you have a preference, Arienh AsTar?"

"I do, Troms el Shiv." She released his hand and smoothed her hair back. "I love Neul Isle. Let's fly."

He glanced at his father and back. "What's your favorite bird?"

She pursed her lips. "Does it have to be from here?"

Thorlu shook his head. "Not now."

"I love red-tailed hawks. Will that work?"

"Yes!" Father and son answered in chorus.

Thorlu chuckled. "I'll see you there. Off you go."

Two red-tailed hawks flashed into being and shot upward. Soaring side-by-side they flew against a background of misty clouds painted by the beginning of the first sunset since the removal of the dome.

Thorlu looked around the empty plains. *So much has happened and there is so much yet to come.*

Shaping his favorite fire eagle, he flew after the two love birds.

41
Neul Isle

Torgin and Gar absorbed the honor bestowed on them by the K'iin while tribal members placed plates full of scrumptious food in front of them. A smile brightened Cadhōla's face as she directed a tribeswoman to set two more places.

Gar looked up from the plate. "You gonna eat with us?"

Her smile widened. "We are about to have guests." She walked over to the entrance oval and touched the center.

When she stepped aside, Thorlu and Elf entered and stood shoulder to shoulder. Something about their demeanor made Torgin put down his mug and look closer.

Father and son grinned and moved apart. Ari, her eyes shining, stepped into the pod.

Gar jumped up, ran to her, and stopped, with his hands on his hips. "Hey, Ari, how'd you get here?"

She laughed. "How do you think?"

Gar's puckered mouth moved right, then left. "I'm bettin' the Universal

VarTerel had something to do with it." He grabbed her hand and pulled her after him to the table. "Sit down and tell us everything. Oh...and *eat*!"

Elf followed them and sat down next to Torgin. "Life on this island is certainly full of surprises."

Thorlu greeted Cadhōla. "Relevart said you needed us?"

The wise woman laughed. "We are so glad he sent you."

She started to close the entry oval, then stepped back as a kestrel glided through, taloned feet extended. It landed and shifted to Esán."

Cadhōla smiled happily. "Our heroes gather!"

Gar waved. "Esán, look who's here!"

Ari stood up.

Esán's eyes widened. After greeting the wise woman, he hurried over and gave her a hug. "Good to see you, Arienh." He looked at his friends. "Now all we need is Brie." He slid onto a seat next to Ari and thanked the timid woman who set a plate in front of him.

Thorlu took a seat and started filling his plate.

Torgin contained his curiosity until a tribeswoman had filled his mug with water. "Well, are the last Vasro gone?"

Cadhōla stepped closer, her eyes wide with anticipation.

Thorlu chewed his first morsel and swallowed. "Neul Isle is free of the Vasro. Relevart transferred the last three into Mittkeer and will leave them wherever they wish to begin their new lives."

Esán nodded his agreement. "I have done a sweep of the island." He couldn't hold back an enthusiastic smile. "I found no further sign of the Vasro or anyone else. Tomorrow, Cadhōla, we double check and then the K'iin can move home."

Cadhōla translated for her people. Excited voices drifted through the Pod while the companions savored the good food and the good feelings that accompany a job well done.

When they finished eating, a tribesman offered to escort them to their sleeping pods. As the Bāoba branches lowered to form the bridges, everyone stood for a moment, eyes upward, absorbing the beauty of the sun's bronze glow warming Neul Isle for the first time since the dome vanished.

Morning arrived with the sun's light illuminating the sleeping pod. Gar, his specs in place, sat on his cot opposite Torgin, fascinated by the changes made by the removal of the opaque dome. His magnified gaze traveled floor to ceiling, then from one window oval to the next, studying the etchings encircling each of them.

Cadhōla had explained that the tribesmen picked the pods when they were small and placed them in the gigantic Bāoba trees, where they became enmeshed in the branches and bark. When full-grown, the tribesmen hollowed them out and painted them with a special preservative to keep them fresh and to strengthen each individual fiber.

The soft sounds of Torgin moving alerted Gar that his cousin watched him. "Morning, Torg!" He opened his arms wide. "I love these pods! Wouldn't it be neat if the street people in New York could live in pods in the trees in Central Park?" Memories of his previous life and the man who raised him held him quiet.

Torgin's arm draped over his shoulder produced a deep sigh. Gar brushed away a sneaky tear and looked his cousin in the eye. "I'm lucky to be here and not living with the rats in the filthy streets of the city." Blinking rapidly, he snorted as his tummy growled.

Torgin laughed and climbed to his feet. "Your stomach's a meal chronometer. Get dressed, and we'll join the others in the main pod." He squinted, pursed his lips, and nodded. "Thorlu and Esán are back from a reconnaissance flight over the island. Let's go see what they discovered."

Gar scrambled into his pants and shirt, pulled on his socks and laced up his boots. In the personal space, he stood for a moment, his hand pressed against the New York logo on his shirt. *I will never forget you, Gin.* Wetting his hands, he rubbed them over his short, black curls, slurped some water, swished and spit, and announced, "I'm ready."

Torgin, fully dressed and waiting to go, laughed out loud.

Gar danced a little gig. "Haven't felt this happy in ages! Yippee, the dome's gone!" He hurried to the entrance oval, touched the center, and grinned. "Bridge's already down. Come on!"

With hopefulness lightening his mood, Torgin followed his young cousin. Cadhōla greeted them with a cheerful smile and motioned them to join their friends at the table.

Gar scurried over. "Morning, Ariehn. You sleep well?"

Ari nodded. "I did." She picked up a flat round cake and plucked a nut from the top. "How about you?" Popping the nut in her mouth, she chewed and licked her lips.

His white teeth flashed. "I slept great." He plunked down on a seat next to Esán. "You've already been out and about, right?"

Esán swallowed a mouthful of berries. "I have, Garon. Fill your plate, and we'll share what we discovered."

Torgin sat down next to Thorlu and nodded at Elf, Ari, and Esán. "Hope you all slept well."

Esán passed him a bowl of dark purple berries. "I slept better than I have in a long time. You?"

Gar jumped in. "Torg slept lots." His imitation of his cousin's snore turned into a snort. "Good thing I covered my head with a pillow."

Torgin joined in the good natured laughter, filled his plate with fruit and flat round cakes flavored with spices and honey. After enjoying a tasty bite, he said, "So, Esán, did you see anything that concerned you on your flight around the island?"

Thorlu answered. "Not a thing. We stopped in the Labyrinth Cavern and told Dri Adoh and Artānga to prepare for their return home. Esán and I thought you and Gar should be the ones to give them the final word once we double check the village."

Again, Gar bubbled over. "I can't wait to tell them! Let's check the village." Torgin noted the twinkle in Thorlu's eye and looked at his cousin. "How about we finish our delicious morning meal first?"

Gar stuffed his mouth full of food, chewed, swallowed. With crumbs flying, he announced, "Finished. Let's go!"

Ari smothered a deep snort with a hand over her mouth.

Elf caught her eye, laughed, and pushed back his seat. "Hey, Garon, let's sit over by the fire pit. Ari and I need a lesson in Inik. Esán told me you're great at it."

Gar grabbed a handful of berries and eyed the adults at the table. "You'd better hurry 'cause I'm ready to go." Popping a berry in his mouth, he plopped down cross-legged on the floor in front of Ari and Elf.

A sparkle of delight lit Thorlu's grey-green eyes. "He's a handful, Torgin. Glad he's in your care. I suggest we finish our meal and head out. I imagine the K'iin are ready to be in their own homes."

Silence settled over the table. Torgin, the first to finish, walked over to talk to Cadhōla. "We're leaving soon to do a last check at the village before you and your people move back to your homes. Is there anything we should look for while we are there?"

Her chin lifted and her gaze grew distant. A nod brought her attention back to him. "Be sure to check the huts of Dri Adoh and Artānga in case the Vasro set a trap." Excitement brightened her solemn face. "Will you come back to tell us everything's fine?"

Esán joined them. "You and your tribesmen prepare to return to the village. Once we know it's safe, Thorlu and I will return and take you home."

Torgin noted her desire to ask questions and then smiled when she chose not to. Instead, she looked at them one by one and said, "Achōsi Tu, for all you are doing. We will be ready."

"Tá Ōmthra, Cadhōla. Your help has made it easier for all of us." He walked over and looked down at his cousin. "It's time."

Gar climbed to his feet. "Elf and Ari, show Torgin you know how to say thank you in Inik."

Ari stood up, offered her hand, and pulled Elf to his feet. Together, they said, "Achōsi Tu."

Torgin put a hand on his cousin's shoulder. "Good work, Garon. You're an excellent teacher. Can they say you're welcome?"

He grinned. "How'd you know I taught them that, too? Show him, guys."

"Tá Ōmthra." Elf and Ari recited the two Inik words with a touch of pride.

Thorlu and Esán walked over. "Time to go. When we get there, Esán and Ari will check Artānga's hut for traps, while Elf and I check Dri Adoh's." He paused.

Gar stuck his chin out. "What about Torg and me?"

Torgin's hand on his shoulder triggered an instant change. The Sanctuary Pod blurred, and a dark blue-black stone tunnel took shape. Torgin hid a grin as realization lit his cousin's expression.

Gar perched his specs on his nose and peered up at him with magnified eyes. "You coulda told me we were leaving, you know."

Torgin couldn't control his desire to laugh. "Ah, but, Garon, surprising you is more fun. Let's find Artānga and Dri Adoh. Thorlu will let us know when we can bring the K'iin home."

Brie sat at the breakfast table toying with her food. *I love Myrrh and always will, but—* She glanced up to find her Aunt Mira observing her with a slight smile. Sighing, she shrugged. "I'm edgy and don't know what to do about it. Everyone I love is elsewhere...except you and Corvus, of course." She caught herself drawing Ari's infinity sign on the tabletop and curled her fingers into a fist.

Almiralyn, her sapphire eyes brimming with empathy, nodded. "I understand more than you realize, Brielle. I suggest you spend today visiting all your favorite people and places. Soon you'll leave Myrrh, and you may never return. Take this time to refresh your memories of where your adventures began."

Brie felt herself on the edge of refusing, but stopped. Memories almost overwhelmed her. She inhaled and smiled. "That sounds like a good idea." Pushing back her chair, she rose. "I'll see you later."

Standing in the back garden, she contemplated not only her past in Myrrh, but where her future might lead. Choosing not to worry about what might happen, she instead closed her eyes and focused on what she wished to see.

After a pleasant visit with Wood Tiffs, Tibin and Sibine and their fast-growing Tiffin, Adin, Brie stood at the base of their TreeOm gazing at the beauty of the Terces Wood. The soft whir of tiny wings made her look up. A smile twitched as two Nyti landed on her offered hand.

"Hello, Mumshu and Ashor! I was hoping to see you."

The two tiny creatures grinned. Mumshu tipped his top hat. "CheeTrann sent us to escort you to Nemttachenn Tower." He bowed.

Ashor fluttered up to look her in the eye. "We've missed you, Brie."

"I've missed you, too. Let's catch up on the way."

Brie listened with a wistful smile as the Nyti shared the latest news of life in the Terces Wood. When they reached the clearing surrounding Nemttachenn, they promised to give her regards to Kieel, their leader. Tiny wings carried them higher in the trees as she stepped into the tower.

The deep rumbling voice of CheeTrann, the Sentinel of Myrrh, greeted her from the hazy blue interior. "Ah, VarTerel Brielle AsTar, what a pleasure. Come closer, so we can see you better."

A soft chuckle drew her forward. She grinned. "Paisley James Tobinette! I didn't expect to see you." Her gaze strayed to the chessboard on the table where he and CheeTrann sat. "I see you are still enjoying your chess matches."

Paisley smiled. "You are much changed, Brielle. I understand you are a VarTerel, the youngest in the Inner Universe." His smile widened. "I am honored to be your friend."

When the pleasantries were over, CheeTrann studied her with quiet intensity. "It is important, Brie, that you visit the Cave of Canedari. Be sure to walk the Stairway of Retu Erath."

Brie gazed up at the imposing sentinel. "I will go there now. Thank you, CheeTrann."

Paisley stood. "May I walk with you to the clearing?"

"I would love that."

Taller than most men she knew, Paisley escorted her from Nemttachenn. His dark eyes regarded her with gentle affection. "Take care, VarTerel. Know I will always keep you here." He tapped his chest over his heart. "Say hello to you sister and friends for me."

"I will do that. Best of luck with your next chess game."

CheeTrann's deep laugh rumbled from the interior of the tower as she teleported.

She arrived in the Dojanack Caverns a short walk from the DeoNyte's central square in Meos. After alerting her friend Zugo with a gentle mental nudge, she ambled along the torch-lit passage. A welcoming shout greeted her when she reached the fountain in the square. The DeoNytes who gathered around it parted to allow Zugo through. Surprise and delight in his pale blue eyes, he hurried toward her. The white fur rippling over his dark-skinned body seemed longer and accentuated the musculature of his matured height. The difference between the boy she once knew and the adult striding toward her reminded her how long she had been away.

When he reached her, they examined each other with hungry interest. Without saying a word, he slipped his furry arm through hers and guided her toward his father's counsel chambers. Once through the double doors, he stopped. "We have both changed since our last meeting. You are a beautiful woman and...a VarTerel."

Brie smiled. "And you are an adult DeoNyte who is following in his father's footsteps. I understand you are to be the next ReDael of your clan."

A throaty laugh brought her attention to Zugo's father. "My son indeed follows in my footsteps, but in ways of his own making. We know your visit is a fleeting one. Let us sit at the round table and catch up."

When they had answered questions and exchanged stories, Yookotay excused himself. "Thank you, Brielle, for choosing to visit Meos one last time. I suggest Zugo walk with you to the Cavern of Tennisca." He rested a hand on her shoulder. "May good fortune always be with you."

After he left, Zugo stood and offered a hand. "Come. The ancients await you in the cavern."

At the door to Tennisca, Zugo's sadness mingled with hers. He clasped her hand between his and bid her farewell. Releasing it, he gazed down at her without speaking, then turned and walked back toward Meos.

A rush of sadness kept her still for a long moment before she opened the door to Tennisca and stepped through. Memories flashed—giests, Seyes Nomed's owl, her capture by the death shadow, Wodash, and Ari's fall from the stairs and out through the mouth of the cavern into the sky above Idronatti. *So much happened here.*

Stepping onto the first step of the Stairway of Retu Erath, she gazed into the darkness and began her descent. Soft whispers stopped her midway down the stairs. "Youngest VarTerel in the Inner Universe, prepare to use your knowledge to restore a world. Focus your gifts on showing the beauty and power of diversity. Your destiny awaits you. Meet it with an open mind." The whispers grew softer. "Evolsefil calls...Evolsefil waits...Evolsefil...Evolsefil... Evolsefil..."

As the voices faded, she gazed at the double purple door into the Cave of

Canedari embedded in a wall of glistening amethyst crystals. Descending the final steps, she drew a cloak of calmness around her and whispered the charm to open the doors. They vanished and ushered her into the home of the Crystal Evolsefil. Its radiance washing over her drew her forward.

Intense quiet held her motionless as she gazed up at the crystal's shimmering beauty. Her lungs demanding replenishment prompted a deep inhale. Euphoria embraced her. All doubt and negativity fled. She placed her hands on the smooth, crystalline surface and closed her eyes.

Evolsefil's vibrational frequency flowed up her arms to her neck. The Star of Truth tingled and grew warm. Blood pulsing through its vascular roots surged deeper and sent strength and power coursing through her. Tears of gratitude streaming down her face, she pressed her forehead against Evolsefil's faceted side, whispered her thanks, and stepped back.

A momentary desire not to leave the Cave of Canedari morphed into anticipation. Darkness replaced Evolsefil's glow. Brie lifted her eyes and laughed softly. *I am in the Intersect.*

After surveying the night sky below her, she looked up at the geode-like arch of jewels overhead. Picturing where she wished to go, she watched the stars blur, and the jewel-incrusted geometric pattern change to the tree roots beneath the Terces Wood. A platform solidified beneath her feet. She climbed the steep wooden stairs, opened the door, and stepped into the tack room in her Aunt Mira's red barn.

42
Neul Isle

Esán and Ari completed their search of Artānga's hut in the K'iin village. Satisfied all was as it should be, they stepped outside. Marveling at the beauty of morning without the dome, Esán surveyed the village with a half-smile and his thoughts circling one way and then the other.

Ari watched him, curiosity blooming like a flower. "What was it like under the dome? I know it resembled the clouds covering the island the first time we visited, but Torgin mentioned the dome turned black."

Esán sucked in a breath. "It was dark as night. The air grew stagnant." He pressed his lips into a thin line. "If we hadn't been able to remove it, I believe all life on the island would have eventually perished."

Ari stepped away, her chestnut eyes searching. With an elated laugh, she swung around to face him, her red curls catching the light in a way that reminded him of her twin. "Something good just happened to Brie."

Joy washed over Esán like a tsunami's wave. "I sense it, too. Can you tell what?"

She laughed. "No, but it was definitely good. Do you know where she is?"

"Nope. All I know is that Relevart took her somewhere safe."

"Ari wrinkled her nose. "So many secrets. Can't wait to complete this quest."

Elf preceded his father around the corner of the hut and stopped. "You two look happy."

Esán beamed. "We both felt something positive happening to Brie."

Thorlu appeared doubtful. "You realize she could be halfway across the Inner Universe?"

Elf flashed a teasing smile. "Yes, but they both love her. Ari is her identical twin, and Esán loves her with all his heart."

Ari grinned. "You are so right, Elf. Hey, did you find anything out of the ordinary in Dri Adoh's hut?"

"We did not, and I gather you found nothing amiss in Artānga's." He turned to Thorlu. "What do you think, Father? Is it time to bring the K'iin home?"

"It is the perfect time! I have already alerted Torgin. Esán and I will bring Cadhōla and her group back to the village." A twinkle intensified the gray-green of his eyes. "I suggest you and Ari spend some time catching up. Ready, Esán?"

Both men vanished from sight.

Sprawled on his sleep-pad in the alcove he and Torgin shared, Gar could hardly contain his excitement. *Today will be the turning we take the K'iin home.* Impatience and not knowing what to expect combined to make him uneasy. He had already called forth his spectacles and sent them away several times. *They won't show me anything...unless Abellona needs to tell us something.* He frowned. *Then they appear on their own.*

The chatter in the cavern suddenly increased. Gar scrambled to his feet, peeked around the edge of the alcove, and surveyed the large main living area. Torgin zigzagged through the crowd, a grin on his face. When he reached Gar, he nudged him further into the alcove.

"Thorlu has been in touch. It's safe to return to the village. Dri Adoh and Artānga are on the way to inform the villagers. Get your things ready."

Gar guffawed. "Ain't got no things." He thumped his chest. "Just me." He cocked his head. "You?"

Torgin grinned. "Just me. Let's go hear the announcement."

When they reached the large living area, the K'iin waited, expectation sparking like a cloud of fireflies around them. Their leaders stood at the front of the tribe. Dri Adoh lifted a hand. The villagers grew quiet. Artānga stepped forward and in the Inik language explained it was safe to leave the Labyrinth Cavern and return to the village.

The tribal members cheered. The rhythmic beat of drums filled the cavern, then stilled. With reverence, the tribe bowed their heads. Dri Adoh recited a prayer of thanksgiving that ended once more with drumming. Women danced, their arms raised, their high-pitched voices contrasting with the lower tone of the drums. With a final swirling turn, the women lowered their arms and stood motionless. The drum's final rhythmic boom, boom, boom ended with quiet restored.

Artānga reviewed the plan for moving back to the village and dispersed his people to carry it forth. Dri Adoh walked over to Torgin and Gar. "Tell the VarTerel we come." His wrinkles etched deeper. "Several of our elders cannot manage the climb up the mountain tunnels. Can you help?"

Torgin and Gar exchanged glances. "How many elders?"

"Seven made it down through the tunnels, but climbing up would harm their health."

"May we have a moment, Dri Adoh?" Torgin asked.

"Yes. I will wait here."

Torgin drew Gar aside. "Do you think you can help me teleport the elders?"

Gar called forth his spectacles. As they settled in place on the bridge of his nose, the rims glowed ember. He smiled. "Yes, and Abellona will assist."

Returning to the shaman, Torgin explained he and Gar would take the elders home.

Dri Adoh looked from one to other. "We thank you, Torgin and Gar."

Gar smiled. "Tá Ōmthra, Dri Adoh."

The K'iin shaman touched his heart. "You honor us by learning our language. Achōsi Tu, Gar Anaru. Come. I will show you where the elders wait."

Close to the main area of the cavern, seven older K'iin sat on a low shelf of rock. Hope filled their wrinkled faces when Torgin and Gar followed Dri Adoh over to stand in front of them.

The shaman translated as Torgin spoke to the elders. No one had questions, so Torgin motioned them to gather around him and Gar. He placed the image of the village bridge in their heads. When they nodded, he and Gar teleported them to that exact place.

Gasps of surprise and delight accompanied their arrival in the village, where Sea Wee Vala greeted them with regal majesty. Their delighted exclamations changed to awe when Thorlu, and Esán, with Cadhōla and her group of tribal members, walked free of Mittkeer, their faces alight with wonder.

Gar, Torgin, and Thorlu joined Elf and Ari off to one side as the two groups of tribal members reunited and paid homage to their Spirit Guardian.

After conferring with Thorlu, Cadhōla took charge and soon Torgin, Elf, Ari, and two tribesmen were helping the seven elders find and move into their own huts. Gar and Thorlu stood ready to help when needed.

Over the course of the next few chron-circles, villagers arrived back from the Labyrinth Cavern. Their eagerness and relief at being home was apparent in their expressions, their laughter, and their increased pace as they stepped from the darkness of the mountain tunnels into the full glory of a sunlit turning.

Men and women who arrived carrying bundles and dragging low carts were met by older children who helped them unload and move into their huts. Younger children, their carefree laughter echoing through the valley, ran free in the sunlit village where they were born. Livestock, the last to arrive from beneath the mountains, ambled into their fenced paddocks, where troughs of water and pile of hay awaited them.

While everyone settled in for the first night in their own homes, Dri Adoh and Cadhōla approached Thorlu. The shaman asked, "When do Inōni and her friends return to the village?"

"I'll contact them when you are ready to receive them." Thorlu's gaze moved over the village and back. "I believe morning would be best."

Cadhōla looked up at him. "Is Inōni still with child, or has her wee one been born?"

Thorlu smiled. "The Universal VarTerel secreted her and her friends in a special place where no time passes. Hopefully, the baby will be born here in her own home."

Dri Adoh fingered a long, black braid and smiled. "I, too, believe morning is best. Everyone needs a night of sleep in their own huts." He looked at Cadhōla, who nodded. "The Sanctuary Pod is ready for your use until you depart Neul Isle. Our wise woman prepared the pods for your stay. She will tell you the Inik words for lowering the Bāoba branches to form the bridges to your sleeping pods and to open the entry ovals. I will see you in the morning. Now, I must check on our elders."

Cadhōla gazed over the village and up at the sky, where the sun slipped through hazy pastel elegance toward the horizon, her eyes glistening. "You and your friends are now part of the K'iin family. By sharing our Sanctuary Pod, you honor us." She then told Thorlu the required words.

With Gar's help, he gathered Esán, Elf, Ari, and Torgin together. A teleported journey later, they sat around the table in the Sanctuary Pod enjoying good food, pleasant conversation, and the knowledge the Queen's Quest was fast approaching its conclusion.

Brie walked from Almiralyn's red barn into the back garden, her head still spinning, and stopped in a patch of moonlight to gaze up through trees. *I love Myrrh, and I always will.* She touched the back of her neck. *Thank you, Evolsefil, for healing the Star of Truth. I will never forget you.*

A raven's caw filled the night. Wing-wind tossed a tendril of hair over her forehead as Karrew alighted, a reflection of the full moon glinting in his ebony eye, and shaped Corvus. Almiralyn, her VarTerel's staff in hand, appeared at Brie's side. Relevart, enclosed in the light from the crystal Froetise, flashed into being. Starlight and eternal night enshrouded them.

Brie, her heart beating a rapid crescendo, fixed her gaze on the Universal

VarTerel. The amber glow of his eyes deepened. "It is time to take Inōni home. Your Aunt Mira and Corvus have agreed to help. Gather closer."

Stardust encircled them. Laughter dispersed it as Penee descended the front steps of Rainbow Cottage and ran toward them. "You're here at last. Inōni is ready to birth her child. We must take her home."

Den waved from the porch where he sat next to the mother-to-be. Inōni's dark-eyes widened to complement her delighted smile.

Brie took in the beauty of Rainbow Cottage, its forest and flower meadows, and hurried up the steps to greet Dri Adoh's granddaughter."

Inōni held out a hand. "I am so glad to see you, Brie. Can I please go home?"

Brie clasped the offered hand. "That's why we're here, Inōni. Please relax. We'll take care of everything."

Relevart took charge. "We must move the cottage and its acreage to the Valley of Tá Súil. It will take a coordinated effort on all our parts to accomplish this. Den and Corvus, shift shape and take up positions in the forest. Penee and Almiralyn take Inōni inside. Brie, stay with me. Be prepared, when I raise Froetise, to help move the cottage to the Incirrata Constellation. From there, picture Rainbow Cottage on Neul Isle in the village of the K'iin. Mittkeer will release us on my command. Positions, please."

A raven and a hawk soared upward. The hawk landed on one side of the forest; the raven landed on the other. Almiralyn and Penee helped Inōni into the cottage and settled her on the couch in the front area. Brie joined the Universal VarTerel.

Relevart looked at Brie. "Call forth your staff."

Brie held up her hand. Her staff materialized. Froetise's power combined with Musette's, creating a rainbow glow that encompassed the cottage and the forest; the garden and the flower-filled meadow.

Relevart tapped Brie's forehead. "Repeat with me, Brielle AsTar.

Words flowed from her mouth, matching his in a chorused chant.

"Universal space and time,
Join to form a fold sublime;
Carry us to the Constellation
Incirrata's marker station."

Relevart raised his staff higher. No Time and All Time formed a swirling tunnel that carried the rainbow surrounded cottage and lands to the Incirrata Constellation.

43
Neul Isle

Restlessness aggravated by the desire to know her twin was safe had kept Ari awake well into the night. When she finally slept, it was fitful at best. Morning light glowing in the window ovals woke her. Dressing quickly, she pulled her red curls back into a low ponytail and made her way to the main Sanctuary Pod.

Gar greeted her with a slight smile and raised a brown pottery mug. "You and me are the only ones awake." He slurped a sip and licked his lips. "Good thing Cadhōla left me some of my favorite juice." He slid the mug toward her. "Try it. If you like it, I'll get ya some."

Ari picked up the mug, inhaled the rich aroma of berries, and took a sip. "Yum! I can see why you like it. What kind of berry is it?"

"It's a frachāno berry, and it only grows on Neul Isle." Gar grinned. "You keep that mug. I'll grab another." He crossed to the food area and returned to his seat. Taking a sip from his new mug, he licked his lips, and said, "It reminds me of cherries and blueberries mixed. What do you think?"

She sipped and swallowed. "It reminds me of the dojanberries on Myrrh."

A nod. "Blueberries and cherries for sure." A sigh finished in a smile. "Thanks, Gar. I needed you to help me settle down."

Gar tipped his head. "How's it feel to have a twin who looks exactly like you?"

Ari took another sip. "It would be really hard if we thought and acted alike, but we don't. What's fun is watching how people try to tell us apart when they've just met us."

Gar froze. His hand flew up and his specs appeared on his palm. "I didn't call so..." A frown bridged his brows and creased his forehead. "Queen Abellona is telling us we're needed in the village."

Ari squinted at the entry oval to the sleep pod bridges. She focused her intent on Elf. His telepathic *"Coming"* let her take a breath.

Soon, he preceded Torgin into the main pod. "Thorlu and Esán are gone." He hurried over to the food storage, grabbed a handful of nuts and berries and a piece of bread, and sat down. We'd better eat and get moving."

Torgin, who had followed his example, popped a nut in his mouth. "Thorlu let me know things are quiet, won't be for long. Eat and let's go." He regarded Ari. "Bet you're excited to see Brie?"

She grinned. "You're right...*and* Den and Penee and Inōni!"

They arrived in the village to find everyone gathered in the open area near the bridge. In the distance, lightning flashed and thunder rumbled. Overhead, clouds roiled, forming what looked like a huge storm cloud. At the center, an opening filled with rainbow light took shape and grew larger.

Elf clasped Ari's hand and edged closer to the crowd.

Gar hurried over to join them. Grabbing Ari's arm, he pointed. "What's that thing that's growing bigger in the middle of those clouds?

Excitement spread through the crowd. Children pointed and hopped from foot to foot. Dri Adoh, Thorlu, and Esán stood together, their gazes fixed on the phenomenon happening above them.

In Mittkeer, the Universal VarTerel nodded at Brie. Together they chanted.

> *"Release us now onto Neul Isle*
> *That Inōni may give birth in style*
> *And conclude the Sun Queen's Quest*
> *With joy and celebration blessed."*

Above the island, the rainbow within the clouds shaped a tunnel that shot downward, forming a pool of light on the ground at the south end of the village. Gar's spectacles glowed fire ember black and red, and his eyes sparked with fire-opal red and green. Jumping up and down, he shouted, "It's Rainbow Cottage! Inōni is coming and so are Den and Penee." He squealed with excitement and pulled Ari with him closer to the pool of light.

Moments later, the cottage and its forest and fields settled on the ground. Brie and Relevart stood at the bottom of the porch steps. A raven and a hawk swooped to the ground. Corvus and Den materialized. The door to the cottage opened. Almiralyn stepped onto the porch and raised her hand.

Everyone grew still, their attention on the beautiful Guardian of Myrrh.

Almiralyn called out, "Inōni is about to give birth. She asks for her mother and the tribal midwife to come to her."

Two women stepped free of the crowd and hurried to the cottage. Almiralyn led them inside. Ari followed and stopped beside Relevart. "Brie is inside, right?"

"She is Arienh AsTar. You will soon be together."

It was not long before Brie walked onto the porch. A smile lit her eyes as she descended the steps and walked over to Dri Adoh. After a brief conversation, he climbed onto the porch and faced those gathered.

Dri Adoh, surveyed his people with an expression of gratitude. "A new tribal member has been born today. She is the daughter of Penesert el Stroma and Den Zironho and is a gift to the K'iin. She represents the sacredness of bringing people together with love and inclusion. Her light and wisdom will bless our tribe for eternity."

Riahtám, Inōni's mother, stepped onto the porch and moved to Dri Adoh's side. After a brief sharing, she faced those gathered and Dri Adoh spoke, first in Inik and then in the language of his guests. "Riahtám wishes to share. She will speak Inik, and I will translate."

Eyes shining with love, she gazed over the tribe. "Inōni and her child are resting. Den and Penee, who gifted us this special child, remain by her side. Tomorrow, we will celebrate the baby's acceptance into the K'iin Tribe with the naming ceremony and feast." She smiled at Relevart. "Thank you, Universal VarTerel, for bringing my daughter and her child safely home to Neul Isle."

From her place at the edge of the crowd, Ari watch Inōni's mother bid Relevart farewell and enter the cottage. Around her, the crowd began to disperse. Feeling dejected, she wondered where Brie had disappeared to and walked over to speak with Corvus and Relevart, who waited near the cottage.

When Almiralyn and Brie emerged and joined them, she felt a rush of relief. Brie smiled and clasped her hand.

Almiralyn regarded the twins with pride shining in her eyes. "You have grown into extraordinary women...just as I knew you would. I am sad to say good-bye, but Corvus and I must return to Myrrh. Please tell your parents, we miss them." She hugged them and moved to Corvus' side.

Relevart gazed down at them. "I, too, must leave, but only for a short time. I will see you at the ceremony tomorrow." He looked from one to the other. "Share time while you can." His staff flashed into being. Almiralyn clasped the rowen wood. Corvus said his good-byes and followed suit. Mittkeer wrapped around them, leaving the place where they had stood empty.

Ari looked at her twin. "What did Relevart mean...share time while you can?"

Brie shrugged. "What's important is that we are together right now."

As one, they moved into each other's arms. After a long happy hug, they looked into each other's eyes and smiled. Hand in hand, they crossed to a bench by the river and sat down. Tranquil quiet settled over them. Words weren't needed. The knowledge they were together, even for a short time was enough.

In her private rooms, Abellona welcomed a smiling Galactic Guardian, her face alight with surprised curiosity. "I am honored to receive a visit from you, Chealim. How may I assist you?"

The magnificent being inclined his head. "Let us sit, and I will share why I am here."

When they were established in the elegant sitting area, he studied her with solemnity that made her heartbeat quicken. Maintaining a dignified silence, she waited, her eyes never leaving his face.

Chealim's full-lipped mouth curved into a smile. "I am here at the request of the Galactic Council to congratulate you, Abellona. Soputto is safe, and Neul Isle is free of its enemies and the dome they created. The K'iin are once again at home, and, as we speak, Inōni and her companions return to the village. We, the Council, feel there is one more thing that must be achieved before your quest is complete."

Abellona's heartbeat pulsed quicker. "Please tell me, Chealim, what must I do to bring my quest to a fully successful close?"

With reverence glowing around him, the Galactic Guardian bowed his head. When he looked up, he met her queenly gaze. "I am here, Abellona, to offer you a place on the Galactic Council."

She caught her breath. Her gaze flew to her regal portrait on the opposite wall and back to the Guardian. "If I accept this honor, who will stand in my place as the Sun's Deity?"

His smile broadened. "You must choose your successor, Abellona, for if you do accept the offer, you will be moving to the Galactic Center."

Abellona rose. "I must consider this with as much care as I know the Council has given their offer."

Chealim came to his feet. "We understand and respect your desire to do so. When you have made your decision, please inform Itarān Cirana, the Leader of the Council of Deities. He will then contact me."

The Sun Queen touched her palm to his.

With his smile blazing, he faded from sight, leaving her standing in the quiet of her rooms. Taking a breath, she crossed to SparrowLyn's portrait and studied her likeness. Stepping closer, she watched thin, fine paint strokes waver like currents in a stream. Colors blended and the painting reformed. Abellona held her breath as her blue-robed figure at the council table took shape on the canvas.

Thoughts racing, she turned to stare at the rooms she had inhabited since her crowning as Sun Queen. Instinct turned her to once again gaze upon her portrait. The blue-robed Galactic Guardian rippled. Paint-stroke by paint-stroke a new portrait took shape, a portrait of her successor and his bride.

⁂

After a night at the Bāoba Sanctuary, everyone but Relevart, who had returned to *El Aperdisa*, gathered around the table, feasting on a special morning meal prepared by Cadhōla and delivered to the Sanctuary Pod with the help of Esán and Torgin.

Brie nibbled a piece of sweet bread and sighed. Relaxation, something missing for some time, was visible in the cheerful faces and laughter of her friends. A conversation between Thorlu and Esán ended with both men grinning. Across from her, Torgin listened to Gar, who spoke with his mouth full, then swallowed and laughed. She looked at Ari and Elf, who sat close, focused solely on each other. *I am so glad we had time for ourselves last night, dearest sister.*

Ari looked up and smile. *"Me, too, Brielle AsTar."* Her attention returned to Elf.

An unexpected need to be alone prompted Brie to carry her pottery bowl to the sink. After washing and drying it, she set it aside and frowned. Her finely tuned instincts informed her something was about to change. She touched the Star of Truth. *Calm and cool to the touch.* She smiled. *Whatever it is, it's going to be good.*

Esán joined her. "Are you alright?"

"I am. Something good is about to happen in the village."

Thorlu walked over and dipped his bowl in the soapy water. "You and I felt something shift in the village." He faced the others. "We need to leave sooner than expected. Let's clean up and go."

Brie and her friends arrived in the village near Rainbow Cottage as the sun crested the top of the Elgnat Range. Morning's warm welcoming light washed the Valley of Tá Sûil. It sparkled on the river pond's calm surface and enhanced the wealth of colors in the forest and fields surrounding the village.

Tribal members mingled together in small groups, their pale umber faces raised to absorb sunlight they had been without for several moon cycles. Childish laughter floated on a gentle breeze, scented with mixed aromas of morning cooking, flowers, and the damp moss covering the stones by the river.

Den and Penee stepped onto the cottage porch and stood side-by-side. The villagers gathered, their attention focused on the man and woman who had gifted them with a sacred child. Dri Adoh made his way through the crowd and joined them. A brief conversation later, he faced his people.

"The time has come to bless the child of Penesert el Stroma, the Girl with the Matriarch's Eyes, and Den Zironho, the eldest son of Relevart, the Universal VarTerel."

Den and Penee moved apart. Riahtám walked onto the porch and stood opposite the shaman. A baby's soft cry announced Inōni's arrival. She paused in the doorway, her wee daughter swaddled in a rainbow-colored blanket in her arms. Her beautiful smile encompassing all those gathered, Inōni moved to stand beside her mother and Dri Adoh.

The soft beat of drums and the chime of tiny bells called forth Cadhōla, who climbed onto the porch to stand opposite Dri Adoh. Together, the K'iin Shaman and the Wise Woman placed gentle hands on the newborn and began to chant,

> *"A child is born to light our way.*
> *Her presence is our guiding ray.*
> *Kīara Aslynn, our Shining Dream*
> *Will lead us forth to joys unseen."*

When they spoke the last word, an astonished cry rose among the K'iin. Hovering above the village, a swirling blue light opened its glowing center. A ray of ebony and gold shot downward, shimmered brighter, and formed a wide staircase. Descending it, each surrounded by an aura of pastel light, and led by Kat, the Goddess of Small Animals, and Aahana, the Sun Queen's youngest daughter, were the representatives of the Deities of the Spéire Solar System. Lining the staircase on each side, they turned their gazes toward the top. The Sun Queen, followed by Nimah and ShioCáni, descended with her scepter in hand. Midway down, she stopped, lifted it in the air and pronounced.

"The Sun Queen's Quest has reached its ending;
Neul Isle is free of those who's rending
Attempted destruction of all we see.
It will now remain forever free."

The scepter created a circle of red light above her head, which expanded. When it circumvented the entire island, Chealim materialized at the foot of the staircase. His deep voice rumbled. "Warriors take flight."

Brie caught her breath as Gar, Ari, Elf, and Torgin shifted to fire eagles and soared over the village. Esán, glowing with the power of the Seeds of Carsilem, floated upward. Relevart and Thorlu hurried to her side, their staffs in hand. Hers manifested, Musette's rainbow light blazing. The trio of VarTerels lifted from the ground and landed with Esán, facing Chealim on the platform at the bottom of the staircase and stepped to one side. Four birds of prey alighted facing them and resumed their human forms.

A rose-pink light enveloped Rainbow Cottage. Pen and Den moved closer to Inōni. Dri Adoh and Cadhōla stood on either side of her.

Chealim, flanked by the VarTerels on one side and the queen's warriors on the other, spread his arms wide. "Today, we celebrate the human child, Kīara Aslynn, and the legacy she represents. Her arrival heralds the completion of the CoaleScence and the beginning of the Quickening, the finale of this Universal Epoch. As a representative of the Galactic Council, I thank those whose choices have brought us to this place in our history. You know who you are; and that your work is not yet done. The Universe's Quickening is the re-establishment of forward momentum and continuing growth for all."

He flashed into being behind Abellona. "Because of the Sun Queen's willingness to lead the quest to rid Neul Isle of its enemies and thus to bring the CoaleScence to a positive finish, The Galactic Council has directed me to inform her and you, her subjects and warriors, of the following decision."

He stepped down beside the Sun Queen and they faced each other. "Your presence, Abellona, is requested at the Galactic Center, where, if you accept the Council's offer, you will assume your new position as a member of the Galactic Council." He met her fire-opal gaze. "Do you accept?"

The Sun Queen's radiance filled the heavens. "I do."

"Have you chosen your successor?"

"I have." She and Chealim stepped apart. Abellona smiled. "May I present the new Sun King and his bride.

Two steps higher up, Nimah and ShioCáni, stood side-by-side Touching a hand to their hearts, they smiled with regal dignity at those gathered.

Chealim bowed his head and vanished.

Gazing at those who had answered her summons and led her quest in the world of Humans, the new Galactic Guardian, raised her scepter. The staircase ascended into Shiór Ridu, taking the VarTerels and their companions with it.

Below, the villagers cheered and Den, Penee, and Inōni waved. Neul Isle grew distant. A swirl of blue light erased it from sight. Brie caught her breath and gripped Esán's hand. White walls surrounded them. Everyone started talking at once.

Brie grinned. "We are home."

Gar pranced from foot to foot. "...in the Holographic Center on *El Aperdisa*!" His spectacles flashed ember bright onto his nose. The queen's voice filled the space.

"You came to my aid when I called. Because you were unflinching in your desire to join in my quest to save Neul Isle, our enemies are banished, and the dome is gone forever. Esán Efre, the Seeds of Carsilem have made claim to you and to Tumu Noci. The key to the space-time continuum now belongs to you. Use it with discretion. Torgin Wilith Whalend, you will retain the information from my book on the space-time continuum. I trust you to use it with honor. Garon Anaru, remember always that you are of my heart. To all of you who gathered here. I honor you as family. Stay true to yourselves and to each other."

The rims of Gar's spectacles dimmed and vanished, leaving him rubbing his throat with one hand and brushing tears from his cheeks with the other.

Brie surveyed those gathered around her. *How extraordinary that we were all brought together for the Queen's Quest.*

The CoaleScence Spins
A web of intrigue thread by thread
A circle that begins its ending
Opening portals that are pending...

A Quickening now picks up the pace
And prompts continuations race
It sparks a journey, one that's fated,
Prophesied, and long awaited.

The End

GLOSSARY

A glossary for the VarTerels' Universe is available to you online at:

www.skrandolph.com/glossary

YOUR OPINION MATTERS!

I hope you enjoyed this book. Your opinion of this book is valuable…to others and to me!

Please leave a review. If you have not done a review before, it is quite simple… just go to where you purchased this book, or perhaps some other review site you like, and leave a few words expressing your thoughts and pick how many Stars you think this book deserves.

When you do a review, please send me an email (SK@SKRandolph) letting me know where you left it. I am interested in reading what you have to say!

Thank you.

S.K. Randolph

P.S. Don't forget to signup with my Readers Group.

https://www.skrandolph.com/readers-group

ACKNOWLEDGMENTS

To Tom, my partner in life: Thank you for joining me in my writing adventures, for making me laugh, drying my tears, and opening my mind to the new and the different. The books we make together are gems!

To my editor, Linda Lane: I thank you for all your work and your encouragement over the past fifteen years. Learning with you has been a magical journey.

To Ann McEntire: Your eagerness to help with the books always warms my heart. You are my beta reader...one of the best!

To Leslie Randolph, my sister and critique partner: Thank you for taking time from your busy life to be part of my writer's village. You always see things others miss.

To Sean Krantz, my consultant on all things Science Fiction: I thank you for sharing your knowledge of drones, spaceships, and all things otherworldly!

A huge *Thank You* to all those whose steadfast support has helped me to become the writer and digital artist I am today.

ABOUT THE AUTHOR

FROM DANCE STAGE TO PRINTED PAGE

STORYTELLER: The pursuit of ballet led S.K. to the art of storytelling through movement. Her dance career spanned four decades of performing, teaching, choreographing, and directing. Over sixty of her original choreographic works were brought to life for theatre audiences in the United States, Canada, Bermuda, and Japan.

DIGITAL ARTIST: S.K. also creates image art. Since 1997 she has been creating original digital art on her computer using a process of her own creation from her photographs.

VOYAGE TO WRITING: In 2010, she retired from the world of dance to tell her stories on the printed page. S.K. lived full-time on her boat for a decade cruising the coast of Southeast Alaska. Anchored in one remote, quiet cove or another, cut off from radio, television, cell phones, and the internet, she devoted her life to honing her skills photographing nature, creating digital art, writing, and catching dinner. She now tells her stories through words and illustrations on the printed 'stage'.

ASHORE: Today, she is reclaiming her "land legs" in the high desert of Western Colorado. Writing and creating art with mule deer looking in her studio window instead of brown bears and humpback whales on the other side of the porthole. S.K. is thriving in her new surroundings...but she so misses Karrew and the other Alaskan ravens.

S.K. at the helm of her forty-foot boat leaving Seattle, Washington. A transformative seventy-five day voyage up the Inside Passage to Sitka, Alaska. Then a decade writing while living afloat in one Alaskan cove or another. 2010

TO LEARN MORE

S.K.'s website:

www.skrandolph.com

Facebook:

facebook.com/skrandolph11

Substack:

skrandolph.substack.com

Join my readers group:

https://www.skrandolph.com/readers-group

Email S.K.:

sk@skrandolph.com

DiMensioner's Revenge: Illustrated by the Author
VarTerels' Universe Book One

630 pages, 79 illustrations

Esán has a dream, but his life hangs in the balance.

The clock ticks.

New friends, creatures from another planet, a beautiful Guardian, and the deadly DiMensioner pursue him across Myrrh, the last remnant of Old Earth.

Will his new friends reach him in time?

Or will the DiMensioner find him first?

ConDra's Fire: Illustrated by the Author
Varterels' Universe Book Two

500 pages, 59 illustrations

DiMensioner Seyes Nomed still wants revenge—the destruction of Myrrh and the death of its Guardian. But he's been evicted from the last remnant of old Earth, his mission unaccomplished and his nephew, Esán, an unwilling companion.

Pursued by soldiers from another planet, twins Ari and Brie and their friend Torgin slip away to rescue Esán.

News of Esán's extraordinary talents spreads through the Inner. Leaders on three planets scheme to make him their own.

Evil forces conspire to destroy all the Guardian of Myrrh holds dear. The water the fountain Elcaro's Eye roils, then calms, revealing what she fears most.

MasTer's Reach: Illustrated by the Author
Varterels' Universe Book Three

690 pages, 61 illustrations

The VarTerels' Universe is in chaos. A galactic drama intensifies. On the surface of the fountain, Elcaro's Eye, pictures flash and disappear:

Esán and his friends, pursued buy the evil Mindeco from RewFaar and a savage creature from the planet TreBlaya, stumble between giant man-eating trees. A rumbling howl pushes them faster. If only they could teleport...

The raven Karrew sits on a makeshift perch, his injured wing taped to his side. Around him, ghosts of violent criminals hover, empty eyes staring. Distantly, he recalls the life he once led...

Wolloh, High DiMensioner od DerTah, lays in a senseless stupor. Only Relevart, the VarTerel of the Inner Universe, has the power to save him. Where is he?

Flames fill the fountain's bowl. A long his echoes through Veersuni. The fire fades. Red eyes of death search the sanctuary.

Water spills from alabaster palms erasing the image, but the evil intention of The MasTer's Reach.

Jaradee's Legacy: Illustrated by the Author

Varterels' Universe Book Four

372 pages, 53 illustrations

Jaradee's Legacy, A Story in Three Parts

Jaradee had no idea when she joined the Vasrosi rebels that her influence would be felt for decades to come.

Floree finds herself enmeshed in the politics of the day and responsible for the life of the boy who will become the most powerful force for good in the Universe.

Rayn pledges to save her people from annihilation only to find herself facing an inner conflict, one that pits her against everyone she has ever loved.

Incirrata Secret: Illustrated by the Author

Varterels' Universe Book Five

430 pages, 61 illustrations

As the CoaleScence begins, the adventures of the VarTerels' Universe continue. New characters join Brie and her companions as their battle to bring balance to the Inner Universe gains momentum.

Those who would shift the scales of justice to suite their evil purposes seek to capture the young people and use their unique gifts to further their bid for power and control.

Corps Stones: Illustrated by the Author
Varterels' Universe Book Six

420 pages, 54 illustrations

The Clenaba Rolas Solar System is on the brink of destruction. Three Corps Stones, powerful crystals that hold the planets to their orbits, have been stolen and transported back in time.

The Galactic Guardians provide Brie, Torgin, and Esán with the tools and the training to create a time tunnel and to live and perform in the dance world of New York City, 1969.

What adventures await them at the end of the tunnel? will they be able to navigate time and find, not only the Corps Stones, but also who stole them and why?

Mocendi's Gambit: Illustrated by the Author
Varterels' Universe Book Seven

340 pages, 36 illustrations

Hunted by evil forces, Brielle AsTar must disappear. The Galactic Guardians warn Esán and Gar they must leave with Brie and tell no one.

Ari's sense of loss triples as Elf departs, her friends are nowhere to be found, and her twin sister vanishes without a word.

The Mocendi's plan unfolds. Events take a frightening turn. Ari remembers a quote from her study of Old Earth's history: United we stand, divided we fall. She shuddered. They had never been more divided.

Queen's Quest: Illustrated by the Author
Varterels' Universe Book Eight

410 pages, 45 illustrations

The Sun Queen paced her royal chambers, her mind racing. Neul Isle and its inhabitants were once again in danger. The time had come to summon her allies to her side.

Brie AsTar stared with shocked dismay through a time window in Mittkeer. Her companions agitated whispers floated through the globe of endless night surrounding them.

Strange events on *El Aperdisa* produced growing uneasiness that prompted Gar, Torgin, and Esán to embark on a perilous journey to Neul Isle.

Uncertainty held Ari, Rethson, and Elf quiet as Relevart explained what he and Commander Odnamo required of them. Ari's confident voice filled the space. "We can do this!"

VarTerels' Universe

Illustrated Novels & Companion Shorts

Milton Keynes UK
Ingram Content Group UK Ltd.
UKHW030707021124
450460UK00014B/133/J